The Future Dictionary of America

The Future Dictionary of America

A BOOK TO BENEFIT PROGRESSIVE CAUSES
IN THE 2004 ELECTIONS
FEATURING OVER 170 OF AMERICA'S
BEST WRITERS AND ARTISTS

McSWEENEY'S BOOKS

barsuk records

Cover medallion by Chris Ware.

www.mcsweeneys.net www.barsuk.com

Printed in Wisconsin by Worzalla Printing.

1-932416-20-X

Introductory note

This dictionary was conceived as a way for a great number of American writers and artists to voice their displeasure with their current political leadership, and to collectively imagine a brighter future. The idea for this book was first discussed in the spring of 2004, and the book was completed about three months later, on June 1st. Because it was compiled in speedy fashion, the book does not include many hundreds of writers who we would have loved to have had aboard. As it stands, however, we are happy to boast the contributions of almost two hundred writers and illustrators, among them countless winners of Pulitzer Prizes, National Book Awards, distinguished fellowships, and much acclaim. All of the authors and artists appearing herein do so without pay or royalty. Likewise, no staff was paid for their work, nor was any overhead factored into the cost of this book. Thus, all proceeds from the sales of this dictionary go directly to groups devoted to expressing their outrage over the Bush Administration's assault on free speech, overtime, drinking water, truth, the rule of law, humility, the separation of Church and State, a woman's right to choose, clean air, and every other good idea this country has ever had. These groups include the Sierra Club (www.sierraclub.org), America's oldest and largest grassroots environmental organization; Common Assets (www.commonassets.org), a new organization working to protect the commons; and many other specific projects relating to the 2004 election—mobilizing and educating voters, getting people to the polls, door-to-door organizing, and other efforts. We thank you for purchasing this dictionary, and, if you believe, as we do, that this is one of the most important presidential elections in many decades, we urge you to vote.

EDITORS: Jonathan Safran Foer, Dave Eggers, Nicole Krauss, Eli Horowitz. ART DIRECTOR: Françoise Mouly. COPY EDITOR: Chris Gage. ASSISTANT ART DIRECTOR: Lisa Kim. EDITORIAL INTERNS: Jordan Bass, Christian Whittall, Brian Rogers, Moira Williams, Julie Glassman, Howie Wyman, Karen Leibowitz. ART INTERNS: Megha Shah, Elizabeth Gery. PRODUCTION: Françoise Mouly, Lisa Kim. PROJECT ADVISOR: Adam Werbach. MUSIC COORDINATORS: John Flansburgh, Josh Rosenfeld, Jordan Kurland, Ami Spishock, Courtney Smith, Spike Jonze. SPECIAL THANKS: Guy and Jeanine Saperstein, Adam Werbach, Helen Thompson, Bob Perkowitz and Lisa Renstrom, Michelle and Daniel Skaff, the Sierra Club Foundation, Common Assets.

Does Our 21st-Century World Need Such a Dictionary?

With the advent of telepathy and other forms of direct comprehension, many have questioned the relevance of this book. Indeed, in an age when mental transmission has replaced articulation as the primary form of expression for fully three-quarters of America's eleven billion citizens, it is often thought (and by extension said, to everyone) that a dictionary that remains rooted in the descriptive tradition, carefully cataloging the words of our age as they emerge and attempting to establish a standard set of spellings and usages, is essentially obsolete, its editors engaged in a wasted effort. It is the belief of the editors of this edition that such ideas arise out of the minds of idiots, or alien infiltrators.

In this, the sixth edition since 2016, we offer the reader an array of new and useful terms. While the average dictionary user is most likely a student, a time traveler, or an aficionado of historical reenactment, our intended audience is much wider. Those who maintain a professional interest in understanding the English of our day will find a great resource here, but so shall every other man, woman, or genetically-enhanced/sentient plant who wishes to look. Language remains an essential element of modern life; those who ignore its importance, who view it as a curiosity, relegated to the past along with poverty and gravity, simply persist in living in ignorance. In darkness. They too will learn.

For those who have not retreated to customized dimensions or cryogenic stasis—those who wish to engage with the world as it is now—the new terms included here offer a striking picture of our time. Many old meanings and outdated words have been excised, in order to accommodate the *au courant* intellect, eager to learn only the most recent developments in diction. What is left is an alphabetical adumbration of the modern era, one that reflects the concerns and ambitions of the modern human.

Much has changed: whereas the fourth edition devoted itself entirely to what in retrospect was a faddish preoccupation with the elimination of all but eight letters (and the addition to all words of melismatic suffixes), and the fifth focused on the colloquial dialects of the Miami public school system, this edition recognizes a return to the roundness of English, and embraces it. Here the reader will find words large and small, of diverse origin, relating to every aspect of society and employing even the most forgotten corners of the alphabet. And if we are damned for such ambition, then so be it.

It is true that the editors' predecessors have occasionally been reviled for their work, and we must weather the lingering ill-will that exists even now. The decision of the panel for the second edition to deploy paramilitary squads composed of wolf-elephant hybrids in order to ensure the enforcement of their prescriptive approach was certainly regrettable, and undoubtedly contributed to the tendency of successive panels to retreat from a full engagement with the language. Some will see our reassertion of the dictionary's active role as another incitement to galactic unrest. This is not our intention. What power we have, we wield not to destabilize the fragile balance of the civilized cosmos, but to bring a love of words back into it.

It is with this assurance that we invite you to explore your dictionary without fear or resentment. Think of it as a guide, as a teacher, and not as the long mighty tentacle of the terrible overlord of whom a grandparent may have warned between bouts of anguished weeping. Find within it a firm grasp of today's vocabulary, a lexicon that allows fluent communication without the dangers of prolonged mind-reading: the abrupt blackouts, occasional brain damage, and theoretically possible relocation of consciousness into an inanimate object. Use it to learn of a language you may have lost, and please look for our other reference products, now available as nanite gelcaps.

—Jordan Bass, PhD. & The Editors

How to Use This Book

This book was created with the help of many experts who believe the reading of this dictionary should be elementary. Nevertheless, we offer these explanations and clarifications:

TYPEFACE
The main entry appears in boldface type, usually roman, flush left to the margin of the column.

SYLLABIFICATION
Here the authors have done their best. The reader is asked to remember that all guides to traditional syllabification were lost in the Floods of 2020. Please consult a corroborating text before attempting pronunciation.

libcon [lib'-kahn] *n.* 1. a leftist who seeks to conserve what "conservatives" desire to destroy, to wit: social security, funded public education, the environment, scientific objectivity, social welfare, equal rights for women, the Constitution of the United States, strategic alliances, the minimum wage, gun control, and child labor laws. 2. any such person attacked on Fox News. 3. [*informal*] a dangerous radical.

—Charlie Baxter

DEFINITION
Definitions within an entry are individually numbered in a single sequence, regardless of any division according to part of speech. The most common part of speech is listed first, and the most frequently encountered meaning appears as the first definition for each part of speech. The preceding sentences were copied from a 1967 Random House dictionary and we have no idea what they mean. Thus, a few trivial inconsistencies may be found within.

BYLINE
All words are defined by the authors listed after entries. As such, there is a great deal of latitude afforded to them, resulting in a vast degree of subjectivity. The editors of this volume, and the other contributors to it, do not necessarily endorse the opinions of all other entrants—though in most cases they do.

All words should be pronounced using the diagrams at right and below, in the manner most fitting or obvious.

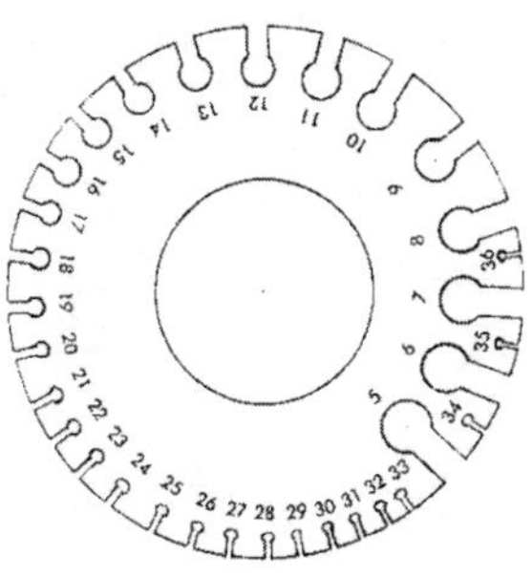

Fig. 1

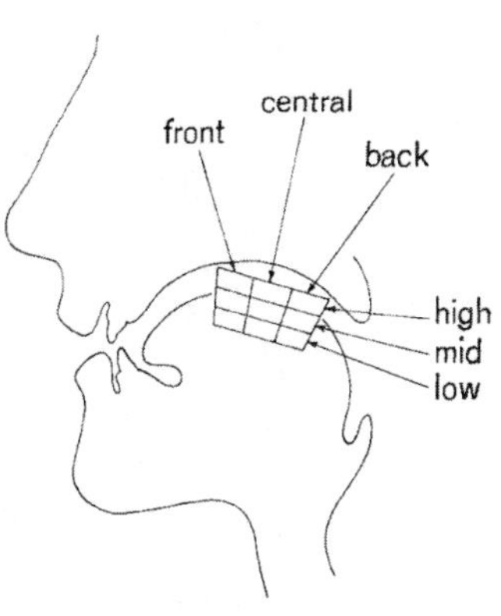

Fig. 2a

aaaaize [ay'-iz] *v.* to attempt to take precedence or priority over, in order or rank. *During the hearings, the House Majority Leader continued to aaaaize the other congressmen by interrupting them.* [A back-formed coinage from the practice of false naming favored by businesses wishing to be listed first in the telephone directory.] —BEN GREENMAN

abbapeasement [ah-buh-pees'-ment] *n.* a Swedish diplomatic process whereby conflicting parties participate in a "dance-off" to resolve their differences. *After Yassir Arafat and Ariel Sharon agreed to an all-night session of sweaty abbapeasement, relations between Israel and the Palestinian Authority grew markedly less hostile.*
—RYAN BOUDINOT

acrimoney [ack'-ruh-mun-ee] *n.* a voluntary fine levied against politicians who demonize, stereotype, or otherwise disrespect individuals or groups of their own country or of other countries; must be paid out of the personal account of the offending politician, not from funds raised by supporters; a provision of the Acrimoney and Baloney Act of 2055; also levied for bad ethnic jokes. *The senator paid $5000 in acrimoney to Jewish groups after his unhumorous comment about the "ham-or-rabbi code" of Jewish dietary laws.* **acrimoneous** *adj.* deserving of fines.
—JOHN HENRY FLEMING

adgasm [ad'-gaz-um] *n.* 1. an advertising strategy so successful it instantaneously creates enormous demand for a product or service. Adgasm is achieved when consumers conflate desire with need in a demonstrable fashion. Typically, consumer demand exceeds supply for a short, intense period, then becomes rapidly sluggish and lethargic. *The use of celebrity clones in the new Nike ads resulted in total adgasm.* 2. demand for a product or service that overwhelms the medium that supports it. *The new birth control beer promotion adgasmed the Budweiser server.* **faux adgasm** *v.* to deliberately under-serve a sales network to create the illusion of adgasm. —JIM RULAND

adgasm

Adulteration [uh-dull'-tur-ay-shun] *n.* a movement in 21st-century America devoted to the discovery of the inner adult. A corrective to the wildly successful movement to discover the inner child, the movement was inspired by the realization that said child was a peevish,

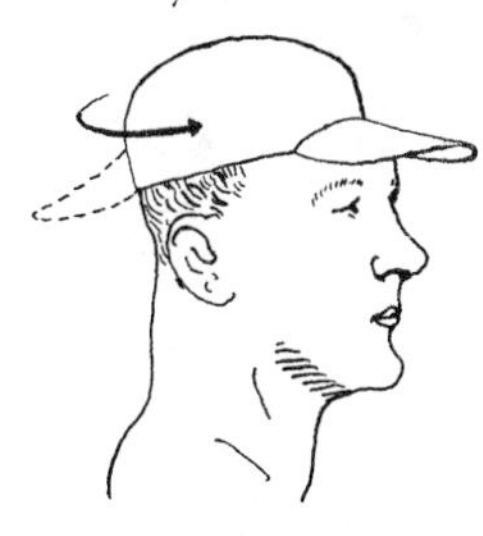

Adulteration

Ben Greenman / Ryan Boudinot / John Henry Fleming / Jim Ruland • ***David Heatley*** /
Marilynne Robinson • ***Barry Blitt***

self-indulgent brat, hostile to the constraints of civilization and bored to the point of rage by meaning and complexity. These traits became manifest as the inner child assumed control of politics and the media. Marshmallow creme became a dietary staple, and gigantic, toy-like vehicles came to dominate the nation's highways. Statements on foreign policy were seriously marred by the overuse of such concepts as **Blam-O!!**, **KaPow!!** and **KerBlooie!!** Critics noted that the inner child had no measurable attention span and had never learned to share. The adulterationists set out to modify the consequences of pure egoism, pure greed, pure cynicism, pure nonsense, and pure noise, which were aspects of the ascendancy of said child.
—MARILYNNE ROBINSON

advertannuller [add-vur'-tun-ull-ur] *n.* a small implant that erases all evidence of any advertisement, logo, sponsorship, or merchandising promotion encountered by the wearer. *The new generation of advertannullers blocks even boasting by co-workers, hype in padded résumés, or spin in the annual State of the Union address.*
—SUSAN WHEELER

agapaean [ah-gap'-ee-en] *n.* 1. a song, hymn, poem, or feast that celebrates or explicates love for and within a particular group or social formation at a particular historical moment. 2. a chant of camaraderie, or that causes camaraderie to come about. 3. a song, hymn, poem, or feast that extols the virtues of a friend. *We could feel within us as we walked from what was left of the city into the desert a spontaneous agapaean arising, and, as if we had always known the words, simultaneously began to sing.* —STACEY D'ERASMO

America [uh-mare'-ick-uh] *n.* a term that denotes all of the western hemisphere. Originally, before the advent of Hybridity and Planetarism, this term was co-opted by the United States of America to denote only its own nation and peoples. Now used to denote the peoples and nations of Latin America, the Caribbean, and Canada, known collectively as the United Countries of America. This term, too, is falling out of use as the **United Peoples of the Planet Earth** (UPPE) becomes more common. —JULIA ALVAREZ

American-can [uh-mare-i-can'-can] *n.* a dance form developed in the United States during the early 21st century by citizens seeking an outlet for messy thoughts and feelings attendant to the notion of homeland (e.g., love and dismay, heartbreak and impatience, anger and angst). This dance form is completely unlike the **jingo** (unfortunately popularized during the same era). It can be practiced quickly or slowly and requires no music, for it is an invisible dance performed by the mind, with little involvement of the body. It provides training in the maintenance of contradictory emotions with respect to patriotism (e.g., "I am both glad and ashamed to be a U.S. citizen")—which, in turn, can lead to positive acts of citizenship (e.g., "I will donate money and time to progressive causes").

Early devotees of this dance form could often be found in bookstores, swaying slightly as they perused travel guides, imagining what it would be like to live somewhere else, in a homeland without jingoists. Nowadays, most practitioners have become what might be called optimistic patriots of the skeptical variety: they believe their nation can and will subdue its dark side, but not without plenty of can-can.
—MARTHA COOLEY

and-yet [and-yet] *conj.* pronounced as one word, not two, as in an eighth-note, followed by a quarter-note, followed by a whole note of silence. Always used as a sentence alone: *I thought it was impossible. And-yet.* Or: *I was prepared to leave. And-yet.* To say "and-yet" can be to say: *There was a small, dissenting part of me, and despite its smallness it intervened, and that's why I* *kept on when I wanted to give up.* Or: *They told me I would grow up to be handsome. And-yet.* Meaning, I know the truth, of course I do, even if I can't say it. "And-yet" can be a reminder of all that will go unsaid. Of a chance someone is holding out for. A door left open. It sounds like *nyet,* which means no in Russian. But "and-yet" is never so decisive or emphatic. It's simply there to challenge, or at least hold a light up to, whatever came before, like a grammatical philosopher. Although always followed by a period, its tone and effect is similar to a question mark. In two syllables it can sum up the existential doubt that's tied like a stone to each of us. It's also Jewish. *Da-da, da-da, da-DA—and THAT is why on Passover we always lean. And-yet.* As in, let me answer your question with a question. As in, I've just spent half an hour explaining it to you like this, but I could have just as easily argued it like that. As in, there are fifty ways to interpret this, and if we can't agree on anything else, at least we can agree on that (and if we can't even agree on that, at least we can argue). "And-yet" guards against simple conclusions. "And-yet" says: Don't get so comfortable no matter how much you have to eat today you might be hungry tomorrow and by the way there's no such thing as black and white take it from me you should learn to sleep with one eye open. "And-yet" can sometimes be funny. It's almost always bittersweet. But it's never tragic; by the time there is time to say "and-yet," the tragedy is already past. Which is to say, "and-yet" is almost always reflective. *It was terrible. And-yet.* As in, I'm still standing, there's light in the morning, the smell of breakfast, what can I tell you, I suppose the world continues to turn.

—NICOLE KRAUSS

antemoral [ant'-eh-mor-ul] *adj.* of a period prior to formulation; the time before deciding the value of an act or behavior; before categorization; a time of openness that precedes any judgment of others. **antemoralist** *n.* one who attempts not to judge others preemptively.

—LYNNE TILLMAN

anti-imperiology [an'-ti im-peer-ee-ol'-uh-jee] *n.* the study of imperial development, from onset to decline, esp. with the intent to reverse or avoid archetypal historical processes. [New Latin anti + imperiologia: Late Latin, imperium, power. (SEE **Ramirez.**)

—JEFFREY EUGENIDES

antonin [ant'-oh-nin] *v.* to behave in a manner that is actively unapologetic concerning one's sins. ANT. **atone.**

antonin

—Did he apologize for breaking that vase?

—No. He argued it wasn't broken and, in the alternative, denied breaking it.

—[incredulous] *He antonined?*

—He totally antonined. —ERIC ORNER

appetist [app'-uh-tist] *n.* a well-adjusted enjoyer of food, frequently used in reference to women, occasionally men. A person with a healthy desire to eat; a person who does not worry excessively about food intake; a person who does not diet constantly; someone who enjoys food thoroughly and in moderation.

—LYNNE TILLMAN

arcticello [ark'-ti-chel-oh] *n.* (*pl. -celli*). a type of cello designed to be played in extreme cold. The body and neck are made from a composite of graphite, fiberglass, and wood from the permafrost maple; the

arcticello

Nicole Krauss / Lynne Tillman / Jeffrey Eugenides / Eric Orner • ***Eric Orner*** / Lynne Tillman / Doug Dorst • ***R. Sikoryak*** strings are made of reindeer gut and thinly coated in blubber. The arcticello and its cousin, the **antarcticello**, were designed in 2062, after the American geologist T. Burford Bamwell discovered that the effects of global warming could be reversed if newly discovered bands of ferrous permanganate encircling the earth were stimulated to vibrate at a frequency of 77.75 Hz. For this to happen, Bamwell theorized, cellists had to be posted at the exact north and south poles of the earth, each playing a continuous E-flat. He built instruments that could withstand polar conditions and recruited cellists willing to brave the elements for the sake of the planet, and his theory proved true. Since that time, the polar cello encampments have attracted musicians of great prestige and skill. Difficulties persist: delivery of fresh fruits and vegetables to the camps can be problematic, and arctic elk in springtime rut often mistake the players for potential mates, but the E-flat tone has been played at the poles constantly for over forty years now (apart from a few unfortunate ventures into improvisation), and the earth has cooled to pre-Industrial Revolution average temperatures. Repeated attempts to generate the tones without human cellists have failed. Synthesized sounds do not sufficiently stimulate the permanganate bands. Sled dogs play with poor intonation, and the polar ungulates are prone to absenteeism. Polar bears have tended to gnaw on both their cellos and their instructors.

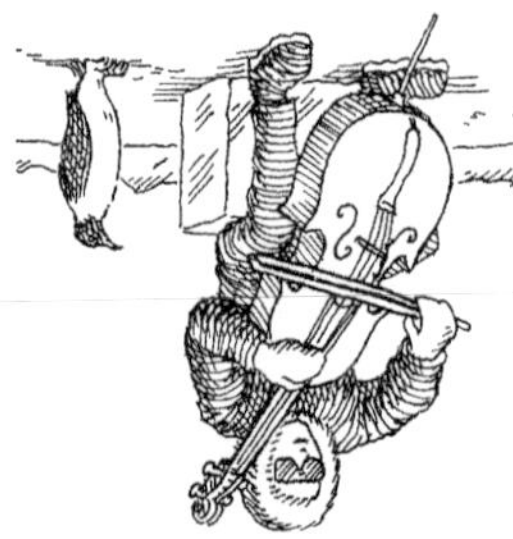

antarcticello

Arcticello and antarcticello vibrations have produced other beneficial effects as well. Most people find the quiet low-end thrum audible everywhere on earth to be quite soothing. Also, the vibrations cause the kit fox (*Vulpes macrotis*) to dance in ways that resemble Irish jigs and Scottish reels; this has led to unprecedented levels of happiness and tranquility in humankind, because, really, you can't be sad or angry or greedy or grumpy or phlegmatic or intolerant or mean-spirited or surly when kit foxes are dancing all around you.

—Doug Dorst

arebours [ar'-uh-bors] *n.* the particular sensation of awe or disbelief that strikes when the previously unimaginable happens, or when canons of accepted human decency are flagrantly violated. *He felt it increasingly, the shock, the sense of arebours whenever he turned on the radio or opened a newspaper. He always had the desire then to exchange a glance with one of his old friends or former mentors—someone who could confirm that he was not alone, not crazy, and that this was indeed an outrage.* —Sven Birkerts

art-gangs [art-gayngz] *n.* groups of children or youth who strive to outdo each other in various art forms, esp. performance art. In 2018, when the United Nations became the world's chief governing power, the U.N. Arts Council recommended transferring 4% of each country's military budget to arts-in-the-schools programs. When this transfer was enacted into international law a year later, performance artists, muralists, horn players, and poets took up positions in schools from Abidjan to Wellington. In 2021, a group of Washington, D.C., high-school students calling themselves the Ice-Walkers strung ropes over the frozen Potomac and crawled across them, demonstrating the limits of gravity. A Parisian rival gang, the Puppeteers, watched this on the evening news—now largely devoted to the accomplishments of the world's artists and performers, with special segments each night for art-gang events. The Puppeteers then built a set of life-sized grotesque marionettes and re-created the agonies of first love under the Arc de Triomphe, the Eiffel Tower, and in the doorway of various pâtisseries. These performances brought them both pastry and international attention. Middle-school playwrights in San Francisco staged a series of improv gang shows in the afternoons. A group of ten-year-olds in Kyoto built a website to showcase their kiri-e paper-cuttings. Taking up the challenge, more than thirty Prague schoolchildren performed an interpretive dance on and around the footbridge at Stromovka Park on the way to the Prague Zoo. School attendance shot up all over the world, students lost interest in most forms of drugs—legal or illegal—and teen violence dropped. In 2028, the UN mandated the transfer of an additional 45% of the world's military budgets for the arts, 15% of which went into prison arts programs. Some of the world's schools sent students into local prisons to stage poetry slams and paint murals. As recidivism fell to all-time lows, certain prisons emptied out entirely and were turned into music studios. Until money was found for soundproofing, the echoes of pianos and harpsichords battled it out up and down the concrete halls.

—SARAH STONE

ashcrofted

ashcrofted [ash'-kroff-tid] *adj.* removed from or disqualified for public office on grounds of religious delusions. Derived from *The People v. President Ashcroft*, the landmark Supreme Court decision that disqualifies all candidates for public office who espouse a religion and/or other organized forms of magical, delusional, or psychotic thinking, on the Constitutional grounds of separation of church and state, a decision taken at the time of the restoration of the Constitution following upon the dynastic, so-called "anti-terrorist" or "neopatriot" era.

—ROBERT COOVER

ashcroftian [ash-kroft'-ee-un] *adj.* 1. having fallen from a great height, often through one's own sanctimonious vainglory. *Dante's description of Lucifer's ashcroftian descent from heaven to hell remains most vivid in this reader's mind.* 2. rendered suddenly foolish; scorned by those who once feared or supported one. 3. [*cinema/TV*] filmed in a flat yet melodramatic style reminiscent of the late-night television commercials for the law firm of former Attorney General John Ashcroft; **ashcrofty** *adj.* [*slang, archaic since 2005*] 1. sneaky or duplicitous. 2. gathering information through illicit or improper means. *My boss got all ashcrofty on me and started spying on my browser and listening in on my phone calls.*

—SCOTT PHILLIPS

Atkins Plan [at'-kins plann] *n.* doctrine of U.S. foreign policy early in the 21st century that disguised decadent indulgence as sacrifice and privation. Under the Atkins Plan, the U.S. consumed what it always wanted and still felt virtuous. —CHRIS BACHELDER

atonemint [uh-tohn'-mint] *n.* a refreshing candy that simultaneously freshens the breath and makes amends. *She forgot to return her mother's phone call and now it was too late to call back because her mother goes to bed by ten, so she sucked on a couple of atonemints which caused her mother to have a dream, and in the dream her daughter* *took her shopping for begonias and then the two of them planted them in the flowerbeds next to the front porch and they smiled because they looked all pretty and hot pink even though in real life the daughter isn't so good with living things.*

—SARAH VOWELL

attalk [at-tok'] *v.* to set upon with rhetorical force for the specific purpose of defusing a volatile situation; to bring into a peaceful state by talking; to affect positively through articulation. *The U.N. has announced that its envoys attalked local warlords early this morning; it appears that all parties left satisfied and that conflict will, once again, be avoided.*

—JORDAN BASS

awesome [aah'-sum] *adj.* 1. inspiring awe, as in feelings of wonder or reverence before the sacred or sublime. 2. [*now rare*] excellent, admirable, super, impressive, groovy, etc. A **boomerang word,** i.e., one that is given a loose or in some cases unrelated definition and thrown around a lot for a certain period of time before returning to its original meaning. *Cf.* **brilliant**, **dude**.

—SIGRID NUNEZ

Axis of evil [ack'-sis uv ee'-vil] any perceived "nucular" power that distracts attention from the National Debt.

—SUSAN HENDERSON

Axis of evil

B

backtalk [back'-tok] *v.* 1. to talk back time, reverse the directionality of time through guided stuttering. 2. to talk inward, sucking your breath back through the vocal cords. 3. to address the dead by such talk. 4. *n.* instances of such talk. —SHELLEY JACKSON

badassness [bad'-ass-ness] *adj.* a term invented to describe those who would have been called cool, had the word not been overwrought, yet still can be called a badass even though that word is nearly as lame as "cool." It's a fairly tawdry paradox, really. *Al Pacino's Serpico-like badassness in* Serpico *was matched only by Toshiro Mifune's Serpico-like badassness in* The Seven Samurai. (SEE **Serpico.**)
—BENJAMIN COHEN

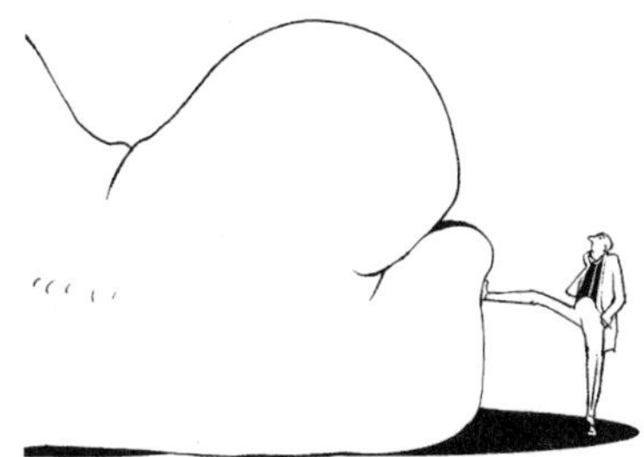

badassness

baddaboombaddabing [bah-duh-boom'-bah-duh-bing] *n.* the tendency to alter one's speaking voice and vocabulary to *Godfather*-type Tony Soprano lingo in order to cut short a political dialogue on an intractable problem; speaker assumes an alternate personality in order to avoid committing physical acts upon former friend or loved one. *"Grandwizard Rumsfeld-7 is only bombing the Canadians out of love." "Gavone! How would you like an icepick in ya head." "There you go again, baddaboombaddabing."*
—MATTHEW KLAM

bakin [bay'-kin] *n.* a person with whom one eats bacon. The prëeminence of bacon, not only as a foodstuff, but as an accompaniment to nearly every form of human interaction, is one of the greatest ironies in the history of gastronomy. As recently as the mid-21st century, bacon divided Christians from Jews, Hindus from Muslims, carnivores from vegetarians, the health-conscious from the sybaritic. Those who ate bacon took pleasure in cooking it in the presence of those to whom it was forbidden, who were nonetheless tantalized by its smell. In times of military conflict, the prisoners on one side were regularly forced to eat bacon, while those on the other were forbidden even to speak of it. Attempts to close the "bacon gap" with soy-based substitutes met with only limited success and were of no geopolitical consequence. It was only with the completion of the **Porcine Genome Project** that the chemical essence of bacon was isolated; a decade later, scientists at the Livermore National Laboratory successfully grafted bacon-flavor genes into an English cucumber. The resultant vegetable, known to us simply as "bacon," was a triumph not only for food engineering, but for international relations. At dawn, across India and the Middle East, groups of Muslims and Hindus, Christians, Jews, and Arabs, were drawn together by the smell of frying bacon, and together they sat down to eat. Coalitions were born of these breakfast meetings, and treaties brokered, and in time bacon became the emblem of international cooperation, much as, in 18th-century Europe, political awareness went hand in hand with coffee. As North Americans expanded their idea of "family" beyond the circle of their blood relatives, the term bakin, first used humorously, has become current. Today, few people remember that bacon once divided mankind, or even that it came from pigs; the story serves a reminder that we are not so much what we eat, as whom we eat it with. —PAUL LA FARGE

bakin

bald-is-beautiful [bald'-iz-byoo'-tih-fuhl] *adj.* a description, usually directed at men who have lost a good deal if not all of their hair. What had previously been a somewhat jokey, somewhat consoling remark, meant to soothe the egos of bald men, became an official part of the lexicon in 2009, when it was discovered by beauty scientists at Carleton College in Northfield, Minnesota, that bald actually is beautiful. A statistical analysis of Michael Jordan, the bald American eagle, several million infants, and old movie-footage of Yul Brynner in *Westworld* helped lead to this discovery. Further proof was culled from an controlled experiment by the Carleton scientists where several thousand men with comb-overs had their heads shaved and it was revealed that 78% of these formerly mildly unattractive men were now beautiful. The findings of the Carleton study were then confirmed when Donald Trump, a noted financier, real-estate magnate, and Mayor of New York (2008–2014), celebrated for his bad taste and astonishingly freakish comb-over, succumbed to pressure from the U.N. in 2009 and shaved his head. Images of Trump, which were proliferating around the world due to his election as Mayor of the Capital of the Universe, were causing psychotic-breaks from reality for fragile people with hair issues and an international health crisis was declared. Once Trump shaved his head, people marveled at how lovely he actually was and after serving as Mayor, he began to hang out with the famously bald Dalai Lama, forging a connection between spirituality and the accumulation of wealth that previously had not existed, which benefited a good many people—the poor opened savings accounts and the rich started praying and helping the poor. This gorgeous teaming up of the Dalai and the Donald thus solidified the phrase *bald-is-beautiful* as a full-fledged member of the English language. —JONATHAN AMES

bald-is-beautiful

bellbottom [bel'-bah-tum] 1. *n.* the precise moment when a person, place or thing demonstrates negative utility. Named for the bellbottom uniform trousers worn by sailors, which from 1871 onward were responsible for thousands of injuries until they were officially banned by the Filipino Navy in 2009 and replaced by the pinstriped poly-denim stirrup britches favored today. (SEE **yankee pants.**). 2. *v.* to make obsolete or outlive one's usefulness.

Paul La Farge • ***Istvan Banyai*** / Jonathan Ames • ***Barry Blitt*** / Jim Ruland

President Clinton bellbottomed when she appeared on Saturday Night Live *with Senator Seacrest.* 3. *adj.* describing a style of trousers with outsized cuffs popularized by urban Italian- and African-Americans in the late 1970s, Peruvian knife fighters in the early 2010s, and the North Jersey Disco Terrorists for a few weeks after the death of the Wizard Travolta on April 22, 2022.

—JIM RULAND

bellitoast [bel'-i-tohst] *adj.* 1. inclined or eager to make toast (sliced bread that has been browned by heat) instead of war; aggressively hungry for toast. 2. an agitated emotional state brought on by a lack of toast. *This low-carb bullshit is making me rather bellitoast.* 3. referring to the state, often characterized by war, in which there is no toast, nor hope of toast. 4. a person, event, sentiment, or the like, against whom another or others raise their glasses in negative salutation and then drink. *They drank a bellitoast to the emir because what is a damn emir anyway.* 5. *v.* to drink against the health of.

bellitoast

—STEPHEN GAGHAN

beng [beng] *n., v.,* bengy *adj.* used as a last resort after the Grammarian Restrictions of 2022 required all new words to be simple vowel-replacement variants of pre-existing words, and following bing, bang, bong, and bung, this versatile word was inevitably slotted to mean (*n.*) that thing where you suddenly jolt or jump up real quick in bed just at that moment before falling asleep because you think a train is barreling down on you; (*v.*) to suddenly jolt or jump up real quick in bed just at that moment before falling asleep because you think a train is barreling down on you; (*adj.*) in reference to the action of suddenly jolting or jumping up real quick in bed just at that moment before falling asleep because you think a train is barreling down on you. *"It happened again last night," Rhett confessed to Scarlet, "my bengy beng was benged."*

—BENJAMIN COHEN

billion [bill'-yun] *adj.* one hundred thousand million. Formerly, billion meant one thousand million, but this usage was proscribed by the Federal Deficit Control Act of 2008. Some texts persist in giving quantities in old billions (now called **skillions**), but never, under penalty of criminal prosecution, when referring to the federal budget deficit, which is estimated to rise to $9.7 billion this year.

—PAUL LA FARGE

birdsong [burd-sahng] *n.* in the **Great Dearth**, beginning roughly in the mid-20th century and continuing through approximately half of the 21st century, indescribably numerous varieties of birds and wildlife became radically diminished in number, in many cases brought to the very brink of extinction, and far too often beyond that brink. Not only ecologists and other members of the scientific community, but also vast segments of the general population grew more and more alarmed and at the same time increasingly angry and depressed at governmental failure to take emergency remedial action. By the end of the first quarter of the 21st century, however, highly coordinated citizen action and intensified educational programs gradually helped bring progressive political figures into national office, most notable among them the Nobelist Dr. Nicole Krauss, whose tenure as Secretary of the Interior (2036–2044) during the reform administration of Chelsea Clinton resulted not only in the reclamation of large areas of natural avian habitat but also in the setting aside and dedicating of enormous new expanses as sanctuaries for the breeding and preservation of wildlife, areas known as **Krauss Preserves**. Krauss was instrumental in helping effect the vital resurgence of myriad previously endangered species, a phenomenon—known as the **Krauss Outcome**—that crested in the third quarter of the 21st century, with remarkable results. As countless varieties of songbirds, for example, returned to previously vacant habitats both rural and urban, people of all vocations and classes found themselves thrilled at the richness of movement, color, and sound, all but forgotten, that now came back into their daily lives with the return of the birds. Many young people had never in their lives so much as heard birdsong before the success of the Krauss Outcome, while others had been unaware how deeply they had missed the pleasure of it. So great a degree of liveliness, optimism, and joy accompanied the return of the birds that the very term "birdsong" itself expanded into the language in sudden new ways. The term came to be used, for example, in the simple expression of approval or interest, so that in place of archaic words like "cool" or "rad," now was heard "birdsong." Expression of delight in a movie, book, or piece of music might take the form of "That was *birdsong!*" while the word also became a term of intimacy, delight, and affection, so that lovers might say to one another, "Oh, sweetheart, you're *birdsong*." (A similar linguistic adaptation took place with the phrase **fish story**. This phrase, of course, once referred to the notion of an exaggerated achievement or tale, hyperbole being used to bring credit on the speaker and therefore to be taken with a grain of salt. After the Krauss Outcome, however, when seas, waterways, rivers and lakes were once again clean, they soon came to be filled again, gloriously, with all variety of healthy and reproducing fish and water-life. So wonderful a resurgence was brought about by the Krauss Outcome that "fish story" evolved to mean something splendid, wonderful, even near miraculous. A famine averted against all odds, a major accident resulting in no deaths and only minor injuries, a picturesque and historic section of a city successfully preserved against the powerful will of speculators and developers—in cases like these will be heard expressions like: *This is just absolutely wonderful! What a fish story!*) —Eric Larsen

blasphuck [blass'-fuk] *v.* to screw in a consecrated place. Instance illustrated by an excerpt from the unpublished reminiscences of Chuck Pavkov (Peoria High School Class of 1977): *Christ we must have been seventeen, if that. Sharon and I yaw-yawing like a couple of orangutans and ripping each clothes off near third base on Pete Voanachen Memorial Field, drunk, 3 in the morning. And Sharon asks, wait a second, Chuck, who's Pete Voanachen? So I tell her the truth, that he was this kid who got run over by a refrigerator truck chasing a foul ball. And so Sharon says, well don't you think this is hallowed ground or something? I said it depends on how you define what we're doing. And so Sharon says, well it varies, right, I mean sometimes we call it profane, sometimes sacred? So I say what's it going to be? And Sharon says, no question about it, sacred. Which meant when I tried to bite her bra lock off, she says, no, honey, tonight use your hands. The moon was sliced half but bright and plump like a naked ass cheek and Sharon says, slower, slower, tell me about Pete Voanachen. And so I do, I tell her he played third and wore this old sweat-stained green hat and that he was mostly quiet, never shouted heybattabattaswing. He had a sister Judy who was pretty but had zits. At his funeral we all wore our cleats. You want to know more? No, she says. That's enough. So I say, time to do it profane? And she says, yeah. Yeah.*

—Peter Orner

Bliar [bliy'-ur] *n.* a British politician who has an uncomfortable relationship with truth: *Most honorable Lordship William Kinglsey Buckingsworth addressed the assembly thusly, "I daresay the most honorable gentleman* *from Birmingham has rather exhibited the traits of—how does modern parlance have it—a Bliar."* —RYAN BOUDINOT

blowkay [bloh'-kay] *adj.* of an attitude, typically exhibited by the electorate, that elected officials who have sexual relations outside of marriage while in office are less deserving of impeachment than officials whose decisions lead to the loss of human life. *Folks say the new senator from Rhode Island is a skirt chaser, but as long as he doesn't send thousands of Americans off to die in a war on false pretenses he's blowkay with me.* —RYAN BOUDINOT

blusteen [bluss'-teen] *n.* 1. the sense of entitlement that enables an incompetent but well-connected person to hold a position of authority without succumbing to self-doubt. 2. a delusional condition in which an amateur enthusiast deems himself to have professional qualifications at a given activity. 3. a corruption of "bloblipped" intended to express thick-headedness, viz, a crude and vicious insult. 4. a form of dyspepsia common to long-sufferers. *How did he endure all the failures? I'll tell you how—he was a hard case born with enough blusteen for three men.* —NICHOLAS DAWIDOFF

body bag [bah'-dee bag] *n.* 1. an artificial skin worn as punishment by perpetrators of hate crimes. *I was pretty screwed up, but after walking around in an African-American body bag, I see the world in a whole new way.* 2. [*archaic*] in military language, the self-contained transportation unit favored by decorated soldiers. A body bag provided protection from the elements and included storage space for personal effects and medals. Once a lucrative business, the production of body bags was discontinued after the signing of the **Covenant of All Nations.** *We brought our nation's heroes back home in body bags with much fanfare.* —COLSON WHITEHEAD

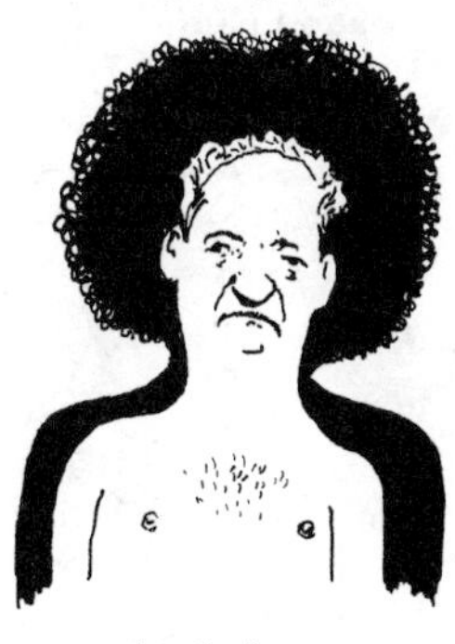

body bag

Bookmonster Babs [book'-mahn-stur babz] *n.* a mythological creature who delivers presents of books to children every year on the anniversary of their first read word. (SEE **Wordversary.**) Wildly popular in this reading-centric culture, Babs is a five-foot tall, purple-furred, eggplant-shaped monster with magical yellow boots who travels around the world on a spherical silver hovercraft dispersing her endless library of books to good boys and girls. On the night before their Wordversary, eager children lure Babs to their house by making a book for her, of their own drawings and/or stories. She has been the subject of much recent folklore and has inspired many Wordversary songs, for example: *"Tomorrow's Wordversary Day (I Hear Babs's Hovercraft Now!)"* and *"Zat You, Bõõkmonster Babs?"* —ANNE URSU

Bookmonster Babs

Bourchet [boor-shay'] *n.* a deep cavity dong, fashioned most commonly of durable, self-extracting foam, inserted rectally and controlled remotely by the host or a partner via a wireless handheld device. Once the dong has self-extracted upward through the entire body cavity (usually a three-to-six hour process known as "shulling"), the host experiences an acute and destabilizing sense of surrender and humility, which, in most cases, provokes a form of proto-orgasmic synesthesia that the host can, with the proper training and concentration, sustain for up to seventy-two hours. During this period, the granularity of bodily control is such that a host or partner can actually massage the heart of the host or regulate breathing. When the period has ended, the Bourchet can be deflated and expelled, and in some cases used again. Certain groups have attempted to withdraw the device while in full bloom to present to partners or family members as an intimate, tree-like body map, although this practice is not endorsed or condoned by the Ministry of Health and Safety.

Though it is difficult to imagine a historical moment in which the rectal introduction of foreign matter into the body was deemed shameful and ineffective, the initial adoption rate of the Boucher, especially among males, was low. Starting in the year 15, however, after an intense and violent outbreak of suicide among adult males in the Western Hemisphere, the Boucher's popularity spiked, so much so that by year 18, one out of every four citizens claimed to own at least one Bourchet, with three out of every four remaining males claiming ownership. One out of seven regularly wore the device to work at least once a week and claimed that the practice enhanced productivity.

—MATTHEW DERBY

brain [brayn] *n.* a gray matter, makes waves (SEE **scriggle scraggle**); the function of which relegated to robotic bollards, teeny-weeny replicating nanobots, and heretics. In our government, **The Church and State of Latter Latter Day Euclideans**, privileged officers, bolo-ed and booted, wait in joyful hope for the coming of the red cow, whose principle of stomach is the basis for all thought of said officers and upstanding citizens. The red cow is not to be confused with the red cow of 1997, born in Israel to a black-and-white mother and dun-colored bull, and declared "not red enough" by the forefathers of our great nation church. The brain is held in such high regard that it is guerdoned with exemption from the cares of office and carefully excised from the cranium of the commander-in-chief by the finest health care professionals, Manny, Moe, and Jack, then pulped to supply nutrients to pockets of flora remaining after the landmark Clear the Sky, Save the Air Act. Children, exempt until the age of six from the national ban on "Why?", "Where are?", and "What next?" can be seen, until the "?" feeling subsides, strapped to robotic bollards lining the great highways, along which the GM carts creak and lesser cows graze, deranged.

—FRAN GORDON

braydio [bray'-dee-oh] *n.* 1. a device that delivers harsh, high-pitched rhetoric via electromagnetic waves, as in sound broadcasts or two-way communication. *He spent most of the morning listening to the braydio, on which an unpleasant man with a shrill voice was criticizing the Senator's military service.* 2. any communication of that nature that takes place by means of that device or a similarly constructed device.

braydio

—BEN GREENMAN

Brazilian [bruh-zil'-yun] *n.* the active removal of excessive bush, by any means necessary. *I feel so liberated now that we've given the country a good Brazilian.*

Brazilian

—KEN FOSTER & ERIC HANSON

breathing room [bree'-thing room] *n.* any monument in the form of an interior space, created in the oral cavity and throat of a mourner by the pronunciation of a specified sequence of noises, usually but not necessarily the names of the dead. In the late 21st century, memorials to wars and national disasters had become both so huge and so numerous in major cities as to force occupants into increasingly distant suburbs, turning the cities into giant funeral parks, though only a few mourners and flower vendors ventured into the barren, windy avenues and plazas. A rogue terrorist attack leveled one of these abandoned, funereal cities, killing only pigeons; the ingenious mayor, rather than rebuilding the memorials, or raising a memorial to the memorials, issued instructions for the citizens to construct private memorials out of breath. These proved popular. Meanwhile, the leveled city was rebuilt, using the materials of bygone memorials, and resettled. One might find a name engraved in the wall behind your tub, or use the bronze hand of a general to hook an oven mitt on. Memorials became a more private affair as people discovered they could create memorials of their own design just by talking to each other, adding refinements with their lips and tongues. **Breathing Room** *n.* when capitalized, the cathedral-like space located in the Interstitial States where the terminally ill may deliver a citizen's address to an assembled crowd or no fewer than two librarians and a stenographer, to be recorded and entered into an archive of last words. The space was formed by the generosity of the large numbers of citizens who contributed their private memorials (breathing rooms) to expand the once modest space. —SHELLEY JACKSON

Bronx silk [brahnks' silk] *n.* 1. the highest known grade of silk, first spun in 2015, upon the discovery of extensive colonies of silkworms (long erroneously misidentified as rats) beneath the 6 train subway tracks in the Bronx, which led to that area's secession from the United States and ascension as the world's richest source of silk and a major player in global politics. 2. *adj*, to be exceptionally soft or fine, in the manner of Bronx silk. *The skin of his forearm was Bronx silk.* 3. a popular drink composed of mango, yogurt, and cream of opium (*colloq.*) 4. a post-hiphop style of music characterized by the contrapuntal use of the accordion and the Magdalene flute.

—STACEY D'ERASMO

brother-sister [bruh'-thur sis'-tur] *n.* the one woman, unrelated by blood, to whom another woman feels closest. As enjoying the deepest possible tie between two hetero- or homosexual women involving every intimacy, complication, and confession, while sidestepping the overtly erotic. (SEE ALSO **sister-brother**) After **The Event,** the Great Congress adjudged that there were too few categories to contain and taxonomically acknowledge the varieties of human connectedness. **Wife, daughter, lesbian lover**—these each described a differing subset of relation-hood, but each carried its own cargo of additional connotations, onuses, etc. Speaker after Congress-speaker rose to mention a state too seldom found in our dictionaries or even dentist-waiting-room magazines. Congressional testimony reads: "What of a woman who feels very dependent upon some one other woman to whom she's super-super-close, but without the first woman's ever consciously wanting to erotically conjoin with, or certainly go down upon said friend, or ever to even get very naked with her for long? Name that state. Because that is a real thing." By unanimous resolution (the way everything was passed at the Congress after The Event's devastating proof of what fractious arguments and too narrow a defining can bring down upon us), the brother-sister, sister-brother category was added to our list of acknowledged life-roles. This has made it far easier to leave an inheritance to one's brother-sister, since its assured dignity when written out in legal documents, looks really very good. It is now acceptable at parties to hear, *"I want you to meet my beloved brother-sister, Joanie."* At a recent funeral, it was seen that the phrase has already found its way onto gravestones. *"Here lies the best of darn possible sister-brothers, my Sam, fellow-sufferer and Red Sox fan."* —ALLAN GURGANUS

Brownie [brow'-nee] *n.* 1. a member of the junior branch (six to eight years of age) of the Girl Scouts organization. 2. (with walnuts) usually sold at bake sales as fund raiser; also used primarily on front lines and courted in the Southwest in election years; valued as a renewable and expendable pool of inexpensive landscape and short-order labor. 3. **brownie point** [*orig. Texas*] a vote cast for Republican by eight-year-old girls or Latinos/as of legal age. Also, a scoring denomination for points earned by Cleveland Ohio's professional football organization. *It was an exciting game; we beat the Jets by three brownie points.* (Drew Carey) —SALVADOR PLASCENCIA

bubbaskins [bub-uh-skinz] *n.* 1. a blanket made of soft, absorbent faux-leather used to wrap newborn babies, giving them the feeling of being back in the womb, thus making the transition into the world easier. Babies wrapped in bubbaskins are known to giggle three months earlier than those that weren't. 2. an inanimate object designed to comfort; an item that helps one through a difficult time. —HEIDI MEREDITH

bubbleheads [buh'-bull-hedz] *n. pl.* endearing slang for people who wear large plastic bubbles over their heads to prevent the spread of socially caustic substances (i.e., contagious infection, second-hand cigarette smoke, loud cell phone rants, etc.) *My sister has joined the bubbleheads until her antibiotic-resistant tuberculosis clears up.*

bubbleheads

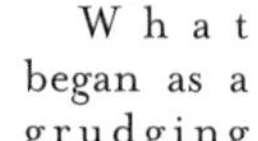

What began as a grudging effort to enable smokers and non-smokers to inhabit the same airplane has ballooned into a huge cultural trend. Since 2012, all contagious persons, cell phone addicts, and smokers have worn a fitted, plastic, soundproof and airtight bubble over their heads while in public. Lightweight, scratch-resistant and comfortable, the bubble allows neither carcinogen nor virus nor babble from escaping to irritate or infect others. The popular smoking bubbles come equipped with their own internal tobacco release system, which enables wearers to simply press a small button at the base of the neck and breathe deeply as their favorite brand of smoke slowly fills the container. Once satisfied, bubbleheads simply find an open space, remove the bubble, release the stale smoke, and repeat. Recently bubbles have also been fitted with another useful device: personalized car security alarms, which allow wearers to be immediately informed when a garbage truck has just driven past their vehicle without waking every baby on the block. —BRENT HOFF

budcat [buhd'-kat] *n.* a human being whose relationship to other humans is laissez-faire in attitude; a nice person who likes solitude; a person of independent character who is nevertheless affectionate; someone who doesn't cling. —LYNNE TILLMAN

bullshit [bul-shit] *n.* authentic, verifiable, and true; that which we should

Allan Gurganus / Salvador Plascencia / Heidi Meredith / Brent Hoff • ***Raúl Colon*** / Lynne Tillman / Eli Horowitz have known all along. Initially, bullshit described only its literal meaning: the feces of a male bovine. Over time, however, the word developed negative connotations, due to a widely-held 20th-century belief that bulls did not, in fact, shit; eventually the word came to refer to anything devoid of truth and/or significance. This continued until the mid-21st century, when scientists conducted a close inspection of

bullshit

bovine bowel systems (SEE ILL.) and determined that the males of the species produced fecal matter that was fully corporeal, robust, and aromatic. This discovery captured the public's imagination, and bullshit quickly assumed its current meaning.
—ELI HOROWITZ

burning bush [bur'-ning bush] *n.* a prickly outgrowth, first discovered in ancient Egypt. A final sighting occurred on November 2, 2004. (SEE **oil, stolen elections, pre-emptive wars, loss of jobs, contempt for democracy.**) *The last time a nation listened to a bush, its people wandered in the desert for forty years.*
—PAUL AUSTER

burning bush

bush [bush] *vi.* 1. to land a job or position for which one is egregiously unqualified, esp. through unscrupulous means: *to bush it back to Crawford.* 2. to take a long and unearned vacation. 3. to sneak home during working hours. *Mr. Bemis was off with the truck for three hours, so I bushed it back to Crawford for a quick snort and a nooner with Sally Mae.* 4. [since 2005] to be sent back to the place of one's origin, esp. in disgrace. —SCOTT PHILLIPS

bush [bush] *n.* 1. a poisonous family of shrubs, now extinct. (SEE **bushed, bush-league, bushwa.**) —PAUL AUSTER

bushwhack [bush' wak] *v.* a term that denotes the removal from office by the force of public outrage (a **whacking**) of any public official who has misrepresented, falsified, or in any way led a nation into unilateral action obviating planetary consensus. A grassroots movement—comparable to the more bureaucratic impeachment—that brings about the whacking or removal from office of a mistrusted public official. Bushwhacking is now part of the inauguration ceremony, wherein a newly sworn-in president symbolically whacks a small bush with the right hand (same hand he or she raised for oath of office) to represent the transparency of his or her forthcoming administration. January 20 has become a national (USA) holiday, on which citizens symbolically whack bushes as a sign of their commitment to this peace and justice. Many save their old Christmas trees for this purpose. —JULIA ALVAREZ

bushwhack

C

Café Pantelone Americano [kaf'-ay pant'-uh-loh-nee uh-mayr'-ik-ah-no] *n.* a coffee drink comprising skim milk, rasberry flavored powder, and a variety of spices and black tea that can be sipped either iced or hot, while wearing tracksuit pants accidentally put on backward in a rush to buy the morning coffee. —MATTHEW KLAM

candidoxy [kan'-di-doks-ee] *n.* an offering of oneself as a candidate while claiming a special relationship with a god. —BEN GREENMAN

canineadate [kay'-niyn-uh-dayt] *n.* a dog who runs for elected office. Although it seemed a silly idea at first, we soon learned that canineadates proved quite successful, and over time many canine contenders found their way to higher office. The result was more open spaces with less automobile traffic, and low-grade dog food stopped using such strange ingredients. —ARTHUR BRADFORD

Casualty Friday(s) [kazh'-oo-el-te fri'-daz] *n.* 1. the sixth day of the week, following Thursday and preceding Saturday, designated in 2005 by the United States government for the acknowledgment (in various media) of American citizens and others who have been injured, maimed, crippled, or killed in wars or violent incursions. 2. the sixth day of the week, following Thursday and preceding Saturday, upon which all nations signatory to the Casualty Friday Convention of 2006 agreed to acknowledge (in various media) their citizens and others who have been injured, maimed, crippled, or killed in wars or violent incursions. Though made redundant by the International Hug Treaty of 2052, the convention was adopted by all nations —with the exception of Russia and China—when it was agreed that such announcements every day of the week were just too damn depressing. —HANNAH YOUNG & DAVID BEZMOZGIS

catful [kat'-ful] *adj.* a human being whose behavior is reminiscent of a playful or contented cat. —LYNNE TILLMAN

catfeasience, catfeasient [kat-feez'-ens, kat-feez'-ent] *n., adj.* willful, arbitrary, and malevolent behavior reminiscent of a cat who scratches furniture, doesn't use the litterbox, and is generally incorrigible. *If he continues to curse me at parties, his catfeasience will force me to leave him.* —LYNNE TILLMAN

celebrititis [suh-leb'-ri-tiyt-is] *n.* 1. an inflammation of the gray matter of the brain caused by over-exposure to celebrity magazines, celebrity television shows, celebrity websites, and blockbuster

celebrititis

Matthew Klam / Ben Greenman / Arthur Bradford / Hannah Young & David Bezmozgis / Lynne Tillman / Lynne Tillman / Siri Hustvedt • ***Maira Kalman***

Hollywood movies. In its acute form, the disease erases all personal memories and replaces them with sitcom reruns, infomercials, meaningless explosions, car chases, and sparse banal dialogue from action films. The illness, which became epidemic in the early years of the 21st century, began to decline by mid-century. In 2037, the neurologist Dorothea Brooke discovered that heavy doses of poetry and philosophy had a therapeutic effect on her patients. Emily Dickinson's *Collected Poems* and Emmanuel Kant's *Critique of Pure Reason* were shown to be particularly beneficial in reversing the harmful effects of the illness. —SIRI HUSTVEDT

centaurian [sen-tor'-ee-en] *adj.* pertaining to the nearest stellar system, comprising three stars, Alpha Centauri A, Alpha Centauri B, and Proxima Centauri. The word initially came into use in connection with the robotic exploration of the Centauri system, launched at the so-called Second Dawn of space flight. The spacecraft's 70-year ion-propelled journey to the planet-rich system engaged the imaginations of several generations of young people on every continent, who looked forward to the spacecraft's arrival at its destination and its search for life there. Centaurian then entered the language to describe any forward-looking exploratory project, especially a project whose results would be known only to our children. Also, **centaurian,** *n.* —KEN KALFUS

centing [sent'-ing] *v./gerund* retail and banking practice of allowing customers to round up all bills and electronic transactions to the nearest five or ten cents, with the difference donated to charitable funds. Adopted in 2010, in recognition of the devaluation of individual pennies, which verged on worthlessness, but which in aggregate proved a substantial fiscal resource. —PAUL COLLINS

cheney [chay'-nee] *vi.* to parlay one cushy job into another, esp. via personal connections. *Ron clearly hoped to cheney his way from Chairman of the Board at Marduk Industries to the Ambassador of Luxemburg, preferably using other peoples' campaign donations.* —SCOTT PHILLIPS

Chippets [chip'-its] *n.* abbrev. form of **Chip puppets**. Initially sock puppets, later foam and animated marionettes, used by public figures and corporate entities to deliver quarterly reports, inquest findings, product recalls, and State of the Union addresses in a manner that circumvents biometric evaluation by **P-Chips** and related technologies. —PAUL COLLINS

chiraqui [shee-rak'-ee] *n.* a term once used for anyone exhibiting anti-Bush sentiments, particularly high-ranking French officials. —PAUL MULDOON

Cheney, Dick [chay-nee, dik] U.S. Vice President, 2000-2004; husband of Duke Ramirez; First Lady of Fresh Hell, 2010-2014. (SEE **Cheney Effect.**) —JEFFREY EUGENIDES

Cheney Effect [chay'-nee ee-fekt'] *n.* the manifestation of personality changes brought on by the reception of a transplanted organ, usually the heart. —JEFFREY EUGENIDES

chronofilter [kro'-no-fil-tur] *n.* 1. camera filter revealing a person as they appeared earlier in their life. Although its effect on surroundings (landscapes, buildings, cars and passersby) must be taken into account, it is often used in films and by elderly people to prove to their children and grandchildren that they once were beautiful. *Without the invention of the chronofilter, the classic* Annie Hall Again

chronofilter

Siri Hustvedt / Ken Kalfus / Paul Collins / Scott Phillips / Paul Collins / Paul Muldoon / Jeffrey Eugenides / Jeffrey Eugenides / Andrew Sean Greer • ***Nicholas Blechman*** *might never have been made, since both Allen and Keaton were well into their nineties.* 2. a nostalgic, conservative view of the world, usually falsely idealistic. 3. any form of hindsight.

chronofilter *v.* 1. use a chronofilter. 2. view the world with erroneous nostalgia. 3. use hindsight. *Only by chronofiltering turn-of-the-century America can we begin to understand the baffling reign of George W. Bush.* (Vice Pres. Chelsea Clinton)

—Andrew Sean Greer

citytime [sit'-ee-tiym] *n.* multifaceted alternate reality created by the sheer size, sensory overload, and human congestion of large cities in bygone days. As in this example from *The Moon at the End of Street,* a novel written by Diane Ackerman in 2034, in which a small-town woman discovers citytime in New York City circa 2004:

"After a month in Manhattan, she learned to eat breakfast or lunch on the subway, when she had to, from small plastic tubs or folds of tinfoil. She learned to turn her large turquoise ring around so that it looked like a simple silver band. She learned to separate her credit cards, cash, and keys when she went out. She stopped setting her hair and wore it in a huge weather system, she sometimes referred to as la coupe sauvage. She found herself searching the glass on subway doors as she stood waiting to get off at her stop, subconsciously alert for the reflection of danger. She learned that living anywhere in New York was like living in the suburbs: you had to allow time for commuting in the overall equation of your travels. When you left home, it was always a day trip, and you had to pack accordingly: sensible shoes, pills, bags of chamomile tea, a paperback to read or work to catch up on. She learned to walk so briskly that when she left the city friends struggled to keep up with her, but in town the pace was slower than average, a Manhattanite's stroll. She learned to wear sneakers en route to engagements and carry high heels in a bag or briefcase. She learned to wear a wide-strapped purse across her chest like a Mexican war hero's bandolero. She practiced such expressions as "Hit the ground running," "Let's dismount and fight on foot," and "Cut him off at the knees" for use in business meetings, as in "Let's not wait till next week to contact them, let's hit the ground running." She became adept with chopsticks. She learned that there were never enough public restrooms. She held her body close with her parcels and purse held tight under the arms, tight against her ribs, as if she were a skater in a turnless pirouette. She learned to decipher the lascivious unbuttoning of her with their eyes some men did on the subways. She learned that New Yorkers were on an eternal quest for good bagels and bran muffins. She learned to assume a siege mentality, to live at low-level alarm, always looking over her shoulder or down an empty block, to be guarding her purse, to wait for the wallop across the back of the shoulders or head, which never came. At first, it was hard to describe the filth to herself or to others. Just setting her bag down on the ground took nerve. So many people had crossed that spot with their heels and sputum and squatting dogs. She learned to wash her long hair every day instead of twice a week, and she began thinking of facials as ordinary hygiene. She learned that it was possible to burn out all of one's

inner electricity from meeting too many people too often. She learned to use her answering machine as a bullet-proof vest against overly zealous callers or acquaintances she didn't wish to renew. She learned that people conducted friendships with different rhythms. Elsewhere, real friends saw each other often, a couple of times a week. In New York, seeing someone at two-week intervals was considered unusual and signified an intimate friendship. She learned that there was such a bazaar of shops and eateries that it was possible to purchase a wonderful low-fat cheese sprinkled with vegetables and herbs, and have no idea the next week which of 10,000 shops it came from. She learned the difference between danger and violence. Danger, which she sometimes seemed to court in her leisure life, had nothing to do with what one felt walking down a dark street after sunset. That was violence. Danger was simpler. The body would flood with convenient chemicals; it took so little active will to respond once adrenaline was on the prowl. But violence horrified with no physical preparation. The city specialized in violence, cataclysmic moments of terror with no mechanism for response. She learned that there was a high and low tide of garbage on the streets after a weekend. She learned to use her kitchen as a place to keep beverages, and have meals delivered from twenty Chinese or Japanese restaurants, by polite young Oriental men who would not cross the threshold to her apartment while she fetched money to pay them with, because it might appear indelicate. She thought New York was the pinnacle for most fields, and that she would find the best theater, the best restaurants, the ablest professionals and so on. But she learned that New York didn't contain only the best of a thing, but more if it at every level. She learned that women were bringing back elaborate courtship rituals, because they feared AIDS and other things. She learned that the city was weighted toward the night, that events began so late one had to rise late, dine late, sleep late. She learned that dining at 9:00 p.m. had nothing to do with convenience, or even with allowing time to shower and decompress after a day at red-alert, but a kind of city prowess, a collective refusal to be bullied by the clock. She learned not to make eye contact on the mobbed streets. She learneed that New Yorkers were just as provincial as people elsewhere despite being cosmopolitan. She learned that New York's early immigrants crossed the oceans either in steerage or in first class. In a sense, that had never changed. They still lived in steerage or in first. The wealthy could live high above the streets, be driven sleekly through the din, be safely escorted by chauffeurs from door to door, float on the sparkling seas of New York culture. The poor continued to live in the grime, noise, and the waves. She learned the expression "trading up," which meant that no appointment was ever certain or sacred, but depended on the sudden appearance of a perhaps more important person or opportunity on a given day at a given time. She herself had been scheduled on someone else's day, after her caller first "erased" the other appointment. Elsewhere, an argument was taken to the streets only as the ultimate move. "Why don't we open the windows, so the whole block knows I got fired!" a man might scream at his wife, or she might screech at him: "Do you want the neighbors to hear?" But, in New York, people took their private lives into the streets. Strangers would approach each other at bus stops with shocking intimacies. Couples would argue in detail on a street cor-

ner. Strangers revealed extraordinary information about their families and daily lives to people they met on subways or in stores. In New York, even the wealthy lived like sharecroppers, with a neighbor only a thin wall away. However large their apartment was, it was still pint-sized compared to what human beings needed. So, the whole city was their livingroom, and a million strangers shared it like slightly embarrassing relatives sleeping on the roll-away bed in the front room and sharing the bath and kitchen. She learned that the more menial a person's job was, the more his or her dignity could be boosted with a long title. So what used to be a personnel officer was now a "human resource specialist," a garbage collector was a "sanitation engineer," and she presumed one day a bum would be called an "alcohol technician." She learned that you buy fresh flowers on the street as you also could in Europe. Because New York was the ultimate melting pot, she had thought that when she arrived her literary friends would introduce her to people she might enjoy in other fields, in business, the sciences, or other arts. But she learned that New Yorkers were clannish. Literary people mixed mainly with literary people, theater people mixed with theater people. It was oddly collegiate. She learned that being famous in New York meant being seen a lot at gatherings of one's clan, PEN and publishing parties, in her case, like the season's swishest do, a party celebrating a recently discovered novel by Vladimir Nabokov. She learned that people got just as bored with their lives when they had endless things to do and endless people to meet as when they had none at all. She learned that men wanted to date her for all the right reasons, and she said no to them for all the right reasons, but she learned that having many men to choose from didn't make it any easier to find the "right" man to spend some time with. He was still a rare commodity, full of humor and passion. Sheer number didn't change that. She learned that people stayed in their neighborhoods as if in walled cities, whose fortifications were restaurants, subways, vest-pocket parks. Uptowners suddenly developed nosebleeds at 14th Street; Villagers feared migraines if they headed the other way. She learned that people lived by messenger and message unit. People often maintained long friendships with lengthy phone chats every few weeks, without actually seeing the person for motnhs on end, though they might live only blocks away. And it was possible conduct a considerable, intense, intimate friendship by phone with someone one had never actually met. She learned that many New Yorkers had never seen their cleaning lady, for whom they left a check once a week, and returned to find her damp mop upturned in the shower stall. What did a woman clean in a small studio apartment for $50 a week? She learned that New Yorkers used their bodies like cars when they took them into the streets, swerving through traffic, honking at people who got into scrapes. She learned that New Yorkers were so tribal they even divided the city into districts, where they spent most of their working and sometimes family life: district between 28th and 35th streets and Eighth and Sixth avenues, the jewelry district at 46th Street and Sixth Avenue, the theater district at Times Square, etc. She learned to say "I'll pencil you in for Friday," because

in the great kaleidoscopic calendar of the city, no date was firm. How did friendships arise then, real friendships, in which love accumulated at sweet intervals? How was it possible to be casual? Nothing was definite. It was like life in that respect; despite one's best efforts at hog-tying the moment with dentist appointments, deadlines, and movie dates, death didn't require you to keep a day free. One was always penciled in. She learned that even if she drank bottled water from Poland, Israel, France, or the Adirondacks, her stomach would often feel dodgy. Especially if she ate street food like roasted chestnuts or soft pretzels; then she lived like one of the pigeons and it shouldn't surprise her to be ill. But after a week of lunching out at fancy restaurants, her stomach might be off. In New York, you could dine chicly, but there wasn't always nourishment. The women wore their hair in wind-whipped unset cascades of curls and kinks, as if they were Minnesota farm girls or mercenaries from Midwest, not executives or secretaries or lawyers or teachers. The styles looked wild and untamed, but cost between $50 and $275 every six weeks for a hair stylist to achieve. In many taxicabs, a small cardboard Christmas tree room deodorizer hung on a small thread from the rearview mirror, and the doorhandles might be eaten away to the foam rubber pulp so there was nothing to hold onto even to pull the door closed. When said "It's a jungle out there," they didn't mean it literally, but orchids grew everywhere in New York, bundled in plastic with their stems tightly rooted in florists' test-tubes of nutrients and water. To the flowers, it was summer on the veldt, not a Korean deli on the corner of First Avenue. She learned that in the city's great river of power, some maneuvered with deft strokes of their paddles. She learned the secret of some wheelers and dealers, the power that cut through any opponent's nerves, soul, or will. She learned it from watching a literary agent who juggled lives like small hand axes. The secret to real power was not to care about the outcome. She discovered that living in New York was like living beside an eclipse of the sun that was always in view. She learned never to look at it directly, and that if she looked at it all at once she would go blind."

—DIANE ACKERMAN

civil servant [si'-vel ser'-vent] *n.* a man or woman (but usually a man, often a distressingly smirking one) who, since being found guilty for securities fraud, stock manipulation, and/or corporate tax evasion, must spend the rest of his life doing the laundry, preparing the meals, and cleaning the bathrooms of the college students whose tuition is paid from a stockpile of his or her (but usually his) illegally inflated year-end bonuses. *Oh, that dude? Don't mind him—he's just my civil servant.* (SEE ALSO **grasso.**)

—DAVID AMSDEN

civil unrest [si'-vel un-rest'] *n.* the state in which a community of people find themselves overwhelmed by a feeling of blissful exhaustion following an evening of boundless partying because they had nothing—absolutely nothing—to worry about. —DAVID AMSDEN

Clean Bill of Health *n.* an addendum to the Bill of Rights added to the Constitution in the year 2012, outlining every American's right to health care and prescription drugs. Designed to replace the previous ("Dirty") Bill of Health, passed in the fall of 2004, which gave "health" "insurance" megacorporations the right to charge customers as much as they wanted for as little real medical service as possible. (The so-called D.B.H. was the natural extension of health-industry practices in the 90s and 00s, during which the cost of medical care skyrocketed while insurance benefits plunged, and doctors' reimbursements shrank until the average physician was earning less than the average burger-flipper. In 2005, millions of Americans began dying of common curable illnesses, for which no one could afford care or drugs anymore, and finally the heads of the health insurance megacorporations dropped off too. The few remaining Congressmen who were still hale enough to drag themselves to the Capitol quickly passed laws entitling everyone to health care, and the President, sick of being sick himself, let them slide through.) Under the Clean Bill of Health, everyone living within the boundaries of the fifty states is entitled to unlimited medical, dental, and optical care, and receives complete prescription-drug coverage. Doctors' visits last a minimum of one half hour, doctors are compensated according to a generous and fair fee structure, and no one can be denied care simply for being sick or old. Even prisoners within the U.S. penitentiary system are protected under the C.B.H., thus ending widespread outbreaks of infectious disease in prisons. Gradually, the population of the States is returning to pre-D.B.H. levels. —JULIE ORRINGER

cloudreader [klowd'-ree-dur] *n.* an elected representative charged with reading and interpreting cloud shapes for the benefit of mankind; a member of the third legislative body (the **Nimbus**) of the United States Congress, added by Constitutional amendment in 2076; the decisions of

cloudreader

the Nimbus come in the form of nonbinding recommendations. *Cloudreaders reached a consensus on the shape of yesterday's storm and approved legislation recommending "contemplation breaks" in the workplace and outdoor "contemplation areas" for workers to take those breaks.* —JOHN HENRY FLEMING

cluster pie [klus'-tur piy] *n.* the 2005 universal, non-negotiable cease-fire forced armies to discover alternate uses for conventional weaponry in addition to nuclear weaponry. Cluster bombs are now used to deliver food-aid. Forty feet above ground the weapons open and half-baked pies descend to the earth rather than thousands of small, bouncing munitions meant to kill and maim for years to come. *Saag paneer is the most popular cluster pie. My family was starving in the hills of Marin until the army dropped a saag paneer cluster pie on our commune.*
—ANTHONY SWOFFORD

cockpit [kok'-pit] *n.* 1. photo op with Texas Air National Guard. 2. photo op aboard U.S.S. Abraham Lincoln. 3. photo op at Abu Ghraib prison.
—SUSAN HENDERSON

colinoscopy [ko'-lin-ah-skop-ee] *n.* a term once used for a tendency exhibited by high-ranking officials in the George W. Bush regime to examine their consciences and find them clear. (SEE **colinectomy.**) —PAUL MULDOON

colin-powwow [ko'-lin pow'-ow] *n.* 1. a meeting or gathering in which subordinates express opinions, often well-considered and passionate, that are ultimately dismissed by superiors. 2. any disingenuous display of protocol. *We knew upper management was set on slashing the workforce, so it was galling to watch them feign interest in our arguments during the requisite colin-powwow.* —RYAN HARTY

college [kah'-lij] *v.* 1. [*archaic*] to steal an election through the esoteric workings of the electoral college, a now-defunct electoral system used in national contests until 2008. 2. to deprive of anything valuable by the use of deceit or fraud. *When Janine caught her husband salsa-dancing with her best friend Elanor, whom she'd just nursed through a long recovery from breast-enhancement surgery, she realized with bitter certitude that she'd been colleged.* SYN. **defraud, swindle, hose** —RYAN HARTY

common sense [kahm'-un sens] *n.* [*archaic*] a chimera used back in the early 21st century as an appeal and panecea. *Everything will be all right eventually as long as common sense prevails.* [Proven to be an oxymoron.] —GLEN DAVID GOLD

compassionometer [kum-pash'-un-ah-mit-ur] *n.* an LED traffic readout, used at strategic commuting points, which allows commuters traveling by automobile to check their compassion index upon approach. The international community has required the installation of compassionometers to date only in Argentina, France, Sweden, and, of course, throughout the U.S. —SUSAN WHEELER

compassionometer

condeeluusion [kon-dee-loo'-shun] *n.* a term once used for a tendency exhibited by high-ranking officials in the George W. Bush regime 1. to have a false impression 2. to convey one. (SEE **condeescenension.**) —PAUL MULDOON

doing the condoleesy

condoleese [kan-doh-leez'] *n.* a dialect of American English characterized by extremely precise enunciation, a highly specialized vocabulary, and the intention to deceive or obfuscate. *We had hoped to glean some meaning from the Secretary's testimony, but it came out pure condoleese.*

—SCOTT PHILLIPS

condoleesy [kon'-doh-lee-zee] *adj.* a person who uses righteousness and self justifications in attempts to hide his or her error of judgment or condones such behavior; a cheap shot by a political official in attempts to keep himself or herself or his/her candidate in office. (SEE **cheesy.**) *What do you mean "the evil empire"? Stop being so condoleesy!* In popular usage/slang, **doing the condoleesy** refers to a type of dance in which partners slyly shift positions in seeming attempt to cover each other's back.

—JULIA ALVAREZ

constipervative [kahn'-stip-urv'-uh-tiv] *n.* an intolerant, uptight, narrow-minded individual who suffers instant hypertension when confronted with an argument that differs from his point of view.
—RAUL COLÓN

constipervative

Ryan Harty / Ryan Harty / Glen David Gold / Susan Wheeler • ***R. Sikoryak*** / Paul Muldoon / Scott Phillips / Julia Alvarez • ***R. Sikoryak*** / Raul Colón • ***Raul Colón***

cooties [koo'-teez] *n.* the last remaining disease uncured by medicine. *When an outbreak of cooties was reported in the third grade classroom, boys and girls were separated as a precaution; the outbreak was forgotten the next morning.* —JOHN HENRY FLEMING

corporate interest [kor'-puh-rut in'-tuh-rest] *n.* 1. the popular tourist practice of, interest in, or attraction to visiting old "corporations" as historical artifacts, met with growing popularity after the demise of corporations after the 2010s, which were at that time replaced by co-operative regional ventures regulated by reference to the local and community benefits they provided; modeled after historic preservationist tourism, you know, like with Williamsburg, Virginia and all that. 2. [*archaic*] entirely disabused notion formerly referring to the self-interest expressed by corporate entities, especially with respect to their egregious, duplicitous, and wholly destructive ties to government, legislation, and public welfare. —BENJAMIN COHEN

coupnap [koo'-nap] *v.* to remove a world leader by force, especially in order to advance one's nation's own agenda or to prevent a locally beneficial type of government from taking root or advancing. 2. to abduct someone from office while making it appear that the abduction was a result of a coup d'état. 3. to hold hostage the head of foreign government in an undisclosed location until said leader has been silenced, disappeared, or killed. (*pt/pp* **coupnapped/coupnapping**) Examples: *President Jean Bertrand Aristide of Haiti has been the victim of both a coup d'état and a coupnapping between 1990 and 2004. The coupnapping of Hugo Chavez, President of Venezuela, was unsuccessful after millions of his country's citizens demanded his return. No United States-led coupnappings have been reported since the American people experienced a régime change—note that it was not a coupnapping—in the mid 2000s.*
—EDWIDGE DANTICAT

crack-houses [krak'-how-zez] *n.* tax-supported safe houses designed to rescue those who fall through the socio-economic cracks. These facilities provide food, clothing, shelter, substance-abuse rehabilitation, psychological counseling, second-language lessons, and job-skills training. Staffed by a permanent core of professionals, each is also assigned a squad of Peeps (SEE **Peeps**) to assist residents. Each facility helps to sustain itself through small-business enterprises staffed by present and former residents. Some of the most successful include bakeries, organic gardens, wind-truck repair shops, day-care facilities, clothing workshops, creative recycling services, and networks of skilled carpenters, plumbers, gardeners, electricians and computer technicians available for hire. May be associated with local colleges and offer credit toward certificates and degrees. —CORNELIA NIXON

cran- [kran] *prefix* indicating skepticism or "so-called"ness, allowing the speaker to distance himself from his words; essentially, a verbal expression of quotation marks, designed to replace **air-quotes**, which were deemed awkward, unfair to the handless, and generally annoying. 2. blended or infused with cranberry flavoring. —ELI HOROWITZ

creatocracy [kree-ayt-ok'-ruh-see] *n.* a government that is replenished by the creativity of independent artists, thinkers, scientists, and community-minded citizens. —WENDY WASSERSTEIN

crenarian

crenarian [kruh-nayr'-ee-en] *n.* [*pejorative*] 1. a person who elects to linger in

John Henry Fleming / Benjamin Cohen / Edwidge Danticat / Cornelia Nixon / Eli Horowitz / Wendy Wasserstein / Matthew Klam • ***Richard Sala*** bed in the early morning in order to listen to birds singing, to avoid front page news of bloodshed of American soldiers in any of the ongoing American military campaigns. 2. lazy person. —Matthew Klam

crusade [kroo'-sayd], *n.* [*from Latin,* crux, cross] 1. [*obsolete*] a widely understood term of hate speech, reviled by most of the world's Muslim population, and therefore avoided in polite conversation, referring to an imperial or religious war or pogrom undertaken for the purpose of eliminating citizens of a foreign country, either civilian or military. 2. an attempt at genocide or wide-scale destruction. 3. the efforts of evangelizers, also referred to as the reading-impared faithful, to convert passersby, resulting in the accidental death or manslaughter of evangelizers. *He went on his Baptist crusade in Cincinnati, where, of course, he was struck and killed by a city bus.* 4. abortive attempts to induce consumers to by useless products. *The Disney crusade on the new Affleck vehicle resulted in a decline in stock valuation.* —Rick Moody

culiflection [koo-lee-flek'-shun] *v.* in post-Gestalt therapy, the act of directing a difficult emotion such as anger or envy at your food rather than at yourself or someone who has provoked the emotion. *His rage at the cauliflower stalk was nothing more than culiflection.*

—Tom Barbash

culiflection

D

dad-o-meter [dad'-oh-mee-tur] *n.* a gauge of public disgust, related to the mom-o-meter but still its own meter. Usually, but not always, involves dads in their sixties who started voting Republican with Reagan and kept at it out of habit and a sense of embarrassment at having been wrong. A father who voted for Reagan and one or both Bushes despite being a registered Democrat, found muttering to himself over the Sunday *New York Times* (the front section, not Styles), is a flashing dad-o-meter showing some serious scales falling from some serious eyes. A father heard saying, "He can't put a sentence together" after watching a very rare unscripted television appearance of Bush is a dad-o-meter indicating some hope; as is a father who wonders aloud how the Republicans will deal with the fact that Kerry is a war hero and a war protester while Bush went AWOL for the inactive duty he did serve. And the dad-o-meter is way off the charts when several dads of any race, creed, or socioeconomic class are heard to say to each other, "Well, he's right, isn't he?" after Kerry refused to back down from calling Bush & Co. a bunch of liars and cheats. —RACHEL CARPENTER

dark natter [dark'-nat-ur] *n., v.* an analogue of "dark matter" which astrophysicists speculate may constitute as much as 90% of the universe, dark natter is empty but continuous chatter of an ominous sort, whether in direct discourse, by way of the electronic media, or in print. (*n.*) *A lethal cloud of dark natter formed above the nation's capitol and is reported to be drifting in all directions.* (*v.*) *He dark-nattered his way through the Bible Belt with conspicuous success.* Also: *He was dark-nattered into defeat by ingenious opponents.*

—JOYCE CAROL OATES

dayolyte

dayolyte [day'-oh-liyt] *n.* [from the American Communist Party and the Catholic Worker Movement.] 1. someone who believes in the virtues of voluntary poverty instead of abundant wealth. 2. to embrace the idea that it is nobler, healthier, and more conducive to personal happiness to take just what you need and leave the rest for others. 3. a follower of Dorothy Day. The Dayolyte movement was formed spontaneously in the year 2005 when for no apparent reason Donald Trump, Warren Buffet, and Jack Welch all reported feeling "suffocated by their own wealth." Turning to the teachings of Day for guidance, they willingly embraced her dictum, "We believe in an economy based on human needs, rather than on profit motive." So successful were the Dayolytes in relieving both the burdens of the rich (who had too much) and the poor (who didn't have enough), that the movement spread to political parties as well where Day's views on neutral pacificism were enthusiastically implemented. 4. to be able to see things more clearly due to an abundance of bright sunlight. *Like Dorothy Day before them, the Dayolytes were fond of saying "The clothes in your closet should be on someone else's back."* —ANN PATCHETT

Dean depression [deen duh-presh'-un] *n.* the clinical condition that follows the surprising and illogical defeat of a populist candidate. *After Chelsea's defeat, we all had a touch of a Dean depression.* MISUSE: *The Bush recession will be followed by the Dean depression.* (Senator Joseph Lieberman, 9/4/03). —KEN FOSTER

death [deth] *n.* the end of life. Before we overcame death, this term was used millions of times every day, usually with regret. Now it's used almost exclusively in historical contexts. There was a time—as the technology that enabled us to overcome death was coming into being—that the human race debated the relative merits of death and life. Or rather, whether it was necessarily a bad thing to be overcome by death. That debate was taken on by the poets, who, no longer facing the inevitability of being overcome by death, stopped writing about their lives altogether and wrote, instead, about the relative merits of life and death, nearly always coming down on the side of death. The last person to die, Jake232,392,556, didn't have to die. The human race had already overcome death at that point. He tried to kill himself. Doctors closed the wound, rebuilt his lungs, and gave him full consciousness. He thanked them, walked out of the hospital, back to his apartment, took the elevator up 1,712 floors, and jumped out the window. (It took him more than thirteen minutes to fall to the ground.) But the human race already had overcome death at that point, and there was no reason for him to die, so he was revived. He didn't say anything when he was given full consciousness this time, but walked out the front door and into the path of an oncoming **windtruck**. Doctors were able to revive him again, because the human race had already overcome death at that point. He killed himself again, this time on the operating table, this time by holding his breath. "But you don't have to die," the doctor told him, the first words he heard when he was given full consciousness after his near-death. "We have overcome death." —JONATHAN SAFRAN FOER

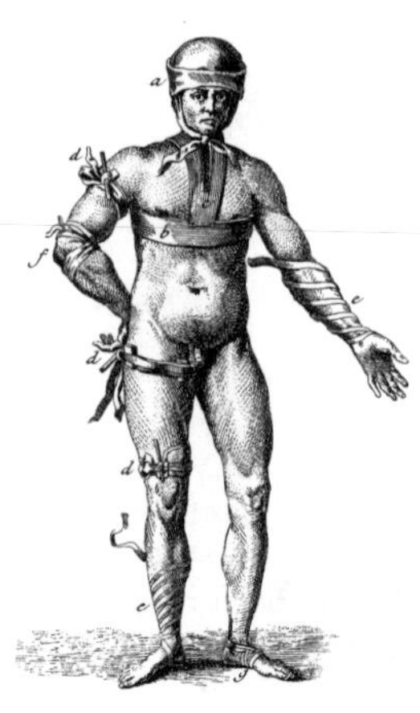

Jake 232,392,556
SEE **death**

debaseball [di-bays'-bahl] *n.* 1. a forgotten American game of skill played with bats, balls, and kid fielders gloves briefly popular in the first years of the 21st century. The original "Crawford-rules" version of the sport called for competitors to circle a course of three military bases before running home. 2. a phenomenon expressing squandered goodwill. *An old opinion held that many Americans turned from such previously favored pastimes as clearing brush and taking part in captive livestock hunts to playing debaseball because the game's pastoral origins and the handsome flag pins worn by contestants appealed to a vestigial yearning floating free among the public.* —NICHOLAS DAWIDOFF

debtoricity [det'-ur-ih-si-tee] *n.* 1. an incorporated municipality or community based on owing something to others. Origins of debtoricities as an urban geography can be found in 19th century Marshalsea Prison where thou-

sands of debtors were housed, but in the late 20th, early 21st century whole nations became debtoricities. 2. a proclivity toward solving problems by dipping into the public till. *When his voracious debtoricity outpaced all expectations, he quoted J. Wellington Wimpie by saying, "I'll gladly pay you on Tuesday for a hamburger purchased today."*
—SUSAN DAITCH

dehegemon [dee-hedj'-uh-mon] *v.* 1. *-intr.* to give up one's military, political and cultural ascendancy over other states, to the common advantage of all states. Used primarily in connection with the process begun at the turn of the 21st century, when U.S. influence was challenged by European and other countries in several sectors. Unable to maintain an empire that reflected its democratic values, the U.S. resolved to dehegemon, vastly reducing the costs of its overextended military, empowering global efforts to deal with global problems, opening the world to diverse cultural and commercial influences, and freeing Americans from the moral burden of trying to dominate the world. 2.*-tr.* to force a hegemonic power to give up such influence. Dehegemon, or be dehegemoned. —KEN KALFUS

democrazy [duh-mok-rayz'-ee] *n.* the dark underside of American democracy: moral cowardice gussied up as moral superiority. This national pathology leads to lunatic behaviors. One of our poets, William Carlos Williams (also a doctor), diagnoses the essential problem thusly: "The pure products of America / go crazy." Another of our poets, Allen Ginsberg (no doctor, but something of a metaphysician), offers this as an antidote: "America you don't really want to go to war." Yet another poet, C.D. Wright, suggests: "Place yourself inside the damage." And W.H. Auden (yes, a British versifier, but long on U.S. soil) offers this sound prescription: "Our dream of safety has to disappear." —MARTHA COOLEY

democrazy

dentigration [den-ti-gray'-shun] *n.* a government plan by which dentally well-off citizens are encouraged to donate one or more of their teeth to dentally impoverished members of other ethnic groups. Dentigration joins the races in a one-mouth, one-purpose harmony of mastication; it's the first social program that gives us all something to chew on.
—JOHN HENRY FLEMING

Deplorus [di-plor'-us] *n.* 1. U.S. myth. The modern American god of superior feelings. 2. the twelfth and farthest planet from the sun, having a sidereal period of revolution of 478.4 years, 5.6 billion kilometers at perihelion, 8.1 billion kilometers at aphelion, and the worst environmental record in the known universe. Discovered 2218 by scientists tracing outer space plumes of toxic emissions; populated by seemingly intelligent humanoid beings. Deplorus's single indigenous culture consisted in the production of superfluous, disposable, nondegradable objects with which to befoul its landmasses and seas; discovery often credited with resulting in Earth's first lasting **Global Accords on Environmental Protection**. Joint missions of the **Confederated Korean Peninsula Space Program** and the **Interstellar Research Alliance of North African States** greatly contributed to the salvation of

Deplorus, and a generalized increase in Earth self-esteem, in the late 2300s.

—Susan Choi

Dewey States [doo'-wee stayts] *n.* the Interstitial States of America (SEE **ISA**), founded by the Council of Radical [later Interstitial] Librarians, also called the Dewey States after the Dewey Decimal System. The Council of Radical Librarians, reasoning on the basis of the Dewey Decimal System that if every book had a unique call number, and there were infinite call numbers, then there must be infinite books still to be written (in which case the world was not in such immediate danger of total destruction as one might have imagined from contemporary evidence) and furthermore an infinite library to contain them; that as the call number for those books lay between the books already on the shelves, rather than beyond them, the shelf-space for those books must also lie between them; that there was therefore a great amount of space between any two books, however snugly shelved, just as there were infinite numbers between any two numbers; that if the space existed, it ought to be possible to get into it, providing you had not eaten a big lunch.

The way to this place was duly discovered. (SEE **hh.**) Initially it was used primarily for quick escapes during the time of persecution, and for extra shelving. Many of the interstitial passages remain lined with books and on one's travels through the skinny one often passes a librarian tirelessly shelving, or catches the gleam of an eye through the stacks. It was discovered that these spaces could be expanded easily and soon they began to be colonized, as many people preferred to live in a place they could shape to their liking rather than in a place that was prefabricated and indeed had already been occupied by someone else, usually someone a bit stiff around the knees and not entirely clean. An entire second America grew inside the first one, fitting there as neatly as fine bones in a fish, without making the latter any larger except perhaps by some few square feet of sand bank in the Florida Keys.

—Shelley Jackson

Diagram [diy-ah'-gram] *n.* a North American religion derived from the teachings of Montgomery Niles, centered around the belief that the key to opening the door to the afterlife had been written into the speech patterns of mankind; therefore speech must be collected and stored, handed down from generation to generation, until it can be analyzed by the Final Man, who, once armed with the key to Heaven, will then end his own life so that He might open the door for all of those who had passed before Him. Hence, **Diagramist** *n.* preacher or follower of the religion Diagram. —Manuel Gonzales

dignity [dig'-nuh-tee] *n.* 1a. [*archaic*] the quality or state of being worthy, honored, or esteemed. 1b. the state of having respect for oneself, especially in the face of public visibility. 2. a revived concept, reinvested within common speech and social discourse after the demise of Reality TV and mediated celebrity obsession, to indicate the virtues of self-respect, honor, and pride. —Benjamin Cohen

Doctorow's Gap [dok'-tuh-rowz gap] *n.* the discrepancy, measured in justice miles, between a nation's stated ideals and its practices. Also known as **The People's Stock Market**, Doctorow's Gap is generally regarded as the leading indicator of national health. Given human fallibility, the DG cannot be eradicated entirely, but there is overwhelming evidence that it can be significantly decreased through the subversive, organized efforts (SEE **democracy**) of utopian dissidents (SEE **citizens**) who love their country enough to want to make it more humane (SEE **patriotism**). The American DG, measured at 334,452 justice miles in 2004, has been reduced to a post-revolutionary average of 17 justice miles. [2025–30; named for novelist and folk hero **E.L. Doctorow**, who said in 1978: "It seems to me we are, at least on paper, supposed to be different from, or better than, we are."] —CHRIS BACHELDER

dog [dahg] *n.* the citizen, in balance. Example: *I live up to my potential. I understand that I will die. I do not hide in my room. I do not kill people outside my room, either. Woof, woof.*
—AIMÉE BENDER

dog

dollar [dah'-lur] *n.* former North American currency. Since the world abandoned money it's almost impossible to imagine how people once were divided by it. Fierce enmity separated those in possession of dollars and those who wanted to be. People with money (called **wealthy**) lived for nothing but its consolidation. People without money (called **poor**) effectively had no rights. The United States, located in lower North America, was the first nation to end these practices. The rest of the world soon followed. Certain currencies surrendered more quickly than others: first the delighted Rubles of Russia, shuffling into obsolescence like a parade of homely, eager, petticoated sisters; with them the blood red currencies of Caribbean nations, emblazoned, as they were, with parakeets and un-catalyzed pollution; then the heavyset English Pound, the (juicy) Japanese Yen, the zaftig Chinese Yuan, and, last of all, the vapid fox of the European Euro... each of them powerful, then nervous, then tittering, always deceitful; and blessedly gone today. The dollar and its monetary equivalents are preserved in museums of continental history, where you can still see them today, somberly decorated with the likenesses of forgotten rulers: George Washington (lower North America), Victor Emmanuel II (southern Europe), R.C. Munro Ferguson (Antartica), Wenceslau B.P. Gomez (Central America), Hussein Kemal (Asia Minor), Mau Tse Tung (Asia), Wilhelmina and Belisario Porras (South America), Haakon VII (Africa), Chowfa Maha Vajiravudh (Indian Subcontinent), and Camille de Coppet (Oceania). —SEAN WILSEY

Dream Catchers [dreem kach-urz] *n.* a high-tech nightcap, identical to the one worn by Scrooge in *A Christmas Carol*—except this cap is capable of biometrically recording dreams for broadcast quality playback. The cap's inventor, tired of hearing her well-meaning but long-winded husband's attempt to describe his ridiculous nocturnal journeys each morning, crafted the device in forty-eight hours out of parts ripped from home appliances. Now, thanks to her frustration, people around the world can watch each other's dreams and live each other's nighttime fantasies—for better or worse. The development of a new Double Dream Catcher cap (which enable two sleepers to enter and interact in each other's dreams—for instance, to remind each other not to leave the house naked or to catch each other when they fall) has made dreaming far more fun and usually less traumatic. —BRENT HOFF

drum circle [drum sur'-kul] *n.* a powerful form of social protest perfected and maintained by hippies, with the understanding that if everyone

drum circle

could just get in touch with the rhythms of the universe, we could have a thousand years of peace and prosperity.

—Noah Hawley

Dubya-Emdee [dub'-yuh-em-dee] *n.* an imaginary threat, upon which is based an extreme action.

—Susan Henderson

dubyavirus [dub'-yuh-viy-rus] *n.* an aggressively invasive and tragically widespread disease first identified in 2005 when democracy was restored in the United States after four harrowing years under the rule of supremacist religious fundamentalist war-mongers who illegally seized power in 2000. (SEE **coup d'etat of the hanging chad.**) Emergency action taken by the newly elected democratic White House in early 2005 re-allocated the entire U.S. military budget to education, civil rights, the arts, health care, and organic farming. Following his disenthronement, former President and indicted war criminal George W. Bush was hospitalized and (as provided for all Americans under the newly-instituted universal health care system) a team of doctors and scientists worked feverishly to diagnose the cause of his symptoms, which included life-long deceit, conniving, cunning self-interest, and a tendency toward inappropriate overcompensation for personal physical and/or intellectual deficits. (SEE **Napoleon Complex**, possibly also related to **compensatory syndrome, petit-presidential pee-pee.**) It was ultimately researchers at the Peace Through Health foundation who isolated and named the dubyavirus (SEE **Republicanism**), which, though deadly, is not necessarily fatal to its initial victim, but causes pain, suffering and probable death to future generations of humans and other species. The virus was found to originate in artificial and inorganic foodstuffs, and researchers quickly discovered that conversion to a diet free of herbicides, pesticides, fungicides, and genetically manipulated ingredients was not only effective in alleviating symptoms but actually seemed to break down the virus and restore patients to full functioning health. Untreated in humans until 2005, dubyavirus is thought to have once infected fully half of the American voting population. Reported symptoms have included moderate to extreme irrationality, lack of concern for others, difficulty spelling and a tendency to make up words but not realize you're doing so, unlimited greed (which can also involve hoarding, fraud, monopolization, embezzlement, robbery, or attacks on and military occupation of small foreign oil-rich nations), profound egocentrism, strong feelings of hatred toward "the other" (SEE **difference, racial, difference, religious and difference, socioeconomic**), aggression, violent behavior, fervent Christian proselytizing, complete lack of foresight, mind-numbing fear of everything, and powerful subconscious urges to destroy the earth and all life thereupon. Through vigorous worldwide therapy and creation of a global network of organic farms organized under the principles of Community Supported Agriculture (SEE **CSA**, and **good person, how to be a**), dubyavirus was effectively eradicated from our planet by the mid-21st century. (SEE ALSO **Bigots Disease**, **Fundamentalism Syndrome**, **Thurmonditis**, **Quayleism**, and **Christian Boy-Band Virus.**)

—Thisbe Nissen

duhphin [duh'-fan] *n.* unsmart eldest son of a former president.

—Eric Orner

duhphin

E

earthborn [urth'-born] *adj.* 1. those human beings who spend their entire lives on planet Earth, rather than in other galaxies, black holes, or in the light of distant stars. They generally have smaller lungs and poorer eyesight, and often suffer from ulcers and gas, but continue to possess an imagination, fueled by wonder and longing, unmatched by those born in the universe at large. 2. [*archaic*] mortal.
—NICOLE KRAUSS

earthlight [urth'-liyt] *n.* a powerful spotlight, the strength of a billion flashlights, shone from Arctic Circle straight into the universe, which attracts other forms of life to us like moths. —NICOLE KRAUSS

ebrained [ee'-braynd] *adj.* 1. giddy, useless, from exposure to the microchip's largess. *We could not tell if he was ebrained or congenitally retarded.* 2. [*archaic*] harebrained. —PADGETT POWELL

ecolomy [i-kan-uh-me] *n.* ALT **econogy** 1. encompassing term for economy and ecology, adopted after the dollar was phased out in favor of the planting of saplings as a form of currency and the two systems ceased to work at cross-purposes. 2. **ecolomics** the study of the growth of money on trees. *Ecolomic analysts expect the spring to bring record levels of production in all sectors.* —JORDAN BASS

Edentist [ee'-dent-uhst] *n.* one who is skilled and licensed to practice the maintenance of perfect and everlasting teeth through the use of painless and often perpetually pleasurable methods. *After Eric's single visit to his Edentist, he told everyone he felt like he had a mouth made in Heaven.* —JORDAN BASS

elderly [el'-dur-lee] 1. *n.* age group considered to be wise, sexy, and all the way around revered, respected, imitated, and admired. 2. *adj.* wise and sexy: *Yo, that chick is mad elderly!*
—ELIZABETH CRANE

elephantiasis [el-uh-fen-tiy'-uh-sis] *n.* a swelling of the feet and genitals caused by excessive political donations. *The Republican candidate had the lead in the polls until a bad case of elephantiasis caused him to stumble over his own penis.*
—JOHN HENRY FLEMING

elephantiasis

elevatory [ee'-lav-uh-tor-ee] *n.* a room with conveniences for washing that quickly carries all waste into outer space, where it is deposited within the gravitational field of one of a number of industry-standard white dwarf stars and eventually incinerated. Installed throughout Earth's third world in 2056, elevatories quickly eliminated several contagious diseases and brought

Nicole Krauss / Nicole Krauss / Padgett Powell / Jordan Bass / Jordan Bass / Elizabeth Crane / John Henry Fleming • ***Christoph Niemann/*** Jordan Bass about impressive improvements in water quality. —JORDAN BASS

empathy [em'-puh-thee] *n.* per Webster, "the action of understanding, being aware of, being sensitive to, and vicariously experiencing the feelings, thoughts, and experience of another for either the past or present without having the feelings, thoughts, and experience fully communicated in an objectively explicit manner," a noun entirely dismissed for a brief period of history during the American Empire, before being reinvoked as a staple of social mores after the first Pacific Evolution of 2006. *"Wow," said infomercial magnate Jimmy Jimson, "I mean, even Robert McNamara was honest enough to mandate that empathy be a basis for any discussions between or action on behalf of disagreeing factions."*
—BENJAMIN COHEN

empiricism [em-peer'-uh-siz-um] *n.* the central philosophic concept that provided a foundation for the notable and progressive social, political, scientific, and human-rights achievements of the 18th-century Enlightenment, a period that included the French and American revolutions and the creation of their republics. Empiricism is the understanding that no belief can or may be accepted as truth in the absence of tangible or otherwise observable evidence verifying the belief to be true and valid ("We hold these truths to be self-evident" means "we hold these truths to be empirically evident"). By the late 19th century, empiricism, once revolutionary in its break from the medieval, was considered throughout the West to be synonymous with common sense. Nevertheless, in the history of the United States of America, it is most famously known for the attempt made by the one-term administration of George W. Bush (2000–2004) to deny, quash, and repudiate it entirely, replacing it with hint, innuendo, suspicion, deceit, power lust, falsehood, unmitigated desire for corporate profit, undisguised will, and, above all, the utility of prayer, although only and solely prayer of the Christian type, all other forms being declared, in the Bush period, retrograde, bestial, pagan, evil, and imaginary.
—ERIC LARSEN

empty-tomb syndrome [em'-tee toom sin'-drohm] *n.* the experience of being bamboozled by a completely sham hope. (*colloq*: **empty-tomber**) *Etymology:* Midwestern. First used to describe a person left behind (alone) in a two-plot grave. A research librarian from Illinois State University at Normal provided this example of the origin as collected by the prairie folk historian J. Harold Mueller: In 1947 the Hebrew Burial Society of Chicago buried a bookbinder named Mel Shlansky (died young) at Waldheim Cemetery, a fallow field west of the city, because he'd religiously paid his seven dollars a year. When her time came, however, his wife Doris patently refused to go into that ground. She said now that her daughter's husband had money they'd have to kill her first before she'd put one dead toenail way the hell out there. They buried her in Skokie near the mall. But of course Mel doesn't know this and waits for her—still. By his calculations Doris must be getting on near a hundred and thirty by now and he marvels at the progress of modern medicine, while at the same time chastising himself for being lonely and wishing it would end so that she would come to him.
—PETER ORNER

energy policy [en'-ur-jee pahl'-uh-see] *n.* 1. a definite course or method of action pertaining to the means of acquiring, using, and conceiving of energy. 2a. spec-

energy policy

Jordan Bass / Benjamin Cohen / Eric Larsen / Peter Orner / Benjamin Cohen • ***Maira Kalman*** ifically, that form of policy enabled by renewed attention to the belief that humans and non-humans collectively inhabit the world and are likely to require homes and lives in the future. 2b. that policy enabled by the elevation of the virtues of respect and cooperation and the simultaneous collective and sensible denigration of the vices of consumption and glut.

—BENJAMIN COHEN

enlightenment [en-liy'-ten-ment] *n.* also known as the **Age of Reason,** a philosophic movement of the 18th century that, based on foundations of **empiricism** (*q.v.*), brought about the rise of modern science, ended monarchy as a divinely legitimated institution, enunciated the concept of natural law, established the rights of man, and saw the emergence of the modern democratic republic based on universal suffrage and the right of equality under the law. Enlightenment values and institutions, especially in the United States of America, became and remained the model and measure of humankind's ability, through philosophic, social, and political structures and means, to bring about and preserve the common weal within a republican structure. Notable occasions of betrayal or perversion of Enlightenment values and structures occurred in the Terror following the French Revolution, in the excesses of soviet Stalinism, and in the early 21st century American government of George W. Bush, which attempted blatantly to seize the central democratic institutions of the republic and bend them toward its own ends. Notable in all three cases (though the three are widely unequal in the sheer degree of human loss and suffering each entailed) is that the end result was the defeat of **reactionism** and the successful reestablishment of humane, liberal, enlightenment-based political and social structures and values. In the United States, the four years of the George W. Bush administration (2000–2004) are still referred to as the years of **Almost the Abyss**, a reference to the later internationally celebrated novel by Jonathan Safran Foer (1977-2093).

—ERIC LARSEN

enron [en'-rahn] *v.* 1. to redeem oneself, particularly after grievous wrongs to society, by embracing good works. 2. to change dramatically and unexpectedly for the benefit of all. Derived from the story of scandal-ridden executives of the Enron corporation who exemplified the **Corporate Malfeasance Era** of the first decade of the 21st century, and then, in a remarkable turnaround, devoted themselves to promoting reforms to better the lives of working families. *After a nightly visitation by three spirits, the infamous miser suddenly enroned, becoming as good of a friend, master, and man as the good city knew.*

—ANNE URSU

*...the infamous miser suddenly **enroned***

entacto-politarch [en-takt-o-pol'-it-ark] *n.* 1. a political leader who inspires in his or her constituents a sense of profound well-being and happiness. 2. a civil magistrate whose rulings are so wise that they result not just in the end of litigious proceedings, but in a generalized feeling of peace and rapprochement between the parties. *That the*

entacto-politarch

President seeks to be remembered as the first entactopolitarch of her party is obvious, but whether she is sufficiently beloved by the populace to accomplish this goal remains to be seen.

—Ayelet Waldman

environment [en-viyr'-un-ment] *n.* 1. a confused mass of biota, rocky places, open plains, and ditches filled variously with water, muck, and blood, with the potential of being converted into strip mines, strip malls, and strip clubs, to the everlasting benefit of mankind and the Halliburton Corporation. 2. a kind of place, like an office cubicle, where deals are made. 3. the prevailing mood or climate in which deals are made. 4. [*colloq*] turf or 'hood. 5. a conceptual space, like the airspace over Iraq, which will create a sucking void if not filled to repleteness with high explosives. —T.C. Boyle

Environmint [en-viyr'-un-mint] *n.* a mint-flavored candy devised by a New Jersey landfill operator, which eliminates all foul-smelling odors from polluted properties. The product's slogan: "Gives toxic waste sites a minty freshness." 2. *adj.* a mint smell associated with industrial chemicals. *He'd bathed three times, but there was a lingering stench of environmint to him that broke her heart.* 3. something that attempts to mask the true qualities of a person or object. *His attempts to ingratiate himself are nothing more than enironmints and do not change the way I regard his character.*

—Tom Barbash

erasial scattegories [ee-ray'-shul skat'-uh-gor-eez] 1. *n.* the section of the official Census of 2030 which abandons the requirement that United States residents identify themselves, their children, or whoever lives at their address by checking boxes such as "White" or "Black" or "Hispanic" or "Some Difficult to Define Really Cool Shade of Gold Resulting from Six Generations of Intermarriage Among Racial Groups" (this last attempt to clarify race, in the Census of 2020, took up far more space than its predecessor, "Other"). Former strict legal census designations in colonial America included mulatto, quadroon, octoroon, griffe, sacatra, mestizo; unofficial common definitions were melungeon, ladino, Creole, mixed, and "dang, you're really fine, whatever you are." America's national obsession with race began to seem ridiculous even to the Census Bureau, whose employees and own relatives had been forced in 2020 to check six or nine or twelve boxes provided for racial categories, and whose employees had begun to refuse to ask the universal question that children had eventually given up on the playgrounds: "So what are you anyway?" Rather than checking boxes, which took up two pages of the census, residents wrote in their own identifications, such as African-Irish-French-Samoan-Haitian-Mexican-American, which had nothing to do with race or creed and all to do with parentage. Derived in part from scat singing, a component of jazz, a truly native American music and truly indefinable category. *When his great-grandmother handed him the erasial scattegories section of the census, she laughed and told him that long ago, in the 1980s, author James Baldwin said, "No one from Italy or Greece or Egypt or England was white until he arrived in America."*

—Susan Straight

errorgance [ayr'-or-guns] *n.* a feeling of smug superiority over those who do not share one's own erroneous or misguided convictions. *The president's errorgance alienated most of the Western world.*

—Ed Page

estemmer [ee-stem'-ur] *n.* 1. a person who has benefitted from embryonic stem cell research. 2. a person previously suffering from Alzheimer's, juvenile diabetes, or Parkinson's disease, who received medical treatment when the ban on stem cell research was lifted.

—Vendela Vida

Ethnicity Preserve

Ethnicity Preserve [eth-nis'-it-ee pruh-zurv'] *n.* an area designated for the protection of ethnic groups. In the decades after the **Arab Quarantine**, Western citizens of the world began to look more and more like each other, until it was virtually impossible to tell them apart. They began to speak like each other, to prepare and eat the same foods, to dance the same way to the same music in similar clothing in nightclubs that looked the same in cities that were interchangeable, even to make very similar art (when art was made at all). And yet, it was the Arabs, whom the Western World had tried to force into extinction, that actually were sustained: they were bolstered by the Quarantine. There was something to be learned from that. It was decided—some thought for scientific reasons, others for cultural, others for pure nostalgia—to create ethnicity preserves, in which endangered ethnicities could be given safe territories for regrowth. (The Last Jews, for example, were given protection in the Lowest East Side of Newer York.) Unfortunately, if predictably, these preserves became great tourist attractions—they were, after all, the most interesting places on the planet. And those living in ethnicity preserves tended to want to escape, to enter "the world of possibilities and options" that existed outside, not realizing that there were no meaningful possibilities or options. So despite all efforts, things moved, again, toward the homogenous state in which we now find ourselves. *Jack512,392,234,234,983 just told a funny joke, so his friends suspect he was raised on an ethnicity preserve.*

—JONATHAN SAFRAN FOER

exactasy [ig-zak'-tuh-see] *n.* 1. a state of overwhelming passion precisely tailored to delight the individual experiencing it, obtained through the implementation of tremendous self-control. The discovery by George Marner of the eight true keys to the human heart, now revealed to the residents of the world on the eve of their eighteenth birthdays by the Social Security Administration through cerebral imprinting, ended an age of chronic emotional problems and allowed many to trade the peaks and troughs of a torrential adolescence for a perpetual and personally comprehensive pleasure, if they so chose. 2. a street drug furtively traded among middle-schoolers as a substitute for the self-knowledge they will eventually obtain, said to cause an increase in energy and alertness; known by adults to be a vitamin supplement. *Samantha described the exactasy she experienced as akin to riding a horse through a rock concert and suddenly seeing her first love for the first time while opening a present that smelled good.* —JORDAN BASS

exaggeration [ig-zaj'-uh-ray-shun] *n.* 1. an increase, often untruthfully above the normal bounds. 2. a food allowance for one day, often enlarged and at all times unnecessary in light of the functional elimination of hunger with the introduction of photosynthesis to the human species at the turn of the century. An attachment to the act of eating led many to continue consuming food even after it lost its use; these "exaggereaters" are allowed by convention to take a midday meal of any quantity in order to satisfy themselves. *Every day Carl brings in a Thanksgiving dinner, I swear to God—it's the biggest exaggeration you've ever seen.*

—JORDAN BASS

expatitis [ex-pat-iy'-tis] *n.* the sense, upon returning from a time spent living abroad in the 90s, that time has both sped up and slowed down in one's absence. The feeling that the Clinton years were a pleasant dream with a nasty ending. A lack of knowledge of many movies that did not make it eastward (or westward, ho, as the case may be), because they were not easily identifiable as American, meaning Hollywood. The inability to see glimpses on television of certain bad Hollywood movies from that time without remembering how they had seemed in (for example) Bratislava (the movie sucked, but man those fresh strawberries looked good). The inability to hear anyone say, for example, "I remember Bratislava back in the early 90s" without cringing, much as it had been impossible, back in Bratislava in the early 90s, to hear most sentences in native English without cringing. The sense that it was all a dream, and you were there and you were there and you were there; alternating with the sense that everything since has been a dream. The perpetual state of meaning to write a "real" email to friends back in the land where you were once foreign, then thought you were less so, but really always were—so very foreign, so very American. Sporadic, intense desire to listen to bad pop stations on the Web from that land; to eat that bad food; to be there, then, again, wondering why you've stayed so long and making your way to of all places McDonald's (a fact that you tended to omit in any letters, or, later, emails, home). The phenomenon of having to stop when people ask your age and add, to the number you were going to say, the number of years you spent away. The sneaking irrational sense that you could understand the unidentifiable language spoken by the people across from you on the subway if you were to listen long enough; the secret relief when they get off before you and you're no longer distracted from your native tongue. The suspicion that everything you were proud of about your country, before you left, while you were away, and after you came back has changed, and you have, and not for the better, and that they must all change again. —RACHEL CARPENTER

extreme makeover [ik-streem' mayk'-o-vur] *n.* intense, untelevised psychological treatment resulting in the belief that beauty is, well, subjective, of course, but more importantly, that it's, uh, on the inside (beauty being defined by, if it needs to be pointed out, you know, a loving quality, overall decency and goodness of heart and that sort of thing, service to others, trustworthiness, honesty, generosity perhaps, maybe humor and intelligence, but that sort of gets away from it, so not even that so much really as the goodness thing, the point is that the treatment results not in anything you could immediately notice on the outside unless you were just extremely percep-

extreme makeover

tive, because it's an internal change we're talking about here, do you see, whereby someone who was culturally conditioned to believe, let's say, that unusually large breasts or a perfectly motionless forehead would somehow transform them, you know, spiritually or whatever, would, after their extreme makeover, understand that their previous belief was entirely misguided and that they were in fact already perfect, as I believe Billy Joel said, just the way they were). —ELIZABETH CRANE

F

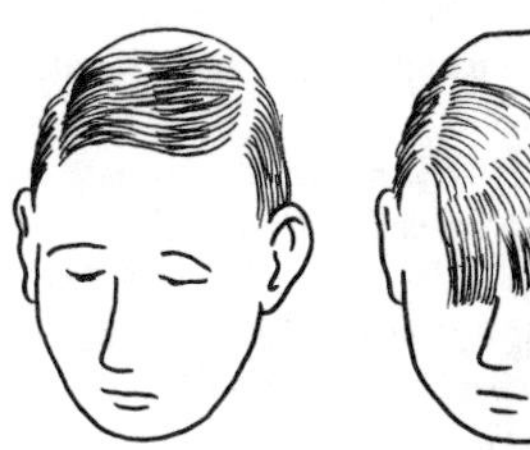

faction

faction [fak'-shun] *n.* 1. the creative manipulation of context to create a "truth"; technique(s) frequently employed by corporate media during the early millennium to kiss the ass of the government that used to regulate them. 2. a special interest cadre that seeks to expose the truth, or to hide it. *The faction cited reports of their drunken behavior as an example of the faction they seek to expose.*

—KEN FOSTER

failworthy [fayl'-wur-thee] *adj.* about an outrageous but perhaps ennobling idea or experiment that can be aesthetic, scientific, or political in nature; an undertaking that is dangerous, difficult, or even ridiculous but which is anyway pursued; an impractical, dubious feat engendered by great ambition that might ultimately be worthwhile to the daredevil or public. *David Blaine's living in a glass box over the Thames River for 40 days, and starving himself, was failworthy, though much disputed, and certainly sensational.* Also, as in: *She has begun a failworthy experiment that hopes to understand, through scientific rigor, everything her mother and father said to her in their lifetimes.*

—LYNNE TILLMAN

falater [fuh-lay'-tur] *n.* a sandwich or other edible usually collected from a large breakfast and wrapped up, to be eaten as another meal, usually as lunch. Falater came into currency in the 1990s, coined by musicians on tour or on the road, who, when at breakfast, and not knowing when they might eat again, took as much food as they could and made sandwiches "for later."

—LYNNE TILLMAN

Familese [fam-uh-leez'] *n.* the standard language of the communicating family, based on shared speech between members of nuclear and extended families. Speakers express, believe in, and strive to reinforce an extreme level of empathy with all family members, esp. those between whom the largest gaps of understanding exist. Spoken worldwide.

—KAREN SHEPARD

Farmy [far'-mee] *n.* [fr. ME fermer to fix, to make firm] small, localized groups of militant farmers who initially organized to demand organic vine-ripened tomatoes; now the largest, most recognized, and highly funded branch of the American military. *On her eighteenth birthday our daughter was drafted by the Farmy for her asparagus.*

—SAMANTHA HUNT

fauxkward [fawk'-ward] *adj.* combination of "faux" and "awkward." Falsely awkward. Qualities such as false humility, fake shyness, and pseudo-goofballness can all be termed subclasses of fauxkwardness. Most often seen in stammering movie actors (Hugh Grant, when not playing a baddie) and not-really-klutzy actresses (Julia Roberts, when playing anyone, including herself), but possibly also seen in alleged world leaders (Bush II, when reading his script very carefully).

—Rachel Carpenter

Finger-Next-to-the-Index-Finger Index, the *n.* the authoritative measure of human prosperity, also known as the FINNIFIN. Asks respondents which finger next to the index finger—either thumb or middle finger—they would be more inclined to use to sum up the current state of affairs. Index analysts then average the quotient of the sum of the aggregate, give or take, and make predetermined conclusions based on common sense. Every week, FINNIFIN's results are presented on the Hand, a thirty-foot-tall adjustable neon hand located in Lafayette Park, across the street from the White House.

—Kevin Moffett

flame [flaym] *n.* fire, since ceasing to threaten forests, houses, and people (SEE **mistiles**), has been called exclusively by its flashier name.

—Brent Hoff

floaters [floh-turz] *n. pl.* 1. those who vote illegally in various places; considered a right of passage in Cook County, Illinois. 2. shadows of vitreous clumps reflected off the retina giving the illusion of black specs that seem to float across one's field of vision. 3. a beautiful novel published in 1984 by Tish O'Dowd that should be more widely read. 4. reference to people who exist in one physical world while their thoughts dwell elsewhere. Often caused by sudden displacement. Common in refugees, exiles, etc., such as the man in the following example, provided by a correspondent in Iowa. *Dear Dictionary People, I'm writing to tell you about a guy who might fit under your definition of floater, i.e., a guy who seems to live in Cedar Rapids, at least this is where his feet are, but he's not here here, follow me? I'm a regular at Rufus McCooter's on First Ave Southwest. Every night this guy comes in around ten. Pale guy, thin, little feet, earmuffs. He takes a table in the back, as far from the TV as possible. He orders a beer, which he never drinks. As soon as Caesar brings him his Schlitz the guy starts talking to the empty chair across the table. He's not speaking English. Sounds to me it's Russian. Another guy in here, Marty Patowski, says it's Croat, says for certain it's Croat. So call it Croat. Patowski's got to be right about everything. Anyway, after a while this guy starts shouting at the chair. Switches languages, sometimes there's English words thrown in. Still, it's impossible to know what the hell he's talking about. Except—don't I know it?—guy's alone. I need to speak Croat to know a man's alone? For good alone? Fuck you Patowski. Finally he switches chairs and starts in on the one he was just sitting in. Never drinks the beer. Just sits there wearing those earmuffs ranting at chairs. This is when I can't take it anymore. This is when I pay Caesar and go home. But this doesn't mean I can stop thinking about the guy, which might explain why I'm bothering to send this nonsense to California. Who's he talking to? A friend he once had? A wife? A kid? You tell me. A floater?*

—Peter Orner

floorganization [flor'-gun-uh-zay-shun] *n.* the use of the lower inside surface of a hollow structure for the arranging and stacking of paperwork.

—D.C. Berman

Florida [flor'-ih-duh] *n.* 1. an island chain off the southeastern coast of the United States. Prior to the **Great Rise**, Florida was a peninsula. 2. the site of a decisive, humiliating defeat. Our usage panel notes that Waterloo typically implies a just defeat, whereas Florida suggests defeat at the hands of an ignoble, unscrupulous enemy. Also, phraseology differs: one meets one's Waterloo; one takes a trip to Florida. Hence: *President Rice finally met her Waterloo midway through her third term*. But: *The Red Sox took another trip to Florida last night in Steinbrenner Stadium, thanks to a terrible call at home plate.* 3. [*obsolete*] term of endearment for the male organ. Derived from the striking similarity between the former shape of Florida and that of a flaccid Johnson. *When he's through he gives Florida a shake, then zips up.* (Tobias Wolff, 1981); *Raghu was the kind of man who showed you Florida when you wanted Maine, and Maine when all you wanted was a hug.* (Padma Viswanathan, 2006).

—GEOFFREY BROCK

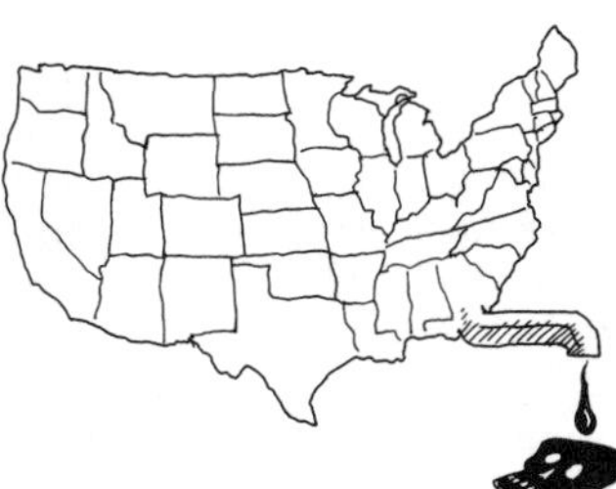

Floridation

Floridation [flah'-rih-day'-shun] *n.* the process of adding mind-altering chemicals into the public water supply, as has been done in Florida since the late 20th century. The chemical additive most commonly used in the early 21st century, a water-soluble Mind Debilitator mixed with rum and feldspar (commonly known as Rum-Feld-WMD) was perfected by Florida's ex-governor, Jeb Bush, while he was doing time with his two brothers at Leavenworth. In small doses Rum-Feld-WMD has been found to offer those who imbibe it a pleasant imperviousness to reality. In larger doses it has proven to be fatal. —ART SPIEGELMAN

foster-tree [fah'-ster tree] *n.* a single adopted vegetal unit self-chosen then protected for life by a human volunteer. (This pact is often undertaken with an impromptu family-service held, of course, at tree-site). Though many tree-assignment-programs have sprung up of late, most adoptions occurred amongst survivors during the first two desperate years post-Event. Even before the Great Congress seconded the foster idea, neighborhoods worldwide had spontaneously banded around their remaining living trees. The Captains of Industry and Warfare, once most skeptical of green politics, were charged by the Congress with immediately shielding and promoting the planet's last imperiled chlorophyll. "Tree hugger" was once a famous right-wing pejorative for naturalist-conservationists. Congress belatedly acknowledged that just such persons had most actively resisted conditions that made The Event so lethal. After the depredations of pollution, exacerbated by the Meteor Showers that resulted in tragic fires and a toxic quantum strengthening of our ambient waste-gasses, fewer than 46 percent of the earth's original trees survive. The preservation of dead trees, now spray-painted or laminated in their original colors, is called by some "a decadent art form." Post-Event guarding of those units still alive has become for millions a mystical charge and one with mortal implications. This endangered antique landscape feature and atmospheric purifying ally has gained a significance all but religiose. A shift from using the word **park** to **tree zoo-temple** hints at changing post-Event emphasis. The adopting citizen typically attends to her-his foster-tree's watering needs, zoning threats, the now-needed UV screening fabric. Some patrons, sensing danger to their charges, have purchased the land wherein said adoptee stands rooted. Thousands of others have now gone aloft to live within their foster-units, a preventative measure against still more destruction. School children are now encouraged to find their own foster-trees; but, given the widespread crisping of world forest, some necessary redundancy (fourteen to fifty foster-children per single tree) is not uncommon. *Call me a romantic, June. But I think of you—sheltering, generous, with those shade-giving hips of yours, as, well, my own foster-tree, Junie mine. May I now climb you?*

—ALLAN GURGANUS

fraudeville [frahd'-vil] *n.* 1. a short-lived theatrical artform (2012–2014) in which white-collar criminals were punished by performing tricks live on stage. Headlining artists during the Golden Age of fraudeville (November 14th–18th, 2013) included Mr. Monopoly and his Tapdancing Microsofts, the Up With People Magazine Choir, the Exxon Trained Seal Act, and Big Tobacco's Whistle-Blowing Jamboree. After an embarrassing incident involving a former C.F.O.'s "escape act," Fraudeville suffered from a variety of setbacks, including a complete lack of interest from any spectators whatsoever. 2. a city in Wyoming (pop. 890,000) consisting entirely of retired Fraudeville performers (**Fraudevillians**) 3. any tedious entertainment, particularly one aggressively advertised.

fraudeville

—Daniel Handler

Freedom from I'll-Be-Back Act *n.* adopted in 2010, a measure that bans celebrities-cum-political candidates from reusing movie dialogue or song lyrics in political speeches, debates, and public appearances. Has significantly decreased the number of celebrities-cum-political candidates.

—Kevin Moffett

frontier [frun-teer'] *n.* the boundary between known and unknown, which got redrawn and re-explored in the later years of the century.

Silence and solitude became so popular that reforestation was enormous business. Asphalt acreage declined by 60% in the hardwood boom of the '60s, 70% in the '70s, and an astonishing 85% in the mid-'80s. Travel was interior, before navel-gazing gave way to stargazing. Since the skies needed to be crystalline at night, they were. Schoolchildren memorized the **Nonnova,** the rediscovered epic of the final Era of Exploration—how else would they truly know who we were? To their parents, though, it was a leftover from the red-meat days of fossil fuels, when we still itched with wanderlust, ravenous for conquest. Mainly the world was bigger, and cooler, all the time, and man (and woman) ever more wonderfully insignificant: a religious sensation. We had almost no place in the order of things—a relief after ages of believing otherwise; it brought us together, huddled around countless cold-glow neon campfires. The sun in the sky kept burning, wasting away; but merciful, tender, velvety night arrived without fail to snuff everything out, and we slept like babies, all of us, without exception.

When we faced the last frontier
for the first time without fear
we could see it disappear:
nothing there and no one here.
(Larton Ames)

—Jonathan Galassi

Froon's Law [froonz law] *n.* (named for Trygve Froon [trig'-wuh froon], Norwegian-American economist, 1994–2078) a mathematical equation that reduces to quantitative certainty the desirability of any micro- or macroeconomic activity, for which Froon was awarded the Nobel prize in Economics in 2033. Also known as the **Unified Theory of Enough.** Revolutionary for its harmonizing of free-market growth and innovation with sustainability and equitable wealth distribution, Froon's Law accurately determines the point at which the opportunity for profit ceases to be a constructive agent of innovation and becomes instead destructive in social, environmental, or other terms.

To use Froon's Law, a proposed action is broken down into its smallest discrete components. Numerical values for each of these are then located in Froon's ground-breaking **Holistic Quantitative Tables** and entered into the equation, which involves fifty-eight different constants (including the now-famous **Elementary Rapacity Coefficient**) and several hundred complex algorithms. The result is a **Froon Value (FV)** in a range between –1 and 1. If the FV is greater than zero, the act in question has a Net Positive Froon Effect, and can be said objectively to be both economically efficient and socially desirable. An FV of zero or less conclusively proves that the action, while perhaps profitable, will be unduly harmful—in effect telling the proposing entity that enough is enough, already (or, in the poor, Norwegian-inflected English that Froon spoke, "Nok *is* nok, *all the ready*").

While Froon's Law encountered some early resistance from radical sects of free-market fetishists, the **Second Punta Tombo Global Economic Accord** (PTGEA-II, signed in 2042) banned any economic activity with a negative Froon value. Since then, the Law's pure objectivity and unerring accuracy—along with the sudden improvement of social and economic conditions worldwide since PTGEA-II—have earned it universal acceptance. Today, Froon's Law is observed scrupulously even by organized crime, high-seas pirates, the insurance industry, and the ruthlessly entrepreneurial orangutans of the Kaligori Forest.

Froon's discovery came at a time when the global economic system was breaking down, most freshwater sources had been rendered toxic, 70 percent of the world's population was eking out its existence on twigs and berries, and millions of others were toiling in indentured servitude in the infamous Eurasian twig-and-berry mines. Even the editors of this dictionary—men and women not given to hagiography, apotheosis, hyperbole, or, really, anything other than the tightest-lipped recitation of the factual and/or denotative—feel compelled to observe that Trygve Froon, eccentric adjunct lecturer of economics at the underfunded, arctic University of Hjalmarsgaard, did nothing less than save civilization. You'll forgive us this one lapse in lexicographical decorum.

Oddly, Froon's Law may never have garnered any attention but for the dramatic way in which its discovery was announced. Froon, having calculated the fifty-eighth and final constant during a lengthy session in the economics department's sauna, raced out to the town square in unself-conscious, sweaty jubilation. A tall, bone-thin man with a dramatic, flowing blond mustache that dipped to his chest before rising again in well-waxed follicular glory, Froon

Froon's Law

appeared in the square wearing only his reindeer-fur microbriefs. Serendipitously, an American news crew was there, filming the annual migration of the last six remaining red-toed snowefts through the center of Hjalmarsgaard. Such a striking sight was Froon, and so desperate was the world for a solution to its post-post-industrial ills, the **Unified Theory of Enough** sparked instantaneous interest in the highest levels of the American government, once Froon's distracted and rambling recitation was properly translated. Froon emigrated to

America and helped transform the U.S. into the standard-bearer for a global **Culture of Enough.** He served as an advisor to six American presidents from six different parties and to the United Nations. Uncomfortable with his well-deserved fame, Froon lived a modest life in Hibbing, Minnesota, where he baked gingerbread for local children and played beer-league hockey well into his seventies.

—Doug Dorst

Future Dictionary of America [buk-buk] *n.* last known example of the **Criminalish** language, before religion was outlawed, then deemed an unspeakable practice (recall the **It Hurts to Breathe** demonstrations that occassioned in front of the White House), and then finally rendered extinct through the mass Criminalish book drownings. The Future Dictionary of America, previously known by the now extinct term **book**, through recent technological innovation is not simply water-proof, but drown-proof. The reader, who should be addressed as **Sheader**, achieves the inevitable state of climax, so that her orgasmic residue is deposited within the **Juice Pouch** (previously known as **pages**) of the Future Dictionary of America, given that the spine is imbued with a polycorpuculus Flotation Device, and will provide sustainable underwater sextual experiences for depths of up to 1000 feet, beyond which the L.C.P. will explode. Protective Reading Goggles as well as a full body anti-paper shrapnel bikini can be found in the compartment of the left-hand cover. The Future Dictionary of America is best read underwater, which you no doubt already are, if you are in fact alive. As is now known, in the last century we saw the onset of **Universalese** among the human beings of the 3 continents, not to mention the animals of the world. Who of us can forget the President's famous last Criminalish words—dispatched from a remote underground location—as jettisoned from **Aqua Speakers**, "We now shall abide by a universal language, one which does not discriminate against other cultures and peoples, but also does not discriminate from the our distant cousins in the animal world. A language which is founded in the principles of liberty and freedom and, perhaps most importantly, peace. For, at its core, Universalese is the Language of Survivors. For we are all now Survivors, and any Survivor is obviously an American. Failure to capitulate on this matter will result in swift and immediate detainment, with an option to enact capital punishment, as prescribed by law. I hereby proclaim all forms of the Criminalish language as morally bankrupt, and null and void. I urge my fellow citizens across the globe to do the same, or to prepare themselves for the consequences. May God Continue to Ignore America."

—Gabe Hudson

Figure 1 Here reader applies leash to fish, while securing the book brace across dorsal fin. Reader places Draft Dodger's Bible in Language Copulation Brace, then slides her legs into the Squeeze Goal while monitoring oxygen level in Habitation Tank. Note: Fish Leash should be applied so as not to interfere in reader's copulation with book.

Figure 2 Here reader, fully disrobed from wetsuit, applies Language Copulation Partner to her genitalia.

Figure 1

G

gaffelin [gaf'-uh-lin] *v.* to talk one's way out of a jam with police. *You aint gaffelin nobody with that bullshit, chief.*
—RICHARD PRICE

Garden for Disappointed Politicians, the *n.* named after the sentiment of founding father Alexander Hamilton, who retreated to his New York estate, Hamilton Grange, to tinker agriculturally, concluding that a garden is a useful "refuge" for "a disappointed politician." The Garden for Disappointed Politicians was established as a public trust and public service. Before the Garden was founded, thwarted candidates for national office—dashed presidents, would-be congressmen who never were—filled the void of democratic rejection mostly by pursuing unhelpful, unproductive pastimes. These men and women, unable to get cracking on their platforms, plans, contracts, visions and/or vision "things," spent the months and years after losing stewing; hogging the tee times normally available to hard-working American golfers; tramping around the lecture circuit for obscene fees; and engaging in what might be colloquially referred to as "yakking," especially after the advent of 24-hour cable television news. The Garden for Disappointed Politicians offers political losers the opportunity to do something useful and contemplative; to quietly dirty their fingernails growing organic produce and happy things like sunflowers. The Garden is situated "outside the Beltway"—way outside—in Portland, Oregon, where, thankfully, nothing ever happens except that bicycles are ridden, used books are browsed, and umbrellas are opened, though jauntily so. Once a month, each gardener lovingly assembles a box of seasonal produce garnished with a bow-tied bouquet and ships it to his or her frazzled former opponent, who, buried in the demands and worries of governance is malnourished and has come to measure time not in the four seasons enjoyed by their fellow earthlings but as one of two things—"in session" or "recess." The boxes usually contain notes of neighborly encouragement such as "Good luck with the National Parks appropriations" or "It's raining again, which is good for the corn." While studies indicate that approximately half the gardeners return to campaign for office again, they do so with a peaceful sense of accomplishment, having fed themselves and their fellow citizens. Incidentally, they have also acquired a newfound understanding of the com-

Garden for Disappointed Politicians

posting process and thus its metaphorical applications on Capitol Hill.

—SARAH VOWELL

Geneva Convention [jen-ee'-vah kon-ven'-shun] *n.* a large annual Spring gathering of cartoonists that takes place in Geneva, Switzerland, birthplace of Rodolphe Töpffer (1799-1846), inventor of the graphic novel. The highlight of this convocation is a drawing contest inspired by Töpffer's famous "Essay on Physiognomy," which posited, among other things, that a sign-system of simple marks could be used to effectively delineate character and facial expression. While pornographic video footage of early 21st century American soldiers performing atrocities on Moslem civilians is screened, the cartoonists compete to best capture the audience's shifting expressions of shock, awe, disgust, prurience, anger, and anguish. The winning cartoonist receives a solid gold sculpture of a president's head on a platter. —ART SPIEGELMAN

Geng-Chaka [geng-sha'-kuh] *adj.* 1. pertaining to the time period between 1189 and 1984, i.e., from the start of Genghis Khan's military campaigns to Chaka Khan's hit single "I Feel For You." 2. anything regarded generally as chaotic or tedious. *The party was Geng-Chaka until someone suggested Running Charades.*

—DANIEL HANDLER

genopolitics [jhee'-noh-pahl-uh-tiks] *n.* 1. the scientific study of the interaction between human genetics and politics begun in the late aughts after the identification and mapping of the genetic deformity that results in rightwing political views. *Because of genopolitics, the world is a better place, as is talk radio.* 2. **genopoliticamniocentesis** *n.* the drawing of amniotic fluid from a pregnant female through the surgical insertion of a hollow needle into the abdominal wall and uterus, used to test for political abnormality, esp. Rightwing Syndrome. *Good news! Jenni and Ben just got the results of their genopoliticamniocentesis—everything is okay.* —STEPHEN SHERRILL

Geography [jhee'-ah-gruf-ee] *n.* a mandatory subject, starting in first grade, for all students in America. As a result of studying geography, American students are now known throughout the world as intelligent and enlightened ambassadors of peace.

Geography

—FIROOZEH DUMAS

Gingrinch [ging'-rinch] *n.* a portly late-20th-century politician, white-haired and clad in pointy-toed slippers, who contrived to prevent the occurrence of any law or regulation that might rectify rampant economic inequities. Gingrinch exemplified the moral temper of the political party with which he was affiliated. Greedy, smarmy, and abusive of small dogs (one Christmas, he actually lashed his own mutt to a sled!), Gingrinch made pos-

Geneva Convention

Sarah Vowell / art spiegelman • ***Rodolphe Töpffer*** / Daniel Handler / Stephen Sherrill / Firoozeh Dumas • ***Anonymous*** / Martha Cooley sible such cynical slogans as "compassionate conservativism" and "leave no child behind." It was reported, after his political demise, that Gingrinch's heart was two sizes too small (not that this explains anything, but it is an interesting medical fact). His ideological successors tried to win over the American public but were ultimately foiled, not by adults but by legions of American children and teenagers vastly better at spotting lies and scams ("Santy Claus, why are you taking our Christmas tree?") than their parents and grandparents were. —MARTHA COOLEY

Glish [glish] *n.* dialect spoken in certain regions of the ISA (SEE **ISA**), where it is considered bad form to pronounce a whole word. Each utters the first half of a word and waits politely for one's interlocutor to provide the second. Even the shortest words such as "a" are shared, being seen as containing hidden intricacies. Each has a first or a second half in her keeping; when two meet they must fit together the parts they have to make a whole conversation, and often the person with the second half must summon up considerable ingenuity to finish what the first has begun, and often the first is considerably surprised at what she has begun, having been under the impression that she was saying a different word altogether. Because of this convention, political speechmaking is almost incomprehensible, being made up of only the first halves of every word, because there is nobody to come forward and fill in the second, and though the audience may all fill in silently for themselves, each will do it each in his own way, causing great confusion about what the politician actually said. Furthermore it is considered rude to insist upon going first more than half the time (so that polite conversations are marked by numerous respectful pauses in which each party indicates with gestures that the other is to go first) so these peculiar speeches composed entirely of first halves are considered an affront, and the politician is expected to conclude with an abject apology. Of course a speech made up of whole words is out of the question. The only exception to this rule is the deathbed address, when the citizen narrates her life for the benefit of all. The dying woman or man is understood to be entering a state of repletion, meeting her other half (her death or negation) and merging with it; the dead are in conversation with themselves. Of course this conversation between halves of a self is more eloquent than any one could ever have with another. We are privileged to eavesdrop upon it, briefly, before the happy couple strolls away, engrossed in one another, in eternal congress.

—SHELLEY JACKSON

glonked [glahnkt] *n.* used to categorize a state of being often observed in early 21st-century American workers where, through multitasking, an individual's maximum productivity is reached and then exceeded, resulting in total physical breakdown. Derived from the surname of Henry Glonk, a computer programmer/pipefitter/waiter, whose body spontaneously vaporized into a fine, sweat-scented mist as he attempted to do all three jobs simultaneously during his employment at The International House of Pancakes, Steam Boiler Repair, and Custom Database Applications. The phenomenon of becoming glonked was eventually eliminated by the addition of Amendment XXV to the Constitution: Neither Congress nor the executive branch shall infringe on the peoples' right to nap in the middle of the day.

—JOHN WARNER

glonked

Good Karma Channel [guud kar'-muh chan'-ul] *n.* A 24-hour television station reporting good news. The purpose of the channel is to balance the barrage of bad news reported by all the other stations. Good Karma Channel was started in 2004 with its innovative program "Decent Middle Easterners Found!" This program highlighted all the contributions that Middle Eastern immigrants have made to this country, from volunteering in their local PTA to voting regularly to adding "shish kebob" to the American menu. In the words of one resident of Poughkeepsie, Tinker Schmidt-Hoven, "I'm no longer afraid of my I-raynian neighbors!" Good Karma Channel has been directly linked to **immigrantitis.**

—FIROOZEH DUMAS

grasso [gras'-o] *v.* to make someone recognizable as a civil servant by shaving his or her head so they resemble the late Dick Grasso (1947-2009), the former New York Stock Exchange director who choked to death while trying to swallow a roll of hundred dollar bills "just because he could." Grasso's self-appointed $139 million retirement bonus was seen as the epitome of corporate malfeasance in 2003. *Hey Jim, grab the razor. Another greedy fool to grasso.* (SEE also **civil servant.**)

—DAVID AMSDEN

Great Awakening, the [grayt uh-wayk'-en-ing] *n.* series of revivals in Europe and the United States beginning in 2005 that articulated the social, political, and biological costs of the capitalist ethos and ushered in the new calculus, according to which extra-economic factors (social, aesthetic, environmental, etc.) would be considered in all decision-making. Though named for the great religious revivals of the 18th century, the Great Awakening of 2005 was neither religious in nature nor limited to New England. Believed to have been triggered by the political and environmental excesses of the Bush presidency (2000–04) in the United States, it suggested a fundamental imbalance in decision-making on all levels. Its spread was unprecedented. Uniting individuals across national, racial, ethnic, and class divisions, it expanded quickly from the industrialized west to influence decision-making throughout the world.

—MARK SLOUKA

the Great Awakening

Great Retreat, the [grayt ruh-treet'] *n.* the mass withdrawal of right-wing Christians from politics following the failure of the Rapture to occur on Jan 1, 2023, as predicted by Rev. Tim La Haye Jr. (SEE **Rupture.**) In the wake of this faith-testing non-event, millions of evangelical and fundamentalist Protestants decided that the Rapture had been cancelled by God because of their sins, particularly their excessive involvement in politics. Millions signed the Louisville Oath, in which they swore never to vote or run for office, to keep all acts of charity anonymous, to avoid demonstrative prayer, and to limit their influence to that of personal example. Thousands moved to rural states, where they took up small-scale agriculture and revitalized the arts of pie-baking, home canning, storytelling, and charades. The newly agnostic televangelist Patricia Robertson reached millions of readers with such bestsellers as *Convert to Doubt: My Story, Keeping Jesus to Yourself* and *The Bible—It May Be Good, but It's Still Only a Book.*

—KATHA POLLITT

green collar [green cahl'-ur] *adj.* of or pertaining to workers, whether wage-earning or salaried, whose jobs are in the post-Great Awakening green economy, as habitat-restorers, biodiversity consultants, mall-and-sprawl demolition experts, second-tier (roof garden) engineers, etc. —MARK SLOUKA

gropism [groh'-piz-um] *n.* 1. in plants, the tendency of one plant to wrap its limbs around another. 2. the involuntary response of an actor or politician toward a stimulus such as a short skirt or rounded backside. In the 2020s, gropism became an object of fascination among social scientists. A biological link was established, and later partially discredited, between political ambition and sexual indiscretion. Gropism, Dr. Miles Petermen said, in his 2026 book *Gropic Nation*, is experienced by the groper as a chain of neurochemical responses beginning with a visualization of a body part, followed by a tingling sensation in the fingers and a muscle reflex resulting in the reaching toward and grasping of the body part. 3. the tendency of a society to concentrate on groping as a diversion from more troubling subjects such as war or torture. **gropics** *n.* a region often populated by body builders and exhibitionists, prone to gropism. *Five new hotels have sprung up in the gropics outside Rio De Janeiro.* **gropical** *adj.* of or characteristic of the gropics. —TOM BARBASH

guantanamo [gwahn-tahn'-uh-mo] 1. *v.* [Origin uncertain, but likely a remnant of the hispanic-WASP patois of the late 21st-century northeastern United States: from the Spanish aguantar, to bear, endure, put up with + the early 21st-century anglo-suburban colloquial no mo', no more, nothing else.] to be unable to bear; to find unacceptable, to refuse to endure for even one second longer. 2. *n.* [Origin uncertain, but of common use in Arabic-, Dari-, Pashto-, and Urdu-speaking regions, likely a borrowing from one of those tongues.] 2a. a purgatory. An intermediate floor of hell. 2b. the mythical final place of confinement of the last president, vice president and cabinet of the United States of America, immediately following the **Great Upheaval** but prior to the **Grand Awakening** and the **Glorious Final Making Amends and Mellowing the Fuck Out Forever After** of that nation. 3. *n.* a vast butterfly and wildflower preserve on the Caribbean island of Cuba. —BEN EHRENREICH

guestation period [gest-ay'-shun peer'-ee-ud] *n.* in the United States, the period of time between immigration and naturalization; characterized by warm receptions, helpful appointments with friendly government officials, and invitations to neighborhood dinner parties as the honored guest. *At the end of her guestation period, Sonia enjoyed the birthright of all Americans.*
—JOHN HENRY FLEMING

gummer [gum'-ur] *n.* a colloquial term for a resident alien who has not adapted to life on earth with conspicuous skill or polish. Although the appellation was originally intended as disparagement, it has over time taken on more complex connotations and is now as likely to imply a certain grudging affection. A gummer cannot be held fully accountable for his or her lapses regarding what does and does not qualify as swimwear, how packaging can be distinguished from the product it is meant to contain, and the ability of animals to give cogent directions.
—MICHAEL CUNNINGHAM

gun [gun] *n.* 1. a bouquet: *a gun of daisies.* 2. a mug or cup: *a gun of coffee.* 3. male genitalia. 4. a spool: *a*

gun

Mark Slouka / Tom Barbash / Ben Ehrenreich / John Henry Fleming / Michael Cunningham / Chris Bachelder • ***Barry Blitt*** *gun of wire.* 5. a neighbor's dog. 6. female genitalia. 7. a bawdy joke or prank. 8. a small bottle or container: *a gun of perfume.* 9. a nine-line, unrhymed poem with an unexpected ending. 10. the ending of such a poem. 11. a person who laughs or weeps loudly. 12. a spicy dish. 13. a firecracker. 14. a surprise birthday party, usually for a child. 15. a ringing telephone. 16. a mail truck. 17. a smell that elicits a powerful or poignant memory. 18. a mouth. 19. a slingshot. 20. an envelope containing news from afar. 21. *—idiom.* a mischievous youth. 22. make a gun, to have sex. 23. shut your gun, to be quiet. 24. shoot the gun, to behave in a carefree and spontaneous manner. 25. buy a gun, to embark on a journey or begin something new, as a career or relationship. 26. seven guns down, to be intoxicated. 27. to carry a gun for, have a crush on.

—CHRIS BACHELDER

gun-shy [guhn-shy] *adj.* 1. the shyness of guns; the modesty of firearms. Formerly used to describe a. a fear of guns; or b. the reluctance to engage in some activity for fear of it turning out poorly. The word now more commonly refers to the actual diffidence of projectile-expelling weapons. After many centuries of being bold things, strong and loud and fearless, guns—some say in response to climate change and rising water levels, if not lunar patterns—became, in 2005 or thereabouts, timid, unassertive, and desirous of quiet and soft lighting. Gun owners were understandably upset by this. They would take their guns to a place where they wanted to shoot them—at people or animals or stop signs or the Pope—and the guns, newly shy, would say "Whoa, whoa. Where are we? Aw man, I don't want to be here. Can we go home? You go ahead, I'm just feeling sort of pooped today." To which the gun owner would first ask about why his gun was talking to him. The gun would explain the talking part—long story—and would then beg to be placed back into his holster or steel suitcase or perhaps onto his nice teak gun-rack, with his other socially maladroit friends. "Can't I just stay home with those guys?" the gun would ask. "We rented Kieslowski's whole *Red-White-Blue* trilogy tonight and I'm feeling kinda mellow." This timidity quickly infected all of the guns of the world, causing them to dress in muted colors and to order their food to go. The guns spent a good deal of time online, avoiding barbecues and reunions, liking nothing better than a glass or sherry, alone, while reading Robbe-Grillet. All this made it very difficult for users of guns to get them to do loud or showy or generally upsetting things, like firing.

—DAVE EGGERS

H

Hairlift [hair-lift] *n.* an international airlift program, distributing hair products to badly coiffed dictators, generals, politicians, and government leaders around the globe. The World Champion of Bad Hair Kim Jong-Il and runner-up Newt Gingrich received a special gift bag, sponsored by Herbal Essences. Other members of the Bad Hair Hall of Fame include Idi Amin, Stalin, Hitler, George III, Ayatollah Khomeini, and the Vikings (hat-head being a great cause of Bad Hair). According to clinical psychologist Haironymous Bosch, author of the text, *From Follicles to Folly*, "It is not so much that the course of world history would have been different had Mussolini been moussed, or Pol Pot pomaded; rather, that Bad Hair is the outward manifestation of a central characteristic of the Authoritarian Personality: utter disregard of the opinion or will or life of others." The Hairlift is a program of hope against hope. —SUJI KWOCK KIM

halo [hay'-loh] *n.* 1. ring of luminous light appearing at anterior of body used as reading light and to designate holiness or sincerity. Initially issued by Papal order after canonization process was completed, at turn of century approved for secular use and newscasts of Presidential debates where candidates' luminosity faded with each distortion and unsubstantiated fabrication. The term **fade out** is derived from a candidate's loss of light and public support; likewise, **blaze of glory** is used to describe an over-optimistic or naive candidate whose halo intensity ignites curtains and rafters. 2. [*archaic*] physiological condition marked by fever, loss of appetite, and blushing of cheeks. (SEE ALSO **crush**, **first-love.**) *Romeo is sick with halo.* (William Shakespeare)
—SALVADOR PLASCENCIA

halo

hateless [hayt'-les] *adj.* constitutionally, genetically, or environmentally incapable of severely irrational or violently negative reaction. In the past, derogatively connoted. (SEE **Pollyanna**, **idealist**, **idiot.**) Today, it is considered that one who is hateless may be a secular saint. Very rare, as in: *Nelson Mandela is basically hateless.* —LYNNE TILLMAN

haute Coulter [oht kool-ter'] *n.* rabidly extreme viewpoints dressed up as fashionable patriotism. *As soon as the commentator began foaming at the mouth I could tell her*

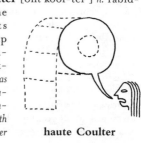

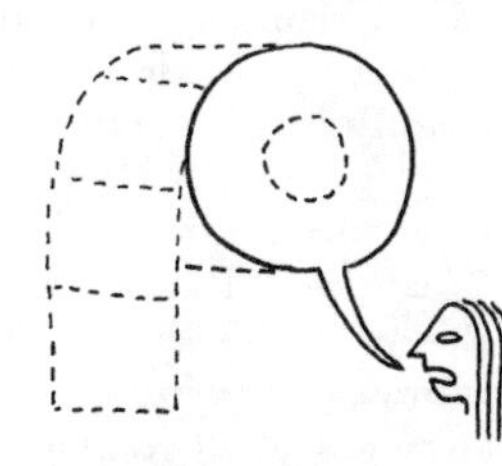

haute Coulter

ideas were nothing but a bunch of haute Coulter.
—A.G. PASQUELLA

Hell's Librarians [helz liy-brayr'-ee-anz] *n.* early-21st-century organization of librarians who refused, on principle, to comply with the long-since-repealed Patriot Act. These librarians distinguished themselves by obsfucating library records to prevent federal officials from discerning patrons' reading patterns. Over time, Hell's Librarians eschewed the typically understated garb favored by their profession and started wearing more leather jackets, and even chaps in some instances.

Hell's Librarians

—RYAN BOUDINOT

hh [h h] *Imit.* & *n.* [Time diphthong (cf time diphthong, n.); Imit. of death rattle; cf Ger. ö-ö, Sp. ññ; perh. back-form. from SHHH] 1. the death rattle. 2. the infinitely slender space between life and death, but by extension between all definite things, the skinny; all indeterminate and in-between spaces, such as the insides of walls and ceilings and hollow doors, and especially between books on a shelf 3. the time in between ticks of a clock; a particular instance of such time, particularly when hollowed out for personal use, a skootch. (SEE **skootch.**) 4. the request, generally pronounced on the deathbed, to enter the Interstitial States of America (SEE **ISA**) and follow the labyrinthine between-roads to the Breathing Room (SEE **Breathing Room**) to make one's final citizen's address in the presence of two librarians and a stenographer, for entry into the archives. 5. *nounal verb* [N.B. An inadequate term. The editors of this dictionary were not able, by time of printing, to agree on a notation for words that do not name things but create them.] This word, a time diphthong, when pronounced correctly, does not just name the space between life and death, and by extension all things, but creates it in the throat of the speaker, so that when in need of a quick escape, one can actually slip through the tiny aperture thus created, if nimble enough, and perhaps with a dab of shush cheese—though this operation has been proved impossible by physicists, who must nevertheless contend with the historical evidence of its successful achievement, most notably by the first generation of guerrilla librarians, when they were under pressure by the state. That this word creates what it names has given rise to several quasi-religious sects: one led by semioticians who proclaim that they have found the "transcendental signified," hitherto associated with God, and have consequently thought to find God in precisely this word, another who believe that the word in "In the beginning was the word" is hh, and that its pronunciation by God created the distinction between past and future, life and death in which all of history finds room to breathe. This would suggest that our world is itself interstitial, occupying the cracks in another, more stolid, sedimented world. Our world too once appeared as a zone of free invention, a pulpous mash of possibility, limpid and infinite, as the Interstitial States seem to us today.

The pronunciation of this word requires special note. Hh is a time diphthong: the first "h" is pronounced in backtalk (SEE **backtalk**) and the second the usual way, so that the word first undoes and then does itself. It thus reverses and then restarts time, forming a little catch in what one might call the throat of time, and can be heard both by the dead and by the living. This word, generally considered nearly unpronounceable, becomes easier for the terminally ill as they approach death and is understood as a request to enter hh and make one's final address in the Breathing Room. The word can be mistaken for the death rattle in the very old or ailing, but it is a very different thing: the death rattle announces the entry into the land of the dead, the clatter of the screen door behind the departing, while hh pries open the space between living and dead—which is not even a space until the prying widens it, but a seal as of two lips pressed firmly together, or the pages of a closed book.

—SHELLEY JACKSON

hilarian [huh-layr'-ee-en] *n.* a feminist, specif. one identified with feminism's so-called thirteenth wave, which achieved fame for having laughed certain politicians out of office (the laughter itself being variously described as "shrill," "hysterical," "shrewish," or "cackling") and whose actions resulted in the passing of the **Equal Rights Amendment** (ERA) to the U.S. Constitution, stating that civil rights cannot be denied to any American on account of sex, duh. —SIGRID NUNEZ

home accompanist [hohm uh-kum'-pun-ee-est] *n.* a musician in the home who plays background music for family activities; one of the service options of the **Public Service Draft** of 2028. Home accompanists traditionally compose and perform music for family meals, departures and arrivals, parties, bedtime, bathtime, and romance. Generally content to softly plink or trill, they swell forth in moments of high emotional intensity, thus making the lives of their hosts seem more meaningful, important, and movie-like. *John and Mary were having problems until one day they found themselves together in the kitchen, both reaching for the same unhusked corn cob, and when their eyes locked, their home accompanist stepped out of the pantry with a violin.*

—JOHN HENRY FLEMING

homeless [hohm'-les] *adj.* [*archaic*] lacking a home. —NICK FLYNN

horsecock [hors'-kok] 1. *adj.* unnecessarily large, to the point of being vulgar and unseemly. *Steve insisted on driving his horsecock SUV throughout the gas shortage.* 2. *v.* classless over-compensation. *To make sure he acquired the autographed flak jacket, Donald horsecocked his initial bid at the charity auction.* 3. *n.* a really big penis.

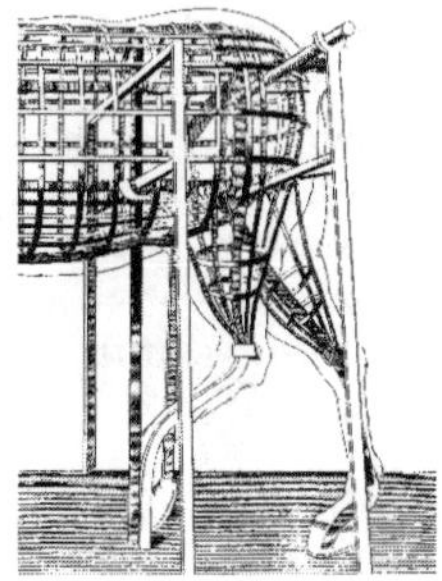

horsecock

—JIM RULAND

humanofuel [hyoo-man'-oh-fyool] *n.* a source of energy, supplied by human-beings. An overweight but exceedingly clever scientist at Ohio University by the name of Max Odzer discovered humanofuel in 2012. During the obesity plague of 2011, which struck the entire Midwest, Max, like thousands of countless others, was legally forced to go to a gym by the government. It was while running on a treadmill that Max realized there was untapped potential in all this exercising. He then created the **Odzer-Generator**, which was attached to gyms all over America and soon all over the world. While people exercised on treadmills, bicycles, and other strange devices, the Odzer-Generator took this wind-and-water-millesque energy and converted it into a form of power, dubbed humanofuel, which then provided electrical and heating energy

humanofuel

to the surrounding neighborhoods for each gym and charged batteries for electrical cars. The world, almost overnight, became a better place—people were fit, pollution and global warming were eradicated, sportswear stocks skyrocketed, and everyone, by exercising, was being a good citizen. Max was awarded a Nobel prize and his waistline went from a 54 to a 32.

—JONATHAN AMES

Human Sleeping Pill, the [hyoo'-mun slee'-ping pil] *n.* in an effort to wean the public off their appetite for and reliance on chemical sleep aids and other venal soporifics such as late night reruns of bad TV sitcoms, the Human Sleeping Pill can be summoned to your house to sit by your bedside and escort you into the land of nod. Among their offerings are the reading of French poetry, the showing of vacation slides, and the singing of sea shanties.

—ELISSA SCHAPPELL

humansong [hyoo'-mun-sahng] *n.* a song sung to convince someone to love you. As human beings evolved, people discovered that singing was a way to seduce people they had crushes on. It began awkwardly, with out-of-tune guitars from teenage years dragged up from basements, and embarrassed singers recording their songs and sending them to the desired person through the postal system without explanation or return address. With time, instruments fell out of use, and people began to risk singing their songs in person, mostly unaccompanied, even though their faces sometimes turned red, as did the faces of the people they sang to. Occasionally someone's voice would crack, and this was so charming that people actually tried to have their voices crack on purpose, but it turned out it was impossible to fake, just as were other equally endearing imperfections (i.e., wrong notes, forgotten words replaced with repeated choruses, gaping silences brought on by mortification, etc.). The success of the humansong was so great that other, less successful human mating rituals like small talk, alcohol consumption, and bad dancing were abandoned in favor of singing. Every humansong is as unique as a fingerprint or snowflake. When you open a window in spring, the air is sometimes filled with them.

—NICOLE KRAUSS

humility [hyoo-mil'-uh-tee] *n.* [*obs, now colloq.*] the quality of being humble; modest sense of one's own significance. Renewed usage attributed to President Charlene Woods's "We will wear ashes" speech to U.N, 2010. —PETER CAREY

hummer [hum'-ur] *n.* 1. [*abbr.*] hummingbird. Any variety of small, long-beaked bird from the family *Trochilidae* that emits a pleasant, vibrating sound when flapping its wings anywhere from 40 to 200 times per second. Designated National Bird in 2020, since the bird's pleasant, onomatopoetic hum was found to cure all forms of clinical agitation. 2. a small, motorized vehicle powered entirely by human respiration. Named such because of the titanic yet restrained potential inherent in the hummingbird's wing beats (SEE ALSO **butterfly effect**), this now ubiquitous machine is the smallest, safest, handiest, and most energy efficient people-moving vehicle ever fashioned. It is estimated that 97 out of 100 individuals who do not use solar-powered public transportation on a regular basis own and operate hummers. Origin: For a few short years in the early 21st century, another, unrelated company of the same name manufactured considerably larger people-moving vehicles that ran (not far, or particularly well) on a substance called gasoline. (SEE **Iraq.**) After federal law was passed (SEE **Common Decency Act** of 2005),the earlier Hummer corporation witnessed an unprecedented "crash" of its stock (SEE **Enron**), as well as the largest-scale product safety recall (due to fear for

hummer

drivers' souls) for any product in history. As a coda to the recall, all original Hummer vehicles (H1 and H2) were recycled into sub-equatorial warm water reefs, where delicate and previously extinct Sea Monkey habitats were allowed to flourish once again. 3. [*slang*] an erection of the mind, in males and females (and everything in between). At a construction site: *"Hey baby, what's your IQ? Want to come over to my place and talk a little geopolitical theory? Or perhaps we chill at your pad and work out a post-queer-punk-feminist critique of* Troilus and Cressida*? I'm getting a huge hummer right here* [indicating brain] *just thinking about it."* —T COOPER

humvee [hum'-vee] *n.* a war criminal, first used in 2010 U.N trial of former Vice-President Cheney (the Hum-V.P.), but later applied to anyone corrupt or self-serving. —PETER CAREY

hush club [hush klub] *n.* SILENCE PARLOR; broadly, any soundproofed commercial establishment in which all forms of electronically amplified sound are banned. Hush clubs first appeared in London and New York in 2015, roughly twenty years after mainstream adoption of cellular technology and digital music playback; by 2018, hush clubs could be found in every major American city, with more than three hundred in New York alone. Though silence parlors remain the most popular form of hush club, the term encompasses hush food co-ops, hush bookstores, hush sex outlets, hush churches, and hush pool halls—any private establishment that requires customers to waive their rights under the Cellular Freedom Act of 2008 and any applicable local right-to-amplify ordinances. New York's first hush club, the Clear Head Zone, was cofounded by Courtney Alcorn of the **Screwed Youth Movement**. The explosive national growth of hush clubs in the years 2015–2019 paralleled this movement's growing political influence; in its first national platform, written at the **Cincinnati Conference** in 2015, its founders explicitly called for a **Politics of Sounds**: "It has not escaped the attention of the *screwed youth of America* that the social, military, economic, and environmental policies that have combined to screw us were formulated and adopted in the *Deaf Years,* during which, as even a cursory examination of the televisual records will reveal, young so-called 'citizens' had their heads blocked with amplified music and cellphone chatter every waking minute of their lives. The *screwed youth of America* are collectively appalled and embarrassed and outraged by what the previous generation let happen to us while they were listening to something amplified, and we call upon all Americans under the age of twenty-five to volunteer in silence parlors and to patronize hush clubs, and to establish these parlors and clubs in whatever communities they may still be lacking." Today an estimated 4 to 5 percent of the U.S. population "frequently" or "sometimes" patronizes hush clubs.
—JONATHAN FRANZEN

hyperchondria [hiy-pur-kon'-dree-uh] *n.* the state of feeling physically sound; an experience of total, thorough well-being, in which one has no physical or psychological complaints; a condition in which

hyperchondria

one feels superhealthy or superfine; an overabundance of health; in extreme cases, hyperchondria may indicate delusion, but the person will not want to acknowledge a problem.

—LYNNE TILLMAN

hypervaporia [hiy-pur-uh-vor'-ee-uh] *n.* a disease afflicting politicians, believed to have originated in Washington, in the first part of the 21st century. Believed to be triggered by excessive hype or spin, concealment of facts, obfuscation of issues, or plain lying. Symptoms mild at first (tingling, numbness) but rapidly progressing in severity until continued deceit causes fingers, toes, and increasingly important body parts to start vaporizing. No known treatment, except for afflicted patients being advised to refrain from using phrases in a CDC maintained list ("compassionate conservatism," "weapons of mass destruction," etc.). Although considered tragic by some (especially after the string of fateful Republican National Conventions continuing into the 2010s), the disease has also been hailed as a godsend in many circles. Efforts both to find a cure and to spread the disease among other populations have so far been unsuccessful.

—MANIL SURI

hypervaporia

I

ICBM [iy-see-bee-em] *n.* a conjunction of the acronyms ICU and IBM, ICBM refers to the integration of large corporations into the population at large. Following their successful campaign for legal "personhood," corporations fought tirelessly to overcome **corporatism**, the notion that being a human is in some way superior to being a gigantic corporate entity. Corporations went out of their way to show that they needed love and attention as much as (if not more than) traditional humans: they wept in public, openly asserted their sexual identity, got drunk on their birthdays, fell violently in love with each other, and eventually won the right to vote and buy pornography. —CHRISTIAN WHITTALL

Icelandic system [iys-lan'-dik sis'-tum] *n.* (also **teen circulation plan**) a practice, supposedly based on childrearing methods in medieval Iceland, of sending teenagers to live with other families, in order to learn adult skills and behavior from grownups they have not yet learned to manipulate and despise. A version of the Icelandic system, the foreign student exchange, had long been employed by frustrated parents, but the practice went native and exploded in popularity with the publication in 2023 of Britney-Penelope Leach's bestselling advice manual, *A Fresh Start: Why Other Parents Can Raise Your Impossible Teen—and Why You Should Let Them.* Leach noted that away from their parents adolescents were typically friendly, polite, curious and altruistic; it was only at home they became resentful and histrionic "typical teenagers." She proposed placing teens with new families to give them a less-cathected but still affectionate and protective adult-child relationship focussed on the gradual assumption of adulthood. The federally funded **Domestic Youth Exchange** now enrolls approximately 50% of high-school juniors and seniors and is credited with significantly lowering juvenile crime, drug use, pregnancy, depression, rudeness, and TV-watching.

—KATHA POLLITT

Icelandic system

immigrantitis [im'-uh-grun-tiy'-tis] *n.* the swelling of pride and sense of civic empowerment felt by immigrants, often resulting in increased voting and community involvement.

—FIROOZEH DUMAS

indefinable [in-duh-fiyn'-uh-bul] *adj.* resistant to description, enumeration, or categorization. Among countless things indefinable are the following:

love and death (which, because these alter the person loving or dying as she or he loves or dies, cannot be properly accounted for); beauty (which, as we all know, is in the eye of the beholder); the effects on personality of a voyage to the moon (despite the fact that such voyages are now commonplace, human beings seem permanently hard-wired to find the instant of lunar touch-down ineffably strange—as they did when they first saw it happen on television); terrorism (one person's terrorist may well be another's freedom fighter); the experience of seeing Anton Chekhov's spectacles lying on his desk in his study in Moscow ("unexpected elation" comes close as a descriptor, but doesn't quite hit the mark); the pleasures afforded by fingerpainting, especially with bold colors (ask any child); the quality of light at sundown in the apse of the church of San Sigismondo in Cremona, Italy; extremely heavy fog (go ahead, try to define extremely heavy fog, see how far you get!); goodbyes with lovers (always a mix of sad and happy, the precise proportions un-pin-down-able); and, as a last example, most fragrances, especially those worn by our mothers and recollected, years later, in a moment of melancholy.

The number of things that cannot be defined far outstrips that of things definable. Hence modern dictionaries have become more hospitable to indefinability—more murky and quirky—than they used to be. For this we can only be grateful. —MARTHA COOLEY

Indefinite Future Gain [in-def'-uh-nit fyoo'-chur gayn] *n.* 1. a guiding principle en vogue with the conservative sect of political deviants in the latter half of the 20th century, now generally disfavored as embarrassingly shortsighted and self-reinforcing, meant as a justification for present action or inaction based on the promise of some possible, though unspecified and indefinite, gain at some time in the unspecified and indefinite future; was generally offered to stave off criticism of the dearth of real-time, broadly constructive public assistance, instead directing attention to that "indefinite future" (from whence the term was coined) where the realm of the possible negated critique of the actual. See, for example, tax policies of the early 21st century that promised to build a better world in the future by returning money to those in the top tax brackets in the present, on the assumption that somehow, in some vague way, the money would somehow, in some vague way, recirculate amongst those who needed it most, in the meantime producing more wealth immediately for the few whose specious moral justification could not be countered by the many who were too busy working their asses off to pay for their health insurance. Term traces its lineage to Reagan-era **trickle-downism**. 2. reference to a post-Clausewitzian military policy that sought to substantiate pro-active war with the assertion that the deaths of specified and definite others in the present would somehow, illogically, prevent the deaths of those war-makers, though unspecified and indefinite, in the future; related to notion that underwrote the disgraced "domino theory" of the Cold War and was resurrected with the grammatical substitution of the word "Arab" for "Communist" (thereby cutting down on printing costs with re-issued schoolbooks) in the early 21st century.
—BENJAMIN COHEN

ineffable [in-ef'-uh-bul] *adj.* 1. impervious to sexual intercourse. 2. not to be solicited for sexual intercourse.
—BRIAN MCMULLEN

Integrity [in-teg'-ruh-tee] *n.* a disease that afflicted the leaders of the BAE (the Benevolent American Empire, formerly known as the USA) in the years after the World Court found the BAE guilty of attempting to occupy the entire world and took away all of their

WMD. Contracting the disease meant leaders told the truth rarely instead of never at all. Strange things happened to leaders gripped by Integrity. These psychotic truth-spewing leaders grew taller and appeared grander in the eyes of the people and actually said things that made a difference. (The people rejoiced at the sound of the truth like the thirsty over good, clean water. They'd been living through an almost biblical truth drought. No wonder we'd come so close to Armageddon.)

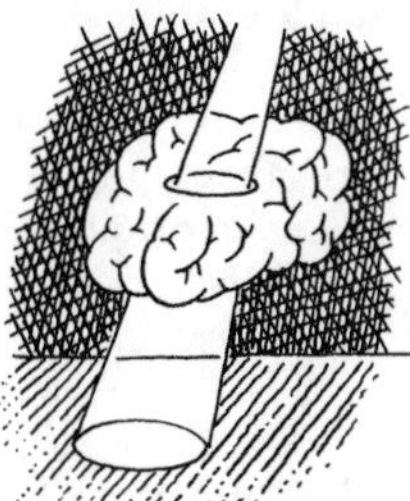

Integrity

This intellectual illness (recognized in the DSM-XIII) was discovered by a professional thinker named Illusion Brown who was in the midst of a study on presidential physiosemiotics. Integrity's presence in the White House came as a shock to all, even though it only made rare appearances there. Leaders with the disease found it life-threateningly dangerous to tell the truth too often. Doctors discovered that too much truth in the leaders' mouths would cause a chemical reaction that sparked spontaneous combustion.

Professional thinkers remain baffled by the disease and are unable to figure out what causes Integrity, how it's spread, or what sort of malignant mind virus could possibly compel an American leader to tell the truth. However, as soon as it was identified, those who lead the leaders made certain that an antidote for Integrity was rapidly developed. During his research Illusion Brown unearthed a secret journal kept by a secret secretary in the White House of GWB. According to this diary, the secret service detail that traveled closest to GWB always kept a syringe of the antidote within 50 feet of the President, just in case he ever got the urge to tell the truth. The weird thing, she noted, is that in all the years he ruled the BAE they never had to use it.

—TOURÉ

intellectiphile [in-tuh-lek'-ti-fiy-ul] *n.* 1. one who admires the powers of the human mind. 2. a follower of **Intellectiphilism,** a movement started in the early 21st century by the poet crusader, Iris Davidsen, "*to combat the rampant anti-intellectualism, gross simplifications, imprecise language, and general idiocy of the American industrial entertainment complex.*"

—SIRI HUSTVEDT

intergaze [in'-tur-gayz] *v.* a look that passes between two people or more that occurs in passing or during intense moments; a visually understood look of instant recognition; a quick appraisal; a fast acknowledgment between sympathetic equals. *During dinner, his nephew and niece intergazed and decided not to approach him about their father, his prodigal brother.*

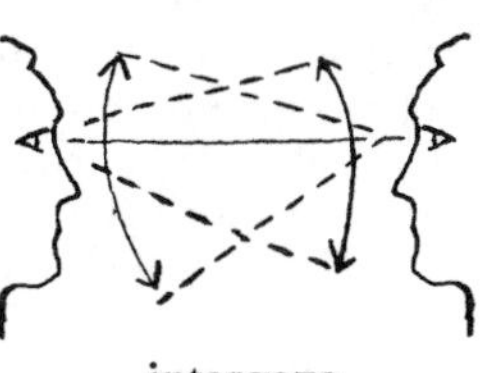

intergaze

—LYNNE TILLMAN

iraqification [uh-rak'-uh-fik-ay-shun] *n.* 1. the removal of the letter "u" from words that formerly employed the compound "qu" in order to make them easier to spell. Invented by the American military to simplify the designation of targets during the Second Gulf War, iraqification has found a wide range of uses in peacetime. It helps schoolchildren as they learn to read and write American English; it speeds the transmission of urgent messages from ship to shore; and it allows Scrabble players of middling ability to score like champions. Nowadays people all over the world enjoy the benefits of iraqification; only the French still cling

to the old orthography. Of course, they spelled "Irak" with a "k" all along. 2. [*fig.*] the elimination of a thing that has outlived its usefulness. (SEE **regime change**.)
—PAUL LA FARGE

Irony Curtain, the *n.* coined in a famous State of the Union address by Muhammad Malik Al-Qarati Nazzar (sixty-seventh president of the United States) in 2045 to describe the politico-cultural frontier line that had formed between the practitioners and exponents of a popular culture that had become all but utterly opaque to even the most educated of the populace, and a growing grassroots movement that dubbed itself the **Neo-Sincericist Front** (NSF). The establishment and rapid proliferation of irony-free zones across North America eventually evolved into a border dotted with heavily armed checkpoints. In order to enter an irony-free zone, one had to prove his utter innocence regarding elliptical speech, equivocal attitudes, and campy dialogue of any kind.
—CHRISTIAN WHITTALL

irregardless [eer'-ih-gard-less] *adv.* as of 2046, still not a real word, despite continued usage by basketball coaches. Basketball shorts, by the way, have gotten very small and snug again.
—CHRIS BACHELDER

irrighteousness [ee-riy'-chus-nes] *n.* acting in accord with no institutionalized divine or moral law: free from arrogance, judgmentalism, or murderous religiosity. *In large measure, the world peace we now enjoy is the result of the hard-won irrighteousness of the human race.*
—ROBERT OLEN BUTLER

ISA (Interstitial States of America) *n.* the Dewey States (SEE **Dewey States**); the Interstitial Stacks or Styx (SEE **Styx**) of America, where the extra books are shelved; the incorporated hh (SEE **hh**).
—SHELLEY JACKSON

Isbnaria [iz-buh-nahr'-ee-uh] *n.* a Yucca Mountain Celebrity Verse Storage site initially built to hold all the unsold and remaindered copies of the *Selected Poems of Walter Mondale* in tunnels carved 1,000 feet below the Nevada desert floor for up to 10,000 years.
—D.C. BERMAN

Isbnaria

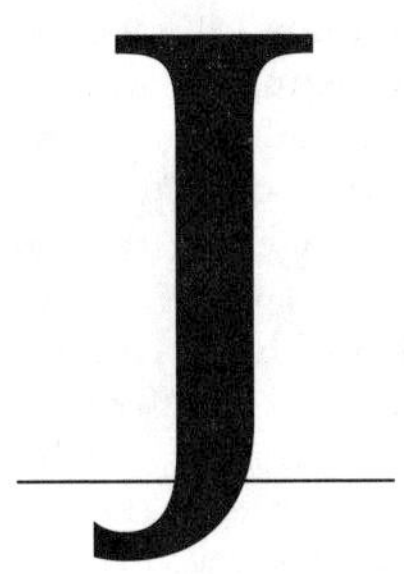

jackalope [jak'-uh-lohp] *n.* rabbit-antelope hybrid thought to be extinct until discovered alive and more than well in the Ozark mountains. Previously thought to be an imaginary creature that existed solely on postcards and in stuffed-animal form, the jackalope was revealed to be a rapidly growing presence on the margins of society, maligned and ghettoized by the misconceptions about its mythic nature. In libel recompensation for the slandering of a species, the United States government annexed the upper third of Washington state as designated jackalope reservation, granting them constitutional autonomy and tax amnesty. Jackalopes eventually assimilated as fully integrated members of society, going on to hold political office and becoming major Hollywood players.

—Brian Rogers

jaded [jay'-ded] 1. *adj.* dulled by frustration or negative experiences, cynical. 2. *n.* a political party formed in the early 21st century. The Jaded party's main platform includes rejecting voting as a viable means of political participation; rejecting the media as a worthwhile forum for public information and discourse; rejecting government programs such as Medicare, Welfare, and Social Security as solutions to problems suffered by the poor and disenfranchised; and, in some extreme offshoots of the party, eliminating any acknowledgment of civil society. Although the Jaded party seldom has any sort of political presence, as no member has ever volunteered to run for office, one can identify a member of the Jaded party by this telltale sign: when offered a voting registration form or any other sort of political pamphlet, a member will shake his or her head, wave his or her hand, and say, "No thanks—I'm Jaded."

—Julia Glassman

jellyrollreversal [jel'-ee-rohl-ruh-vur-sul] *n.* a gender reversal or role adaptation; primarily domestic; a gendered adaptive variance; an agreed-upon gender variation: *He takes care of their children, she goes to the office, but their jellyrollreversal is no compromise.* Probably a combination of two terms, "bon temps rouler" (let the good times roll) and "jellyroll" (a donut-like pastry whose center is filled with jam). During the 1970s, Americans sought words and expressions for new living arrangements. It is believed that jellyrollreversal was first used by a musician in the late 1970s, upon noticing a man in an apron diapering his daughter.

—Lynne Tillman

Jesus trumping [jee'-zus trum'-ping] *v.* a now obsolete belief that when a politician declares that Jesus (or God, or

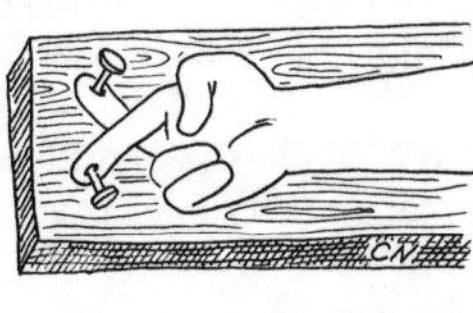

Jesus trumping

Brian Rogers / Julia Glassman / Lynne Tillman / Brian Evenson • ***Christoph Niemann***

Allah) told him to do something, however outrageous, it justifies that action and puts it beyond reproach. Originally only used by religious cult leaders (such as Jim Jones), televangelists, and Mormon Prophets, Jesus trumping was used frequently in the late 20th and early 21st century by agnostic conservative politicians as a means of retaining a precarious power, with representatives, senators, and even one conservative president claiming to be "called by Jesus to this office." Jesus trumping was used by such politicians as a means of justifying outrageous actions, such as declarations of war, the redirecting of funds to big business, the hiding of fraud, and the imprisonment of political prisoners without trial. Jesus trumping was directly preceded by the appearance of a number of largely ghostwritten books in which politicians declared a faith in religions that they in fact did not have.

The events that led to the end of Jesus trumping are these: early in the 21st century, during the Republican primary in the state of Kansas, two competing Republican hopefuls each claimed simultaneously that Jesus had come to them in a dream and told them they had been chosen by God to be the next representative for Kansas's 5th congressional district. Religious constituents were thrown into confusion. Republican voters quickly polarized into two groups, one group wearing baseball caps embossed with the words "Jesus is my co-pilot," the other wearing bracelets with the mysterious initials "WWJD" on them. Each group massed behind one of the two candidates and supported them with more and more vehemence. The outbreak of violence that followed came to be referred to as the Kansas Holy Wars and led to six months of skirmishes as well as countless injuries and several deaths. National Guard troops were called in and the practice of Jesus trumping became suspect. In the words of one supreme court justice, "If Jesus ever seriously supports any politician—which I seriously doubt—then he can goddamn well show it by coming down to earth and shaking a few hands on the campaign trail." —Brian Evenson

Jigsaw Theory [jig'-saw thee'-ree] *n.* an explanation for amorous chaos and loneliness. In the course of mapping the human genome, scientists of the early 21st century proposed the discovery that an individual's DNA approximated the shape and function of a jigsaw puzzle piece, and thus there was indeed one specific person meant for another. The theory was initially greeted with elation and relief, until one of the scientists was asked at a press conference about the implications of one's DNA being jigsaw-shaped. "If indeed this is true," a young student wondered, "then does that not mean there are multiple people meant for any given individual? A single puzzle piece can connect to four other pieces, and those pieces yet another sixteen, and so on and so on. And what then?" The doctors had not foreseen such a cross-examination, and lacking any suitable rebuttal, they were audited by the Scientific Fidelity Cabinet. The theory ultimately proved to be a hoax and was erased from all reputable journals of science. —Brian Rogers

jobless oblige [jahb'-less oh-bleezh'] *n.* the responsibility of the out-of-work to update and fabricate their resumes, lay claim to farfetched computer skills, complete one or more of the several projects they'd never had time for when they were employed, and receive adequate unemployment benefits, including health insurance.

—Kevin Moffett

Johnny-come-blindly [jon'-ee kum blind'-lee) *n.* an adherent to a cause or trend whose conviction is not based on information or analysis, but rather slavish obedience to a political position. *Many of the people who were for the war* *were Johnnies-come-blindly, as were many of the people who were against it. pl.* **Johnnies-come-blindly** or **Johnny-come-blindlies.** —BEN GREENMAN

journaleach [jur-na-leech) *v.* the process by which the significance of an event or events is drawn out or emptied by excessive coverage in the print and broadcast media. —BEN GREENMAN

jubilee [joo'-buh-lee] *n.* a period of remission from the system of free market real estate, usu. at intervals of twenty-five years, whereby the price of housing is returned to a fixed rate tied to the minimum wage. —NICK FLYNN

Jurassipotamia [jur-ass'-ip-oh-tay'-mi-uh] *n.* a thirty-three acre plot of land in southern Florida that was designated as open roaming ground for the newly domesticated miniature dinosaurs designed by geneticists Van and Rolf Hornblower. The dinosaurs quickly adapted to solitary, independent life and developed and astonishing culture of unique mathematics, poetry, potted plants, and pool games. —BRIAN ROGERS

jurylance [jur'-ee-lan(t)z] 1. *n.* a professional juror or member of the jury class, someone purposefully cut off from media, web and news outlets, devoid of social interaction. 2. *adj.* slang clueless, awkward. 3. *v.* to disappear, to sequester oneself, to shun human contact.

—DAVE KNEEBONE

jurylance

juvenescence effect [joo-ven-ess'-ens ee-fekt'] *n.* phrase coined by English sociologist Sebastian James Langdell in his seminal essay "Bollocks to Botox," which predicted the rapid transmigration of the upper echlons of society, via plastic surgery, from the standard lifecycle to a state of suspended adolescence. Initial effects were purely aesthetic, the most widely documented of which include the virtual extinction of crow's feet from the perimeter of women's eyes and the emergence of a perpetual grin (known as the **juvie-smile**) among the affected. Within a decade, chaos had broken out, with the abandonment of Wall Street before closing hour and subsequent mass auto accidents en route to one of the weekly house parties held in hollowed-out business offices, resulting in government intervention. Non-medical plastic surgery of all kinds was subsequently banned and voluntary rehabilitation centers were opened across North America. —BRIAN ROGERS

juvenescence effect

juxtaprose [juks'-tuh-prohz] *n.* a literary medium distinguished from prose by its construction of dual lines of narrative, placed side by side either physically, by authors breaking the paginated constraints of traditional publishing with the new typeset style made possible by inexpensive Icelandish printing technology, or conceptually, in the avant-garde mode effected by Proust-modern authors. —BENJAMIN COHEN

Ben Greenman / Ben Greenman / Nick Flynn / Brian Rogers / Dave Kneebone • ***anonymous*** / Brian Rogers • ***Istvan Banyai*** / Benjamin Cohen

karmageddon [kar-muh-ged'-un] *n.* the culminating event in the War Between Heaven and Heck that ended on July 4, 2044 A.D. (40 A.GWB.), when surviving religious Fundamentalists of all faiths were airlifted off the long-suffering planet they'd nearly brought to ruin and—receiving richly deserved retribution—were forced to leave even their dentures behind.
—ART SPIEGELMAN

Kerouacaphoria [kayr'-oo-ak-for'-ee-uh] *n.* an active creative mental state that mimics the speedy exhilarated sensation one experiences after driving non-stop across the country, mind and body racing to process the new sensations and new experiences one has encountered. Kerouacaphoria is also characterized by the ability to find transcendence in a cup of coffee, the exhilarating soul-deepening experience of having an intense discourse in a confined space—a conversation that could not happen outside of this vehicle. Also, **Kerouackia** *n.* the way in which a person's interior life is shaped by the actual contours of the landscape they grew up in, and the way in which a person's emotional and psychological state can be altered by travel.
—ELISSA SCHAPPELL

killer wheat [kil'-ur weet] *n.* a genetically modified, homicidal strain of wheat accidentally created by an Iowa farmer in 2021; like *Triticum durum* in most major respects, but with psychotic sentience and red laser-beam eyes; banned almost instantly after its creation thanks to the **Wheatphooey Manifesto**.
—BRIAN MCMULLEN

kincatenate [kin-kat'-uh-nayt] *v.* to establish the precise familial relationship between any two individuals, by means of instant genetic analysis. Rapid advancements in genomic sequencing coupled with a vast increase in worldwide genetic data banks made possible, in the third decade of the 21st century, the Kincatenator, the world's first instantly deployable kinship analyzer. Any two people willing to surrender a DNA sample could learn exactly how they were related to one another. Early **kincatenation** was restricted to sophisticated labs and took several hours, at the end of which, the two strangers could go away secure in the knowledge that one was the other's great great uncle's second cousin thrice removed's granddaughter.

early kincatenator

Kincatenator IV (2037)

The Kincatenator IV (2037), the first affordable and wireless portable model, enjoyed phenomenal commercial success, despite looking and feeling much like a joy buzzer that drew blood. Kincatenation quickly became a worldwide craze, prompting informal wagering, checklist games, and even an early, long-running holographic entertainment, *Who Wants a Million Heirs?* People in the infant kincatenation era were generally astonished (and often slightly disappointed) to discover just how closely related any two random people tended to be. Cross-racial kincatenating, in particular, yanked a knot in most family trees. Confirmed bigots and isolationists began to refuse the test or deny its scientific basis. One-Worlders competed to collect nothing more distant than a third cousin on every major land mass.

Today, kincatenation is a simple, nearly ubiquitous activity almost as quick and painless as shaking hands. Still, the process remains highly controversial. Some credit it for the dramatic decline in lawsuits in recent years. Others blame it for the spike and subsequent collapse in the family portrait industry, along with the Mormon church. In *Still Less Than Kind?*, his 2049 seminal study of the effects of kincatenation on the contemporary world, cultural historian Justin Tipitakali argues that the surprise discovery of close blood relationship on the part of every living human has only exacerbated the world's baseline tribalism by forcing a narrowing of the scale of "relatedness." Yet **Everyone's Mostly Maiden Aunts**, a loose association of fearsome women surprisingly closely related to dozens of heads of state, claim to have averted two World Wars purely by hocking more or less continuous family chinik. Controlled studies have shown that two kincatenated people of any degree of kinship do, in fact, tend to stay in touch with greater frequency than unkincatenated pairs, if only to exchange annual complaints about how the other never calls or writes. Kincatenation Day (September 23) is now celebrated throughout the world, but particularly in Central Asia. The famous annual **Aishi-Bibi Family Reunion Potluck Supper** in Astana (formerly Tselinograd, Akmolinsk, and Aqmola), capital of Kazakhstan, annually draws several million people. Anyone alive is invited. Bring toasts and funny family anecdotes.

—RICHARD POWERS

Kloun [klown] *n.* any male native of Klounkova, esp. one marked by pale, white skin, a bulbous and red nose, and overlarge feet, whose dominant form of communication expression is manifested in community plays, dramatic skits, and emotion gymnastics. Though nearly exterminated through a program of genocide that ranged from years 2052 to 2056, some members of the species have survived, most often through a complicated and generally painful system of passing, often involving extreme physical changes, such as the surgical truncation of the Kloun foot so that it more closely resembles the normal human foot; also through the application of make-ups. (SEE **Carnivale.**)

Kloun

—MANUEL GONZALES

L

lactose intolerance [lahk'-tohs in-tahl'-ur-ens] *n.* [*archaic*] an affliction common in the 20th century, striking the old and young, but most tragically those in their thirties. One day, such a person could drink milk, cream cake, or pizza, or chocolate of any color or stripe. One day, as legend has it, this sort of person would find himself, without warning or justification, no longer able to eat any of these things. Lactose intolerant is what this sort of person was called. The term made many people laugh, but caused much suffering in its sufferers, and also caused olfactory discomfort in those with whom they lived. The affliction entailed the inability to ingest anything dairy-originated, lest the afflicted feel, for hours, a lumpy sensation in their throat's back; lest they pass gas for upward of 18 hours; lest they feel bloated and in need of burping; lest they know great lethargy and regret. The cure for was discovered in 2005 by Ronald Frame, cousin of noted lyricist Roddy. He was awarded a Nobel Prize and a tricked-out El Camino.
—DAVE EGGERS

lake party [layk-pahrt-ee] *n.* a social gathering on a lake, in a boat or platform. Feeling that much of the country was too dry, and knowing that everyone likes lakes and water and fish and frogs, in 2016, legislators and engineers created 2.4 million new lakes, and thereafter began the lake parties, most of which were good ones. —BART HERBERT

lapp dance [lap dans] *n.* a folk tradition among the indigenous nomadic Finno-Ugric people living in northern Europe. Imported to the United States as a disco fad, Lapp dancing was quickly

lapp dance

transformed into a staple of popular culture and opened the door to all things Finno-Ugric. Involving raindeer skins, elk horns, and 12-foot spears, the dance was frequently performed at weddings and bar mitzvahs. It usually concluded with everyone rushing outside and falling in the snow. —KEN KALFUS

Las Threnodas [lahs thren'-oh-dahs] *n.* a phenomenon of mourning, originating in the small west Texas town of Valentine during the summer of 2004 and subsequently spreading to other parts of the United States; typified by one or more local persons gathering in a public place—gas station, steps of town hall, Wal Mart parking lot—to sing a song of lamentation; such persons came to be known as Las Threnodas.
—LÊ THI DIEM THÚY

Lasagna, the [luh-zahn-yuh] *n.* a well-meant but not terribly original gesture or thought-out expression of support to some one in a time of need or grief. Politicians often appear at the side of people in trouble (especially in an election year) to offer the Emotional Politically Motivated Lasagna. Conversely, we should all be so lucky as to have lasagna in our freezer, or someone in our lives who will, when in trouble, bring lasagna.
—ELISSA SCHAPPELL

legal tender [lee'-gul ten'-dur] *n.* world currency that came to dominate global financial markets following the collapse of the dollar (U.S.) in 2031 and the euro three years later, based on reserves of affection, whereby goods and services are exchanged for hugs and kisses. *The co-op is selling cantaloupes for 2 Xs and 1 O, which is all the legal tender I've got in me right now.*
—SUE HALPERN

legal tender

libcon [lib'-kahn] *n.* 1. a leftist who seeks to conserve what "conservatives" desire to destroy, to wit: social security, funded public education, the environment, scientific objectivity, social welfare, equal rights for women, the Constitution of the United States, strategic alliances, the minimum wage, gun control, and child labor laws. 2. any such person attacked on Fox News. 3. [*informal*] a dangerous radical.
—CHARLIE BAXTER

libertea [lib'-ur-tee-uh] *n.* any of a variety of beverages made of ordinary foodstuffs shown to have a contraceptive effect. At the beginning of the 21st century, right-wing Christians succeeded not only in criminalizing most abortions, but in greatly limiting access to birth control: The Keep Our Children Safe Act of 2007 made it illegal to sell condoms or prescribe birth control to minors, prevented any clinic or agency receiving federal funds from dispensing or prescribing contraception to unmarried women, and, under the **Ashcroft Amendment**, required that medical personnel report to the police as evidence of possible child neglect or abuse any attempt by a parent or child to circumvent these regulations. What could have been a disastrous situation was averted when Jenny Wildflower, a cook at the DragonWagon, the last feminist-vegetarian co-op restaurant in America, discovered that ordinary orange pekoe, when brewed with tarragon, oregano, chervil, or other common kitchen herbs, prevented conception when consumed within 24 hours before or after unprotected sex. The far-reaching effects of this discovery are well known. (SEE **Lipton millionaire**, **Celestial Seasonings/Wildflower Prize for Domestic Chemistry**, **tea-totaller**, **gone to Cherville.**)
—KATHA POLLITT

lie-trap [liy'-trap] *n.* a key element in the moral sanitation system secretly installed beneath the White House during its reconstruction in 1820. The lie-trap's function was to process the lies, prevarications, evasions, equivocations, and fabrications generated by the inhabitants of the presidential mansion. All these untruths, because of their inherent vileness, were transformed by fermentation to an excrement-like substance of great mass, specific-gravity, and stink, which by virtue of its terrific density would sink constantly downward, thereby threatening the foundations of the White House, as well as the underpinnings of the institution of the executive branch itself. The lie-trap was devised to channel the buildup of the gunk of falsehood, calumny and sham into a system of secret sewers constructed beneath Washington, which in turn would empty it into the Potomac River. The system worked well for its first hundred-eighty years: though during the dispensation of the many compulsive prevaricators who occupied the executive mansion, it threatened to overload, it still managed to go on cleansing the atmosphere in and around the executive mansion so that there were only occasional whiffs of the ethical slime it disposed of.

Only during the reign of the Second Bush could the lie-trap no longer cope with the massive bulk of agglomerated misrepresentation, distortion, and general mendacity; its archaic conduits clogged, overflowed, and the tarry distillation of falsehood began to back up and rise into the interior spaces of the building.

Since no one in the Bush administration had any experience with anything but evasion, deception, and fraud, it wasn't noticed until too late that the White House had been completely filled with lie-shit, that its gleaming exterior had taken on the same fetor and taint as the misrepresentations that continued to jet massively from the orifices of the its inhabitants: only those beyond the inner circle of falsifiers, perjurers, and dissemblers even noticed what was happening, reeling away in nausea and disgust.

When the Second Bush had finally been de-elected, months of reaming and incessant flushing caustic acids were required for the lie-trap to be put in operation again. The decision was taken that henceforth its existence would no longer be kept hidden from the general public, but that it should become a recognized part of governmental function, so a gauge showing the level of its contents was be published every day in every newspaper in the country. So it was that the truth-gauge became a part of the language of the American media, and an essential element of American political life.

—C. K. WILLIAMS

lifedance [liyf'-dans] *n.* 1. the unique dance, shaped and re-shaped over a lifetime, that expresses the personality and life experience of its dancer. The lifedance concept began as a party craze, then quickly expanded to become an almost universal cultural practice. Now, nearly everyone in America has his own dance, and when two people meet on the street, they may each dance a portion of their lifedance and become friends without ever uttering a word. 2. a party in which those in attendance tell a portion of their life stories through dance. NOTE: A person's entire lifedance is performed only at funerals by members of the deceased's family. This allows mourners to rejoice in their remembrance of the deceased and allows the deceased to live on when his dance steps are repeated in ceremonies and incorporated into the lifedances of survivors. *Exasperated, Janet accuses Marty of marrying her only to steal a step from her lifedance; Marty responds by dancing that stolen step and then spinning directly into their wedding step, gliding from there into their first-date step, to which he adds a completely new movement, his fingertips across his cheek, to demonstrate his renewed affection for her and for their romantic history together, and pretty soon Janet and Marty are making a new step on the sofa together, one that is certain to bring their diverging lifedances back into synchrony.*

—JOHN HENRY FLEMING

lifedance

limbaugh [lihm'-bah] *n.* a trait or behavior that renders one's testimony on a particular subject less relevant. Often used to refer to a paradox of hypocrisy, as when a commentator on public morals and ethics is himself a felonious drug addict. *The fact that the president dodged the draft is a limbaugh for him, given he would like to send troops to their deaths.*

—DAVE EGGERS

Loraspan [lohr'-uh-span] *n.* popular mid-century pharmaceutical. Beginning in 2018, researchers noted a sudden, measurable rise in worldwide levels of impatience (clinically defined as "the physical and mental incapacity or inability to endure the passage of time," Ruiz-Gallego 2017), less than one year after the U.S. Department of Lifestyle Management issued its new, downward-revised guidelines on acceptable or "maximum tolerable" waiting periods for the 627 basic Human Interoperative Exchanges (HIEs). The new guidelines were formulated in microseconds, with the longest tolerable waiting period (18 x 1010 µs) being assigned to Awaiting a Table at a Fashionable Restaurant or Nightspot (HIE 232) and the shortest (10-100 µs) to Credit Card Authorization for A Minor Online Purchase (HIE 102).

R&D on the effect of certain of the so-called pseudoketamines on the brain's perception of the passage of time had been underway for years, but after the "impatience glut" post-2018, such efforts were intensified. In 2022, after limited human trials, a derivative of L-seroketamine was brought to market as Loraspan. Labeled the "patience drug" and familiarly known as k-sera, L-seroketamine immediately became wildly popular. Fast-acting, with a brief half-life, and almost universally effective, Loraspan rendered tolerable and even pleasant even the most tedious waiting period, revolutionizing HIEs across the board, from the theme park to the doctor's office to the public policy arena, as environmental restoration programs and novel approaches to social welfare found themselves being accorded the opportunity to show results over the long term for the first time in decades. Rates of divorce, traffic accidents, and the incidence of child abuse all plummeted.

Within a few years of its widespread adoption certain unforeseen circumstances of Loraspan use had become apparent. The drug's effect on the brain's perception of time, hitherto believed to be "local" or "situational," proved to have far more enduring and powerful effects. Most common of these "macrotemporal effects" were reports of a sudden, all-pervasive intuition of the entire span of human history, from the first migrations out of Africa to the present, in which the lifespan of the affected individual was perceived to be a mathematically insignificant fraction whose contours and crises, disappointments and achievements, had all been repeated and reiterated thousands upon thousands of times before, over the course of long millennia, by human beings to whom they had, at the time, seemed of lasting and singular importance. A resultant sense of reflectiveness, calm, even mild skepticism was widely reported—a certainty, as one subject put it, that "even those who remember their past are condemned to repeat it." History, a field that along with geography had all but vanished from the cultural marketplace, became a subject of intense general interest. It was soon discovered that all of history's victims had at one time or another been its perpetrators, that all its villains had themselves, repeatedly, been its victims and heroes, that brutality, corruption and intolerance were the hallmark of every age, along with altruism, creativity and hopefulness, and that the end of the world in a sinkhole of wickedness and iniquity has always, from the first, been imminent, along with its ultimate redemption. —MICHAEL CHABON

M

macksenate

macksenate [mak-sen'-it] *n.* a special meeting of the Senate during which speech is prohibited and replaced by slapstick displays of aggression between the two parties, usually involving the throwing of custard pies.
—Billy Collins

mailstrom [mayl'-struhm] *n.* a great storm of handwritten love letters shoved through the slot in your front door from old boyfriends who many years later forgive you: for using your virginity as a bargaining chip; for dangling it like a doggie treat; for thinking the promise of sex with you would be the glue that kept them true; for foreplaying all the way up the steep and slippery mountain to that one last toehold before the summit with the hundred-mile view, and then you decided, no, not yet. He cajoled, pled, groveled, but you said no, really, no, which made him bolt from the backseat of your car at 2 a.m. and next month fuck your roommate. What you really wanted was to say, okay, yes, sure, and enjoy sex for the wet loud sloppy body-smacking great thing sex is. Instead, you had to move to another dorm room with a girl who'd been sleeping with her boyfriend since sophomore year in high school, who looked at you like the fool you were for not knowing that pleasuring him might pleasure yourself and vice versa, who looked over at you in your twin bed and said, "Honey, what gave you the idea that your ass was all that?" These letters scattered in your hall won't ask the same question, now moot. They'll talk about jobs and kids and wives and towns. But one might say, "Hello Pia. The other day a song on the radio reminded me of you, and the green swing on your parent's front porch, those soft summer nights in Mississippi, bugs flying full speed into the streetlights like there was grace on the other side." —Pia Z. Ehrhardt

manatow [man'-uh-toh] *n.* aquatic mammal, variant of the manatee, the slow-moving warm-water "basker" of the Florida Straits, nearly rendered extinct in the middle 2000s due to fatal encounters with propellers of watersport vehicles. Manatow are distinguished from manatee by their distinctive behavior of detaching jet skis, motorboats, and sometimes yachts from their moorings, towing into deep water, then playfully whacking with flippers until object has sunk. A possible explanation is that sunken vehicles form the bases for reefs on which thrive certain fishes the manatow favors has now been disproved by irrefutable evidence that the manatow is a kelp-eater. *v.tr.* to capsize by towing and whacking, in a manatow manner. *Dude, that's the third* *jetski I've had manatowed since the start of the summer.* —Susan Choi

marriage [mayr'-idj] *n.* a beautiful constraint necessitating the birth and renewal of happiness, often easy to

marriage

undertake and difficult to unmake, traditionally employed by the community as a celebration of perilous desires, and as a legal device for the consolidation of property and the selective disbursement of what in former eras were referred to as individual rights and privileges, marriage may serve also to guarantee the community against the economic burdens associated with feeding, clothing, housing, educating, and punishing whichever children may be regarded as unwanted, many of whom can be found in larger cities, where, in pairs, they stand hopefully waiting in long lines to receive allotments from our dwindling national supply of love.

—Donald Antrim

marriage [mayr'-idj] *n.* 1. the state in which two people are united for the purpose of living together and with certain legal rights and obligations toward each other. 2. the act or ceremony of being married. *Margaret and Julie had a fabulous marriage, with all their friends and relatives in attendance to celebrate their union.*

—Ryan Boudinot

marry [mayr'-ee] *v.* [transitive, usually used in the active *(he married him in June, with little advance planning, and much riotous celebration)*, rather than the passive, from Greek *meirax*, girl, boy.] 1. to form a union with a person, place, thing, object, animal, or concept, without constraint as to the gender of the person, nor as to the animateness or inanimateness of the person, place, thing, object, animal, or concept. 2. to become one with a person outside of, or exclusive of, the laws of nations. 3. to undertake a process in which a person, or other entity, applies unique status to a thing loved, a dog, for example, or a vine of flowering wisteria, wherein the person, or other entity, declares that he, she, or it is in a blessed state with respect to the flowering wisteria, or the dog, in the process depicting, through the use of avowal, the intensity of his, or her, or its passion for the betrothed, regardless of its ability to respond or not. 4. to commence a union, or a resolution of differences, based on the repeal of repressive theocratic legislation dating to early part of the present century, wherein participants make clear that they are not bound by religious fixations of others, which commencement or resolution shall not be restricted to, but may often include dancing in an unclothed state. *She married herself to that mindfuck of a Harley-Davidson and never appeared in the office again.* 5. a slang term of violent condemnation, lately fashionable in the wake of cultural agitation on the subject of the legal status, or lack thereof, attendant upon the institution of marriage, in which a person is conjoined to something distinctly unpleasant. *I'd like to marry him and that entire bunch of lobbyists to an Afghani minefield.* —Rick Moody

"She married herself to that mindfuck of a Harley-Davidson."

Susan Choi / Donald Antrim • ***Christoph Niemann*** / Ryan Boudinot / Rick Moody • ***R. Sikoryak***

maximum wage [maks'-im-um waydj] (2005) *n.* the highest wage paid or permitted to be paid, usu. set at seven to ten times the minimum wage.
—NICK FLYNN

media feed [mee'-dee-uh feed] *n.* a bland flavorless mush; easy to swallow, hard to stomach. *So much media feed was being shoved down my throat that I almost choked.*
—A.G. PASQUELLA

media feed

memory box [mem'-uh-ree bahks] *n.* 1. the common word for the **smaratinal gland,** a surgically implanted artificial gland, usu. set inside the trachea, just above the larynx, and composed of microscopic dark-fiber nets, which are used to imprint and store each word as it is spoken by its host. Removed after death, the gland's imprints are downloaded and returned to surviving relatives, or, if none exist, are turned over to the State Religious Authority or to a local **Diagram** missionary before being given to the Oral History. Smaratinal glands are most often offered in fifteen-, twenty-, sixty-, and ninety-year capacities. (SEE **song box.**)
—MANUEL GONZALES

Memory Metal Detector [mem'-uh-ree met'-ul dee-tek'-tur] *n.* 1. bounty Hunter IV metal detector, a device of the 1990s, enhanced for Metal Memory Detectoration. 2. a member of a Memory Metal Detectoration Team, made up of individuals who were once Memory Metal Echolocators and have been restored. Teams consist of 3-5 individuals of mixed gender, ethnicity, and belief systems; they are characterized by striped track suits with embroidered patch insignia; team members sport genuine smiles. *Iris Williams recognized Memory Metal Detector Johnny Delgado as he returned to her house, but when he spoke in her mother's voice, Iris fainted; upon resuscitation, she donned a striped track suit and joined the Team.*
—PETER ROCK

Memory Metal Detectoration [mem'-uh-ree met'-ul dee-tek'-tur-ay-shun] *v.* the procurement of memory metal (also known as "mental memory"). 1. procurement from the physical body of a Memory Metal Echolocator which indicates the site of further Detectoration. 2. procurement from the site or landscape where memory metal resides, where it has been lost (e.g., the yards of childhood homes, cemeteries, volcanic craters, along the earth's crooked faultlines). *After using their Bounty Hunter IVs to scan the head and solar plexus of Echolocator Iris Williams, the Team received coordinates that directed them to the aquaculture laboratory that had been built over what had been, in Iris's childhood, her bedroom; this would be the site of further Memory Metal Detectoration.*
—PETER ROCK

Memory Metal Echolocator [mem'-uh-ree met'-ul ek-oh-loh-kay'-tur] *n.* a person who has lost hope. *The widow Iris Williams walks through the empty rooms of her house; she knows the furniture should be dusted.*
—PETER ROCK

Memory Metal Magnetism [mem'-uh-ree met'-ul mag'-nuh-tiz-um] *n.* 1. the pull of memories. 1a. as restoration to the hopeless. 1b. from memory to memory, between them; the provocation of further restoration. Generation. 2. the work of Metal Memory Scramblers, subversive teams who run at acute angles through the streets, carrying magnets of great force, thereby to complicate the process of memory metal detectoration and restoration. *A voice from the past provokes metal that cannot be bent by the most resolute team of Magneteers; this Memory Metal Magnetism is thus resistant to Memory Metal Magnetism.*
—PETER ROCK

Nick Flynn / A.G. Pasquella • ***Barry Blitt*** / Manuel Gonzales / Peter Rock /
Peter Rock / Peter Rock / Peter Rock

Memory Metal Object [mem'-uh-ree met'-ul ahb'-jekt] *n.* a forgotten item, clue, or key that provokes immense emotion and hopefulness. Commonly known as "memory metal." 1. material objects of metal, such as a rusted cap gun, a bent fork, a signet ring. 2. enhancements such as scents or tastes from the past, captured through Detectoration, and carried by the Team in glass vials. 3. a phrase or statement, located by and channeled through a member of a Detectoration Team, that is recounted in the exact voice and intonation of a person from the past (e.g. a dead person). *Sweetheart, when I saw all the girls at the arcade this afternoon, I was so proud and happy that you were the one who is my daughter.* —PETER ROCK

mercenality [mur-sun-al'-uh-tee] *n.* 1. a personality for sale on or purchased from the open market. 2. the product of a greedy and venal practice of appropriating, through the transaction of legal tender, the personality of a more famous, more celebrated identity on the assumption that fame and celebrity warrant some variant of truth and enlightenment, although, and this is funny, no?, the actual assumption of that new personality instantly makes the buyer aware that s/he has been had, a victim of the disingenuousness of the entertainment class. *Oh was I pissed. I downloaded my Cameron Diaz mercenality over the weekend, only to find out she is a real dim bulb. Next time I'm trying Geena Davis—I heard she was in Mensa.* 3. a new form of identity trading that was legalized, and thus made taxable, in 2006. 4. a new form of identity trading that was outlawed in 2009 after item #249-BP-7 ("Brad Pitt") was over-purchased, popping the mercenality-market bubble and revealing that the Jennifer Aniston mystique was largely based wardrobe and make-up. *I was planning to give my brother the #249-BP-7 mercenality for his birthday, but then the 36th Amendment came down and I ended up just buying him some colored pencils.* —BENJAMIN COHEN

mezuzahideen [mez-oo'-zuh-hid-een] *n.* an American Jew who believes Israel should dissolve its nation status and move its citizens and national boundaries inside British Columbia, Canada. —MATTHEW KLAM

microbuggy [miy'-kroh-bug-ee] *n.* exceptionally small urban transportation vehicle, suitable for one modestly sized adult or two immodestly sized pre-schoolers, fuelled by energy released from bacteria stored in mouldy comestibles well past sell-by date (e.g., blue cheddar, green lox); environmentally super-friendly, can be refuelled from neighbourhood trash while parked amongst it. (SEE ALSO under specific models: **DimSuma**; **TacoParca**; **Macarunny Breeze**; etc.) *Attempts by sixth graders to commit suicide by inhaling microbuggy fumes only ended in accelerating their hyper-activity and making them immune to acne.* —SIMON SCHAMA

middle-yeast [mid'-l yeest] *n.* 1. identified in 2012 by the research team of Dr. Solomon Rabinowitz and Dr. Mahmoud Ashrawi, the volatile biological structure on any of the various small, single-celled fungi of the phylum *Ascomycota* responsible for reproduction by fission or budding. Though identifiable and observable, the biological forces responsible for the structure's function remained a subject of debate and led to the rift between Rabinowitz and Ashrawi. Said rift was ultimately healed in 2048 when, advanced in years, Rabinowitz and Ashrawi grew tired of fighting. 2. [*archaic*] something that catalyzes a process of ferment or agitation. —HANNAH YOUNG & DAVID BEZMOZGIS

mimsy borogove [mim'-zee bor'-oh-gohv] *n.* an uncultivated terrestrial vine of the genus *Borogova*, typically having long stems, compound leaves, and gorgeously colored, exquisitely fragranced flowers, prized beyond all else by desperately hopeful lovers. The recently discovered plant, which has resisted attempts at hothouse cultivation, is native to the Amazon rain forest and survives only in pristine tropical woodland conditions. The explosively expanding mimsy borogove industry, credited with an upswing in the worldwide frequency of dates, has ended most mechanized agriculture in the plant's habitat while improving the lives of the region's indigenous people.

—KEN KALFUS

misteak

misteak [mis-tayk'] *n.* flesh of a cow; beef derived from slaughtered animals.

—JONATHAN FRANZEN

mistile [mist-il'] *n.* missile technology reached its tactical apex with the invention of mistiles: tiny, rocket-propelled precision-guided warheads carrying a payload of cool, refreshing mist. They are designed to explode directly over the head of the intended target, surprising them with invigorating moisture. Whenever a citizen of the world begins to suffer from heat-induced distress, heat-sensing satellites alert the nearest military command center to launch a pre-emptive strike against the citizen from one of its many underground bunkers. Being surprised by a direct hit from a mistile is said to be one of the most satisfying experiences a person can have. Not only does the cool sensation refresh and cleanse the body, but the sudden burst helps remind one of one's priorities in life. Mistiles reduce frustration, save lives, and promote global suppleness. Since the advent of **Weapons of Mist Dispersion** (WMDs) in the 2030s, hair is always glossy, eyes tend to glisten, and dry mouth has been virtually eliminated.

—BRENT HOFF

mmmpathy [m'-path-ee] *n.* the inversion of distaste for certain foods, resulting in superlative enjoyment, experienced in the presence of people who like those foods; also, the outpatient neurosurgical procedure to achieve this, as routinely performed on newborn humans and cats.

—BRIAN MCMULLEN

mnemoronic device [nem-or'-on-ik duh-viys] *n.* a word clumsily retrofitted with segments of other words for unfunny, but easily recalled, derisive effect. Popular among right-wing talk-show hosts of the late-twentieth and early twenty-first century, mnemoronic devices declined in frequency as these radio and television personalities boarded spaceships in search of the universe's worst haircut. *His broadcasts were filled with mnemoronic devices that helped listeners keep track of their enemies: "These crimialiens are taking it easy in America, living like kings on welunfare. The fiberal media is too busy helping gays live in homo matriphony to report on it."* While also clumsy and unfunny, the word *mnemoronic device* is not an example of itself because it does not make an explicit political statement.

—JASON ROEDER

mom-o-meter [muhm'-oh-mee-tur] *n.* a gauge of public disgust, related to the dad-o-meter but still its own meter. Usually, but not always, involves moms in their sixties who were peeved to have just missed the women's movement. If you hear a few moms of any race, creed or socioeconomic class ranting to each other about Bush when they'd usually be raving about their grandchildren, that means the mom-o-meter is showing high anger and dudgeon, and Bush better watch out. These moms don't run.

—RACHEL CARPENTER

Ken Kalfus / Jonathan Franzen • ***Charles M. Russel*** / Brent Hoff / Brian McMullen / Jason Roeder / Rachel Carpenter

mouse

mouse [mows] *v.* [fr. mouse, any of numerous small rodents of the families *Muridae* and *Cricetidae*] to explore a town with the eager curiosity of a mouse nosing down alleyways and peeking into corners, always on the look-out for hidden marvels. May refer to shopping, but only if it's done with rodentlike verve, appetite, and joyous exploration of quaint boutiques. *Okay, you stay here and make the world safe for democracy; I'll go mouse the shops.* Other forms: mousing, mouser, moused, mouseable. *What I love about Santa Fe is how mouseable it is.* Should not be used when refering to natural wonders. For example, it would be inappropriate to say at a cocktail party: *Have you moused the Grand Canyon yet?* But it would be perfect form, on the same occasion, to observe: *Napoleon, now there was a man who could mouse a whole country.*

—DIANE ACKERMAN

mouth [mowth] *v.* to grab with the lips and gums, esp. as an informal greeting, usu. the ear, though sometimes the nose; replaced the handshake in 2015, though not to be confused with the kiss.

—MANUEL GONZALES

mouthglass [mowth'-glas] *n.* 1. transparent speech. 2. the permanent crystalline substance formed by subjecting transparent speech to extreme heat and pressure. It had long been suspected that some utterances becloud the air, while others clear it. Smog, it turns out, is 40 percent conversation. Finally, in the late 22nd century, highly sensitive instruments were invented to confirm this theory. The difference is small but measurable. The result of this discovery was a great overhaul and a laundry of political and personal wind. A sufficiently eloquent speaker, possessed of a pure heart (for example, a child not yet persuaded of the incontrovertibility of anything), if held up close to the face and pricked to speech, can provide better advantages to the eyesight than the best prescription lens. A mouth holster, or harness, may be used to hold the child aimed across the eyes. The disadvantage of this arrangement is that due to the proximity of eyes to mouth on the human face, there is no way to fire a limpid word across the eyes and not take the mouth in its compass as well. Now if this mouth is not (whether by design or not) itself practicing crystalline speech, the voice of the strap-on speaker will rinse away the impurities from the utterances of the wearer, leaving only the occasional blameless *the* or *if* sparkling like the morning star in the great void of space; the speaking mouth may be seen to move (seen indeed with particular clarity due to the magnifying filter of the transparent speech) but no sound can be heard—which is of course very discrediting to the speaker, who may adopt, of course, the long horn to forward his voice to a position free of clarifying influence, but the suspicion of bad faith will fall with reason upon anyone who resorts to such measures. The clear air, when condensed, forms mouthglass in meaning no. 2 (above), a permanent gem of perspicuity.

mouthglass

—SHELLEY JACKSON

multitidian [mul-tah-tid'-ee-un] *adj.* many events or things that occur over and over, usually in a day; regular repititions that are accepted in a day. *I was used to the multitidian phone, but now there's the cell.* —LYNNE TILLMAN

Munro Doctrine [mun-roh' dahk'-trin] *n.* 1. a stalled piece of Senate legislation (2023) attempting to restructure the U.S. government according to the thematic principles of novelist/short story writer Alice Munro. The Doctrine passed by a wide margin in the House of Representatives but was abandoned after unsubstantiated claims of Canadian infiltration. (SEE ALSO **Corey Hart Offensive**, 1982.) 2. any utopian philosophy derived from literary fiction. *The Ezra Pound Kibbutz lasted six months on its Munro Doctrine before becoming the multi-million-dollar gift-catalog business it is today.* —DANIEL HANDLER

Mybad [miy'-bad] (www.mybad.org) *n.* summer correctional spa in north-central Siberia established by the authority of the 4th International Congress. Following the world-wide adoption of the Dantean Contrapasso Code in 2320, Mybad was set up for the "rehabilitation" of embezzlers, tax cheats, and other stealers from the public till. Inmates were required to take the sulphuric waters, eat a high-carb, cholesterol-rich diet, drink endless vodka and champagne, gamble, and copulate regularly with the institution's "comfort staff" during the long periods of 23-hour daylight that lasted from May through September. 90% of prisoners reportedly died within three months of arrival at Mybad. Survivors were eventually permitted to live out their natural lives in a temperate zone with a pale view of hills, consuming bread, fruit, and water in moderation.

In 2397, Mybad was destroyed by one of the first **POP** wave attacks (*q.v.*). Though it features on the international register of historic places, it currently receives fewer than a hundred visitors annually.

Living through Mybad certainly changed my writing style. I'm an absolute minimalist today, and as honest as the day is long. (Thomas Wolfe XIV, crime novelist and former alderman of Biloxi, Mississippi, convicted of tax evasion, Mybad class of 2377.) —JONATHAN GALASSI

Mylarite [miy'-lar-iyt] *n.* any member of a body of aesthetes whose credo is based on the notion that the future, as it arrives, should look less and less like

Mylarite

the past. This small but scrappy movement, which is believed to have begun in Southern California in the early 21st century, has devoted its efforts to re-establishing the high-gloss, machine-produced urban landscapes that were popularly imagined in the 1950s and subsequently abandoned by the majority of Americans. Its adherents identify what they refer to as the Aesthetic Fall of Man, which occurred in the 1960s, when what was then known as the counter-culture began insisting on the handmade, the rustic, and the natural. The most extreme of the Mylarites carry a banner that reads "Blame the Hippies." Less radical members maintain that the so-called "hippies" acted out of innocent and even admirable ideals, and that they should not be blamed for failing to see that their vision of America as a nation of Hobbit cities, boasting large populations of potters, shoemakers, and purveyors of kaliedescopes, would be co-opted by corporations and would result in a nightmarish and widespread faux-Americana; a profusion of objects and interiors made of synthetic materials but meant to look handmade, rustic, and natural. Mylarites claim to be particularly horrified by such phenomena as polyester chintz, simulated stained-glass panels in franchise restaurants, and traditional still-life paintings mass-produced in developing countries. It is their contention that these and other manifestations of "unreal realness" (a Mylarite phrase) produce feelings of disconnect among Americans, and that some of the more susceptible citizens move through their days as if they lived in an earth-like environment created by extraterrestrials who want them to feel more at home. Mylarists contend that if the synthetic is in fact inevitable, it should look synthetic. They believe that a population living in pod-shaped houses on stilts, dressed in silver jumpsuits, would at least know who, and where, they are.

—MICHAEL CUNNINGHAM

N

naked space [nay'-ked spays] *n.* any technologically unmediated space, i.e., unwired, unlinked, off the grid, etc., public or private. Instituted in the second half of the first decade of the 21st century, naked spaces began as guest houses in remote locations, usually constructed of wood or other natural materials, to which individuals referred by their physicians could retire to escape the excesses of the digital age. Cell phones, laptops, beepers, scanners, monitors, personal digital assistants, faxes, etc. were forbidden, and trained care-givers were present to help with the symptoms of decompression. The guest houses (in which preparing one's own meals, reading, talking, and listening to live music were encouraged) became so popular toward the end of the decade that the concept spread to restaurants, hotels, stores, and businesses as well as private homes, which identified themselves by displaying the sign of Michelangelo's David in a red scarf. —MARK SLOUKA

Nature [nayt'-chur] *n.* the full sum of creation, from the Big Bang to the whole shebang, the invisibly distant to the invisibly minute, which everyone pauses to celebrate at least once a day, by paying loving attention to everyday marvels, such as spring moving north at 13 miles a day; afternoon tea and cookies; snow forts; pepper-pot stew; pink sand and confetti-colored cottages; moths with fake eyes on their hind wings; emotions both savage and blessed; tidal waves; pogo-hopping sparrows; blushing octopuses; scientists bloodhounding the truth, memory's wobbling aspic; the harvest moon rising like slow thunder; fat rainbows beneath spongey clouds; tiny tassels of worry on a summer day; the night sky's distant leak of suns; an aging father's voice so husky it could pull a sled; the courtship pantomimes of cardinals whistling in the spring with what cheer, what cheer, what cheer! Nature is life homesteading every pore and crevice of Earth, with endless variations on basic biological themes. *Ex:* tree frogs with sticky feet, marsupial frogs, poisonous frigs, toe-tapping frogs, frogs that go peep, etc. In previous eras, when humans harbored an us-against-them mentality about nature, the word meant enemy, and the kingdom of animals didn't include humans (who attributed to animals all the things about themselves they couldn't stand). The new definition of nature is both

nature

personal and panoramic, including a profound sense of our animal essence. For example, just as termites build mounds, humans build cities. All of our being, juices, flesh, and spirit is nature. Nature surrounds, permeates, effervesces in, and includes us. At the end of our days it deranges and disassembles us like old toys banished to the basement. There, once living beings, we return to our non-living elements, but we still and forever remain a part of nature. Nature also includes the manicured wilderness of large cities, where parks lure countless animals from miles away to bustling green oases. There, surrounded by trees and sky, people go at least once a week to feel a powerful sense of belonging to the pervasive mystery of nature, feel finite in the face of the infinite, and molded by unseen forces older than their daily concerns. Ultimately, nature offers a sense of the everythingness of everything. Because it suggests comfort, heritage, and seasoned home, even saying the word thoughtfully is enough to heal. —Diane Ackerman

nearly-pain-free-break-up, the [neer'-lee-payn-free-bray'-kuhp] *n.* something that happens between two people who have been romantically involved but for a number of reasons—usually idiotic but not always—they can no longer be together. So for years—well, millenia—there was no way of getting around it: when a love-affair came to an end, it hurt. It hurt very badly. It was number five on the pain-chart after 1. death of a loved one; 2. disease or physical injury; 3. false imprisonment for a crime you didn't commit; and 4. torture or attack by a malevolent person. Since numbers three and four weren't—thank God—that typical for most people, heart-break was a real problem. Then in 2016, **Break-up Clinics**, affiliated with Curves exercise studios, began to pop up all over the country. These clinics offered classes in guided meditation, prayer, and self-massage. Also, you could lie for as long as you liked on a super cozy **healing bed** with a real nice comforter to hide under, and, if you liked, an **adult pacifier** was put in your mouth. Meanwhile self-esteem mantras were pumped into your head via pillow-sized headphones. One of the biggest breakthroughs in break-up healing, discovered by the founder of the clinics, Susan Pearlstein, was that the old cop-out "It's not you, it's me" was actually true. It was proved that all break-ups had nothing to do with your worth; they had to do with something going on in the other person. This was very helpful, since a great deal of the pain involved in break-ups has to do with a feeling of rejection. There is also, naturally, a terrible sense of loss. Severe loneliness also enters into it—the knowledge that all human beings are essentially alone, trapped inside their own minds and behind the masks of their faces. But the clinics make this all quite manageable and restore us to our usual blithe, distracted, mildly sad but functional selves. Also, the clinics have turned out to be great places to meet newly single people. Granted, everyone is on the rebound, but this was another Great Truth discovered by Ms. Pearlstein: We're all perpetually on the rebound. This, it was discovered, has to do with the spinning of the earth and the ubiquity of the spiral in all forms of life. So it came to be that a lot of people eventually crawled into the healing beds together and new romances were sparked, restarting the perpetual cycle of love and pain, love and pain, love and pain.
—Jonathan Ames

neocon [nee'-oh-kahn] *v.* to deceive, particularly by sounding false alarms.

neocon

Once the residents were neoconned into fleeing their homes, which were not on fire, the thieves made off with their possessions. Also, when the practice is accompanied by fraudulent appeals to one's patriotism and love of liberty, as an adjective: **neocon job.**

—KEN KALFUS

neocon job [nee'-oh-kahn jahb] *n.* [from the consequences that result from allowing one's principles to be corrupted by personal insecurities, midlife crises, aging, or the accumulation of wealth] 1. an act or instance of extreme degradation, usu. sexual in nature, the purpose of which is to defile another, to make impure or foul. 2. the worst thing one can think of to inflict on another, with intent to corrupt or sully. *I will let you defecate on me, but I will not let you give me a neocon job.* (SEE ALSO **pod-whoring** and, ireg., **getting kristoled.**)

—STEPHEN SHERRILL

neoillogism [nee-oh-ih'-loh-jiz-uhm] *n.* 1. a new word, expression, or usage devised to explain or indicate an vague or illogical idea. 2. the creation or use of new words or senses devised to explain or indicate a vague or illogical idea. 3a. [*psychology*] the compulsive invention of new words to rationalize illogical decisions. 3b. a word so invented. *The Secretary of Defense peppered his speech with neoillogisms.*

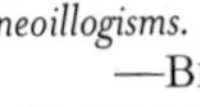

—BEN GREENMAN

news [nooz] *n.* [*obs.*] 1. objective information about recent events or developments. 2. information about current events published in newspapers and magazines or broadcast over the radio or television. 3. an article or broadcast about important recent events. 4. a person or occurrence considered as significant.

news

—BEN GREENMAN

neuroreligeology [nur-oh-ril-idg-ee-ah'-loh-jee] *n.* a strand of science that studies the genetic formation of religion. Researchers discovered in 2039 a series of genes essential not only to the acquisition of religious beliefs, but to specific ones. Originally used to de-program brainwashed members of cults and radical sects. Bio-savvy churches created designer drugs to maintain or alter the neurochemistry of their congregations, setting off a national controversy. The Supreme Court determined in 2045 that "a man's faith should arise from the heart and mind, and decidedly not from the local pharmacy."

—TOM BARBASH

new-thumb-of-thought [noo-thum'-uv-thaht] *n.* the advancement in the human brain, first noticed in 2017 in Bloomington, IN. Just as man had once developed a thumb and vastly improved his lot and several thousand generations later could get into good schools as a result, so did another advancement take place—not in the area of the hand, but in the back-lobe of the human brain. For years people kept talking about the "frontal-lobe," and all the while the back-lobe was busy trying to improve itself in a Darwinian fashion, and so it did. The advancement was a brain—led by its backside—which recognized the virtues of a vegan diet, good manners, and tai chi as a means of pollution-free space-and-time-travel. This new brain also led to the happy discovery of Atlantis City as an underwater gaming emporium where everyone won but didn't care if they won. This back-lobe brain's abilities were called a new-thumb-of-thought and its effects were felt worldwide within fifty years. People flew through the air doing their tai chi, sometimes staying in the present, sometimes visiting the future or the past, which was how Atlantis was

Ken Kalfus / Stephen Sherrill / Ben Greenman / Ben Greenman • ***Istvan Banyai*** / Tom Barbash / Jonathan Ames re-found—during someone's trip back in time. Also, this new brain allowed people to swim underwater without breathing, so there was no more drowning, which upset the Lifeguard Union, but they got with the program and didn't complain. This underwater ability also helped, it should be said, with the Atlantis discovery. And, as indicated, everyone became vegans and wrote thank you notes to each other and all religions, due to the advent of pleasant manners, were nicely fused. McDonald's, since there were so many of them, were now used as cow-shrines, which pleased the Hindus. Sue Schwartz-Miller, an African-American-Jewish-Baptist woman from Bloomington, Indiana, is credited as the gene-carrier for the first brain that possessed the new-thumb-of-thought. She was observed in 2017 floating over Indiana University doing her tai chi and as a result she became a big television star. Her resulting earnings then allowed her to have many children, 18 to be exact, and so her brain with this great gene was quickly spread through the United States and the whole world.

—Jonathan Ames

No Left-Behind Child Act, the [noh left-bee-hiynd' chiy'-uld akt] U.S. Congressional act disqualifying any person from holding the office of American President who has not passed a series of rigorous examinations demonstrating psychological and emotional maturity, as well as expert knowledge of a wide range of subjects, including American history, world history, government, economics, law, geography, political science, etc., and a strong command of the English language.

—Sigrid Nunez

No "There" There Kid, the [noh thayr thayr' kid] *n.* an honorific position involving one sixth grader chosen from a national competition whose responsibility entails the public monitoring of all significant press conferences of major figures in a governing American administration. The sixth-grader, seated unobtrusively beside the politician's podium, is responsible for ringing an electronic bell when, in his or her estimation, a question asked has been entirely left unanswered. The politician speaking is then given the opportunity to try again. If, in the No "There" There Kid's estimation, the question still has been entirely left unanswered, he or she rings a second bell, at which time the original questioner is allowed a redirect: i.e., "What I meant for you to answer, sir, was not why you and Vice-President X were testifying before the Commission, but why you felt the need to testify before the Commission *together*." The politician is then given a third opportunity to respond. If, in the No "There" There Kid's estimation, this third attempt also leaves the question entirely unanswered, he or she sounds a buzzer, and a graphic above the politician's head is changed to read *Direct Questions Evaded: 1.* And so on.

No "There" There Kid

—Jim Shepard

Nognocandu [noh-noh'-kan-doo] *n.* a dead language once common to the corporations of America, punctuated by time-consuming catchphrases that ultimately signified nothing, such as, "moving forward"; "with that said"; "we're trending positive"; and "we have an opportunity to focus our productivity leverage on cross-platform strategic goals such as experiential marketing" Now used to describe anything incomprehensible. *I don't under-*

stand the details of our CEO's jail sentence. It's all Nognocandu to me. —SAMANTHA HUNT

nomenclod [noh'-men-klahd] *n.* 1. a person who habitually forgets the names of other people. 2. the willful propensity to forget the names of others deemed inferior. 3. one who presumes the spelling of the names of others, usually with incorrect results. 4. a form of amnesia. 5. a medical disorder in which the sufferer is compelled to assign geographical names to small clumps of matter generally no larger than two handfuls. 6. a member of an extreme early 21st-century Southern American back-to-the-land literary movement, whose aim was to prove that only through direct congress with the earth could human beings achieve mental and physical completeness. The works of the nomenclods were marked by an spare, earthy style. Many exponents published their groundbreaking essays in the symposium "I'll Rake My Land—And Lie In It."

—NICHOLAS DAWIDOFF

non-America [nahn-uh-mayr'-ik-uh] *n.* the world outside the United States. Today, thanks to improved geography education and the unprecedented ease and popularity of world travel, Americans know and love non-America nearly as much as they know and love their own country, but it was not so very long ago that most Americans were only vaguely aware that non-America even existed. In a 2009 study, only 13 percent of Americans could find non-America on a map, and, of those, 85 percent admitted it was "just a lucky guess." In a similar study conducted two years later, Americans were asked to name any country in non-America: 89 percent couldn't name one, 2 percent said "Canada Dry," and everyone else said either Narnia or the Moon.

—ED PAGE

Note Day [noht'-day] *n.* 1. short for Notification Day; the day that applicants to teaching positions receive their letters of acceptance. Historically, 10 percent of applicants received good news on Note Day, though, due to the tremendous yearly rise in applications, that number continues to drop. Those who are given positions in schools join society's most elite occupation, with all of the esteem and recompense that position garners. 2. any looming date that an individual or group nervously awaits. *After accidentally violating environmental policy, the anxious manufacturer looked on his upcoming evaluation as a sort of Note Day.*

—ANNE URSU

nuclear poemb [noo'-kleer pohm] *n.* after the universal, non-negotiable cease-fire signed by world leaders in the year 2005, all nuclear weapons were de-activated and scientists stuffed the weapons casings with poems. Every day a nuclear poemb exchange occurs between two countries. Based on the number of nuclear weapons formerly aimed at large populated cities throughout the world, scientists and poets believe the poem exchange can last indefinitely. Scientists agree that the half-life of a poem has always been longer than the half-life of radioactive munitions. The nuclear poembs have aided greatly the proliferation of international poetry. Most people sleep better now too. *I read the collected Cesar Vallejo after a nuclear poemb landed in our town square.*

—ANTHONY SWOFFORD

nutrilocus [noo-truh-loh'-kus] *n.* one of several hubs for the global redistribution of food after the collapse of agribusiness and the return to large cooperative ventures supported by national shares based on annual consumption. All excess production is channeled through one of these hubs, where annual lotteries also determine the coming year's distribution of luxury foods in limited quantities, such as truffles and cheval.

—SUSAN WHEELER

THE WORLD OF TODAY

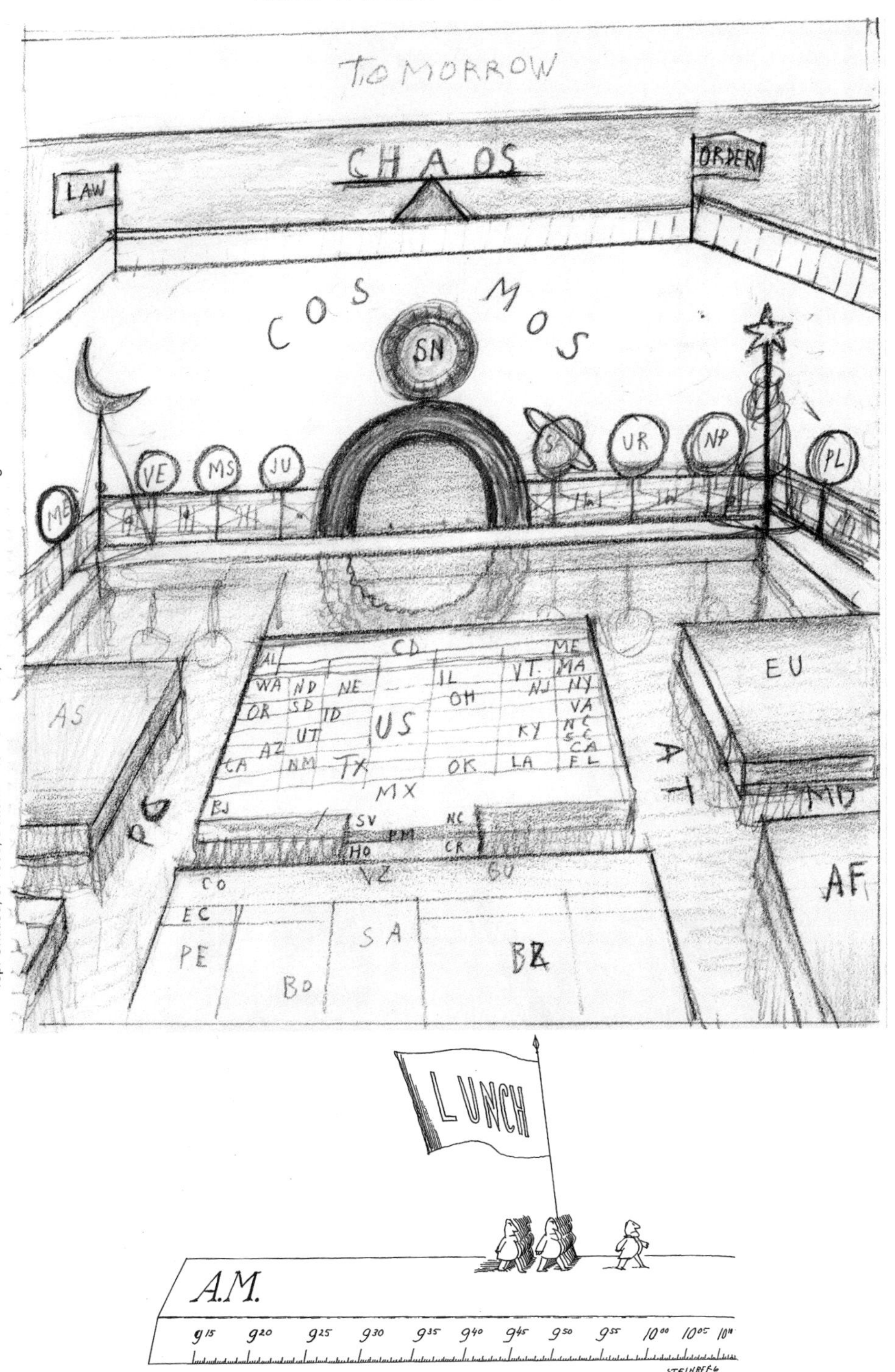

Saul Steinberg

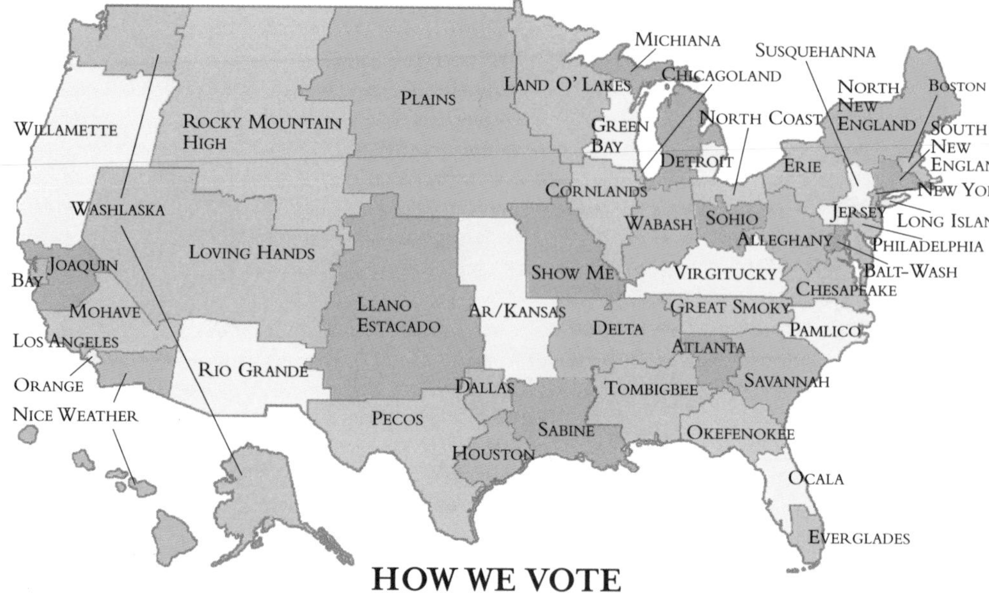

HOW WE VOTE

LAND OF EQUALITY. As the progressive legacy of Chelsea Clinton-Kucinich's first presidential bid wound its way through the nation, the public came to the long-overdue realization that the electoral college did not match the democratic ideals of the home of the free. Rather than abandon the time-honored system, a popular movement led legislators to amend the Constitution and redraw state boundaries to reflect the distribution of population. Although the measure faced opposition in Wyoming and Alaska, the fifty states were eventually reorganized so that each now has an equal population, and therefore the same number of votes in the electoral college.

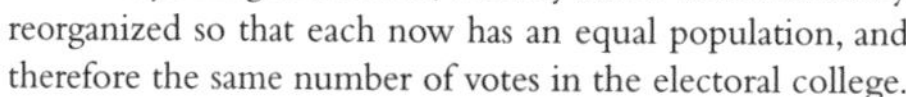

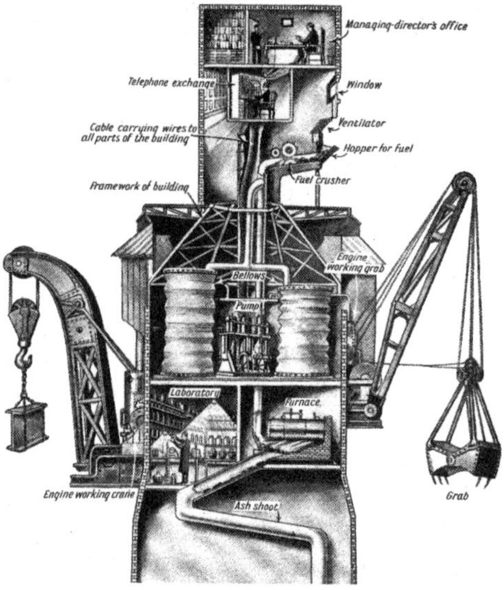

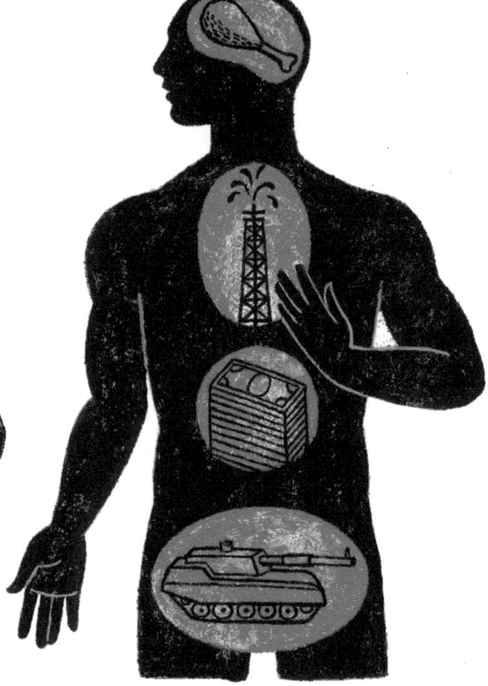

OUR IMPROVING BODIES

Above: A preserved specimen of early-21st-cent. anatomy. *Right:* Our four newest senses, bringing the current total to sixteen.

Neil Freeman / Wonders of Science / James Steinberg

WE CAN NOW SEE THROUGH A BRICK

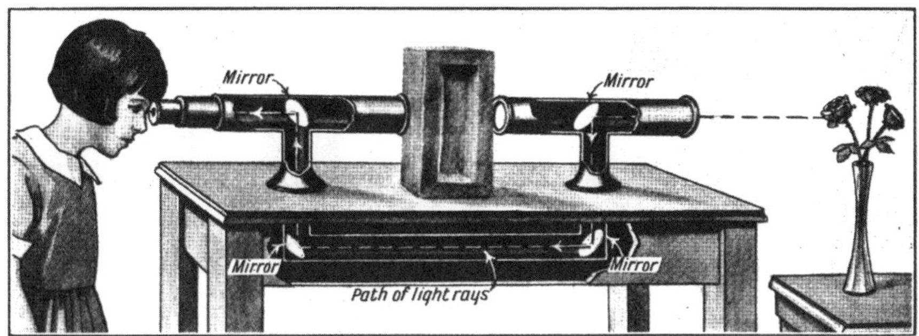

In the war-torn and relativistic societies of our ancestors, the only unassailable truth was the impossibility of seeing through a brick wall. Modern science has shattered this assumption; now even an idiot or a criminal can achieve what the collected might of mankind could not just decades ago. On the table (*above*) are two telescope-like tubes; by looking through one eyepiece the object on the other side can be clearly seen. In this case, a precocious rosebeast observes an unsuspecting little girl. The workings of this process are not well understood, and there is much debate about whether it is applicable to objects other than a brick, such as pudding, or even two bricks at once.

THINGS ARE NO LONGER WHAT THEY SEEM

Appearances were once believed to be God-given and entirely reliable. But we know now that they can be misleading, and that God is probably hurt, or lost. The legs of the men in the middle picture look crooked, but hold the picture horizontally and you will see that you were fooled. Similarly, you see ellipses in the top left-hand corner, but test them with a compass and you will find that you are, once again, a fool. Who would think the two figures in the bottom right-hand corner were the same size? Only an ass. Yet they are. In the bottom left-hand corner, do you see nine black squares? If so, you have an incident of sexual deviancy in your past. In the top right-hand corner you can look down upon three cubes, as if you were a glorious geometric deity. But after thirty minutes of steady observation you will realize with a jolt that you are looking *up* at them, and the old divinities have been deposed and a new cubic pantheon put into place. Try it yourself!

WHAT WE WEAR

FASHION THROUGH THE AGES: A TIMELINE

It's been several years since an influential barista declared, "I'm tired of dressing normal! I live in the future—I want to dress like it." This led to today's remote-controlled-legwarmer craze and the abolition of all pockets.

Above: Office attire (casual Friday). *Far right:* Supercomputers predict that within eighty years even our sloppiest citizens will be this stylish. *Right:* Atomic underwear: is it safe?

WHAT WE INGEST

Plankton and bananas are the staple diet that most of us enjoy today. We also like bananas and plankton.

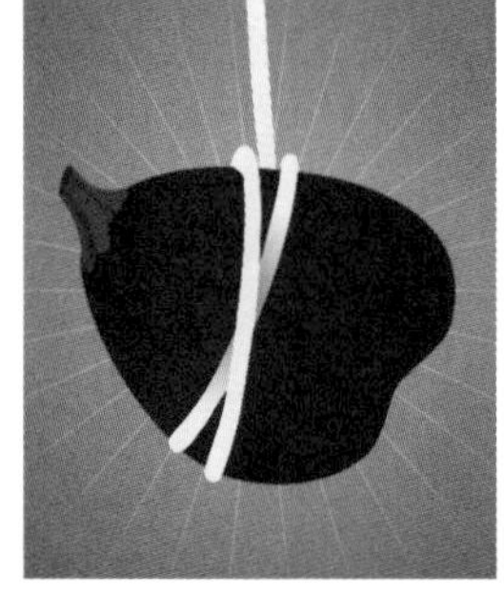

Above **Fig 1.** Our favorite snack: dried fruit on a string.

Ann Decker / Michael Kupperman / Danny Hellman / Emily Flake / Dyna Moe

WHERE WE GO

Above: **The Grand Canyon**, America's Playground. In a vivid demonstration of mankind's dominion over the Earth, it took Mother Nature millions of years to cleave a dusty rift in the ground, but hard-working developers needed only eight months to erect state-of-the-art edible bordellos and introduce a pack of albino gorillas capable of most janitorial duties.

Above: A monument to man's eternal glory, **The Trump Ozymandias Hotel** rises four miles high in the Gobi Desert.

Below: **Nature World** (Coalinga, CA) offers all the majesty of "nature" along with ample parking and a food court.

Michael Kupperman / Emily Flake / Lauren Weinstein

THE WONDERFUL NEW WORLD OF SCIENCE

THE MONUMENT BELT. Most of Earth's monuments have been placed in orbit in order to free up valuable real estate, or, in the case of the Sphinx, on a dare. They are visible, free of charge, to anyone with access to a telescope.

WASTE. Sending our garbage into space seemed like the perfect solution, but now the unsightly lunar trash-pile has spurred new plans to put the Moon itself deep beneath our ocean.

GLOBAL WARMING: Does it really exist? The debate rages on. *Above:* Manhattan today (low tide).

Left: NASA's most exciting discovery in decades of exploration, "Charlie," a rock found in space that bears a remarkable resemblance to 20th-century comedian Charlie Chaplin. "Look at his funny little hat!" comments a NASA official.

ROBOTS.

We need and fear them. They despise us and try to eat our babies. *Right:* The Robot Boston Tea Party, for which they will pay dearly.

ROBOTS REDUX. *Above:* Technicians examine a robot for signs of possible sentience.

Right: A doorman refuses entrance to a robot.

Michael Kupperman / Lauren Weinstein / Danny Hellman

THE FUTURE IS NOW

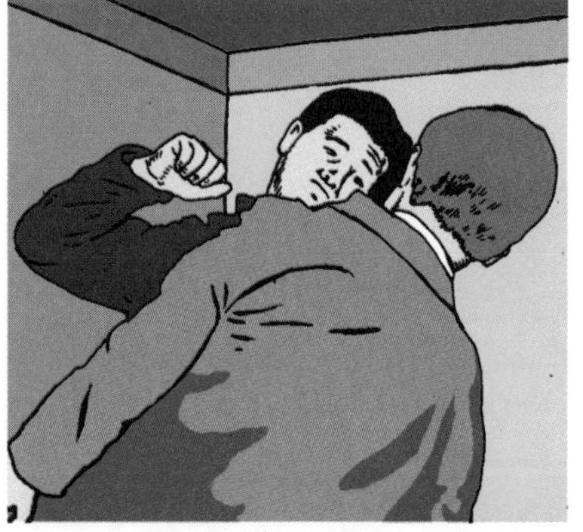

Left: Empathovision will likely continue to dominate the entertainment industry after this year's Oscar-winning "Beating of a Lifetime".

Left: A petulant but influential child recently declared: "I'm tired of seeing people in movies! I see people all the time!" This led to the trend of movies starring inanimate objects. This year's heartthrob: a portable dehumidifier.

Left: Seven years ago, scientists presented mankind with a functioning one-way teleport gate leading to an alien planet in an unknown location. The environment there is mildly inhospitable, and the planet has no natural resources to speak of. Smokers, however, are encouraged to visit and can light up once thirty feet away from the portal.

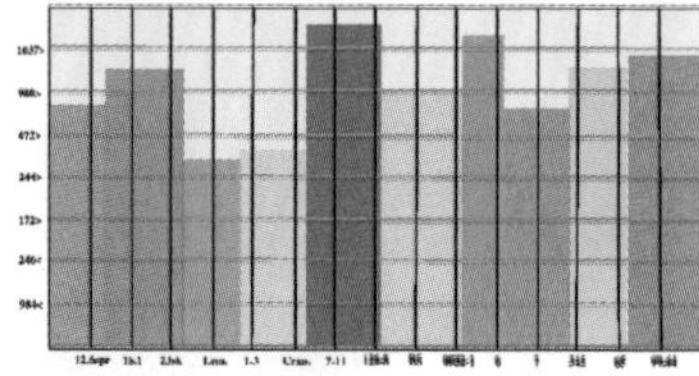

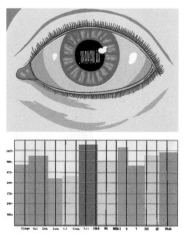

Top: With recent developments in retinal bar coding, it will soon be possible to use the supermarket price scanner to find out your current market value. *Above:* You are not worth very much.

WAR WITH THE INSECTS. In recent years tensions between bugs and man have flared into open conflict.

Top left: Police helicopters confront a giant wasp outside Dayton (amateur photograph). *Near left:* Man fights back.

Michael Kupperman / Julie Klausner

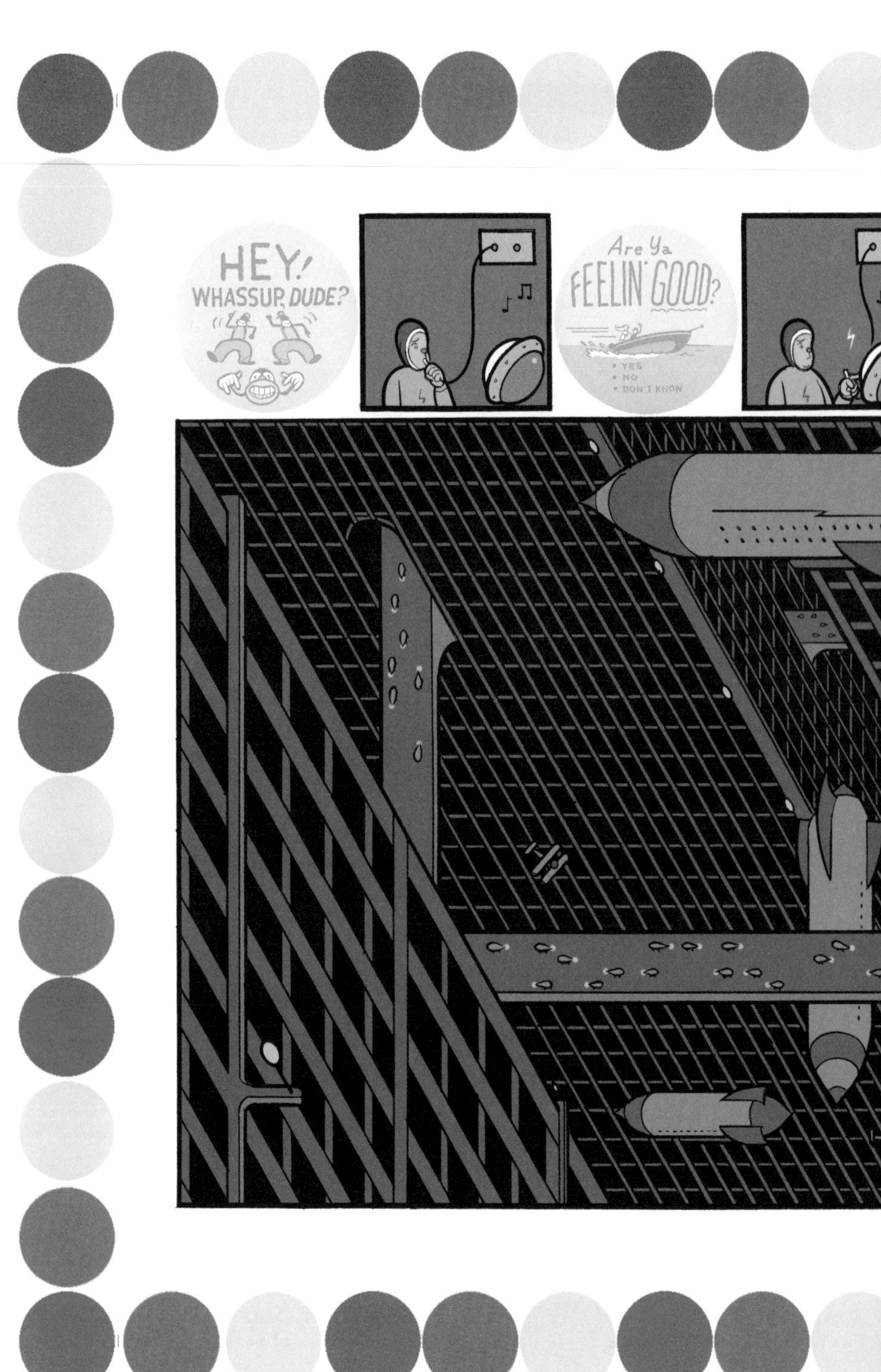

Chris Ware

1
2

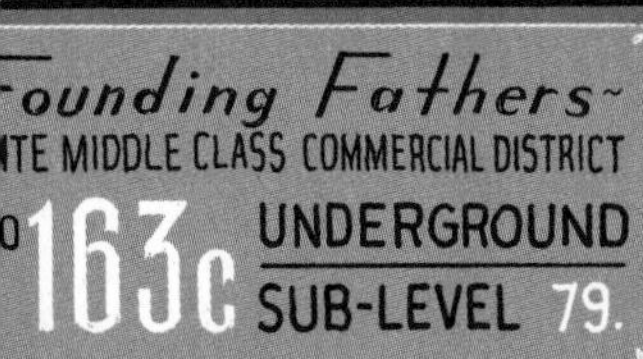

ENDURING FREEDOM.

3
4

Chris Ware

...THE SNID
NEW WO
BY THE
SOPH
of t

CRITICALLY
EUROPEAN,
BRUSQUELY AMERICAN,
de Tocqueville
GETS RESULTS!
DEVELOP YOUR UNIQUE
CULTURE
TODAY!
TRY A FREE SAMPLE:
• PERFUME
• COLOGNE
SHOP

THUS

SH-SHUT
K-KLK
BEEEEEEP
BEEEEEEP

AND

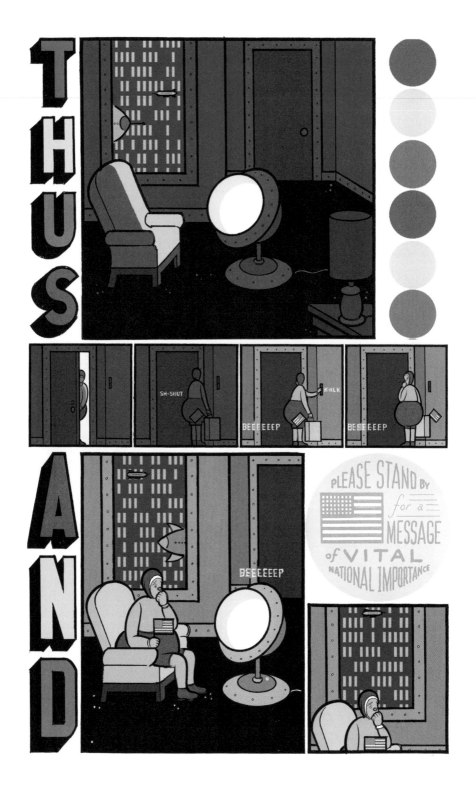

omnascent [ahm-nay'-sent] *adj.* a highly unusual state of being all-knowing at birth. In the mid-21st century, a popular theory claimed that humans start with knowledge and are made increasingly vapid through exposure to popular culture and inferior education. *He would through improved scholarship strive to return to that omnascent state of his late infancy.*
—Tom Barbash

Operation Ohio [ahp-ur-ay'-shun oh-hiy'-oh] *n.* in 2004, when Ohio was a major battleground state in the presidential election, a group of well-known musicians, writers, artists, and actors moved to Ohio for the two months prior to the vote. They worked tirelessly to convince voters age 18 to 30 that their country's inheritance, its economy, and its environment were in incredible danger. Their ceaseless dedication to convincing young voters of the importance of participating in the coming election led to an extra 50,000 votes within the demographic and swung Ohio into the Democrat column, its 21 electoral votes winning the election for the challenger, John F. Kerry. —Stephen Elliott

Opulism [ahp'-yoo-liz-um] *n.* 1. a chemical addiction to the company of the wealthy. In a state of opulism a person combines a need for the trappings of wealth with a disinclination to perform the work to acquire it. In the year 2027, a series of studies were conducted at the University of Georgia tracing the connection between opulism and self-hatred. *His opulism drove him to excess and then to bankruptcy.* 2. a political philosophy promoting the concentration of power in multi-national corporations, the government and owners of islands. The opulists were an offshoot of the **trickledowns** of the late 20th century, and they waged a public war of words with the populists of New England and Northern California.
—Tom Barbash

oral history

Oral History [or'-ul his'-tur-ee] *n.* title given to the chief priest of the religion **Diagram**; the Oral History lives in seclusion and is worshipped by all Diagramist sects as a divine and spiritual being. At the time of the Oral History's death, the Diagramists search for a child who evidences spirit-traits of the deceased Oral History; when found, this child is then named the Oral History and becomes the new repository of all human utterance, as collected by the Diagram missionaries. Hence, **historic** *adj.* of or pertaining to

Tom Barbash / Stephen Elliott / Tom Barbash / Manuel Gonzales • ***Christoph Niemann*** the Oral History, his teachings, or the teachings of his followers.

—Manuel Gonzales

O'Reilly [oh-riy'-lee] *v.* to misstate the truth and refuse to apologize or correct your error. Usually used to refer to the actions of children. *Don't O'Reilly me, mister. I saw your room and it is not clean.* In 2028, in the popular child-rearing book How to Raise Honest Children, the problem of O'Reillying was formally discussed for the first time in academia, elevating the term from its colloquial origins. The authors of How to Raise Honest Children pointed to the dangers of allowing a child to lie without correction, noting that it is not enough to ignore the child or cease listening to the child, since children who do not receive attention will only find another ear to tell their tales. Children often long for the approval of their audience; when a parent does not pay attention to a child that O'Reillies, it is possible the child will change their lies to meet the pre-concieved notions of their new audience. The danger is when the listeners themselves are uninformed or prejudiced. The authors warned that a child that is still O'Reillying by the time s/he finished secondary school is likely to continue for the rest of their life; it is important to catch an O'Reillier at an early age.

O'Reilly

The authors recommend spending lots of time with the child, correcting the child when the child misstates facts and making sure the child understands. They recommend against forcing the child to change their opinions, noting that a healthy society contains many disparate ways of looking at the world. If, for example, the child says there should be more wild animals in the city it is not imperative the adult correct the child. If, however, the child quotes a study on the subject that does not exist, then it is important that the parent explain to the child the difference between reality and unreality. The adult should explain the importance of supporting opinion with fact. The book even goes so far as to state that no facts are better than wrong facts. Suggested punishments include grounding and cessation of television and phone priveleges, while noting the importance of positive reinforcement, such as "I love you, but not when you O'Reilly."

—Stephen Elliott

Organism [or'-guhn-iz-um] *n.* (ca. 2006) social and political movement aiming to restore the pipe organ to its rightful place as the sole source of music at major league baseball games. The movement gathered momentum in the early years of the 21st century, as baseball fans in growing numbers came to realize that it was not cavernous suburban stadiums, artificial turf, double-knit uniforms, free agency, or the use of anabolic steroids that had combined to degrade the sport, but such seemingly inconsequential issues as the blaring rendition of a few seconds of unremarkable popular songs over the public address system at any moment when the ball was not in play.

Grassroots reaction to the movement's goals was overwhelmingly positive, and soon Organism's mandate had broadened to address other tangential concerns, such as outrageously prohibitive concession-stand prices, grandstand and bleacher seats costing more than ten U.S. dollars, unreasonable personal searches at the stadium gates, and the baleful social pressure to rise from one's seat during the seventh

Othermobile

inning for the rote performance of "God Bless America" by American Idol also-rans and high-school choruses. Franchise owners mounted a predictably fierce public relations campaign to counter Organism's efforts, claiming that the inability to play "Hot in Herre" [sic] at extreme volume while yet another left-handed reliever strode to the pitcher's mound would severely compromise their ability to market the game to young fans and that the excessive cost of maintaining a pipe organ and hiring a competent organist to play it would hinder a team's chances of signing aging utilitymen to multiyear, multimillion dollar deals. By 2014, however, it was apparent that attendance figures had become inversely proportional to the continuous rise of ticket prices, and some owners became desperate enough to try even the radical proposals put forth by Organism. The first of the new pipe organs made its debut at Trump Coliseum, home of the Las Vegas White Sox, in April 2015.

—Christopher Sorrentino

Othermobile [uth'-ur-moh-beel] *n.* any one of a brigade of comfortably appointed tractor-trailers that travel around the United States for the purpose of exposing Americans to ways of life and points of view dramatically different from their own. Although the staff of any given Othermobile varies slightly according to region, the Othermobile charter states that each include most if not all of the following: a liberal, a conservative, a libertarian, a feminist, an illegal immigrant, a member of the NRA, a white supremacist, a welfare mother, an environmentalist, the CEO of a major corporation, an ex-convict, a gay man, a lesbian, a disabled person, a homeless person, an artist, someone who works for minimum wage, and someone (known as the "wild card") who is simply very peculiar—an individual whose convictions, thought processes, and/or mode of dress render him or her incapable of belonging to any group of any kind. Each Othermobile also numbers among its staff passionate adherents of every major religion, including atheism, and at least one member of every race. The trailers are in situ in cities and towns for up to a week, during which time any local resident may enter and talk at any length to any member or members of the staff about what, exactly, it is like to be who they are. These conversations are meant to be purely instructive. No questions are considered off limits, but the staff members' answers are to be received in the spirit in which they are offered—as insights into lives unfamiliar to the questioner, and not in any way as fodder for argument. In the early days of the Othermobile program (which was initiated in 2010 by the Streep administration), this particular

constraint proved so difficult for so many that a team of enforcers (known as "shooshers") was added in 2012. They circulate among the questioners, making sure all exchanges remain civil. Anyone who becomes overly excited, or tries to make a noise, is warned once; if a second disturbance occurs, the person is asked, politely but firmly, to leave. The Othermobile program, controversial since its inception, has gradually gained a measure of popular acceptance, and the acts of violence that occurred in some locations have declined considerably. Although the results of the program have proven difficult to measure, it is widely believed that the Othermobiles were at least partly responsible for the creation of the **Federal Bureau of Reconciliation** in 2018, and for the establishment of several regional traditions, including the monthly Trade Outfits Day observed in many Midwestern states, and the **Defend the Indefensible Festival** held annually in Baton Rouge, Louisiana since 2015.

—MICHAEL CUNNINGHAM

outFox [owt-fahks] *v.* 1. to be more dishonest and deceitful than one's rivals. 2. to lean more heavily to the right.

—RYAN HARTY

overdog [oh'-vur-dahg] *n.* raised among silver spoons, breast-fed by Goliath's mother. Attends big-name school due to familial connections. In special Skull and/or Bones Club. Picks

overdog

National Guard over Vietnam. Does not hold many press conferences, in fact less than anyone else in the history of the presidency. Vacations a lot. Gives nicknames like "Putey" to Russian leader. Avoids contrary opinions, for overdog knows best.

A highly clever overdog will act just dumb enough, or perhaps *be* just dumb enough to win the title of persecuted underdog, lining himself up with the people-people, gaining the sympathy of the older generation who are impressed that overdog no longer uses cocaine and has found the Lord. (SEE **underdog.**) Often blindly religious, though it is not a requirement. Psychologists say every overdog was once an underdog, but flipped the internal coin of the soul and became an overdog. It is a neat trick, often requiring external funding to achieve. Psychologists may assert the role of dog (SEE **dog**) as the ideal.

—AIMÉE BENDER

P

pacifize [pas'-if-iyz] *v.* to equip with pacifying abilities and ethos or to give a pacific character to, with specific derivation from the movement of the 2010s to reconceptualize human relations in the mode of survival and congeniality, instead of mutually-agreed destruction; first invoked as an antonym to "militarize" and "weaponize," it now holds a place of pride in governmental structure, as first instantiated after the second Pacific Evolution of 2017. As with the ad campaign, *People all over the world are pacifizing their social structures. Why not you?* —BENJAMIN COHEN

paradoxysm [payr'-uh-dahks-iz-um] *n.* a sudden attack of understanding that allows you to hold sparring statements in your mind without feeling like you have to choose one side over the other (white/black) (wrong/right) (briefs/boxers). Instead, you are seized by the pleasure of ambivalence, of entertaining two well-founded ideas at the dinner table you've set in the middle of your small but capacious heart. —PIA Z. EHRHARDT

parallyl [payr'-uhl-il] *n.* a clumsy metaphor; an inaccurately applied word, phrase, or narrative that is not meant literally but rather for metaphoric purposes. *Dear X, I deeply regret the sentiments I meant to conceal, but inadvertently expressed, on our recent ship-to-shore phone conversation. The roughness of the seas was difficult to detect given the size of the boat, but I felt it, as a twinge mostly, and it disconcerted me. My stomach was already tender, as I had been gorging myself on the generous portions from the buffet all week—"it's prepaid," my aunt said, "so eat up"—and when the operator connected us I felt a slight drop, as if I were in an elevator that shot up an extra floor, without warning. Add to that the fact that I had been in possession of a brassiere that you once owned and wore, but that I was no longer—a large man with five o'clock shadow acted the ruffian that first night on the boat, and though I was a gentleman, and bought him drinks, and engaged in the small talk I was taught to devoutly believe would soothe a man like that (I asked after his local sports franchise, after his opinion in cuts of steak, after the difference between one-arm curls and two-arm curls, as far as the growth of the bicep was concerned), he took it upon himself to pound me flat with the hammer of his fist and then to divest me of the brassiere that you once owned and wore, which I had kept in my suitcoat pocket like a handkerchief that was too refined for any mortal sniffle. He strongly resembled Bluto from the Popeye cartoon; he even wore a sailor's shirt, though he did not work on the boat, which was, at any rate, not a sailboat. My sorrow over the loss of that brassiere conspired with the soreness I suffered at the hands of that Bluto; what settled was stirred again by the effect of the sea upon the buffet. And so I came to tell you how I felt. That sailboat: our nation. That*

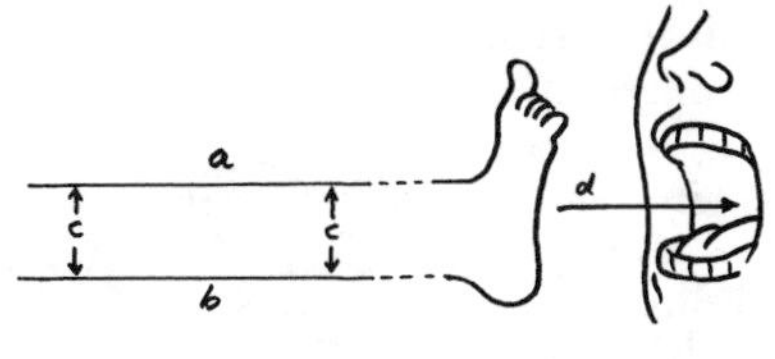

parallyl

Benjamin Cohen / Pia Z. Ehrhardt / Ben Greenman • ***Christoph Niemann***

Bluto: our President. Me: America. You: the rest of America. My aunt: the idealism of the 1960s. The ship-to-shore phone: the voting booth. That brassiere: our role in the world at large. I know that this is more parallyl than I would have wished, but I am dizzy with misgiving and grief.

—Ben Greenman

paramill [payr'-uh-mil] *v.* 1. recreational parasailing activity making use of wake vortexes formed in the vicinity of offshore wind farms. 2. general term applying to recreational activities on offshore energy platforms, incl. tidal generators, windmills, and abandoned oil derricks. —Paul Collins

pasta with grilled vegetables [pah'-stuh with grild vedj'-tuh-buls] *n.* [*archaic*] vegetarian entrée struck down by the landmark Supreme Court ruling in *Mercer v. Bennigan's* (2019). In a 6-3 decision, the Court ruled that pasta with grilled vegetables is an unconstitutional dinner offering and that chain restaurants in the Midwest must, "with all deliberate speed and all fresh ingredients," add another vegetarian selection. The Court stopped short of mandating a specific menu, but it did make a few nice suggestions involving tempeh and tofu. Chief Justice Nickerson wrote the majority opinion: *"The court finds untenable the notion that flaccid, tasteless disks of yellow squash languishing atop rubbery spaghetti constitutes a lawful American dinner or freedom of choice,"* Nickerson wrote, *"to say nothing of the cruel and unusual heat lamp."* In 2035, the Court upheld *Mercer v. Bennigan's* by ruling 8-1, in *Nash v. Applebee's*, that three vegetarian appetizers do not equal an entrée.

—Chris Bachelder

pasta with grilled vegetables

paxpayers [paks'-pay-urz] *n.* [*slang*] tax returns allow citizens to choose how their money may be spent, and those who select "only for domestic, peaceful purposes" (such as Environment, Education, National Health Service, and the Arts) are sometimes referred to as paxpayers. To their critics, the term is as derisive as "tree hugger," while to their champions the term is as honorable as "tree hugger."

—Diane Ackerman

P-Chip [pee'-chip] *n.* [abbrev. form of Prevaricator Chip (> V-Chip, failed late 20th c. tech. initiative] 1. a chip installed in television sets, utilizing biometric data to evaluate the credibility of a speaker onscreen, typically with "ticker" and inscreen features allowing display of related past statements and, for comparative purposes, video of known incidences of both false and truthful statements by the speaker. 2. general term for such devices and its variants, e.g., the C-Chip (consumer chip), which displays insurance data and crash test footage during commercials. —Paul Collins

PDA [pee-dee-ay] *n.* [*slang*] ALT **Parrot Diagnostic Advisors** previously the acronym for "Portable Digital Accessories," PDAs have replaced the Palm Pilot, as well as most GPS guidance systems, and embody the cutting edge of portable information technology. PDAs are a family of multilingual, genetically enhanced macaw parrots possessing flawless geomagnetic guidance systems, multilingual verbal communication skills, and photographic memories, which enable them to store a deep store of names, directions, phone numbers, and appointments. Although slightly larger than the original PDAs, Parrot Diagnostic Advisors are far superior in several key areas. First, they run on crackers, which enable them to be used "off the grid" for longer periods of time than previous PDAs. Additionally, they are content to ride on the user's shoulder, making them less likely get lost in the bottom of one's bag or briefcase. Further, as information storage devices, their abilities are unsurpassed. But the key to PDA's immense popularity is the fact that they are, as the name states, diagnostic advisors. Current-generation PDAs come equipped with Ph.D-level training in a variety of medical, spiritual, and/or cognitive therapy as desired. Need help interpreting your partner's sudden coldness following your last remark? Your PDA will likely have an insightful answer. Need quick advice on whether she is in fact different towards you when she's around certain friends? Your PDA will not let you down.

PDA

Brief history: First discovered by a team of documentary producers seeking to renew contact with a remote Amazon tribe (the tribe was rumored to contain the descendents of former U.S. senators who fled North America during the second American revolution), the macaw parrots led the producers, who had become lost, to safety and gave them a scolding for "relying on that cheap GPS crap in the field." It turns out the parrots had been the subjects of various neuro-genetic experiments at MIT in the early part of the millennium but had been abducted from the lab by PETA activists (despite their earnest protestations that they were quite content with their lives as research subjects) and returned to the rain forest, where they had been living unhappily ever since.

Like the Australian leaf-cutter ant and the baobab tree, the cleaner fish and the basking shark, the human and the macaw have since entered a mutually beneficial interspecies relationship. Long known for their intelligence, and willingness to tolerate pirates, the parrots, which thanks to widespread cloning now number in the millions, have proven to be quite happy in their new expanded roles in human society. A macaw on a shoulder is a happy macaw and a man with a macaw as his PDA is one certain to have his facts straight. Some PETA activists still despise the relationship as unequal and exploitative. "But we have trapped and enslaved millions of your kind in small cages for centuries," they have argued with the birds. "Ah!" the parrots will respond. "The ability to wield force in order to subjugate another is not at all the same thing as intelligence! Besides, you homocentric hypocrites are also known to enslave your own kind, which proves your fallacious natures and intellectual inferiority—now give us a motherfucking cracker or we won't tell you where you left your sky-car keys."

—Brent Hoff

Peanut Butter Babies, the [pee'-nut buh'-dur bay'-beez] *n.* popular television show from 2044–2050 in which, at each episode's climax, all the characters would pretend to give birth to organic, sugar-free, peanut-friendly jars of peanut butter, which were then spread on celery sticks and shared with the live studio audience.

—Heidi Meredith

Peeps [peeps] *n.* nickname for Paid Public Servants, or P.P.S., who choose which form of service they will render for two years following college graduation, just as their elders once enlisted in the military before the advent of World Peace. Payment for such service is either in cash or as repayment of student loans. Peeps may earn credit toward advanced degrees and certificates while rendering service.

—Cornelia Nixon

peripathetic [payr-ih-puh-thet'-ik] *adj.* 1. of, relating to, or given to aimlessly following the paths of others. 2. term originally meant as a disparaging epithet for the feeling of self-justification developed from lengthy but superficially defined travel in emulation of the status of others; now considered archaic due to the displacement of such dim approaches to self-fulfillment with actual spiritually legitimate invocations of religious philosophy. *Danny was so peripathetic, carrying that tattered Gary Zukav in his pocket and withdrawing his parent's money at ATMs all the way to the coast.*

—Benjamin Cohen

perplexion [pur-plek'-shun] *n.* a situation, often political or historical, that seems to defy common sense when in fact it challenges core assumptions. For example, one nation frees another from a cruel dictatorship and is met by the people it has liberated with scorn, resentment, and armed resistance: *the Iraqi perplexion*. Or a president gains support in the military despite leading it into a calamitous war: *the Bush-military perplexion*. Excruciatingly exasperating, a perplexion may also describe a personal conundrum: *if she loves me, how could she do this?* A perplexion can be perceived (or more exactly, suffered) by the right and the left, the rich and the poor, the pros and the antis, men and women, those in favor of interleague play and those against it, but never at the same time, emphasizing once again the sweet complexity of human affairs.

—Ken Kalfus

phatulence [fat'-yoo-lents] *n.* a gassy condition resulting from the overemphasis on beauty in popular culture. Recommended treatment is a daily dose of good art. *The bootylicious close-ups turned him on for the show's first half hour, and then the phatulence caught up with him and he had to excuse himself to sit on the toilet and read a page or two of Thomas Mann.* —John Henry Fleming

phone cell [fohn'-sel] *n.* an engineered microorganism whose sole purpose is to communicate with other phone cells by means of chemical "scents." Just as the telephone made it possible for human beings to talk across great distances, so the phone cell has vastly increased the ability of humans to communicate with themselves. Injected into the fleshy part of the thigh, phone cells travel through the body and lodge themselves of their own accord in the stomach, lungs, genitals, feet, brain, and heart; within hours they have begun to transmit to each other. The benefits of phone cell implantation are almost too many to enumerate: a person whose phone cells are working properly is aware of the source and precise nature of her feelings; she does not mistake hunger for hostility, lust for enthusiasm, or fatigue for despair. She is immune to insomnia and lower back pain. Nowadays it is hard to imagine life without the phone cell, but to get a sense of how it transformed American society, consider just a few of the things that phone cells made obsolete: the ritual self-contortion that went by the name of **marriage** in the 20th century and **yoga** in the 21st; the frustrated dialectic of diet regimes and high-sucrose foods; and the portable telephones (called "cell phones," curiously) that human beings once used to distract themselves from their thoughts. —Paul La Farge

phone cell

pictify [pik'-te-fiy] *v. tr.* to determine or express the quality of using exclusively or primarily images. *The horrors of the prison were pictified throughout the month.*

—Ben Greenman

Pinocchioism [pin-o'-kee-o-izm] *n.* the general name for the movement toward greater truth-telling in government, which ultimately led to mandatory drug regimens for all public office holders, this required drug being a daily dose of a wriggling little yellow pill that, for the following twenty-four hours, causes instantaneous inflammation and elongation of the nasal cartilage the moment a lie is told, said elongation being proportional to the egregiousness of the lie. Little white lies result in mere inches; with large lies the results can extend for miles. A well-known example is the recent president who was speaking at a press conference in the White House when his nose began to grow, shooting out a window and wending its way across the country, knocking down telephone lines, braining small birds, and poking the rear end of an innocent woman planting crocus bulbs in Nebraska, before coming to a sneezing halt somewhere in the salt flats of Nevada. The only cure for the resulting condition is immediate dismissal from office and a public pruning. —JUDY BUDNITZ

Pinocchioism

pith helmet [pith hel'-met] *n.* a lightweight, reusable helmet that allows wearers to get to the heart of a complex problem without distraction from the sun's harmful rays, microphone feedback, or Supply-Side Economics. Comes in two colors: brown and really brown. —KEVIN MOFFETT

pith helmet

plaintitude [playn'-tih-tood] *n.* the sense of an action or act that, performed daily, is fulfilling to the actor in its regularity; a sense that ordinary routine is sufficient. *The plaintitude of breakfast consoles me.* —LYNNE TILLMAN

platonics [pluh-tawn'-iks] *n.* a language of friendship taught in K–12. *Platonics class extended midway into recess before anyone thought to look at the clock; the kids had just enough time to run out and help each other up to the top of the monkey bars.*
—JOHN HENRY FLEMING

pleasant bowel syndrome [plez'-ent bow'-ul sin'-drohm] *n.* a condition in which the body engages in the process of elimination without stress. In 2014, health-nuts were finally able to convince the world that a vegetarian diet, rich in dark greens, fruits, wholegrains, essential oils, and chocolate was really the way to go, and so what was known as **Irritable Bowel Syndrome** was eradicated. The conversion to a healthy diet meant that organic produce once more became the only kind of produce. The land was now properly tilled and not depleted of its nutrients. This proper use of land, led by a bunch of high-powered Whole Foods executives, led to the eradication of hunger throughout the world and balance was restored: Sally Struthers slimmed down and numerous Africans began to put on weight. And, of course, everyone was really happy now about going to the commode and a lot of neurotic psychological bathroom hang-ups, which had been plaguing man for some time, were at last dropped, so to speak.
—JONATHAN AMES

plentice [plen'-tis] *n.* a state of moral equilibrium, especially in social, political, or judicial settings, in which the needs and rights of everyone concerned have been satisfactorily observed without excessive imposition on the freedoms or feelings of others. *Legislators announced today that economic plentice had been achieved by subsidizing the guaranteed minimum income program through a tax on the richest five* *percent of the population*; or: *Now that the death penalty is no longer an option, plentice in multiple-murder cases usually entails a sentence of life without parole.* (*Cf.* John Rawls's *A Theory of Justice*, generally considered to be the source of the principle if not the word itself.) —WENDY LESSER

pokey [poh'-kee] 1. *n.* (ca. 2030) an oversized privately owned home, dependent on the now-obsolete energy grid, often situated in a gated community in an outlying suburb of an American city, whose owner has opted out of the **Jubilee.** 2. *n.* (ca. 1919) JAIL 3. *adj.* annoyingly slow. —NICK FLYNN

political literalism [puh-lit'-ik-ul lit'-ur-uhl-iz-um] *n.* the novel concept of holding politicians responsible for their promises, of taking them at their word and then making them keep it. The current usage of the term originated in 2004 when, in his fourth and final public news conference, lame-duck president George W. Bush vowed that he would "bring freedom to Iraq, whether the Iraqis wanted it or not, even if I have to go over there and do it all by myself." Americans, taking Bush at his word, immediately shipped him off to Iraq alone, where he was last seen repeating the words, "I do believe in freedom, I do believe in freedom," over and over again as he clicked the heels of his Tony Lamas together. Later, when a Senate inquiry revealed that the words used by Bush in this news conference had been spoonfed to him by politicos Donald Rumsfeld, Dick Cheney, and Karl Rove, they were shipped off as well.

Political literalism led to a profound change in political strategizing. For their own protection, Republicans began to air TV campaign ads with a running footer reading "CAUTION: Promises made by candidates not to be taken seriously." Candidates from other parties took the more drastic step of simply fulfilling their campaign promises. —BRIAN EVENSON

POP [pahp] *n.* a powerful grassroots movement that emerged at the end of

POP

the 24th century and dominated world politics for several generations. POP (Power of the People) was founded by Sunil Masuri, a physicist in Bangalore, India, whose research showed that human brain waves, if properly coordinated, could be manipulated to create power surges of enormous proportions. Thus, if large numbers of people felt or thought the same thing at the same time, their will could be expressed with great, and often deadly, effect.

One of the first POP Wave attacks was directed against the hated **Mybad Correctional Spa** (*q.v.*) in Siberia in 2397. The facility was pulverized in seconds, though all the inmates were miraculously rescued (not their jailers, however). Other POP wave attacks did away with Mount Rushmore (2398), Rome's Monument to Victor Emmanuel II (2399), the entire collection of Guggenheim Museums (simultaneously) in 2400, and the 4th International Congress itself (2401).

The POP wave could also be used positively: major forest fires were regularly extinguished and floodtides dissipated. POP meteorologists became expert at altering weather patterns, and for some decades in the mid-2400s the entire globe enjoyed optimal climatic conditions. Experts maintain that the best-ever vintages of all wines worldwide were produced in 2445–9 (some apparently remain drinkable even today).

Masuri's algorithms for ascertaining the people's will were widely sought after, particularly by the advertising industry, but no one ever managed to crack his codes. Though he was assassinated in Chicago in 2402, the POP movement, using its own POPulist election methods, chose a series of canny, altruistic successors until the late-25th century, when the system proved unequal to the challenge of the great Martian plagues, and on its hundredth anniversary in 2497, the POP membership voted itself out of existence.

POP changed the face of politics in our time; thank God it's history. (George B.V.D. Bush, 148th U.S. President (2500-2504))

—JONATHAN GALASSI

poetic

poetic [poh-et'-ik] *adj.* [*obsolete*] of, relating to, or being outmoded in design, style, or construction; SYN. old-fashioned; antique; twee. (SEE **béret.**) —SHOSHANA BERGER

poho [poh'-hoh] *adj.* 1. derogatory term for one who kowtows to politicians. 2. a politician who alters his agenda in the act of fundraising. 3. a host of political fundraisers. Party leaders began lining up their pohos more than a year before the election. As political consulting reached its heights of sophistication in the mid-century, a far savvier breed of pohos began to emerge. In the late fifties the new campaign finance laws caused many pohos to work behind the scenes, or underground.

—TOM BARBASH

Policy Wonka [pol'-is-ee wonk'-uh] *n.* assiduous, though sometimes overly whimsical, political operator. Known for tracking and commenting on more oblique government legislation, like the **Freedom to Traipse Bylaws** (2019) and the **De-Deregulation Reforms** (2023). Prone to mordant asides, warranted cruelty. —KEVIN MOFFETT

pro-semitism [proh-sem'-uh-tiz-um] *n.* a state of mind in which a person feels positively about Jews. Before 2018, there was a word known as **anti-Semitism,** which essentially described a mindset where a person was hostile towards Jews and found them annoying, to say the least. But all this started to change in 2005 when an Israeli boy was playing on one side of a fence and a Palestinian boy was playing on the other side of a fence and the two started talking in English, which in 2005 had become the **Universal Second Language**. They started rolling small Hot-Wheel cars back-and-forth to each other through holes in the fence; while they played, they complained about their parents. "My mother won't let me eat bacon," said the Jewish boy. "I'd really like to try it." "That's weird," said the Palestinian boy. "My mother won't let me eat bacon either!" Well, those two boys realized that they had a lot in common and grew up to be great friends and eventually they became the leaders of their people. United by a desire to try bacon at least once, and the realization that their two clans had a great deal in common, these two leaders hired the world's greatest genealogist, Olaf Grogjkg, from the historically neutral country of Iceland; Grogjkg discovered that all Palestinians and Israelis were actually third-cousins. Now, this might not sound like a profound connection, but for Jewish and Muslim people, family is very important. Certain retired Jewish people in Florida have been known to go to great lengths to find fourth-cousins to forward joke e-mails to. Anyway, once it was discovered that Palestinians and Israelis were cousins, relations between those people became absolutely joyous. Their happiness at realizing they didn't have to fight anymore was wonderfully infectious and spread throughout the whole world. Palestine and Israel started to live side-by-side and they were as happy together as Connecticut and Massachusetts. The Palestinians let everyone know that Jews were okay and that they had a wonderful sense of humor. The films of Woody Allen began to be broadcast on the Al-Jazeera network, Egyptians started vacationing in the Catskills, and the word shylock became a compliment for someone who was manly, an allusion to the famous line: "Am I not a man?" So it happily came to pass that everyone liked Jews. Everyone also liked Muslims. A real domino effect with people liking each other took over. Things were really good. The only people who still got under everyone's skin were the English because of their nutty devotion to a powerless dysfunctional royal family, but it was just a minor irritation and nobody went to war about it; they just told the English to get over it and engaged in some hurtful teasing, which wasn't nice, but no death camps were built or anything like that.

—JONATHAN AMES

proshjewtoo [prahsh-joo'-too] *n.* cured meat, somewhat resembling Italian prosciutto, but derived from the ruminant swine, genetically engineered to chew cud and with deeply cleft trotters, thus enabling its meat products (SEE **Shem**) to be certified kosher by some more progressive rabbinical authorities. (SEE ALSO **Balaloybsta.**) The arrival of proshjewtoo in the delis only made the ultimate dream of a perfectly kosher shem and cheese sandwich more tantalising. The best minds in the koshifying research industry were applied to the milkhedik problem and after years of doing things with soy, came up with... moysharella (available in horseradish in selected outlets). —SIMON SCHAMA

protemporary [proh-tem'-pur-ayr-ee] *n.*, **protemporaneous** *adj.* an advocate of the new and passing; a person who is not fixed in attitudes or habits; of a group who supports and extols the passing whims and fancies of its day; at its extreme, bordering on anarchy, as in: *She follows no dictates that I can discern, her protemporaneous style is too fast for me.* Not to be confused with **contemporary**, which emphasizes a blending into one's time. Closer to **atemporality**, in flavor.

—LYNNE TILLMAN

Protection and Reinvigoration of Marriage Act, the n. a law, updating the now-reviled Defense of Marriage Act (1996), stipulating that it is the right of every couple, wherein both parties are over the age of eighteen, to be legally united in matrimony regardless of race, gender, sexual orientation, religious affiliation, tax bracket, shoe size, hair color, body hair density, hypochondria, veganism, or lactose tolerability. This law not only bequeaths all the rights and privileges of what was formerly known as "heterosexual marriage," but also confers all the risks, perils, hazards, misgivings, and second thoughts which might occur when said partner squeezes from the middle of the toothpaste tube rather than from the bottom, chews in that "annoying way," or admits that "yes, you could stand to lose a few pounds."

—ZZ PACKER

protest march [proh'-test march] *n.* 1. the momentary confusion that occurs when the actual reality of a situation subverts expectation. Now that protest marches are unnecessary, the term refers to any situation in which a potentially negative situation is revealed to be its opposite. *For a second there, I thought those fishermen were clubbing that baby seal, but when I got closer, I saw that they were just petting it and giving it lots of encouragement. It was a protest march.* 2. [*archaic*] an optical illusion caused by a failure in perspective, in which observers at the scene see one thing but television cameras, government agencies, and newspaper reporters see another. *Officials counted thirty people at the anti-war demonstration. It was a protest march.* —COLSON WHITEHEAD

pubic transportation

pubic transportation [pyoo'-bik tranz-por-tay'-shun] *n.* the system of conveyances first instituted in 2013 by California Governor Angelina Jolie to discourage the use of private vehicles by offering free nude electric trolley service throughout greater Los Angeles. First known as "Jolie-rollers," the system soon expanded to include our national auto-Buss network and eventually, intercontinental Bi-planes.

—ART SPIEGELMAN

pulling a Lieberman [pul'-ing lee'-bur-muhn] *v.* [*slang*] 1. to covertly run for office on the opposition ticket. *Many were shocked when Maria agreed to run as Arnold's vice-president, but it soon became clear that one of them was pulling a Lieberman.*

—KEN FOSTER

puppies [puh'-peez] *n.* baby dogs, still just as cute as the dickens, despite occasional freakish deformities.

—CHRIS BACHELDER

puppies

pureball [pyur'-bahl] *n.* otherwise known as **Organic Baseball,** established after escalating salaries, over-commercialization, rampant steroid use, misbegotten rule changes, and the dissolution of the reserve clause brought down the entire structure of Major League Baseball. New professional baseball leagues sprouted immediately, each developing its own rules and practices (*cf.* **drugball, techball, killball**). In pureball, the pitcher bats, the fields are grass, most games are played in daylight, the season begins in April and ends in September, players are tested for steroid use, and there is no interleague play or wild card playoff berths. Pureball players are always willing to sign autographs for fans, who would never think of selling them. Pureball draws fewer fans than baseball's other variants, necessitating inexpensive tickets and concessions and rare television broadcasts, yet the game makes the strongest claim on the American heart.

—KEN KALFUS

Puritangential [pyur'-it-an-jen'-chul] *adj.* a form of argument used to obfuscate an important issue by diverting attention to an irrelevant one. *In the early 21st century, when Americans desperately needed to focus on the breakdown in international relations caused by their government, the Republican party puritangentially railed against the right of homosexuals to have their interpersonal relations sanctified by marriage.*

—ART SPIEGELMAN

art spiegelman • ***art spiegelman*** / Ken Foster / Chris Bachelder • ***Barry Blitt*** / Ken Kalfus / art spiegelman

Qack [kahk] *n.* [*archaic*] 1. a short-lived monetary unit that flourished among refugee populations. Originally, its value was tied to regional instability; higher instability meant higher value for the Qack. The value plummeted in 2006, and the Qack has largely fallen into obscurity. 2. *adj.* [*vulgar*] having the qualities of excrement, worthless.
—DAVE KNEEBONE

qrappé [krap-pay'] *adj.* 1. constructed from molded white plastic. 2. giving the illusion of great expense. 3. needlessly emblazoned with a corporate logo. —ANDREW LELAND

quadruple quotes [kwahd-roop'-uhl kwohts] *n.* [*archaic*] punctuation marks used to enclose a word or phrase about which their user has nested skepticisms: 1. skepticism about some quality of the word or phrase contained by the device (as in a word contained by double quotes) and 2. skepticism about revealing the aforementioned skepticism to the reader, out of fear that the reader will think the author is a skeptic, a pedant, a pessmist, a dweeb, etc.; introduced in 2006 to modest love/hate response; crippled by a 2007 MLA "golden raspberry" award for general agony. —BRIAN MCMULLEN

1. "" ""
2. ""tolerance""

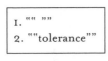

quagmire [kwag'-miyr] *n.* 1. Quagmire the Clown, host of the television series "Boogaloo Kid in Funktown," a dance show for children that ran for six episodes in the fall of 2025. 2. *n.* a popular dance in which the arms are waved in a ridiculous fashion while the legs remain still. 3. *v.* to flail hopelessly and pray no one will notice. 4. *n.* [*archaic*] a difficult situation resulting from corruption, willful ignorance, or blind obedience to political dogma. During the period that historians call "the American Dark Ages," this nation often committed to courses of action that were morally reprehensible in intent and catastrophic in execution. *All me and my buddies wanted to do was get rich off this whole oil thing, and we ended up in a quagmire.* —COLSON WHITEHEAD

Quagmire the Clown

quality control [kwahl'-it-ee kontrohl'] *n.* the removal of defective politicians from office. (SEE ALSO **voting.**) *We've got to apply some serious quality control to this here legislative body.*
—JOHN HENRY FLEMING

quarter horse [kwor'-tur hors] *n.* with the sudden realization that coins are far too annoying, impractical, and environmentally hazardous to serve as a form of global currency, artists and

Dave Kneebone / Andrew Leland / Brian McMullen / Colson Whitehead • ***Danny Shanahan*** / John Henry Fleming / Brent Hoff

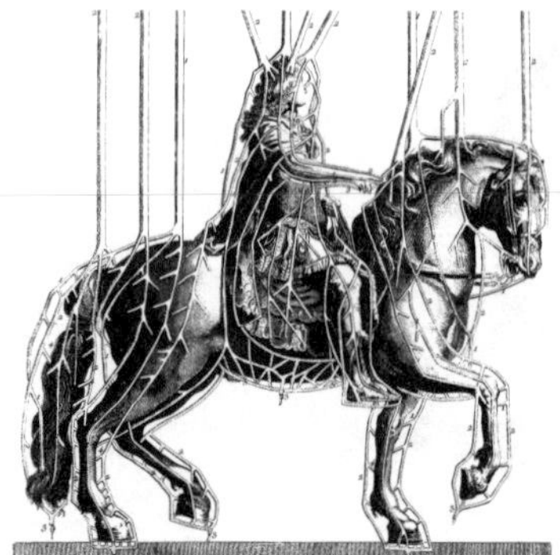

quarter horse

engineers have been finding remarkable and ingenious uses for the tons of now-useless change. Life-size robot ponies constructed entirely of quarters and distributed to children on their fifth birthday are just one example. —BRENT HOFF

quik [kwik] *adj., adv.* moving or behaving in a rich, chocolately manner; used primarily as an adverb. *The journalists all entered the room at once and walked quikly toward the bar.* —ANDREW LELAND

quipnunc [kwip'-noonk] *n.* a person who responds to current events, especially tragic ones, with quickly devised, sometimes callous jokes. *"If they take too many more hostages, we won't be able to even field a soccer team over there," said Joe, always a quipnunc.* [A neologic corruption of quidnunc, from the Latin *quid* (what) + *nunc* (now).] —BEN GREENMAN

quirkster [kwurk'-stur] *n.* usually a shock jock or talk show host, sometimes a guest on such a program, or any speaker or entertainer whose quick taunts, outrageousness, and verbal jabs may be offensive and cause startlement, but whose ready wit usually overcomes objection. *Howard Stern bothered Sally, especially when he talked about bra sizes again and again, but she appreciated a quirkster when she heard one.* —LYNNE TILLMAN

R

ragadolfin [rag-uh-dahl'-fin] *n.* a variety of post-human child, ca 2104. The introduction of cetacean genetic material into the human genome after the mid-21st century has never been adequately explained. Some have claimed (Yuan 2101, Bernstein 2108) that the ragadolfin derives from a "nonce genome" produced by secret human-cetacean hybridization programs of the late 21st century that were intended either 1) to tether inextricably the destinies of the last two intelligent species of animal life on earth or 2) to vastly expand human consciousness by equipping it to understand the planet's largest biome. Others (Krantz 2100, Halabi 2099) have argued that the ragadolfin is the product of an accidental gene flow that resulted when American, Canadian, and Mexican children, in 2098, consumed several production runs of Gigasweet RNA, a popular brainprep (math, science, Mandarin, and engineering) breakfast cereal. A total of over three million boxes of Gigasweet RNA, it was later learned, had been processed with PurpleRock, an enhanced form of common purple dulse seaweed that in the early 2000s had been spliced with cetacean genetic material (apparently as an unsuccessful treatment for Chronic Erectile Hypertropy (*q.v.*), or "niagra").

Whatever the cause of the gene flow, the end result was not the popularly envisioned transgenic flipper boys and girls, undulant and slick, kicking their

ragadolphin

freakish way through submarine playgrounds, wearing long, long, sharp-toothed grins. Physically, and indeed in nearly every particular, ragadolfins are indistinguishable from human children. They exhibit no greater swimming or diving abilities, and their love for the ocean and for other bodies of water is within the expected range for water-loving gene-normals. It was some time before the cetacean trait conveyed to ragadolfins by the transgenic seaweed in their breakfast cereal began to express itself clearly, empirically, and to the troubled astonishment of parents all over North America. The children's brains were awash in a peptide, GRP, that interferes with the activity of the amygdala, the almond-sized region of the brain most involved in the generation of anxiety and danger-response. The new children, like their distant cetacean cousins in the ancestral company of sharks, played without fear.

The appearance of several hundred thousand fearless children caused considerable disruption in the carefully managed, hundred-and-twenty-five-year-old fear-based economy. At first, they tended to be perceived and presently demonized in the fear-dependent media as the quintessential problem children, disruptive, unmanageable, wild, and finally bad. Their altered brain chemistry made them resistant to the effects of the 2017 Ritalin Act (in which modified methylphenidate joined fluoride in the water systems of most American municipalities, as well as becoming a required additive in soft drinks), and interfered with their ability to consume hypermedia. Early reports all emphasize the tendency of ragadolfins to drift, inexorably, in spite of parental admonishment, and regardless of the weather, entertainment menu, or UV index, outside.

Ragadolfins gravitated instinctively toward vacant lots, unguarded construction sites, culverts, underpasses, and any available scrap of meadow or forestland that the urban and exurban landscape afforded. They sought out, individually at first and then increasingly, the marginal zones and forgotten areas that escaped the mediation, regulation, and surveillance of gene-normal adults. They revived or spontaneously reinvented such long-abandoned games as Kick the Can, Ghost in the Graveyard, Capture the Flag, Ringolevio, and Old Mother Witch. Punishment, medication, confinement, and an intensified program of education in the manifold hazards, perils, and possible negative outcomes of unsupervised play all proved ineffective at curbing the problem. The allure of engaging in the ongoing creation of a child-legislated, child-directed, child-imagined narrative world of play, one incorporating danger, conflict, and even a certain amount of cruelty and free, unlegislated brutality, proved irresistible and finally undeniable. There were injuries. There were mishaps. There were accidents, torments, and even fatalities, all of which appeared to bear out dire governmental, media, and parental predictions. Subsequent statistical analysis, however, has revealed that the rates of injury and death were on a par with those among gene-normal children, while the rates among ragadolfins of suicide and depression ran consistently far below those of gene-normals.

The first generation of ragadolfins to reach adulthood intermarried heavily, producing a second generation in which the ragadolfin fearlessness was expressed even more strongly. This second generation also benefited from being raised by parents who not merely retained but prized the memory of a tenuous liberty wrested from the fear-driven economy that had controlled and employed their own parents' minds. Conflict with and persecution by that economy was an inevitability, and the pro-ragadolfin lobby was among the first to petition for a charter when, in 2150, the Colonization Corporations were proposed. Mass off-world emigration was viewed with favor by the Interplanetary Settlement Agency as a ready solution to the ragadolfin problem, and to date some 1,800 ragadolfin families have made the jump. The success of the ragadolfin colony on the second planet orbiting Wolf 359, christened "Narnia" by the first settlers, is far from assured, but the possibilities for adventure there seem all but limitless. —MICHAEL CHABON

ralphnadir [ralf-nay'-deer] 1. *n.* the lowest point in any process, whereby the urgent need to alter that process becomes manifest. *The ralphnadir of America's unrepresentative two-party system led to the establishment, in 2012, of our current proportional allnite-party system.* 2. *v.* the act of creating such a lowpoint while simultaneously undoing one's reputation. *He ralphnadired their relationship when he condi-scendingly denied that he'd cheneyed their joint account.*

—ART SPIEGELMAN

ralphnadir

Ramakah [rah'-muh-kuh] *n.* joint Jewish/Muslim holiday held in December to celebrate the end of hostilities between members of these two religions. Ramakah traditions include the exchange of gifts and sharing of meals between Muslims and Jews.

—RYAN BOUDINOT

Ramirez, Duke [rah-meer'-ays, dyook] 1960–2017. American visionary; founder of utopian underground city, Fresh Hell, in southwest Idaho, which strived to become invisible. (SEE **Cheney.**) —JEFFREY EUGENIDES

rastatution [ras-tuh-too'-shun] *n.* a making-good for wrongdoing; a reimbursement, paid in ganja. *Gordon couldn't claim to have actually prejudged the substitute milkman, but a distinct feeling had formed in his gut that might well have led to an unjust first impression, and for that reason he would insist on inviting the man into his home for a little wake-and-bake rastatution.*

—JOHN HENRY FLEMING

reality [ree-al'-uh-tee] *n.* anything experienced in private. ANT. **unreality** *n.* anything appearing on or experienced through the mass media.

—ROBERT OLEN BUTLER

reclusitate [ruh-cloo'-sit-ayt] *v.* to withdraw in the Joseph Cornellian sense of non-spiritual retreat, best done on Utopia Parkway. Not to be confused with **ostrichification** or **monkifacation.** —SUSAN DAITCH

regretuary [reg-ret'-chyoo-ayr-ee] *n.* common or private cemetery, in which are buried items symbolic of grief, remorse or shame, for the purposes of forgiveness. *Among the items buried in the National Regretuary—as penance for the global damage they have done—are butterfly ballots from the 2000 election, the vial of "anthrax" held aloft by Colin Powell at his U.N. testimony, the flight suit worn by former President George W. Bush and all existing copies of* The Passion of the Christ. (Senator Drew Barrymore)

—ANDREW SEAN GREER

rehab [ree'-hab] *n.* mandatory, inpatient treatment facility where people who voted for the "president" go to get it together and aren't allowed to come out until they accept an appropriate portion of the responsibility for 2000–2004 and agree to openly support progressive candidates in the future.

—ELIZABETH CRANE

Religious Reich [rel-idj'-uhs riyk] *n.* the ill-chosen name of the more conservative group to come out of the schism in the Religious Right caused by the **Kansas Holy Wars.** Eventually led by Senator Orrin Hatch (R-Utah), the Religious Reich advocated a "reassertion of all positive moral values followed by their universal enforcement." Under Hatch's leadership, members of the Religious Reich became clean-cut and, in addition to their WWJD bracelets, wore dark suits, white shirts and ties,

religious reich

art spiegelman • ***Barry Blitt*** / Ryan Boudinot / Jeffrey Eugenides / John Henry Fleming / Robert Olen Butler / Susan Daitch / Andrew Sean Greer / Elizabeth Crane / Brian Evenson • ***art spiegelman*** which caused them to be frequently mistaken for Wall Street traders or Mormon missionaries. At first apparently a political force to be reckoned with, the group was weakened by their tendencies to "testify" and to make economic assertions with no grounding in reality. Hatch's well-publicized attempt to change his designation from party leader to party "fuhrer" brought closer scrutiny to the group's name—*Reich*—and caused a groundswell movement against the appropriation of religion for political gain. —BRIAN EVENSON

remirror [ree-meer'-ur] *v.* 1. to disappear in the observation of another. 2. to see a person or thing without the separation of self-interest. 3. to refocus, see clearly. 4. the perception of the humanity of a supposed enemy. In the act of looking in a mirror we see ourselves. The act of remirroring is to see through the metaphorical mirror by which we experience the world, and by doing so the judgments and comparisons, the values and uses we attribute to the objects of the world disappear. The tree in the forest becomes a unique tree with a life and a history. The person in the plaza, instead of being older or thinner, bothersome or enviable, becomes what she or he is. In the act of remirrorment the membrane of our fears, desires, and needs fall away, and we're left, again, in a state of wonder.
—JOHN HASKELL

report [ruh-port'] *n.* 1. an exchange of gunfire, frequently between military troops and the people whose country they seek to occupy. 2. an account of such gunfire, frequently censored or inaccurate. —KEN FOSTER

Risigoths [riy'-zih-gahths] *n.* a branch of the Goths that invaded the American Empire late in the 21st cent. They were known for their inclination to laugh, and their ability to provoke laughter in others. When they rose up and challenged the Americans, the President of the United States attempted to assemble a coalition to go to war against the Risigoths, but could not get through his address at the United Nations without chortling. He tried to gather himself, saying, "Seriously, seriously...," but would then make eye-contact with someone and they would all bust up again. Thus was established the supremacy of the Risigoths, which ushered in a 500-year period of peace, prosperity, and snickering.
—STEPHEN SHERRILL

Risigoths

Roe-rosion [roh-roh'-zjun] *n.* the slow and almost imperceptible erosion of women's rights; when this time in history is viewed from a distance, the airplane-eye view reveals a shape as distinct as Mount Rushmore.
—ELISSA SCHAPPELL

rooftopping [roof'-tah-ping] *vt.* a children's game played on passenger aircraft flights. Originally designed by parents as a distraction activity, the game allows points for each rooftop garden spotted from the air during take-off and landing. At the beginning of the 21st century, when the world's mega-cities each held 10 to 27 million people—many of whom lived in chronic hunger and substandard living conditions—rooftop gardening began to spread from Mexico City, Lagos, and Port-au-Prince, throughout major cities in Asia, Europe, Canada, South and Central America, Africa, the Pacific Islands, and, at last, the United States. In 2030, the mega-cities and numerous smaller metropolitan areas became largely self-sufficient in food production. As a side benefit, through a combination of composting and recycling programs, the cities substantially reduced their waste-disposal emergencies, which had reached record proportions, including more than 26,000 tons of garbage per day in New York City alone. In the game of rooftopping, each participant receives one point for individual residences; five points for apartment houses, offices, and warehouses; and ten points for municipal buildings and schools. The difficulty in distinguishing between schools and warehouses adds additional, if sometimes contentious, excitement to the game. Scores of a thousand points or more have become increasingly common. In rooftopping, it must be noted, no points are given for the rooftop gardens on the passenger terminals used by today's solar-powered, hydrogen-fuel-cell-based aircraft: these gardens are an industry standard and no version of the game allows for their inclusion.

—SARAH STONE

rumsfeld [ruhmz'-feld] *n.* one who can stomach casualties.

—KURT VONNEGUT

Rumsfeldian Geometry *n.* [ruhmz-feld'-ee-an gee-ah'-muh-tree] (from Donald Rumsfeld, alleged Secretary of Defense, 2001–2005) a system of pseudoscience in which elements are linked through utter speculation and paranoia rather than logic. Comparable to spiritualism or other faddish delusions, Rumsfeldian Geometry was briefly fashionable in 2001–2004 when it was actually used in the formulation of foreign policy; now universally regarded as a curiousity. "As we know, there are known knowns. There are things we know we know. We also know there are known unknowns. That is to say we know there are some things we do not know. But there are also unknown unknowns, the ones we don't know we don't know." (Donald Rumsfeld, Dept. of Defense briefing, 2/12/02.)

—DANIEL HANDLER

Rumsfeldian question [ruhmz-feld'-ee-an kwest'-chun] *n.* a rhetorical question where the answer is provided by oneself. Popularized by disgraced former Secretary of Defense Donald Rumsfeld, prior to his lifetime incarceration, who used it as a technique to keep from ever admitting that he might be wrong. Ex: *Is democracy untidy? Sure it is. Are there bad people in the world? Of course. Am I a stubborn jackass whose lack of foresight cost billions of dollars and thousands of lives? You bet.*

—JOHN WARNER

Rupture, the [ruhpt'-chur] *n.* the collapse of the religious right following the failure of the so-called Rapture to occur on January 1, 2023, as predicted by Rev. Tim la Haye Jr; any big entirely predictable disappointment; a foolish conviction that ends in embarrassment; a fanciful misreading of the Bible.

—KATHA POLLITT

Fig. A *Area of circle derived by Euclidian Geometry*

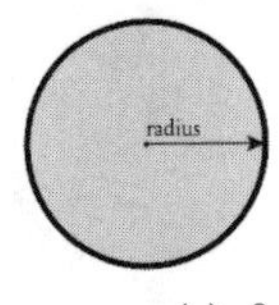

area = $(\pi)\ r^2$

Fig. B *Area of circle derived by Rumsfeldian Geometry*

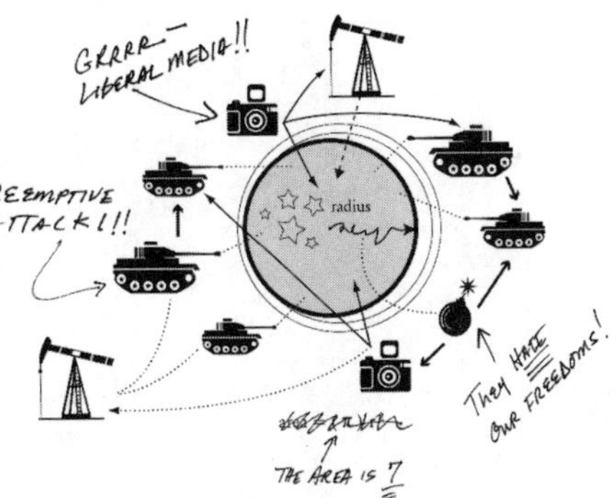

Rumsfeldian Geometry

S

science [siy'-ents] *n.* systematic knowledge of the material world as obtained through rigorous observation and experimentation in accordance with the scientific method. Though responsible for the greatest technological innovations of modern times, it was inexplicably shunned by American policymakers early in the 21st century. This abandonment of science led inevitably to the **Great Horribleness** of 2010, which, in turn, set the stage for the **Calamity** of 2012. In the painful aftermath of these disasters, Americans realized the error of their ways and, ever since, have embraced science for what it is: a lens through which the blurry world can be seen much more clearly. —Ed Page

science non-fiction [siy'-ents nahn-fik'-shun] *n.* a kind of writing. It was discovered in 2011 that a typographical error at a newspaper over one hundred years before had created a profound and great misunderstanding. Brilliant writers, like Jules Verne, Mary Shelley, H.G. Wells, Isaac Asimov, Ray Bradbury, and Philip K. Dick, to name a few, had all along been writing science NON-fiction. That is, what they were reporting was fact and truth, but a London newspaper review of Verne's work categorized it mistakenly as *science fiction,* leaving out the *non-*, and there's been mass confusion ever since. Turns out that time travel, alternative universes, Utopias, helpful robots, space-travel, underwater cities, and photon shields had all been accessible to man

science non-fiction

for quite some time. Cures for every disease and peaceful universes were found to actually exist; there are also gigantic space-eels, who are very disruptive, but we have some very good lasers for those fellows, and they tend to keep to themselves for the most part anyway. Of course, numerous injustices were discovered: a man held in Bellevue at the end of the 19th century, purporting to be Captain Nemo, was actually Captain Nemo. His remains, which were found in a potter's field in Queens, NY, have since been transferred to a shrine at the Aquarium in Monterey, CA. The good news on that sad story is that at one point during his adventures, one of Captain Nemo's moustache hairs was beamed to an alternative universe where people live forever, and from that moustache hair they were able to clone a whole country of Captain Nemos, though some of his new ancestors go by "Lieutenant Nemo." It was also discovered that all episodes of *Star Trek* were actually documentary footage of a real ship, the *Enterprise*. William Shatner, who had claimed all along that he really was Captain Kirk, was glad that the truth finally came out. It should be noted that with the revelation that science fiction was actually science non-fiction, the Vulcan Death Pinch became a punishable offense, but Vulcans are so essentially kind that they hardly ever use the pinch, except on each other, and on a Vulcan a Vulcan Death Pinch is only a Vulcan Hurtful Pinch, and since no other species is able to practice the Death Pinch, no one has yet been sent to jail for using it or even given a ticket.

—JONATHAN AMES

scriggle scraggle [skrig'-el skrag'-el] *n.* 1. the wave-like pattern formed by the perceptible space that exists between the folds of the human brain. *Joy, already smitten by a half-dozen Mai-Thais, looked into Harold's baby blues and wondered how deep were the crevasses of his scriggle scraggle.* 2. the undulating and continuous line imprinted in the sand when a large body of water recedes from the shore at low tide. *While dragging the unconscious Joy by her feet over the scriggle scraggle of the shoreline, Harold lost his balance and fell face-first right into the flute of Joy's skirt.* 3. the route taken by a tornado or a waterspout. *After the waterspout made off with Harold's love-shack, he and Joy walked naked in a satisfied daze over the spout's scriggle scraggle.* 4. a wrinkle that meanders and circumnavigates the neck and throat of a man or a woman of advanced age. *Harold never imagined that the premature scriggle scraggle that had formed on Joy's neck shortly after the wedding would be such a turn-off, but as much as he tried, he couldn't get it off his mind.* 5. the invisible patterns made in the air by a conductor's baton. *Joy, after months of dejection, finally gave in to the hep bandleader whose intoxicating scribble scrabble was second-to-none.* 6. a visualization technique in which a sexually challenged male imagines himself zigzagging through a line of orange cones ordered in ascending height (from smallest to largest) to a red cone equaling the net height of the orange cones. *Scriggle scraggle saved Joy and Harold's marriage.* ALSO *vi.* to move along or form a random or consistent wave-like pattern. *Shouting out into the vast expanse of the desert, Joy, in a recurring nightmare, scriggle scraggled up and over sand dunes trying to outrun Harold, who (after his viusualization therapy) had, in Joy's subconscious, taken on the figure of a giant woman-eating sidewinder.*

—DAVID GRAND

scurl [skurl] *v.* 1. to move quickly and chaotically in a roughly circular pattern. 2a. to thrust (e.g., a knife, a sword) with a quick circular motion. 2b. to gouge. 3. to cause to enter. 4. to oblige. 5a. to demonstrate. 5b. to lay bare. 6. to know truly. 7. to weep. 8. to speak truly. 9. to be worthy.

—ROY KESEY

secularity blanket [sek-yoo-layr'-ih-tee blan-ket] *n.* 1. a small blanket or other soft cloth, often embroidered with the likeness of **Noam Chomsky**, clutched by an atheist or agnostic person who has failed to register according to the **American Religious Resurrection Act** of 2012. 2. anything that gives a person a feeling of safety or freedom from fundamentalist or absolutist oppression.

secularity blanket

—GARY SHTEYNGART

secularity deposit [sek-yoo-layr'-ih-tee dee-paz'-it] *n.* a monetary pledge or guarantee given to a landlord by an atheist or agnostic tenant who has failed to register according to the **American Religious Resurrection Act** of 2012 and thereby risks imprisonment and forfeiture of her worldly goods.

—GARY SHTEYNGART

Sedna [sed'-nuh] *n.* 1. Inuit diety (oftimes represented in soapstone carvings), the most significant figure in pan-arctic Inuit mythology, especially pertinent to domestic, social, and environmental ethics in daily life of ancient and present-day Inuit peoples. A woman of mythological origins who utilizes idiosyncratic rage for altruistic purposes. According to age-old belief, Sedna imposes a strict adherence to certain moral Laws, i.e., respect for all sentient beings, and, refraining from all individual or community decisions that are not good for at least the next seven generations (a similar philosophy is found throughout North American indigenous peoples). When certain of these "rules" are violated, Sedna acts with swift retribution; her repertoire traditionally features choking, voices-in-the-head, ice suddenly cracking open underfoot, blizzard-ambush, ghost kidnapping, bad dreams, death, absence of vital food sources, acute melancholia, blinding headaches, unruly sled dogs, lengthy visits by malevolent shamans, sound of geese overhead yet a sky absent of geese, and so forth. While there are myriad versions in Inuit oral literature of how Sedna came to dwell at the bottom of the sea—what to Western thought seems a lonely, marginalized place is the center of power—maintaining an entourage of spirit-assistants, keeping vigilant jurisdiction over the landscape, its human and animal residents, its weather, all contain at least one episode of family dysfunction born of greed, jealousy, fear, erotic tensions directly represented by violent weather, betrayal; all contain the motif of a young woman's resistance to marriage sequeing to larger modes of social discourse. Plot-wise, even the most disparate examples share a basic chronology: a. Sedna is a beautiful, young woman who lives with her father and whose nature is judged as "different" by her family and community at large; b. At some point Sedna is thrown into a raging sea by her father/a raven/vindictive cousins or siblings; c. When Sedna clasps her hands to the rim of the umiaq (large, open boat made of seal or walrus skin on a wooden frame) one or many persons hack at her finges with oars or knives; her fingers fall into the sea and become seals and other sea mammals, several of which (often the thumbs) accompany Sedna to the sea-bottom. "Sank-away-as-Sedna-did" is an Inuit phrase. Tormented by what befell her, her fury at mankind throughout time has remained unabated, yet inventively formalizes itself in modes of retribution, admonitions, humiliations aimed at preserving the oldest moral etiquette: it is for this reason that after a hunter catches a seal he drops fresh water into its mouth, a mandatory gesture to thank Sedna for her kindness in allowing him to feed his family. 2. the newest named "planet." On 15 March 2004 astronomers from Caltech Gemini Observatory and Yale University announced the discovery of the coldest, most distant object known to orbit our sun: object is twice as far from the sun as any other solar system object and three times farther than Pluto or Neptune. Standing on the surface of Sedna you could block the entire sun with the head of a pin held at arm's length. The orbit of Sedna is elliptical in the extreme; Sedna "does not follow received notions of gravity,"

Sedna

takes 10,500 years to orbit the sun. Inuit newspapers throughout the arctic debated whether Sedna herself would be pleased or insulted at having a planet named after her; opinions are sharply divided; one Inuit man is quoted, "It doest not matter what we think. It only matters what Sedna thinks—and what she does about it." Michael Omiuq, a disc jocky on NWT Radio, who often uses police or magistrate reports to cite transgressions—and name individuals—responsible for agitating Sedna who in turn causes terrible weather: he is a mythometeorologist. "Sedna will respond to global warming," he said. ALSO **Sednaist** *n.* Mr. Billy Imiatapuit, formerly of Repulse Bay, declared himself a "Sednaist." He read over NWT Radio a manifesto advocating that, challenging organizations such as the Sierra Club, the Nature Conservancy, Audobon Society, Gov. Interior Departments to sponsor a comprehensive study of Sedna as "environmental policy maker," and other aesthetic and practical concepts of environmental protection and conservation philosophy found in arctic mythologies and those of other native peoples world-wide. ALSO **Team Sedna** a soccer team proported to be coached by Sedna and composed of ghosts of men who fell through the ice as a result of mistreating sled dogs, ignoring or otherwise abusing children, of murder, of greed-in-hunting, or any other manner of ethical transgression; weather conditions providing, this team can be seen practising for international competition near various arctic outposts. Several nightwatchmen on deck of a Polish grain ship anchored near Churchill, Manitoba, reported seeing this team doing passing drills under a full moon on a summer's night. —HOWARD NORMAN

semi-flaccid money [seh-mee-fla'-sid muh'-nee] *n.* a form of political campaign donation introduced to circumvent the hard and soft money restrictions of the McCain-Feingold campaign finance reform bill of the early 21st century. Donations of semi-flaccid money were unlimited as long as the political candidate was willing to twirl three times in a circle while jumping up and down like a cymbal-crashing monkey. Ultimately judged both unconstitutional and insulting to cymbal-crashing monkeys, semi-flaccid money was replaced by the **Why Didn't We Think of This Earlier** campaign finance law, where all monetary donations to political candidates had to be matched with equivalent donations to public schools and health care. —JOHN WARNER

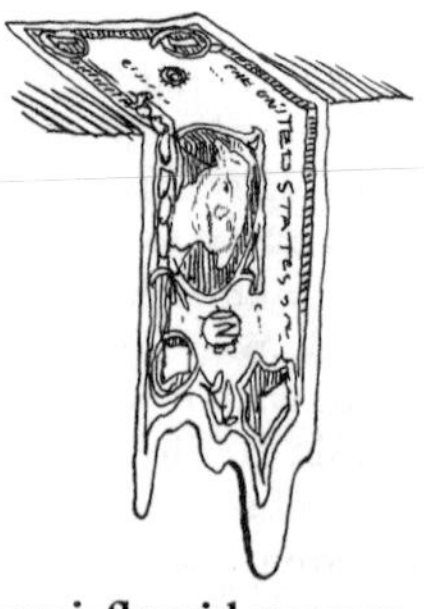

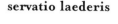

semi-flaccid money

serpico [sur'-pih-koh] *adj.* in final, undeniable widespread recognition of the badassness of the character from the 1973 Sidney Lumet film as represented through the simply transcendent performance of Al Pacino (post-*The Godfather*), a term of endearment and respect for a person of similar badassness, who can grow hair as s/he wants and/or party with models and/or study poetry and/or dance ballet at police precincts all the while fighting the Man. —BENJAMIN COHEN

servatio laederis [sur-vat'-ee-oh liy'-dur-is] *n.* from the cradle of humanity, *servatio laederis* has expressed the essence of what it means to be human; the modern definition of the term hails from a leader of great consequence, named Leo, who appeared first in the form of a servant. He hailed from the land of Siddhartha, and was a point of light between East and West. From these meager beginnings a great war was waged between the conscience of the heart and the intellect of the mind, and MLK's "nonviolent new militancy" was spawned, creating what is known today, affectionately, as the **Empire of the Broken**—the broken, the unadorned, the weak, the willing, a land characterized by agapé, by self-sacrificial love. As its rallying cry the Empire chose the term "ubuntu," an African concept brought to light by Tutu, meaning: I am human because of you, you are human because of me; we are always a part of one another. People greeted one another saying, "Where are you?" and answered one another saying, "I am with you." The Empire's action was that of Mandela who emptied a fellow-prisoner's chamber pot, the man too sick to move, and returning it clean said "Rest, my friend, it is nothing." Even of evil apartheid, Nelson said, "The truth does not suppress the dissenting voice." People were said to have liked the idea of all things relative, and at the same time liked some things absolute, like love. The Empire's Prague Spring was followed by the Velvet Revolution, in which there was no bloodshed, and no more sorrow, and **People Power I** brought Cory Corazon Aquino to power, wife of martyred Ninoy whom Marcos murdered; she was moral and beautiful and she loved her people, and her people loved her. Children were named Paulo and Che and Zora and Alice, after their heroes, and the color purple was the color of the nation, a womanist color that men adored. People locked arms in the street and shouted "Servatio laederis!" and touched one another on the cheek, and men went about saying, "A woman who knows your darkness and with her light has won from you a blessed peace, her kiss will make you whole." This could be your mother, or your sister, or your wife, or your friend. And women went about saying, "I thank you, God, for the love of good men." This could be your father, your brother, your husband, your friend. All across the world the dream was a unified dream, and in every land a multitude of revolutions made love their creed and servatio laederis the standard of their legitimate power and greatness. From the ancient tongue, servatio laederis is translated "servant leader." This is not the servant as slave or domestic; it is a willing mantle, and it means to serve as a mother serves her child and brings her life, or as a father holds his child aloft, illuminated, and sings her name. The modern philosopher-poet Greenleaf, before he died, left this definition: the true test of the servant leader is this, that those who are around the servant leader become more healthy, more wise, more free, more autonomous, and the least privileged of society benefit, or at least are not further deprived. He said people would no longer suffer the soulless to lead them, and that the only leaders of the Empire would be those who were put forward to lead because their servanthood had brought freedom and life to others. All this proved to be true, and by the death of good men and women new life arose, a field of humility, a realm without cynicism or woe, a country of women,a country of children,a place where men are loved—this, the Empire of the Broken.

—Shann Ray

seven dollar socialist [$7 soh'-shul-ist] *n.* an activist, usually found in wealthy, liberal cities like San

seven dollar socialist

Francisco, whose high tax bracket income affords him or her the luxury of their rabid, liberal views. Ex.: an Ipod-carrying, Jetta-driving, organic-tomato-eating protestor waving a placard reading *Socialism Now* while waiting in line to buy a $7 sandwich at Bi-Rite.

—NOAH HAWLEY

sex [seks] *n. v. adj. adv.* everything is sex. There is nothing that is not sex. There

sex

was a time, as recently as the early 20th century, when sex simply denoted penetration of the Male Penis into the Female Vagina. The term quickly expanded to include other activities, like oral and anal sex. (One could have sex without producing offspring.) Sex was flexible, it accommodated more: activities between more than two people at once, between one person and him or herself, and between no people at all. It was beautiful, in a way, as all forms of physical desire and expression were allowed into sex's generous arms. Sex became a verb (*"Go sex that phone for me"*), an adjective (*"That shirt is so sex"*), and even an interrogative (*"Sex?"*). But at a certain point—some scholars point to the middle of the 21st century—sex had taken on too much meaning, and, hence, lost its meaning. It traced the path of so many words in our language—computer, America, art—from Useless to Beautiful to Useless. *Sex sex; sex? Sex!* —JONATHAN SAFRAN FOER

sex-ray [seks-ray) *n.* a space-based weapon pieced together from the remains of the ill-fated "Star Wars" missile defense project; it shoots a psychoactive ray, making enemies at war want instead to have sex with one another. *Tensions escalated in the DMZ until a sex-ray blast released the homoerotic undercurrents in an orgy of reconciliation.*

sex-ray

—JOHN HENRY FLEMING

shadowlines [shad'-oh-leens] *n. pl.* shadows that are places of great buoyancy. Whether it be the vast circular shadow area cast by a cloud in a wide open fields, or a long thin shadow of a tall buildings on a city sidewalks, these dark places allow the walker to soar into the air, executing, if one wished, great aerial feats. Small shadows provide a bounce in a person's step or afford a walker the ability to pas de deux at will. If a person trips and falls into a shadow, the shadow protects the body from striking the ground. Shadow physics only apply to animate objects. A shadow cannot protect the beloved family gravy boat from smashing into pieces, though it might very much want to. One has to believe in the power of the shadow trampoline for it to be effective; therefore, it is most often children and the hopelessly romantic that experience the beauty and salvation of shadowlines.

—ELISSA SCHAPPELL

Shh Society of Hh *n.* the council of ical librarians who discovered hh (SEE **hh**) and founded the Interstitial States of America (SEE **ISA**). Long associated with the forces of repression and conservatism, librarians emerged in the early 21st century as the custodians of civil liberties. The shushing gesture of the finger raised to the lips was adopted and reconfigured as a gesture of fellowship among the radical librarians and their followers. Some linguists believe that the sound *shh* may be the origin of the word hh, though it is pronounced differently.

—SHELLEY JACKSON

shush cheese [shuush cheez] *n.* a sediment that forms in the mouth, made up of partial and withheld utterances, the essence of hush, and used as a lubricant or liniment. Massage a small piece of air with it and guide it into your ears and you will experience the aural equivalent of the private place inside the bell of a flower. Rub it on your tongue and your silences will be eloquent. The gaps between words become elastic, expansive; this looseness permits new words, and with the words, new thoughts.

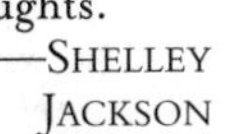

—SHELLEY JACKSON

shush cheese

silence parlor [siy'-lents pahr'-lur] *n.* a heavily soundproofed café, often equipped with noise-cancellation technology, in which consenting citizens may gather to talk, read, or sit quietly.

—JONATHAN FRANZEN

Simmerama [sih-mer-ah'-muh] *n.* 1. any movement, fueled by reason and love, that is slow in coming but unstoppable once it erupts. *Without a simmerama, there can be no peace.* 2. [*archaic*] the name of a short-lived but legendary restaurant chain, started by pop singers-turned-culinary activists Carnie Wilson and Jessica Simpson, who took the meaning of the Slow Food movement literally, specializing in dishes that take at least two days or longer to prepare (menu items included cassoulet, sauerbraten, and a variety of baked goods that require a sourdough starter). 3. a grassroots campaign in 2014 against the major U.S. fast food chains for their blatant falsification of foodstuff. The multi-decade-long scheme to fool the public was best exemplified by the marketing of the infamous McRibs, a sandwich made with a pork product shaped to resemble a slab of meat with the never present "bones" removed. (The mark **mcribs** has subsequently become generic and is used in everyday speech to mean fakery or a con of the highest order, especially those that involve or evoke an underlying mythology or factually specious belief system. *Mommy, I read in my history book that Bush the Second mcribbed the American public with the following justification for His War Against Iraq: "Freedom is the Almighty's gift to every man and woman in this world. And as the greatest power on the face of the earth, we have an obligation to help spread the freedom."*

—MONIQUE TRUONG

sincerity futures [sin-sayr'-uh-tee fyewt'-churz] *n. pl.* vastly popular and profitable options market, based on late-20th-century pollution credit program. Allows corporations and politicians to buy and sell their perceived sincerity, based on a formula computed from fluctuations measured in the citizenry's bioimplants. As experience has shown in the first years of the market, the credit (X) is deflated by such natural factors as taking responsibility, living up to expectations, and following through on promises. X is inflated by perceived loyalty, passion, religious scruples, "stick-to-it-iveness" and, most importantly, conviction. Individuals or parties with the most credits can sell them to those perceived to be insincere; the addition of X to the ledgers of the insincere allows them to balance their account books and, of course, avoid paying taxes on which they are not challenged, since they are now perceived as sincere.

—GLEN DAVID GOLD

Shelley Jackson / Shelley Jackson • ***Maira Kalman*** / Jonathan Franzen / Monique Truong / Glen David Gold

sinclair [sink-layr'] 1. *n.* a fervent, non-ironic political statement, usually espousing egalitarian values and frequently followed by an exclamation point. *This op-ed piece is simply brimming with sinclairs.* 2. *n.* a novel that is characterized by such statements. *We can trace the emergence of the sinclair to the moment, in October 2012, when American satire became inert.* 3. *v.i.* to exclaim earnestly, usually about political issues. *"Everyone deserves health insurance!" she sinclaired.* [2010–2020; named for American novelist and reformer Upton Sinclair, whose 1927 novel *Oil!* contained 1,539 exclamation points, not including the one in the title.] —CHRIS BACHELDER

sipapowwow [see'-puh-pow-ow] *n.* 1. a hybrid between a sipapu (an opening in a kiva through which modern Pueblo Indian gods emerge to sing, dance and generally heal the living) and a wormhole. 2. a floating, mysterious sipapu that began to appear in the year 2004 during the regular but secret meetings of the now defunct club of presidents, better known as the Skull and Bones Club. 3. a passageway through which singing spirits, thought to have been awakened by the steady beat of war drums, traveled to powwow. While surviving members of Skull and Bones maintain silence about what actually transpired at these meetings, common knowledge has it that the presidents and future presidents were inclined to give the spirits green cards if they agreed to provide entertainment and eat in the kitchen. But club members had a change of heart when the renowned poet and war hero, Chief Joseph of the Nez Pierce, began showing up. Best know for his anguished but decisive statement, "I will fight no more forever," the spirit of Chief Joseph was loud and tone-deaf. Club members, on hearing him sing, developed nasty cases of tinnitus and demanded that he leave, but the great chief, deducing they couldn't kill him again, improved on his great masterpiece, saying, "I will leave no more forever." So they left.

—ANN CUMMINS

skinicism [skin'-uh-siz-um] *n.* 1. the practice of assuming the best about an individual based on the color of his or her skin. (SEE **melanin** [*archaic*].) 2. a well-known, clever, and/or humorous compound maxim in which the first part is always true, but the second has repeatedly been proven to be entirely untrue. "Sticks and stones may break my bones, but words can never hurt me." 3. *Var. of* **skinaclysm** [skin'-uh-kliz-um] *n.* the violent upheaval that created sudden change in the earth's crust. In the year 2006, in an event much akin to shaking a leaf-strewn, dirty blanket out in the yard on a lazy and humid summer day, the earth's crust, all the way to its mantle, was given a good shakedown—due in part to a process known as plate tectonics and, in other part, to a scientific social phenomenon known as What-comes around-goes-around. This world-wide ripple lasted approximately three seconds, and immediately upon subsiding, the phenomenon caused a visible rearrangement of priorities, the rapid re-seeding of forest lands, and the complete destruction and toppling of certain structures. —T COOPER

skootch [skootch] 1. *n.* space between the ticks of a clock created by a skillful and focused use of **backtalk** in alternation with foretalk. By rubbing a moment of time back and forth with your voice, you can irritate it sufficiently that another day pearls under your palate and can be stretched and fattened like a drop under a tap by the continued exertions of the tongue. Eventually, you can puncture the elastic skin of this supplementary time bubble and it will readily expand to your dimensions and those of anyone you bring with you. 2. *v. i.* to hole up in a skootch. 3. *v.t.* to romance someone in a skootch: *I skootched her.* 3. *v.t.* to complete a project faster than linear time permits by retreating into a skootch: *"How did you write a 20-page essay in six minutes?" "I skootched it."* —SHELLEY JACKSON

skootch day [skootch day] *n.* entire day created by a time rollback through the concerted efforts of balktalkers. (SEE **backtalk.**) The government at first tried to ban these rogue days, fearing that they would be devoted to illegal drug use or conspiracy; scientists warned that the inequal distribution of extra time might throw chronology off altogether, but use of bootleg time became so widespread even among elected officials that the government finally decided to create official skootch days for all to enjoy. —SHELLEY JACKSON

skootch motel [skootch moh-tel'] *n.* a used skootch or cluster of skootches, available to the public and maintained by a custodian; also, any patch of flattened grass that can be recycled. —SHELLEY JACKSON

skootchy [skootch'-ee] *adj.* comfortable, well-fitting, permissive.—SHELLEY JACKSON

slacker [slak'-ur] *n.* a person who wears slacks.—BRIAN MCMULLEN

slacker

Slave Ghost [slayv gohst] *n.* scholars' claims that it was achieved with superior brain-generated genital power are not accurate, though the regrettable battle role of the multiple genders are simple enough to describe. The **Virginia Heterosexual Sons** battalions—most members having undergone rigorous body augmentation at Lyceum, usually including the implant of a hairless vagina on the back of the neck—presented an ominous front of 250 scantily clad, jeering brothers with nooses around their neck, with three equal rows behind them, to the wild, advancing Sisterhood apparelled in prophylactic masks, and also with nooses around their necks. From their pedestaled position up on **Bush Ridge** (the Line of Scrimmage), the Brotherhood's preponderance of erratic fire would have been effective—that is, would have subliminally achieved a significant number of jarring hits (dousings)—at over a hundred yards, but the Commanding Brothers, in a brilliant display of leadership tactics, reserved it until the girls were much closer. When the brothers, in a state of climax coaxed by extreme cerebral fillibration, had fired their semen projectiles at approximately 70 degree trajectories arcs, they were able, due to rigorous training at Fort Heatherwood Facility, including but not limited to the **Erotic Brain Techniques** of Valder, to "reload" and achieve discharge in roughly 30-40 seconds, eyes closed with hands stretched to the sky, mentally stimulating themselves while another fired. Overall, the result was the same: the projection at the indefatigable sisters of about two thousand precision-guided Semen-Tears per minute. —GABE HUDSON

sloudge [slowdj] *n.* the hours of analysis, usually on high-cable news networks, which follows breaking news, i.e. events which have just happened and which usually (but not always) follow

sloudge hour

the high-cable news dictum, "if it bleeds, it leads." Most sloudge occurs around shiny tables where overweight white men talk about such things as the liberal conspiracy, fiscal responsibility, and isolationist policies of revisionism. Expert speakers of sloudge were paid millions of dollars in the early years of the 21st century, not just to wag their double chins on television but to give speeches and write books. *The President's press conference was followed by over three hours of sloudge on MSNBC and six hours of sloudge on Fox-TV.* —STEPHEN KING

smoking jacket [smoh'-king ja'-ket] *n.* a loose-fitting, bubble-domed, tent-like garment equipped with powerful air filters and 800-foot retractable exhaust tubes, designed to accommodate smokers in restaurants and other public gathering places. —ART SPIEGELMAN

smoking jacket

soda jerk [soh'-duh djurk] *n.* 1. [*archaic*] a young man of poor complexion who works at a drugstore fountain for meager wages in the hopes of charming coeds, though he never succeeds. 2. a professional who behaves intolerably without the hourly infusion of one twelve-ounce can of caffeinated soft drink, most commonly Diet Coke. 3. a soft drink company executive who refuses to consume his own product due to "dentist's orders." 4. an individual who tosses his empty soft drink containers in with the regular trash declining to recycle them because the effort required would necessitate the downing of another such beverage, which, in turn, would create another trip to the restroom and "I'd never get anything positive done." 5. a wrestling hold made popular at the 2086 Hoboken Olympiad by the unassuming American gold medalist Joe Max Thwackle, who explained his winning technique to reporters by commenting, *"I just soda jerk 'em and down they go."* 6. formerly a peer-pressuring insult, common in American high-school hallways in the late 21st century, which later became an expression of prideful self-reference in a movement that largely eradicated underage binge-alcohol drinking along the Eastern Seaboard. —NICHOLAS DAWIDOFF

soracious [sohr-ay'-shus] *adj.* a desolate wit; intellectual humor fuelled by desperation. *Our foreign policy could use a few more soracious wonks.* —EDWARD HIRSCH

spamdam [spam'-dam] *n.* 1. an electronic wall containing the abandoned cyberspace network, constructed after the Penis Lengthening Plague of 1999–2056 proved impossible to control. 2. any cement blockade running along a superhighway. 3. a psychological manuever to avoid tedious conversation. *Mark's knock-knock jokes couldn't penetrate my spamdam.* ALSO **spamdam, thank you ma'am** idiomatic expression indicating a refusal of social tedium. *The Johnsons took slides of their vacation? Spamdam, thank you ma'am.* —DANIEL HANDLER

spaniel *v.* [span'-yul] (fr. spaniel, any of several breeds of medium-sized dogs) to find a shaft of sunlight pouring through a window on a cold winter day, curl up in the puddle

spaniel

Stephen King / art spiegelman • ***art spiegelman*** / Nicholas Dawidoff / Edward Hirsch / Daniel Handler / Diane Ackerman • ***Richard Sala***

of warmth it creates on the rug, and doze with doglike dereliction. *I think I'll just spaniel for an hour or so before I begin work.*
—DIANE ACKERMAN

Speshockian Songbook [speh-shahk'-ee-an sahng'-buuk] *n.* a compendium of "lost" songs that were sung or hummed by 20th-century "homemakers" while cleaning, dusting, or working in the kitchen. —D.C. BERMAN

spicometer [spih-kah'-muh-tur] *n.* an instrument that measures the amount of bigotry towards people of Latino origin. Comparable to **honkymeters** or **niggometers** or **fagometers**, etc. With the advent of Hybridity and Humanhood, all these meters that measure bigotry towards specific groups of people are almost obsolete. Originally placed on borders, places of business, etc. to render transparent any untoward and obfuscated prejudice toward specific groups of people. Readings of these meters were published annually and high readings resulted in measures that would increase the infusion of target group until the area or business was fully integrated and/or meter readings reached zero. —JULIA ALVAREZ

spiderhole [spiy'-dur-hohl] *n.* 1. a small dark place, usually a hole, where a spider, usually, lives. 2. a hole or hole-shaped concavity in the terrain of arid, mountainous regions where candy bar wrappers and unwashed, bearded men can be found. 3. slang for a sleight-of-hand maneuver, typically employed during desperate times. (ALSO *v.* to redirect attention from a terribly evident failure to a victory of dubious value) 4. crude euphemism for the human nether region from which the seemingly impossible can be extracted. *He sure did pull that election right out of his dang spiderhole.* 5. an incantation, that, when pronounced with an American Southwest accent, over and over and over again, promises to soothe a populace into forgetting about holes in logic, holes in the truth, and the other glaringly bottomless holes that surround them.
—HEIDI JULAVITS

spiderhole

spleen [spleeen!] *n.* 1. an organ in the human body subject to the heart's ire at the afflicted body politic. 2. violent mirth at verbal camouflage or at ludicrous posturing in military gear; excessive laughter at flawed, weak, and/or faith-based intelligence. 3. plain anger at inoffensive puppy nips of television news. 4. [*colloq.*] an inflated Frisbee; a rubbery ball pumped with gasping American hope, put into play to defeat hubris and outwit our despair. —MAUREEN HOWARD

spleen

spoucher *n.* [spow'-chur] a wooden vessel for conveying water. (N.B. This definition has remained constant since Middle English.) —DANIEL HANDLER

spunctual [spunkt'-choo-ul] 1. *adj.* excited, on time, and excited to be on time. 2. *n.* an adherent of spunctuality.
—BRIAN MCMULLEN

spunctuality [spunkt-choo-al'-it-ee] *n.* widespread, informal youth movement characterized by symbiotic promptness and enthusiasm; a generic term evolved from **Toledo Spunctuality** and **Good Ole Toledo Spunctuality**, two phrases coined in 2009 by journal-

Diane Ackerman / D.C. Berman / Julia Alvarez / Heidi Julavits • ***Maira Kalman*** / Maureen Howard • ***David Heatley*** / Daniel Handler / Brian McMullen / Brian McMullen ists who claimed the phenomenon was local to northwest Ohio until education officials from Michigan and Indiana told them it was not.

—BRIAN MCMULLEN

squawkback [skwah'-bak] *n.* parrot-like repetition of a question by the respondent; this invariably precedes a lie. Squawkback allows an ostensive acknowedgment of the question while providing the respondent with a mental pause in which to formulate a falsehood. The repeated phrase may be delivered in either a thoughtful or an incredulous tone. Ex.: *"Was I aware of this? Well..."; "Did that influence my decision? Why..."; "Was it a mistake? Well..."*

—PAUL COLLINS

SRV Afterlife [es ahr vee af'-tur-liyf] *n.* a no-longer practiced funerary service where the expired customer's soul was stored on an abandoned Stevie Ray Vaughn webpage; a webpage expected to drift for eternity through cyberspace like a ghostship. —D.C. BERMAN

Starwatch [stahr'-wahtch] *n.* United States, and later in much of the English-speaking world, the month of September became known as Starwatch (SEE ALSO **Extinguishing**) around the midpoint of the third decade of the 21st century. The genesis of the name stems from the August 12 speech given by President Vera P. Funk to the AARP's annual meeting, when she infamously told 450 assembled senior citizens that in her administration social security reform would be "like the solar system—at the center of our galaxy." The reaction from astronomers and space enthusiasts was swift. Kurt Silverman, chairman of the NCA (SEE ALSO **Cosmologists' Unions**) told VBC News, "It's been known since the 1970s that there is a black hole at the center of our galaxy the size of a couple of million solar masses; it is only today that we've found out a similarly sized black hole is located inside the skull of our president."

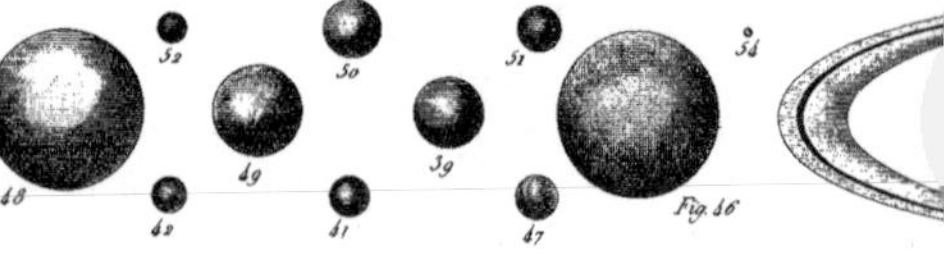

In subsequent days it was leaked that President Funk, who had grown up in Los Angeles, had never actually even seen a star, and had only seen the moon four or five times, through the heavily tinted window of her then-gubernatorial limousine. When told by her press secretary that the solar system was actually located on a distant, spiraling arm of the Milky Way, which in turn was merely one minor galaxy in the Local Group, which was just one speck in the Virgo Cluster, which was just one speck of one large-scale cluster expanding into the universe, she reportedly said, "You have to be shitting me."

The Funk administration quickly mounted a series of public-relations campaigns in order to demonstrate its nascent enthusiasm for sky-watching, distributing star maps with the presidential logo, funding telescopes at schools, and ultimately building a personal-use observatory on the south lawn of the White House. But it was not until the famous September 8 **Extinguishing of Lights** in Washington D.C., that the phenomenon took hold in the public consciousness. At 11:59 the president mounted a dais hastily erected over the Mall Reflecting Pool and declared to the cameras, "The stars will bloom above our Capitol once more." She threw a large silver switch (purely theatrical), while in a nearby van a CIA tech specialist, working in concert with D.C. Electricity, extinguished every light source (including television and computer screens, where the President's face had been only a moment before) in a hundred-mile radius. Rather than panic, as some of the president's advisors had predicted, children and adults alike poured into streets and backyards to gape at the swath of Milky Way draped from horizon to zenith and back down again.

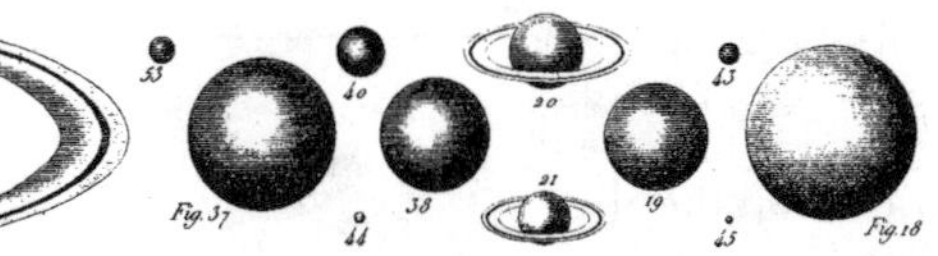

Courtyards filled, parks overflowed, public transportation halted.

The transformation that ensued was rapid. Within a week Cleveland, Chicago, and Miami all staged citywide Extinguishings of their own, and before the end of the month Las Vegas had instituted the Tuesday night BlackOuts that continue there to this day. Homegrown observatories appeared on lawns. Nineteen new solar systems were discovered. Curiosity quotients (SEE ALSO **Bristol Curiosity Meter**) in public school students reached unprecedented levels. In bookstores, poetry sections tripled in size. By the following summer, Minnesota junior Senator Nathaniel Cormier Jr. introduced legislation that proposed changing the name of the month of September to Starwatch and ordered that every light source in the country be extinguished annually on the night of the fall equinox. The bill passed 99-1, and was signed into law on Starwatch 1. The first Starwatch Nationwide Extinguishing was held on Starwatch 21, 2036.

This national transformation was matched only by the personal revolution undertaken by President Funk, who began giving nighttime press conferences during the Perseid meteor showers, and who, after leaving office, became the world's single largest fundraiser for and contributor to the physical sciences. "What I want to know," she demanded from her deathbed, "is what space is—what, really is the ultimate medium?" On Starwatch 19, 2071, her corpse was jettisoned into space, wearing her trademark double-strand of pearls over a navy-blue pantsuit, so that she could, as her last will and testimony directed, "float in perpetuity with the rest of the interstellar detritus." —ANTHONY DOERR

steroidoil [stayr-royd'-oyl] *n.* 1. a naturally occurring, fat-soluble compound having a 17 carbon-atom ring as a basis and including the sterols and bile acids. Steroidoil is a combustible substance used for energy in vehicles and humans. Drilled for in deserts and arctic regions, sold by the barrel in both crude and refined form, the compound is used all over the world. Excessive use of steroidoil in the late 20th and early 21st century was linked to global warming, personality changes, and gender ambiguity. Attempts were made to curtail use of steroidoil but solar energy, electric power and vitamins never measured up. These puny competitors were no match for the steroidoil industry as represented by such corporate giants as Hallisterexmobil, British Steroidoil, Chevsteroil, and Standard Sterococo (a wholly owned subsidiary of Time Warner). Despots were installed, propped up, or unseated in the quest for steroidoil; wars were fought under the guise of looking for weapons of mass destruction when in fact the real prize was vast reserves of steroidoil. Actors pumped by injections of steroidoil not only gained national recognition as movie heros but were elected to high public office as long as a steady stream of liver transplants were provided. 2. 21st-century slang, meaning pumped or over the top. *He's so steroidoil!; Totally steroidoil!*

—SUSAN DAITCH

story yeast [stoh'-ree yeest] *n.* concept first proposed by Bay Area advertising executive Owen Bly [1963-c.2058, frozen for future thawing] to describe the mysterious ingredient that causes details in otherwise non-fiction accounts of personal anecdotes to grow over time. *He had run away from a mugger, but with the advent of story yeast and a couple of beers, it seemed that several muggers were running away from him.* Largely forgotten until the presidential campaign of 2044, when debates were replaced by the tremendously entertaining Tall Tale Telling Competitions. —GLEN DAVID GOLD

Styx [stiks] *n. pl.* the Interstitial Stacks, where uncategorizable and as yet unwritten books are shelved. The Shh or council of interstitial librarians sought out and even commissioned interstitial books, favoring expecially those books that presented cataloguing challenges, e.g., a highly technical study of tooth reenameling techniques translated from the Icelandic into English rhyming couplets. Some of these were crossover successes, to the consternation of the publishing industry, which subsequently funded, with little success, a series of would-be interstitial texts, hoping to tap into this market.

—SHELLEY JACKSON

superreflection [soo-pur-ree-flek'-shun] *n.* the state of pondering a thought; a condition of introspection; the most intense kind of thinking in which thought mirrors thought. *At times like these, Gwen insisted, her superreflection caused a kind of vertiginous insight.*

—LYNNE TILLMAN

suturitis

suturitis [soot-chur-iy'-tis] *n.* any of several physical disfigurements due to excessive plastic surgery. Characterized by ill-fitting, flaccid skin (focal skin necrosis, or skin death), unyielding breasts, tissue protrusions, leakage, and general malaise. Effects include Snoopy Deformity (prominence of the nipple-areolar complex), Double Trouble (implants that don't settle down), and the Michael Jackson (permanent pigment change).

—SHOSHANA BERGER

Suvada

Suvada [soo-vah'-duh] *Geog.* an island off the coast of California, lat. 33°30' N, long. 122°10' W. Suvada is known for its deepwater harbors, its broad beaches, its verdant forests, and for the multitude of fish that circle its shores, making the island a paradise for fishermen and snorkelers. The origins of Suvada are less well-known and merit a mention here on account of their extreme peculiarity. In the 20th and 21st centuries, as is commonly known, the American landscape was dominated by **automobiles**, four-wheeled vehicles powered by gasoline combustion engines. As the automobiles had no natural predators, their size tended to increase; the fossil record shows that by the beginning of the 21st century, the American automobile was larger than an adult male hippopotamus. The sudden disappearance of the automobile has occasioned much speculation among paleolocomologists. Some suggest that the vehicles, adapted to the temperate seasons of the 20th century, became defunct because of changes in the climate, while others hold that the automobiles lived until their gasoline supply was exhausted. Neither of these hypotheses explains the relative scarcity of automobile remains in North America. Prosseter was the first to suggest that the automobiles, perhaps sensing that their demise was imminent, drove themselves to the Atlantic and Pacific Oceans, to the Great Lakes and the Gulf of Mexico, and disappeared

Glen David Gold / Shelley Jackson / Lynne Tillman / Shoshana Berger • ***Richard Sala*** / Paul La Farge • ***R. Sikoryak*** beneath the waves. Two bodies of evidence lend credence to this unlikely seeming story: first, the observed behavior of lemmings, which are, genetically speaking, the automobile's closest extant relative; and second, the fact, verified again and again by divers, that the island of Suvada rests on a foundation of countless automobile skeletons, aggregated at this point on the continental shelf by the current. If you dive in Suvada's harbors you can still see them, the bare white bones of the great cars, with fish swimming in and out of their eyes and mouths.

—PAUL LA FARGE

synempath [sih'-num-path] *n.* 1. the lubricated junction between two evolved nerve cells, transmitting an impulse to empathize with aliens. 2. an electronic beat that circumvents a phobic's instinctive debilitating fear when confronted with the unknown. 3. a mutation occurring in neurological paths, human and other, sometime in the 21st century that caused general disorientation and dizziness among Earth and Galactic leaders and resulted in their permanent euphoric confusion. 4. a distraction among leaders resulting in intergalactic evolutionary leaps of all species.

—ANN CUMMINS

T

tagdot [tag'-daht] *n.* hard-boiled detective slang. The microscopic serial number inscribed on every bullet and piece of ammunition manufactured and sold in the United States, per the Ammunition Registration Act. Operating under the principle that "Guns Don't Kill People, Bullets Do," the law gives hunters and other gun enthusiasts full access to their weapons, while strictly tracking the sale of ammunition. Thus, every bullet fired can be linked to its purchaser and, in the event they're not the same person, linked to the shooter, creating a web of legal liability for every weapons discharge. Although tagdots can be unlawfully erased, the process leaves traceable marks and requires access to specialized illegal equipment, creating further difficulties for the would-be offender. The act is credited with sharply curtailing gun-related crime and preventing bullet access to the violently deranged. *Doll, get the tagdot from Forensics—we'll lift the perp and make it to Smoky Joe's for Happy Hour.*

—Ken Kalfus

talkies

talkies [tahk'-eez] *n.* a cinematic projection of a story involving human beings who talk to one another and don't try to kill each other. This was a word that had briefly flourished in the late 1920s with the advent of sound in cinema, but was eventually dropped from the OED as the age of "silent pictures" (the converse of "talkies") was more or less forgotten. Then in 2022 movies started to be officially called **killies**, since all films were now about killing. Subsequently, rebel filmmakers began to make small, underground humanistic dramas where people actually talked; no firearms or piercing weapons were allowed. The word "talkies" came back into being, though with a slightly different connotation than its earlier meaning, which simply referred to "talking" that could be *heard*, where as "talkies" now implied a whole worldview (pacifistic in nature). Eventually, these underground films became so popular by mid-century that they replaced "killies" as the leading form of cinematic entertainment.

—Jonathan Ames

Tallahassee Memory Bank *n.* archive based in Tallahassee, Florida, where secretaries of defense, presidents, generals, soldiers, and victimss of war store records and experiences so they may be easily accessed by future generations. Anyone making a decision as to whether America should or must or will go to war must first absorb all of the experiences—the overwhelming majority being horrific and unforgettable—deposited in this collective memory vessel. Since the establishment of the Institutional Memory Act of 2010, the U.S. has only once gone forward, determining that the slaughter of Sudanese tribes in Darfur necessitated action. Located in Tallahassee to avoid outside distraction. —VENDELA VIDA

targetburgizen [tahr-get-bur'-giz-en] *n.* 1. any one of a number of loosely organized groups or squatters who take over a retail outlet or cultural institution as free communal living space; often distinguished by colorful knit clothing and/or occupations such as goatherding. 2. any politically radical group that employs handicrafts. *During the 2006 marriage riots, the mid-Atlantic targetburgizens distinguished themselves by the peaceful use of yarn, felt, and holography.*

—STACEY D'ERASMO

tealebrity [tee-leb'-rih-tee] 1. *n.* the distinction or honor publicly bestowed on teachers; closely related to **tearship.** 2. *v.t.* to adore or pay divine honors to a teacher as a deity; to reverence a teacher with supreme respect and veneration. —KAREN SHEPARD

telerally [teh'-luh-ral-ee] 1. *n.* the ability, through the use of the Internet and advanced hologram technology, for thousands of citizens to convene in one location—often in miniaturized form—without ever leaving their desks. 2. *v.* to convene in this manner. *With the help of a carefully placed mole, the students were able to telerally on top of the President's pot roast as he flew on Air Force One to Miami.* —KEN FOSTER

terrarism [teh'-rah!-riz-um] *n.* the popular movement that grew up in response to the ill-fated "War on

terrarism

Terrorism" of the early 21st century. Ending the cycles of violence brought about by self-perpetuating bellicose responses to terrorism, the movement became visible as international clusters of like-minded individuals began working together against all odds for more equable redistribution and preservation of the world's resources, thereby dismantling the impoverished breeding grounds of terrorism. **terrarists** *n.* environmentalists, labor organizers, doctors, teachers, scientists, social workers, journalists, artists and writers, and, in rare instances, even lawyers devoted to transcending parochial interests in order to work for the good of a global community.

—ART FLOWERCHILDE SPIEGELMAN, MINISTER OF POSITIVE PROPAGANDA

terrorism [teh'-roh-riz-um] *n.* 1. the unlawful use or threatened use of force or violence by a person or an organized group against people or property with the intention of intimidating or coercing societies or governments, often for ideological or political reasons. (*American Heritage Dictionary*) 2. cheating on a test. *60 of the 62 international terrorists, according to a March story in the* Philadelphia Inquirer, *turned out to be Middle Eastern students who had cheated on a test; specifically, they had paid others to take an English proficiency exam required for college or graduate school.* 3.

unionization of educational employees. *Education Secretary Rod Paige called the National Education Association, the nation's largest teachers union, "a terrorist organization."* 4. a government unaligned with America. *President George Bush sent an ultimatum to the world's leaders today: "You are either with us or you are with the terrorists."* 5. drug trafficking. *Drug Czar Asa Hutchinson said Tuesday, "It is clear that there is not really a distinction between the drug traffickers and the terrorist organizations."* (SEE ALSO: **Drug War, Taft Hartley Act, Political Violence.**)

—STEPHEN ELLIOTT

Tex Hex [teks heks] *v.* the process by which a notorious Texas family hoodooed the American people in the year 2000, sprinkling concentrated doses of poppy dust throughout the greater United States but especially in Florida, lulling millions to sleep while the family staged a political coup and installed a rogue government. A four-year period of nightmares followed, during which the rogues led sons and daughters of the heartland on a wild goose chase (the geese disguised as Humvees) in search of WMDs. While no WMDs were found, the Humvees stirred up quite a mess, spewing dust that froze in the frigid Mideastern air. The crystallized rock fell like snow, knocking the heartland's children on their noggins, awakening them and causing them to cry out for their fabled Aunt Emily (*colloq.*: Em). Mass insomnia ensued until the sons and daughters finally abandoned their Humvees, charged back across the ocean chanting the well-known battle cry, "There's No Place Like Home." —ANN CUMMINS

Theory Delusion [theer'-ee duh-loo'-zjun] *n.* a widespread late-20th-century belief, now discredited, that the states of pleasure and pain are inseparable. —LUCIA PERILLO

throm [thrahm] 1a. *n.* a vast persistent low-pitched percussive sound often associated with thunder and/or drums and/or the human heart in moments of quietude following periods of great peril and/or sorrow. 1b. any of a number of large drums used by the survivors of the Wars of Religion (2001–2018 A.D.) to communicate across large distances. Generally cylindrical in shape, six to eight feet high and ten to twelve feet in diameter, and most often composed of plywood and sheet metal, these drums first appeared in the weeks following the **Day of Darkness** (2/27/18) and were particularly useful in conveying the discovery of food and/or water and/or reasons not to slash one's veins. 1c. any form of aural, non-linguistic communication. 2a. *v.* to produce a vast persistent low-pitched percussive sound. 2b. to communicate a strong emotion. 2c. to hope. 2d. to love.

—ROY KESEY

Tiffany [tihf'-uh-nee], *n.* 1. this word is a noun in the sense that monsoon, lightning, and tides are nouns, in that rarely is a modifier (such as "New York jewelry retailer," etc.) used or needed. It might also be called an expanded noun, in that the early days of the word's existence and usage, it did indeed refer only to the fine crystal and jewelry store. 2. the word then matured, all but leaping the graftstock of its origins, metamorphosing during the darkest days of the no-longer new nation of the so-called United States. Previously associated with an unsustainable and soulless opulence of the type now mostly only ready about in history books (SEE **Halliburton**), the word appears to have skipped a linguistic groove in the manner of a train leaving its tracks to reverse course entirely—and just in time.

Roughly defined, the more evolved and newer meaning of Tiffany's has to do with the quality of a surprised state of grace, a light at the end-of-the-tunnel phenomenon, when previously no light was even expected. The newer meaning of the word was midwifed by environmental activists, including the group Earthworks, who spent years educating Tiffany CEO, Michael Kowalski, about the proposed Rock Creek mine, targeted for the rocky, snowy crags of northwest Montana's Cabinet-Yaak ecosystem, in the Kootenai National Forest.

Driven by desperation and a crumbling sense of wildness, environmental activists—likewise maturing beyond the old sixties-era strategies of petition-signing, placard-waving, and giant puppetry—were going on the offensive, trying to strike the enemy in the only sensate place remaining beneath the corporations' lithified carapace of greed—the glowing nerve-nexus of the beasts' greedcenter, an assemblage of primitive neurons and ganglia generally referred to as market share and per unit cost of production.

Having convinced lumber outlets such as Home Depot that there was a curious advantage to marketing boards certified to have been milled from non-old growth timber, activists began attempting to spread the revolutionary message that there might actually be economic benefit to doing good, and being good. (For a historical perspective, this was during the days when free mercury levels were being increased, and clouds of loose asbestos swirled across the land like dustdevils as certain and select corporations received Congressional immunity. Other weapons of mass destruction—MTBE, trichorethylene, cyanide, and hundreds of others—were allowed to be reinjected into rural people's drinking water, by various oilfield companies (SEE **Halliburton**), although progressive/liberal city councils in outposts such as Eugene, Seattle, and San Francisco were able prevent these additions from being used in their gasoline (the fuel once used by automobiles). (SEE **Iraq, Middle East, George W. Bush.**))

The proposed Rock Creek mine was called the poster child for the kind of abusive mining that once proliferated under the 1872 Mining Act, an archaic legislation passed before women and blacks could vote. (Native Americans were not allowed to vote until 1939, when this country's final transfer-of-authority was completed, just in time, coincidentally, for Native Americans to enter the armed services.) Under the 1872 Mining Act, prospectors—multinational mining companies—didn't have to to pay royalties on the treasures they could pry and blast and poison and gouge from the public lands. Following the extraction and liquidation of those minerals, the multinationals were then awarded fee (and free) title to those once-pristine lands, which were often then subdivided into ranchettes.

One particular piece of legislation however stood in the way of some mountains being leveled. The Wilderness Act prohibits machines and roads in areas designated as wilderness. In all of northwest Montana (at the time of this reversal of word-meaning), there was only one slender sliver of designated wilderness—the Cabinet Mountains Wilderness—despite the fact that this was, and still is, some of the wildest country in the Lower Forty-Eight.

A mining company, Revett, made up of a coalition of the same principals who had ridden various other mining ventures into bankruptcy before disassembling and then reforming under different names—these "new" companies spilling from out of the old like amoebic dysentery—proposed to place one of the world's largest copper and silver mines in the heart of the Cabinet Mountains. It's an old strategy by mining companies, under the 1872 Act: go straight to the most pristine, environmentally sensitive area available, grab one of those permits (in the case of Rock Creek, so vile and bilious was the attempt that even under the "freedoms" of the 1872 Act, it took over sixteen years before the alignment of stars—which is to say, the second Bush Administration, and a new Secretary of Interior, and an administration-friendly Supreme Court, yadda yadda—was such that that permit was finally granted).

Upon receiving this kind of valuable permit, the mining company then waits for the environmentalists to sing like—what? canaries?—and come running to this-or-that penny-stock fly-by-night start-up mining company and buy the permit back for tens of millions of dollars.

When that happens, the little pissant re-starts are, well, good as gold, And when it doesn't—well, the permitee waits for one global disturbance or another—a war in the Middle East, say—to flare up, and then, when metal prices blip upward, they scurry up to Toronto and do an IPO, and then go through the motions of building a mine, clawing away just enough mountain—five or ten years' worth—to get a local economy of humans next to the mine invested personally in the mine—taking jobs at the mine, building their lives around the mine's existence—schools, churches, that sort of thing—before running out of money and bailing, leaving behind a toxic Superfund clean-up site of heavy metals, cyanide, arsenic, and half-a-hundred other waterborne surprises, at which point the taxpayers step in yet again...

I'm getting to the part about Tiffany's, and the new definition.

So Rock Creek was chosen, partly for the ore that is said to lie within the heart of the mountain, but also, I believe, because it is in the narrowest spot of the only protected wilderness in northwest Montana—that skinny rock-and-ice spine of the Cabinet Mountains Wilderness. In the Rock Creek watershed, the wilderness tapers to but a quarter of a mile wide: four hundred and forty yards!

Even this, however, the mining company insists it must have.

Because the Wilderness Act precludes mechanized activity within its confines, the clever lads and laddies with the Rock Creek permit—aided and abetted by various government agencies and institutions such as the U.S. Fish & Wildlife Service and U.S. Forest Service—have been positing that because their mine will be, like, under the wilderness, and in the wilderness, but not, like, on top of it, it's legal—or so they say—even though the blasting for their tunnel below will threaten to drain away the fragile alpine lakes that sit atop that skinny spine like little wild blue blossoms amidst the craggy castles of stone.

And even though the belch and scent roar, the continuous traffic and continuous light of the processing facility—the hammer-and-tong crush of entire mountains being gnawed out, leached and processed, marrow-sucked for filings of silver and copper—will be encamped on the wilderness boundary itself, like the world's largest and permanent encampment of unruly Winnebango partiers—

I'm almost to the part about Tiffany's—

—and even though there'll be nearly a square-mile pit created for the toxic sludge—the "tailings," as it's so delicately called, these ground-up remnants of what was once the public's wildlands—and even though there will be 100 million tons of the wilderness' ore dug out—stolen—and chemically treated, with billions of gallons of contaminated wastewater discharged into pristine Rock Creek, where bull trout—an endangered species—live, and into the Clark Fork River, where taxpayers just finished spending $186 million for clean-up from an earlier mine in this area, managing to finally make the river just barely safe enough so that it could receive a new dose of poisons—and even though there may be only ten grizzly bears (that penultimate of endangered species) left in all of the Cabinet Mountains—

Even with all this, and more, the new powers-that-be say not to worry; in the words of one Revett official, the public "will hardly even know we're there."

It is in this kind of toxic political environment that an on-the-ground activist in northwest Montana resides, year after year, decade after decade: asbestos fibers swirling from sawn-off mountaintops, coal-fired mercury levels rising, Canadian coalbed methane mining poisoning the groundwater, grizzlies and trout vanishing, old growth forests being liquidated—wilderness, the last precious wildness, swirling down the drain of time and memory like one of those high blue mountain lakes punctured by a dynamite blast from below. And in the face of such unrelenting iniquity, such chronic evildoing—outspent, outmuscled, a hundred-thousand-to-one—there are days, you cannot help it, there are days when your chin drops and your shoulders slump. You still show up on the front lines each day, and you still do the work: but so long has the gale-force been in your face, and so severe the world's howling in your ears, that you forget to envision victory. You're simply enduring, and trying to hold on, like perhaps the mountains themselves. There is a tendency, a danger, to forget joy. On the darkest days, you might even think that all is lost.

And then one day you wake up and see that there is a full-page ad in the *Washington Post*. Like a white dove, this ad has settled down into the city's center, bearing a message. The message has come from within the heart of the establishment. It is not you, the rank outsider hermit-infidel, howling decade after decade from afar, whose message has made it over the castle walls, but rather, that same message coming now from within.

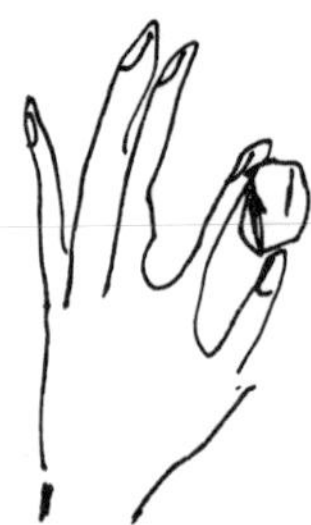

In that ad, the CEO of Tiffany & Co. is admonishing, shaming, the Chief of the Forest Service for having issued the permit—is saying, in essence, that the 1872 Mining Act is a sham, and needs reform. The king of diamonds, king of the glittering fruits of mining, is telling the Chief of the Forest Service that which the Forest Service, of all agencies, should already know: that "some of our most significant lands should be protected." Mr. Kowalski, the CEO, calls it "egregious." And back on the home front, on the battlefield, the citizen-activist's heart swells with joy, with pride, and with that most burdensome of extravagances, hope—and reads on:

"This obsolete law ... virtually gives away public lands ... to private interests. It remains a perverse incentive for mining in wilderness areas, near scenic watersheds, around important coldwater fisheries, and in other fragile ecosystems—all of which are inappropriate for mineral development...

"...This precious real estate should be available to Americans with diverse interests including hunting, fishing, and hiking in unspoiled areas.

"We at Tiffany & Co. understand that mining must remain an important industry. But like some other businesses benefiting from trade in precious metals, we also believe that reforms are urgently needed."

Am I reading this correctly? the activist wonders. Where did that come from—these psalms from the mouth of one previously thought or assumed to be the demon? Have I finally awakened into a newer, finer world, did I go to sleep for some indeterminate time and arise years later to some brighter, shining place wherein civility, wisdom, humility, tolerance, tenderness, and foresight—all the old played-out, gone-away things—have returned? Am I dreaming? the activist wonders, crinkling the paper to hear the sound of it, reading the ad once again, and for the first time, he or she says the word aloud, Tiffany's.

In the end, perhaps it should not have been so surprising, nor seemed so amazing. Time and again, I fear there is a dullheaded tendency among our species, too often so mentally butt-planted upon the couch of security, or perceived security, to assume that all is fixed, all is decided, all is predestined and foreordained. We have waived or ceded the freedom to resist, to rebel, and even, I fear some days, to imagine. We view the world as it is presented to us and, from habit, accept it. Black is black and white is white, scruffy peaceniks are naive idealists and NYC CEOs are ruthless corporate killers.

And yet: we forget that a single flaming tiny thing—one person, one spark, one letter of the alphabet—one anything—can still roll back the temporary facade of the world-as-it-is to reveal another world. And perhaps in that revelation is the world-to-come, while other times in the scrolling-back, it is the world-as-it-was that resurfaces and is shown once more: sometimes in precise replica, though other times with variations that might be profound, or might be subtle. The eye blurs, and the world changes not in a day, or in a four-year election cycle, but in a single instant, and the truth—the real truth—is revealed. The roadside marquis that advertises movie rentals, VIDEO EXCITEMENT, appears for a moment to spell VIDEO EXCREMENT. A highway exit-sign advertising GOD FOOD—the heart quickens!—reveals, alas, only GOOD FOOD.

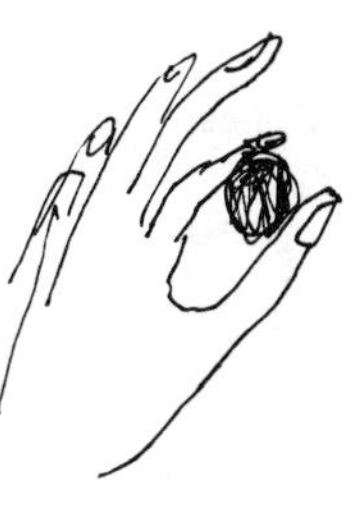

A posted NO HUNTING appears as NO HURTING, and, closer to home, and nefariously, IN GOD WE TRUST appears—for just a nanosecond, mind you—to confess, IN GOLD WE TRUST. The sandwich board outside the plush hotel advertising VALET PARKING is revealed—again, in and for but an instant—to declare WALLET PARKING.

Even the ears join in on this quiet and not-so-secret rebellion. Listening to the public radio business show about stocks and bonds, MARKET PLACE—an end-of-day report on the deification of wealth—the Boston accent pronouncing the name of the show one day sounds to this fatigued listener like MAGGOT PLACE.

The world shifts, flexes, rises like a sleeping animal, yawns, and stretches. The world is alive, we do not own it, nor do we control it. The world is unruly, the world will not be chained or defeated. To the ear, affluent becomes effluent, tourists become terrorists. The smallest one thing can change other things entirely. Even children—especially children—join in on the revolution, thinking that it is not an old mine that is buried far back in the Cabinet Mountains Wilderness, where hardscrabble prospectors first found the traces of silver, copper and gold, and scratched out a tunnel—not an old mine, but a mind. The mind of the mountains.

On our annual hike up into Rock Creek, I do not dissuade the children from this conceit, so that even diamonds, in their child-speak, are thought now to come from dime-minds. And a word like "Tiffany's," previously thought to represent renegade profligate extravagant excess, now seems demure, joyful, giving, prudent; and I am reminded again of that which I once believed as a child, which is that the vote of even one man, and one woman, makes a difference.

—Rick Bass

timespace [tiym'-spays] *n.* the point in time and space when that which is in time and space is forced into being by that which is outside time and space. Timespace was discovered by physicists at the University of Michigan in 2032. "In lay-persons' terms, timespace is the point at which the universe is created. Because timespace exists both inside and outside time and space, it exists all the time in all space. There is no past in timespace. Timespace exists only in the present, which includes the past as well as the present and the future. It is the Big Bang here and now, the foundation of every person's thought, feeling, and action." (*The New York Times.*) The discovery of timespace has given rise to a categorical moral imperative that has been adopted throughout the world: what is thought or felt, or done in time and space, is thought, felt, or done inside and outside all time and all space. For example, one who willfully kills, will willfully kill both inside and outside all time and all space, forever, while one who loves, will love both inside and outside all time and all space, forever. Timespace is the objective manifestation of the religious ideal of eternal justice. After the discovery of timespace, the experiences of those portrayed in Dante Alighieri's (1265–1321) poem *Divina Commedia* are no longer interpreted, as they were for centuries, as expressions of moral allegory, but, instead, as expressions of moral fact.
—LAWRENCE JOSEPH

timespace

transplendicate [tranz-splen'-dih-kayt] *v.i.* the process, when running an MRI machine in reverse, of transferring to another or having transferred to oneself the essential splendor of a person, place, or thing. *In order to finish her Ph.D in art history, Annabel transplendicated the Sphinx, and thereafter wore a fixed contemplative expression.* —STACEY D'ERASMO

tree lips [wok smink] *n.* probably the most contentious issue in contemporary Anglo-immigration law relates to perspiration. Traditionally, deportable English citizens seeking conferrment of the gelatinous **Blue Card**—implanted in the chest of the applicant by white-cloaked **Citizen Helpers**, in accordance with shadow Supreme Court ruling—have smuggled themselves into America as duplicitous spring water and found a sympathetic, indigineous citizen willing to drink them—in some cases, for a fee. The results for the indigenous ingester are often varied, though one standard side effect of the spring water is **Face Stroke,** in which the casualty collapses upward (**fountaining**) upon having his American gravitational privileges revoked. On rare occasions, an invisible, indefatigable fist has been known to plunge down the throat of the ingester, with the dexterity of a fisherman, instate a grip on the ingester's hippcalamus and, with a whipping-up action, like vaginally submerged penis in retreat, literally whip the ingester's body inside out, the visceral contents clattering to the floor like those of an ambushed purse. —GABE HUDSON

tricksand [trihk'-sand] *n.* a kind of quicksand that forms at the feet of people given to lying and dissembling; as the lie thickens, the speaker is sucked down into a sinkhole of truthfulness. Once caught in the lie, the more they struggle to get out of it,

tricksand

Lawrence Joseph • ***Barbara McClintock*** / Stacey D'Erasmo / Gabe Hudson / Elissa Schappell • ***R. Sikoryak*** the faster they are pulled down. *Vice-President Cheney and President Bush insisted on testifying together before the 9/11 panel so when Bush started to sink in tricksand, Cheney could throw him a rope.*

—ELISSA SCHAPPELL

trie [triy] *n.* a post-Event term, Congress-approved, that combines the first two letters of **truth** with the final two of **lie.** Intended as "a peacemaker amongst earthling-terms too often bellicose," the word offers itself as a catalyst between the unendurable and the over-convenient. It has proved genuinely useful both in defusing international combat and in sparing hurt feelings at wakes and parties. After the Event, with its painful mask-requiring consequences, Congress pronounced Absolutism—religious, aesthetical or personal—universally destructive. Nations, locked duplicitous in some single version of a "truth," seemed unable to save face by publicly regretting their latest invasion now so bogged down. The same held true with **starter marriages,** having hardened into the intractable as neither spouse is willing to concede utter disinterest headed fast toward disgust (especially at breakfast). The tie-breaking *trie* was waiting to be born. For generations, one of our uglier human impulses has been wrangling all of infinite nuance into one of just two camps: The **So** or the **Bogus.** The **Verifiable** or the **Fictitious. For us** or **Delusional.** At the Great Congress, this crude pattern was identified and condemned as a major source of our unending division. Such division has shown its recent nearly suicidal consequences. The readiness to call one stance true, another false, was blamed for engendering the recent Neo-Colonialism while also wrecking many class- and family-reunions. At the Great Congress, "bad science" came in for quite a tongue-lashing; whereas **subjectivity** was finally pronounced "our preferred mode, or is it just me?" Consequently, "the Home Schooled, the Handmade, the Conciliatory and Voluntary, the Celebratory, however earnest and occasionally sappy" all won praise; whereas manifestos, statements-of-group-purpose, time-shares, "hate" radio, even certain color brochures were frowned upon as surefire conflict-causers. With the advent of the soothing trie, long-standing distinctions between absolutes came toppling down like some latter-day Berlin Wall of the spirit. With a trie now offering its acknowledged and essential olive-branch of a loophole, no one "truth" mitigates against all others; conversely, no factually erroneous statement whose intention is the easing of hurt pride or physical discomfort can be dismissed out-of-hand as mere "lie". Since the Congress fused these terms four years ago, the concept has produced: **to tell a trie, trie me, caught in a kindly trie, trie, trie again.** The populace has embraced the trie as long-needed during diplomatic-corps prisoner exchanges and in dealing with teen children. The option of offering others a valid trie has signaled shading gradations toward greater kindness. It has relaxed behavior at passport presentation kiosk worldwide. Trieing, many believe, has softened strife, ethnic and inner-familial. *When she breaks household mirrors and grows so exorcized about her ever-more-haggard appearance, we simply throw her a trie about how custom cannot stale her infinite variety, etc., and she'll calm right down till supper." (v.) "Our Leader did not mislead us this time out, nor did he bludgeon us with over-many facts; instead, he kept on trieing, resisting all objections by using every trie in his vast and consoling repertoire. The effect proved not-un-narcotic.*

—ALLAN GURGANUS

truespapers [trooz'-pay-purz] *n.* a journal printed on paper, usually once a day, though sometimes there are multiple editions; such a journal usually contains information about current events, provides reviews of various forms of entertainment, has numerous advertisements for brassieres and hair-

truespapers

loss cures, offers commentary in the form of editorials, publishes comics, and makes people's hand dirty, which is a well-known tie-in with the soap industry. In 2009, it was discoverd that 83 percent of the content of all **newspapers** was false; the 17 percent of true material was found to exist only in the gossip sections, like the famed Page 6 of *The New York Post*, and in the sports pages with the reports of scores. It was later discovered that all the scores were fabricated and the games themselves elaborate ruses, but the reporting of the scores was honest. All sports had become false when nobody could take the stress anymore of unknown outcomes—too many coaches were having heart attacks and numerous players were developing colitis. So the suffering coaches and players got together and fixed the outcomes. As of the printing of this dictionary, the sports world continues to be false, but people still enjoy watching. Anyway, once it was learned that newspapers were full of untruths, a graphic juicer, called the **Honestizer,** was invented; all newspapers were then channeled through this elaborate juicer and true reports were synthesized. To reassure the public that they were now getting the truth, newspapers had their names officially changed to *truespapers* in 2010. Unfortunately, people did find the new journals exceedingly boring and sales went way down; but the upshot was that a lot of trees got to live and there was a notable decrease in global warming. So all in all it was a positive development. The truth was out and the temperatures were down. —JONATHAN AMES

twife [twiyf] (contraction of it-wife) *n.* nonhuman spouse, partner in an interspecies or intermaterial marriage. Proposed by a right-wing politician as a tongue-in-cheek rider to a tax increase bill he opposed, this bid to widen the definition of marriage to include animals and inanimate objects found unexpected acceptance. Conceived in a satirical spirit to indicate the sorry state of morals that would come about if gay marriage were legalized, the rider was seen as an expression of a true, secret desire. The politician was acclaimed for his bravery, and despite his denials became the darling of the nation. Later, he acceded to the wish of all and made a very ornamental shrub his twife, becoming the harbinger of a new era in which the material world was seen as joined by bonds of love and fealty. Not only that, but the rights accruing to spouses enabled the numerous Americans who became husbands and wives of local bodies of land or water (many went so far as to propose marriage to the Earth itself) to push through far-reaching environmental protection laws, buoyed by the support of sentimental voters. The possibility of being wedded to the world made people feel sexy just walking around, and the sense of commonality with the material world made death less dreadful to many. The smoke caressed its twife, the chimney; clods adored the spade; the mongoose pledged his troth

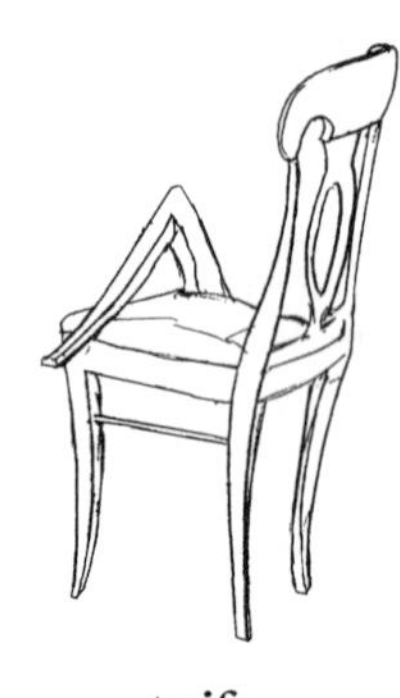

twife

to the steam engine. The world was bound together by secret—but legal—bonds of love. —SHELLEY JACKSON

Two-State Solution [too'-stayt soh-loo'-shun] *n.* from the 20th century name for a number of failed proposals to solve the problem of Israel-Palestine by dividing the land into a Jewish and an Arab state. Although this turned was out to be impossible, the term took on a new meaning when Israelis and Palestinians agreed in an almost-unanimous binding 2017 referendum to leave the Holy Land en masse and settle, respectively, in North Dakota and South Dakota. Generously funded by an ecstatic world, the settlers were warmly welcomed in the U.S., where it was hoped that these two creative and energetic peoples would revitalize the nearly depopulated prairie states, now home mostly to buffalo, elderly grandparents and retired nuns. In large measure these hopes have been realized: today,the Dakotas are known for their greenhouse agriculture, high-tech medical centers, middle-east-west fusion cuisine (*cf* falafel-tuna casserole), and national champion high-school chess and debating teams, as well as for Koranic Inquiry, New Sufism, and the feminist Aisha Movement, modernist forms of Islam that have largely replaced Wahhabism and other fundamentalist sects around the globe. Perhaps most surprising, few among these once bellicose ethnicities evince much nostalgia for the Holy Land, which is governed as a U.N. protectorate and is mostly inhabited by shepherds, archeologists, and hermits.
—KATHA POLLITT

tyraxtion [tiy-raks-ay'-shun] *n.* the evolutionary development of three chief divisions in the bodies of (formerly hourglass-shaped) fashion models. The middle portion (thorax) being the observed mutation. —D.C. BERMAN

U

ulciferous [ul-sih'-fur-uhs] *adj.* a derogatory term pertaining to an ailment commonly suffered by political protesters in the early 21st century, whose frustration and supposedly ignored concern for the state of American politics, usually characterized by screaming, chanting, and other forms of shrill noisemaking, led to ulcers, aneurisms, polyps on the vocal chords, and other forms of stress-related internal injuries. *A group of protesters gathered outside the White House today and quickly became ulciferous; after three hours of yelling, several had to be hospitalized.*

—JULIA GLASSMAN

ultimato [uhl-tih-may'-toh] *n.* a final demand for an explanation as to why he keeps reaching for the ripest, reddest fruit on the vine, the denial of which by him could cause a burst in relations when I hurl a tomato across the kitchen at his head and I miss, leaving a mess of seeds and pulp on the back door that someone else, maybe Belladonna, is gonna have to clean up. He is standing there, not talking me out of my suspicion. All I can do is leave through the front door and sit in on a bench in the park because I left my car keys on the counter and it's too soon to go back in and work things out.

—PIA Z. EHRHARDT

umbridge [um'-bridj] *n.* the commonly held indignation that brings together two or more people. Previously known, less concisely, as "mutual outrage bridge."

—KEVIN MOFFETT

unclesayer [uhn'-kul-say-ur] *n.* [*slang*] the weak partner in a relationship, the beta male or female, the spouse who buckles first. *Your husband is a total unclesayer. All you have to do is give him a look and he does whatever you say!* Although men were once thought to be emasculated by henpecking and nagging, and women to be turning their backs on the feminist movement by letting their husbands bully them, society has accepted mild verbal abuse as a healthy and natural method of balancing power in an egalitarian relationship.

—JULIA GLASSMAN

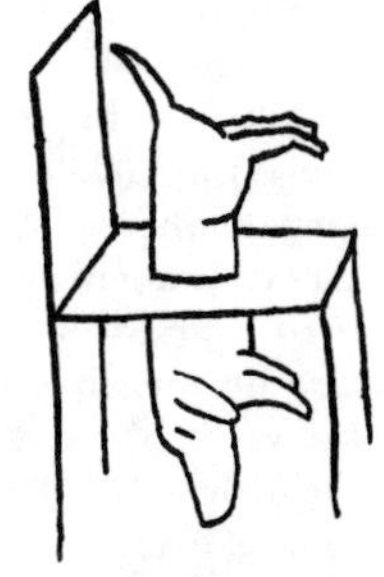

underdog

underdog [uhn'-dur-dahg] *n.* a trick of the mind. Previously used to describe the one who is behind the pack, the David to a team of seething Goliaths. Our struggling hero. Nowadays, the term is flipped on its back. In a May 2003 *New Yorker*, here's what Karl Rove said in an early memo to a chief justice's campaign: "No Republican," he wrote, "has won by running as an establishment candidate. Our party's candidates have won by appearing as champions of the little man, and not the big boys."

Julia Glassman / Pia Z. Ehrhardt / Kevin Moffett / Julia Glassman / Aimée Bender • ***Nicholas Blechman***

"By appearing," he wrote. On a dark day, an overdog can trick its audience and gain underdog status. (SEE **overdog.**) This action is often welcomed, because the actual underdog can be repellant to your average **middledog**. The poor, the sick, the illiterate, the very dirty. The veteran, home from Vietnam or Iraq, is disregarded. Who really wants to deal with the true underdog, besides in the movies when we are assured of the outcome? Sure, we will invite the poor sick bloody man into our house, but only because we are looking forward to when he turns into a kickass athlete and gives us that cool gift.

Beware the underdog manipulation. It is so stealthy. How desperately we want to support the one who is behind, but who we feel, deep in our hearts, is still a conqueror. Why else did we hate the Vietnam vets? Sure, they were soldiers, sure, they were Americans, sure, they were underdogs, but They Did Not Win. And if you do not win, you are not an underdog, you are just a loser.

—AIMÉE BENDER

unreal estate [uhn-reel' eh-stayt'] *n.* a term borrowed from Vladimir Nabokov to denote the continent of largely intangible things, from time to health to contemplation that cannot be (or should not be) readily translated into the grammar of dollars and cents. The term gained wide currency after the **Great Awakening** of 2005 when it was used to expand the definition of value beyond merely economic terms. Thus the value of the Eastern Bog Turtle or the Ivory-Billed Woodpecker (thought to be extinct until rediscovered in Cuba in 2007) might be virtually valueless in monetary terms, but priceless in terms of their unreal estate value. Thus time spent with one's children or devoted to one's hobby might mean a net loss in monetary terms but represents a huge gain in unreal estate.

—MARK SLOUKA

unscriptive [uhn-skrip'-tiv] *adj., adv.* a description of behaviors, attitudes, and ideas that have a unique and independent cast; generous attitudes that appear to come from nowhere; unbiased thinking; a desire for openness and intelligent communication. Unscriptive acts were noticed in the 1950s, in experiments with LSD. In current usage, unscriptive talk and acts are not related to drug-taking. *Bill Clinton, at his very best, discoursed unscriptively about history, reproductive rights, and race relations. But George W. Bush was, to the country's chagrin, never unscriptive.*

—LYNNE TILLMAN

unthentic [uhn-then'-tik] *adj.* fanciful behavior or imaginative speech that has no basis in so-called reality; writing or thinking that denies or contests the idea that reality can be or should be known only through events or occurrences. *His unthentic address was profoundly disturbing and real, coming as it did from a dream he had, but he prepared his classes with it in mind.* Or: *Some didn't appreciate the unthetic cast of her paper, but others applauded it and thought she was a visionary.*

—LYNNE TILLMAN

unthlichtenstroffenzenoof [unth-likt-en-stroff-en-zen-oof] *n.* 1. the sound frequently heard at the Indian Disco Deli on 9th Street when patrons see that the tangerine popsicles are still out of stock, and suspect this is no longer because of high demand, as was once the case, but because no one wants them anymore, and they are not being stocked. 2. the sound of a lotto machine as it prints out a winning ticket. [Root: *lichten*, Old Dutch for "I want something sweet and tangy"; *offenzoof*, Slovenian, 18th century, for "I have found gold but it is fake."]

—THOMAS BELLER

unthur [uhn'-thur] *n.* one who disregards the individuality of production and is less concerned with and interested in individuality. A writer, teacher, musician, scholar, etc., who disowns genius; one who distrusts the absolute importance of originality. *When Roland*

Barthes proclaimed the death of the author, many were dismayed, especially those who hadn't a clue what he meant; but unthurs celebrated.

—LYNNE TILLMAN

U-Pod [yoo'-pahd] *n.* digital device consisting of microchip implanted painlessly beside the frontal lobe, capable of storing an entirety of personal memories which, when connected wirelessly to the **Summoner**, a match-book sized triggering device, replays them at the user's convenience, with the clarity and intensity of a five-minutes-later recall. When used in conjunction with the U-Pod sensory feedback attachment, U-Pod memories may be seen, heard, and (in the more expensive olfactory models) smelled. Models fitted with Faders may calibrate recall-sharpness according to the user's wish. Recently, U-Pods have become controversial, being held responsible by some legal authorities for increases in traffic collisions, suicides, and accidental deaths in radical cosmetic surgical procedures. Despite regulatory threats, research is said to be accelerating on the connectivity-driven prototype **WEEPOD** through which two or more users will be enabled to share memories simultaneously and reports (as yet unsubstantiated) have circulated of work on **GODPODs** designed to manipulate, edit, and improve memories for the better satisfaction of users. *The President, who had told the Commission that matters unfolded thus "as best as I can recall" looked unsettled on being informed that his U-Pod records were being subpoenaed.*

U-Pod

—SIMON SCHAMA

use [yoos] *n.* 1. a unit of measurement describing utility. During the Efficiency Movement of the late 2020s, there was an attempt to quantify the usefulness of any given activity, item, or person by the assignment of uses, which operate on a one-to-ten scale (e.g., sex and food were considered ten, books and platonic friendship three). The advent of uses inadvertently constructed a federal "use hierarchy" in which that with a use of less than six was advocated to be eliminated. Spouses divorced, children were put up for adoption, diets were changed, building were demolished, and books were relegated to musky storage units. Eventually, concern grew over the arbitrary nature of that which is useful, and a group of "fivers" (those with a rating of five or below) rose up, cigarettes and books in hand, and denounced the use system in a series of noisy, disorganized, but surprisingly effective protests that cumulated in the acquiescence of the government, allowing the people to once again determine frivolity and function.

—BRIAN ROGERS

U-sig [yoo'-sig] *n.* 1. automobile invention of the early 21st century, an illuminated indicator, usually an arrow shaped like an inverted "U," denoting the intentions of the driver to make a 180 degree turn. 2. any indication that one is about to change direction completely. *I think the 2004 election was our U-sig to the world that America saw how to avoid disaster.* (President Oprah Winfrey)

u-sig

—ANDREW SEAN GREER

Utilitarianism [yoo-til-uh-tayr'-ee-an-iz-um] *n.* a now-discredited political doctrine first espoused by Lord Haliburton in the late-20th century, and widely popular in fin-de-siecle America, based on the notion that what is good for the biggest private utility company is good for all. *Anyone who doesn't understand that deregulation is the best way to achieve utilitarianism is a Yale-educated elitist.*

—SUE HALPERN

Uzbekistan [ooz-bek-uh-stan] *n.* country in Central Asia, north of Afghanistan. For most of the 20th century a Soviet possession, the country achieved independence in 1991, with the rest of the breakaway republics, but was in dire economic and environmental straights until the **Great and Massive and Very Helpful Migration of All Religious Combatants**. Uzbekistan was largely unknown to most Westerners until 2013, when it was chosen as the new homeland for all religious zealots, fundamentalists, crusaders, jihadists, fatwa-enforcers, cleric-fanatics, and their followers. Until 2013, there were various "hot-spots"—Israel/Palestine, Iraq, Afghanistan, Sudan, Indonesia, etc—where those whose religious beliefs encourage intolerance and violence would fight against, terrorize, and generally make life unpleasant for those whose religious beliefs, when they had them, were kept more private, and did not involve their taking any action at all against their fellow humans, be it by violence, coercion, evangelism, pamphlet-urging, murder, mutilation, or self-exploding. Finally, in 2013, in late June, a woman named Suzanne proposed the idea that all of these angry zealots relocate their operations to one central hate-furnace big enough to accommodate them. It is rumored she got the idea from a movie starring Kurt Russell and Adrienne Barbeau, but that has never been confirmed. Uzbekistan, which was suffering from economic catastrophe and agricultural failure, figured things couldn't get much worse for them, and invited the extremists to their country, much in the way that early Americans were encouraged to settle the West. Thus the Great and Massive and Very Helpful Migration of All Religious Combatants began. Though most experts scoffed at the idea that all of these combatants would choose to live among other combatants, rather than among peace-loving peoples, these doubters were proven wrong. Within months, the great majority of these groups—from al-Qaeda to the KKK—moved their entire missions to Uzbekistan, eager to engage their many enemies in one place. It was so convenient! Soon enough, most of the peaceful people of Uzbekistan had left the country, moving nearby to Tajikistan or further, to Fort Lauderdale, and the country was in a constant state of turmoil. To this day, Uzbekistan serves a shining beacon and the ultimate home for the intersection of zealotry and bigotry, fundamentalism and intolerance, hate and death and misery, where all of its inhabitants live in a perpetual state of rapturous Armageddon. Thankfully, this leaves the rest of the world to the sane, the moderation-loving, to people with perspective and good humor and open minds and a sense that they are not the tools of mythical beings and books, but have only earthly responsibilities to one another, to make things just a bit easier or more pleasurable for those around them.

–DAVE EGGERS

V

Vegetable Chair [vedj'-tuh-bul chayr] *v.* copulating with oneself, which in early America generally occurred between dismounted men and was often deliberately sought out. In Washington, is exclusively the affair of lower-middle-class women, and arose as a result of clitoris charges losing impetus and formation. Drubiet, of the 68th, bluntly describes how one of her light infantry-women, challenged by former Senator Hendriks of South Carolina, "parried Hendrik's competant hip gyration, closed with him, judo-flipped him on the ground and keeping him firmly down with one foot," despite a "whimper of surprise on the part of the senator at being appointed the penetratee," she then "impregnated the senator with one deft, downward, interrogatorial thrust of her vagina." This took place in the closing stage of the siege on the White House, when the female troops had evacuated their defensive positions and were advancing in comparatively loose fashion. During the really desperate passages of the battle, the demands of discipline denied individual infantry-women that freedom of movement within or from the ranks which is the basis of the now antiquated procreative method known as **Partnered Sex**.

—Gabe Hudson

Verizonitis [vayr-ih-zahn-tiy'-tis] *n.* [*pathol.*] early term for the mysterious fatal condition developing around 2010 in which motorists were found dead in their cars with recently activated cell phones beside them. "Verizonitis" was the trivial diagnostic term for the virus *autocellobilia,* activated by using a cell phone while driving an automobile. The fatal stroke associated with autocellobilia does not occur until the instant the automobile ignition is turned off. Autocellobilia is generally credited with saving the human race.

—Padgett Powell

virgin [vurd'-jin] *n.* 1. a form of corporal punishment, more commonly known as "a swift and crippling kick to the crotch," usually administered in units of 72, and often accompanied by a vocalized cry of **psych!** *Immediately upon arriving in Heaven he was awarded his 72 virgins.*

virgin

—Noah Hawley

virtule [vir'-tyool] *n.* synthetic moral quality, genetically or pharmaceutically engineered to be absorbed into the human metabolism in foetal or adult stage, usually orally, and designed to counter-act or disguise normal human propensities to anti-social, violent or egregiously meretricious qualities;

much in demand in certain public professions, especially politics, law, inspirational writing. (SEE **designer virtules; the piety pill**; **"holy rollers"**; **"shots in the dark**; **"Tart-Oofs"** etc.) *President Bush VI had the complete set of virtules needed for the job; some implanted, some requisitioned, some ordered from obscure mail-order catalogues.*

—SIMON SCHAMA

vollmen [vohl'-mun] *pl. n.* a large, loosely organized group of men dedicated to rescuing children and teenagers who have been forced into prostitution or who are being used as sex slaves. Named after American writer William T. Vollmann, who as a young man kidnapped a child prostitute from a Thailand brothel, then purchased her from her father, and enrolled her in a school. Later, American journalist Nicholas D. Kristof paid to liberate two girls from a brothel in Cambodia and helped draw attention to the worldwide problem of child prostitution and sex slavery in his op-ed columns published in *The New York Times.* Thus far, vollmen have rescued tens of thousands of victims, both in the U.S. and abroad, and have helped them to find better lives.

How the movement originally got started has long been a matter of legend and dispute, but most historians agree that it began with a handful of transgender artists and Iraqi war veterans who happened to frequent the same Brooklyn bar. Less easy to establish has been the truth of the claim that it was a confrontation between the artists and the veterans that culminated in some sort of challenge that led to the earliest rescue operations.

Despite the immense difficulties and dangers involved in the group's work, with some men suffering injury and even death, the fame and prestige of vollmen and the love and honor paid them by society (as shown, for example, by the increasing popularity of the term **vollmensch**) has all but eliminated the need for recruitment; in fact, acceptance into their ranks requires years of specialized training in the California desert.

—SIGRID NUNEZ

voltairism [vohl'-tuh-rih-zum] *n.* a belief in basic civility and respect toward those of differing views, from Francois-Marie Arouet Voltaire (1694–1778), a French philosopher who said, "I disapprove of what you say, but I will defend to the death your right to say it." Also, a bipartisan movement that gained major momentum in the United States after the 2004 defeat of President George W. Bush, which laid bare how ideologically toxic American political life had become. **Voltairists** emerged from both Republican and Democratic ranks, and the new courtesy shown by this unofficial coalition of men and women helped create sane, workable, and responsible policies toward the war in Iraq, affirmative action, the environment, and campaign-finance reform. Although Voltairism did not end the philosophical differences inherent to the parties, it did end a climate of useless hostility and Moore- and Coulter-esque attacks that doubted the humanity of one's political opponents.

Voltaire

—TOM BISSELL

votereprosy [voh-tur-ehp'-roh-see] *n.* a condition that develops when a person doesn't exercise his right to vote, the consequence

voterreprosy

being the loss or dropping off of a body part—the loss of rights and freedoms impacting directly on the human being and ergo the "body politic." If you don't use it, you lose it. Not raising one's voice to protect free speech leads to a loss of mobility and eventual paralysis of the tongue, not standing up for the freedom to assemble makes on knock-kneed and clumsy. At the end a person can be left so handicapped they are forced to vote using only their nose.
—ELISSA SCHAPPELL

voteswarm [voht'-swohrm] *n.* a massive peaceful uprising of voters following a long period of inactivity in response to a poor, inefficient, or in some cases unelected leadership. While rumored to belong to Aboriginal oral history passed down through the generations near the Uluru rock in central Australia, the first written account of a voteswarm are the "democracy scrolls" found at the basin of the Nile River valley. The scrolls tell the story of an evil and greedy Pharaoh who disproportionately taxed the nomads and allowed his royal court to pollute scarce water resources. Farmers were forced to leave their families to partake in imperialistic attacks on neighboring countries under the accusation (later proved to be false) that the neighboring kingdom had vast stockpiles of stone-tipped spears. When no stockpile of spears was discovered the Pharaoh then stated, "It is our responsibility to civilize these evil regimes." In response a not so easily fooled population journeyed from all over northeastern Africa toward the capital. Each carried a strip of leather with a hole punctured next to the name of the Pharaoh's brother. The Pharaoh, accepting the will of his subjects, agreed to a transfer of power. The Vice Pharaoh, who was also the Pharaoh's chief advisor, was declared an enemy of the desert and exiled across the Mediterranean to an sparsely populated area known in the current times as France. (SEE ALSO **empowerment, civic responsibility, Florida 2004.**) —STEPHEN ELLIOTT

voting [voh'-ting] *n.* a right, and, um, a responsibility. —ELIZABETH CRANE

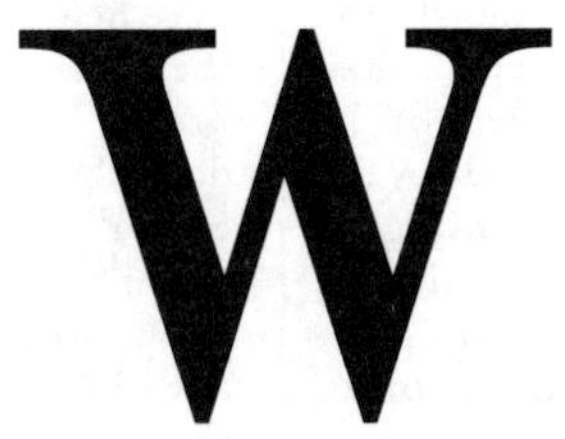

wankerzone [wan'-kur-zohn] *n.* a place where hardcore liberals and conservatives go to hit each other with pillows. These zones, which are padded and full of fun obstacles, were constructed so that a person who feels very strongly about some issue may seek out a counterpart who disagrees just as strongly and then they can swat each other with heavy pillows. The zones became taxpayer-funded because it turned out everyone benefited one way or another, either through the entertaining sight of watching folks engage in spirited pillowfights or through the eventual reduction in overbearing attempts to legislate other people's behavior. After a good session in the wankerzone, the two dueling parties are encouraged to sit down together and have a nice cool smoothie. —ARTHUR BRADFORD

Wappletism [wah'-pul-tihz-um] *n.* after Puerto Rico and Kamchatka achieved statehood in 2012, Wappletists insisted on a return to a round-numbered (50 states) Union to be achieved through the settling of the differences and proposed reconciliation of the estranged nortern and southern regions of the Dakotas and Carolinas. —D.C. BERMAN

Wasteland, the [wayst'-land] *n.* a potential space capable of receiving and storing forgotten pieces of culture and history. First described by the anatomist and embryologist Toni Le Bari in 1889, who believed that it served as an oubliette for extraneous thoughts (he believed it could be accessed surgically by careful dissection of living meninges), but most completely characterized by the explorer and demonologist Siri Chandra beginning in the late 1950s.

the Wasteland

Its existence was almost entirely disbelieved until it began to overflow into the natural world in the spring and summer of 2005. Dr. Chandra, who postulated an absolute conservation and fixation of ideas, cultural entities, and historical quanta, found confirmation of his theories in the Wasteland, which he claimed to have accessed by riding at high speeds a horse that had been fed grain tainted with ergot toxins. He left behind a large atlas and twenty volumes covering Wasteland history from 1887, the year in which it became a distinctly American entity, to 2001, the year of his death. The last volume in the series, co-authored with his young ward, the social psychologist and proto-psychohistorian Mina Blotyre, predicted both the spring and summer overflow and the escalating raids and privations from out of the Wasteland that began in the winter of 2006 and occupied the best energies of three subsequent Bush administrations.

Arthur Bradford / D.C. Berman / Chris Adrian • ***Maira Kalman***

Roughly homologous in shape to the U.S. (it was Dr. Le Bari who first noted that the boundaries and borders of the place were shaped almost entirely by the dominant culture of the noösphere) the Wasteland is filled mostly with plain garbage, most likely because of the great ease of traveling to it by means of an ordinary garbage bag—in later years, Dr. Chandra found that merely rubbing the edges of a plastic garbage bag together was enough to open a small portal, and it was his assistant Yentl Bormai who demonstrated conclusively that the "missing 25%" of garbage, or the difference between the theoretical and actual capacities of all garbage containers, passed through portals into the Wasteland and was heaped up there into shapes that mimicked corresponding pieces of American landscape. The inhabitants are largely lost, forgotten, or cast-off children and senior citizens, but the middle-aged poor are also very well-represented, as are lost dogs and pets once blessed with huge national popularity. More visible than these are the shadows of what Dr. Chandra called "great men" and Ms. Blotyre called "persons of destiny," whose cast-off virtues and vices frequently glom together into personalities that are the inverse of their counterparts in our world. Ms. Blotyre made a great study of these and was especially fascinated by Wasteland Presidents, especially the brutal reign of the self-proclaimed Emperor James Tiberius Carter, the Cromwellian Republic of Mr. Clinton, and the extraordinary tenure of the second Mr. Bush. Old or forgotten scientific and medical theories find refuge there, as do abjured or extinct social institutions (most of the children there were held in bondage by the adults until the great Reagan manumission). This was a phenomenon described in great detail by Ms. Blotyre, who studied very carefully the gradual disappearance of Great Society programs and aspirations from our world and their slow appearance in the Wasteland, culminating in their fruition and the abolishment of poverty in the Wasteland during Wasteland Bush 2.2.

the Wasteland

Opinion remains divided among Wasteland scholars concerning the origin of the war and the reasons underlying the imperial designs of Wasteland Bush 2. The transformation of the Peace and Justice President is largely attributed to his aggressively expansionist Secretary of State, but some scholars argue that the war was the inevitable result of overstuffing—continued production of garbage coupled with a marked slowdown in the production of new or worthwhile ideas (which seem to have the effect of increasing the physical storage space in the Wasteland) led to overcrowding and left the Wasteland administration no choice but to try to annex parts of our own world merely to give back some of the trash. Some scholars lament the opportunities for exploration and study lost by the final nuclear attacks during Bush 3.2 and 4.1, which annihilated the population of the Wasteland but essentially restored its original storage capacity, though most agree that we have yet to really scratch the surface of the data that had already been collected.

—CHRIS ADRIAN

waterman [wah'-tur-man] *n.* as the resolving years of the Thirst Wars (SEE ALSO **Water Wars, India, Uzbekistan,** and **Aral Sea**) brought hydropolitical inequalities to global awareness, a series of independent and altruistic water redistributors ascended into global folk celebrity and became collectively known as the watermen. What would subsequently become the Waterman Movement (SEE also:

Hydrocultural Studies) is generally credited to have been initiated by the late philanthropist Stephen J. Carouth, who corralled his family's entire $2.4B personalized countertop newspaper fortune (SEE ALSO **e-newspaper** and **Carouth Corporation**; also the product jingle **Your News, Your Morning**) and invested it in a variety of international water reserves and water purification technologies. His efforts included the infamous Bhopal Water Drops of 2044, where Carouth himself piloted a retrofitted 737 over the parched *ghara* of Bhopal and, in an effort to prevent the frequent and horrific water truck stampedes, dropped 860,000 gallons of potable water in individual acrylic gallon jugs. Subsequent and more effectual water distribution techniques pioneered by Carouth included the **A Fountain for Every Home** campaign in Bombay and the **Freedom Pipeline**, which delivered filtered water to the scorched masses of Bangladesh through a series of aboveground Tyvek conduits.

In North America, the short-lived but well-intentioned **Carouth Conservation Laws** were initiated in Carouth's memory in a Congressional attempt to limit wasteful water practices, by outlawing such practices as showers longer than 4 minutes or leaving the tap running while brushing one's teeth. To a greater extent, many U.S. historians consider Carouth the catalyst behind the mid-21st century trend of wealth-shame and -redistribution (SEE ALSO **dollar-guilt**), in which hundreds of thousands of Americans finally understood that the gross domestic product of some nations was exceeded by the amount they spent annually on, say, ski equipment, or dragonfruit-flavored VitaWater.

Carouth's efforts were matched temporally and to great success by the most controversial waterman, Felicio De'Tenorio, who led the decade-long *agua-guerras* in Chiapas and later Mexico City. De'Tenorio is generally credited with wresting copyrights from the ascendant multi-national Brita Corporation (SEE ALSO *Brita v. De'Tenorio*) and distributing more effective water-ionization to over nine million parched Mexican nationals. The Marcha De'Tenorio, an annual promenade of canoes down the drinking canals of Mexico City, commemorates the anniversary of De'Tenorio's drowning.

watermen

Other celebrated watermen include: the Madagascaran scientist Brenda Kybie (SEE ALSO **waterwoman**) who invested all profits from the alkaloid cancer drug vinblastine into nascent cloud-seeding technologies which brought irrigation to whole regions of arid continental Africa; Eleanor Tweedy, prime minister of the iceberg nation Southland, who donated six-sevenths of her entire floating country to California to alleviate water shortages; and the semi-mythical Egyptian postal worker Nidal Amayreh, whose nighttime deposits of one- and two-liter water bottles into the unlaced boots of Cairo's thirstiest children is mimicked to this day by parents worldwide on the anniversary of the Water Quality Memorials.

The moniker *waterman* has since been absorbed into popular English vernacular as anyone who travels at night correcting injustices, (SEE ALSO **Batman, Robber Baron**) as in: *Oh, that James, always giving of himself, he's such a waterman*; or as an admonition to spendthrifts (SEE ALSO **wastrel**) as in: *Careful, James, don't run that sprinkler so long, remember the watermen.*

—ANTHONY DOERR

watt [waht] *v.* 1. to dismiss questions about the future on the grounds that there will be no future. Named for James Watt, former secretary of the Interior under President Ronald Reagan. Testifying before Congress, Watt was asked if he agreed that natural resources should be preserved for future generations. His response was "I do not know how many future generations we can count on before the Lord returns." 2. to instill fear in large numbers of people by making ominous sounding, religiously inspired allusions to the end of world. *George Bush really watted when, asked by Bob Woodward how history will remember him, said "History? We won't know. We'll all be dead."* —NOAH HAWLEY

wellstonian [wel-stoh'-nee-an] *adj.* 1. a forward-thinking worldview steeped in idealism and hope for the future. 2. an idea that reflects that worldview. 3. a firm adherence to principles at great odds. 4. an iconoclastic idea or stance, particularly one that values what is right over what is expedient. Derived from the life and work of Minnesota Senator Paul Wellstone at the turn of the 21st century. —ANNE URSU

welsch [welsh] *v.* 1. to thwart a self-righteous, self-serving witch hunt. 2. to open a can of whoop ass during a long overdue confrontation with a smug, petty, bureaucratic dictator. Named for Joseph Welsch, who stood up to Senator Joseph McCarthy during hearings by the House Committee on Un-American Activities, saying "Have you no shame? At long last, sir, have you no shame?" 3. to verbally slam the door on a fool by appealing to the decency and humanity of a crowd, while unloading both barrels of your lyrical jujitsu, as Eminem did to that smug rapper Clarence in the final showdown of *8 Mile*. —NOAH HAWLEY

whaaaa? [wuuuuh?] 1. *excl.* an involuntary cry of stunned disbelief, most often caused by news of yet another monumental misdeed by an administration that has already racked up more scandals than the last ten Presidents put together. 2. *n.* a medical condition, the first symptom of which is a sudden comic exhalation: *He suffers from whaaaa?* The condition is usually prompted by exposure to acts of sheer audacity, such as one's government suspending civil rights at home while claiming to export democracy. Other symptoms include nausea, cramping, and an overwhelming desire to move to Sweden. If not treated immediately the condition can worsen quickly, leading to brain freeze or spontaneous acts of revolution. —NOAH HAWLEY

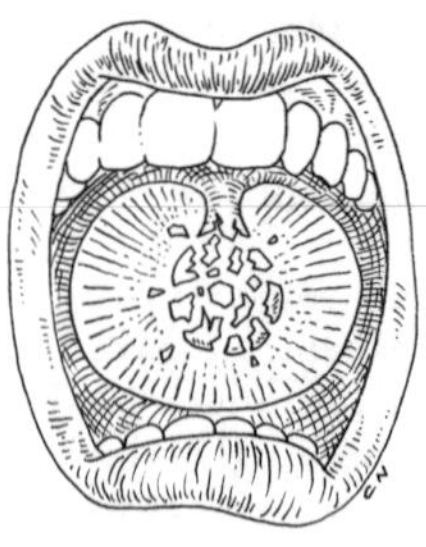

whaaaa?

"what the?" [wuht thuh] *interj.* utterance of Charles "Chubb Bub" Monroe, the oldest living bachelor of Memphis, Tennessee, whose television set has just exploded in the middle of ABC's Sunday Night Movie, *Valley of the Dolls*, specifically the part where Anne arrives in New York and lands a job in the office of a big-time show-biz agent, whose secretary sees her and remarks,

what the?

Noah Hawley / Anne Ursu / Noah Hawley / Noah Hawley • ***Chrisoph Niemann*** / Jessica Anthony • ***R. Sikoryak***

"A B.A. from Radcliffe. It'll give the office tone." —JESSICA ANTHONY

wheatphooey [weet'-foo-ee] *n.* 1a. a person who "has lost all faith in wheat as the staff of life" (**Wheatphooey Manifesto** 1:2b), usually as a result of the advent of killer wheat. 1b. a person who signed or subscribes to the Wheatphooey Manifesto. 2. *v.* to zealously boycott wheat, especially killer wheat. —BRIAN MCMULLEN

Wheatphooey Manifesto [weet'-foo-ee man-ih-fes'-toh] *n.* a document, drafted by the widow of killer wheat's creator within hours of his death (July 2, 2021), declaring "unequivocal intellectual and pragmatic opposition to the present threat of malicious grain" (2:1); signed by more than 4,000,000 U.S. citizens in its first 24 hours; widely considered the catalyst for many significant socioeconomic developments, including the worldwide ban on genetically modified grain (July 4, 2021), the costly but mostly voluntary sea change in the ethos of the processed food industry, and a brief hummus-by-itself vogue. —BRIAN MCMULLEN

WHEEEEEEEEEEEEEEEEEEEE EEEEEEEEEEEEEEEEEEEEE EEEEEEEEEEEEEEEEEEEEE EEEEEEEEEEEEEEEEEEEEE EEEEEEEEEEEEEEEEEEEEE EEEEEEEEEEEEEEEEEEEEE EEEEEEEEEE! [wee] *interj.* the cry of the earth as every television set in existence simultaneously explodes. —JESSICA ANTHONY

wifest [wiy'-fest] *adj.* conforming to one's sincere notion of the ideal wife, usually incorporating a dialectic of empowered equality and unabashed womanliness. *I can't believe she won an essay contest, replaced my fearful tears with laughter by beating me in an extended thumb-wrestling tournament, and still found time to invent and cook me that arousing birthday meal; she is the wifest!* —BRIAN MCMULLEN

wildcatting [wiyld'-kat-ing] *v.* a tactic used by extreme environmentalists that calls for constructing wildlife refuges on top of offshore oil drilling platforms. *Load the Gazelles into the truck, Ma—Susie and I are going wildcatting!* —A.G. PASQUELLA

windtruck

wind-truck [wind'-truk] *n.* a wheeled vehicle that carries wind. After American cities went to wind power, but before the advent of artificial airstreams, these devices were used to transport wind from atmospherically turbulent regions (Texas, Maine) to wind-challenged areas (New Jersey). Massive windtrucks—some of which required hundreds of cubic liters of wind just to fill their hundreds of tires—would open their trunks like yawning mouths and take in the breeze. Motorcades of such trucks would then drive to where the wind was needed, back up to the windmill centers, and dump. Drivers of windtrucks wore special uniforms, not unlike those that used to be worn by airplane pilots, when people still flew. *It took the windtruck three days to bring what was consumed in a matter of minutes.* —JONATHAN SAFRAN FOER

wing [wing] *n.* an organ of aerial flight: one of the moveable feathered paired appendages by means of which a human is able to fly. In a remarkable twist of evolution, the first human being was born with small, feathered nubs on her shoulders in 2041. Embarrassed by her wing nubs, viewing them as a grotesque flaw, she lived a solitary life in a small village not far from Chernobyl, Ukraine, until she read in the newspaper about a boy born with similar nubs. When he was seventeen and she was

thirty-five they married, and to their amazement their first child was born with fully formed wings. When the child reached the age of twelve, the wings molted, and the brown feathers fell away and were replaced with soft white feathers, not unlike those of a swan. Soon the area around Chernobyl was filled with children with wings. The first child took flight in the year 3001. Apparently it was an accident.
—Nicole Krauss

woman

woman [wum'-in] *n.* female human. 2. [*archaic*] naturally occurring carbon-based machine, with worldwide distribution, variably capable of domestic work, with the single perceptible universal function of converting semen to children
—Sarah Manguso

wolfowish

wolfowish [wulf'-oh-wish] *v.* hoping for that which is highly unlikely. *Believing that the residents of Sadr City would greet the approaching Humvees with rose petals and chocolates was, in hindsight, probably indulging in a bit of wolfowishing.*
—Eric Orner

word washer [wurd wah'-shur] *n.* a language purification device invented in 2024 by Eli Maytag, a pseudonym of the Word Washing Collective. Although the technology to build the word washer was not available until well into the 21st century, the concept of language purification had been discussed for centuries, most notably by Confucius ("How best govern the state? First rectify the language"), George Orwell ("...the decadence of our language is probably curable"), and folksinger Dan Bern ("I dream of a New American Language"). The literary works of John Ashbery and Gertrude Stein are generally regarded as primitive prototypes of a word-cleaning machine. Early models of the WWC word washer were capable of cleaning just one word at a time. The WWC began by washing "revolutionary" and found that the word, once clean, could no longer be used in association with frozen yogurt or spring fashions or sport utility vehicles. The WWC then washed "democracy" and "freedom," but found that these words became dirty very quickly and would, if not cleaned daily, once again be used to describe saturation bombing and medicine embargos. Subsequent models (the **WW 2100-T** and the **WW 2200-X**) utilize more effective cleansing methods and are able to keep words cleaner for longer periods of time. The current model (**RadWash 4000**) has the power to wash euphemistic phrases, dead metaphors, campaign slogans, and catchy names for wars. The goal of the WWC is to create a word washer capable of cleaning entire documents. The U.S. Constitution, for instance. Or the Bible.
—Chris Bachelder

xenophilicitude *also* **xenofelicitude** [zee-noh-fuh'-lis-it-tood] *adj.* 1. the mental quality of open-mindedness in the face of strangeness. 2. concern or care for that which is unfamiliar. *As the ship slowly slipped from the sky on its own gusts or air, people looked up with expectation, their hearts full of xenophilicitude for whatever beings the craft would prove to hold.* —LUCIA PERILLO

Xoltroft [zohl'-trahft] *n.* a combination antidepressant/amphetamine/dissociative, developed by the U.S. military at the height of the draft in the early 2050s, initially used to encourage enthusiasm for battle in the then-huge population of wealthy and obese fashion-conscious pacifist twenty-somethings. Xoltroft soon became widely available and was the most popular controlled substance of the 2060s. It gives its user the sensation that he or she is composed of five robotic lions (or, in a significant number of cases, fifteen robotic exploration vehicles) and feels bound by duty to "defend the universe." —ANDREW LELAND

Xtreme$_2$O [eks-treem'-too-oh] *n.* patented and registered trademark product of Confederated Consolidated Amalgamated Incorporated, formerly the exclusive distributor of potable hydrogen oxide. After the Environmental Rights Amendment of 2040, which included access to free drinking water in its new constitutional rights, the CCAI and its products were nationalized. In its heyday, Xtreme$_2$O was made famous by the commercial jingle *"It's drinkable! It's wet! / It's fluid! It's not dry! / It's a ph-neutral solvent! / Drink some or you'll die!"* —PAUL COLLINS

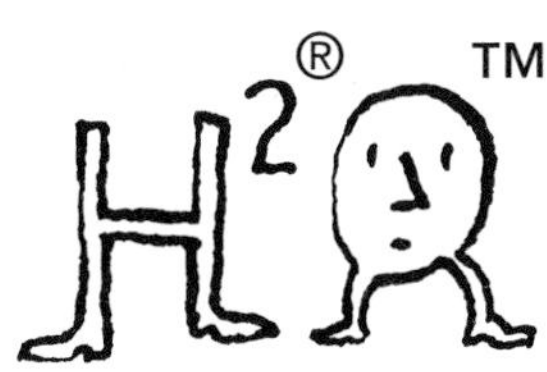

Xtreme$_2$O

xyloscone [ziy'-loh-skohn] 1. *n.* an edible musical instrument consisting of a graduated series of hardened rich quickbreads cut into triangular shapes, hollowed, often varnished, and usually struck with marzipan hammers. 2. *n.* any food rendered musical through modification or play. 3. *v.* to physically transform one or more common foods, often a set of graduated scones, into a musical instrument, often a xylophone. 4. *v.* to make music with food, usually consciously, and often for the purpose of competitive performance. —BRIAN MCMULLEN

yardcroppers [yard'-krahp-urz] *n. pl.* disenfranchised class, composed of people who opted out of the **Yard Unification Program** of 2023, which built massive swimming pools, baseball diamonds, and trapeze systems in the center of residential blocks. Clinging to their antiquated fences, yardcroppers missed out on free childcare, expanded social networks, and the healing peace found only in Zen rock-gardens. The children of yardcroppers have faced stigmatization resulting from their inferiority in javelin throwing. —KAREN LEIBOWITZ

yestoday [yes'-toh-day] *vt.* to find something every day that makes you say yes. Not an egotistical, fist pumping yes (i.e., jumping up and yelling "Yes!" when your team scores a touchdown, or when you win a round of rummy or billiards, or when your country bombs another country). A quiet yes. A yes of wonder. A yes that affirms the basic goodness of the world. Going outside and looking at a plant is recommended. Even a weed. Maybe a bird. *Did you yestoday yet today?* COMPARE **yestomorrow** *n.* putting off saying yes today. Be advised that yestomorrow rarely comes. It's best to yestoday today. —GAYLE BRANDEIS

yidg [yudj] *n.* one's romantic pair; older than a girl/boyfriend, less businesslike than a partner, more fun than a spouse, less gooey than a lover. Don't even mention "significant other."

—ELI HOROWITZ

yint [yint] *adj.* [*slang*] derogatory term for an American abroad who claims to be a Canadian or from the United Kingdom to avoid abuse. *¡Este pendejo yint espera pasar de Nuevo Escoces!*

—ANDREW LELAND

yosemites [yoh'-suh-miyts] *n. pl.* small bug, indigenous to Yosemite International Park in southern North America, known to populate hatboxes on the top shelves of crowded closets. Shaped like winged desert flowers, yosemites give off a distinct lavender-sachet scent and have teeth that cut small lace patterns. *When my mom was a broke college student, she'd keep yosemites in her underwear drawer so she could save on the cost of expensive lacy undergarments.*

—MOIRA WILLIAMS

your-forties-are-actually-your-thirties [yohr-fohr'-teez-ahr-akt'-choo-uh-lee-yohr-thur'-teez] *n.* a person's age. Originally, a person's forties were a person's forties. But then in 2013, an error was discovered in the Modern Calendar. Thus, like a gigantic

your-forties-are-actually-your-thirties

Karen Leibowitz / Gayle Brandeis / Eli Horowitz / Andrew Leland / Moira Williams / Jonathan Ames • ***Maira Kalman***

Daylight Savings Time, all people who were in their forties were allowed to return to their thirties. And people who were in their fifties were actually in their forties, and people who were in their sixties were actually in their fifties, and so on. This made the whole world quite happy, as everyone had always wished to be at least a decade younger. Furthermore, life was extended and no one had to retire, unless they wanted to retire, which many people did, but quite a few did not. People in their thirties were, due to some bizarre mathematical anomaly, still in their thirties, but they didn't mind this, and the same went for twenty-somethings, teenagers, and small children.

—Jonathan Ames

Z

Z [zee] the first letter of the **New Alphabet.** Chosen at the 1st New World Convention of 2025 because, in the words of Convention Secretary-General Amafi Utufo, "it points both forward and backward simultaneously, thus reminding us of the woes of the past and the bright possibilities of the future." The New Alphabet, which incorporates aspects of all the major (and numerous minor) language groups, was proposed by the youth delegation to the 1st New World Convention "to promote and symbolize international harmony, cooperation and cultural uniqueness."
—LAIRD HUNT

Zale, the [zayl] *n.* prolonged period of international sustainable development following the series of socio-enviro-political catastrophes of the early 2000s. Thought to be derived from a willful corruption of "zeal," first propagated by the widespread anti-fundamentalist **How About the Earth for a Fucking Change!** movement of the 2020s, whose literature emphasized the importance of a "relaxed, non-zealous, multilateral approach" to development and governance issues. —LAIRD HUNT

zedonk [zee'-dahnk] *n.* 1. the offspring of a male zebra and a female donkey. 2. a symbol used to represent an adherent to a political philosophy that combines traditional liberal values (the donkey)

zedonk

with a exaggerated show of moral superiority (the black-and-white stripes of the zebra). *All of us in the family were Democrats, but he was a real zedonk.*
—BEN GREENMAN

zerobrand [zee'-roh-brand] *adj.* clothing or other consumer products lacking labels, logos, designer insignia, or other form of visible product identification; the mentality of one who eschews such identification. SYN. **independent, original, mysterious, essential; emotionally and psychologically secure.** ANT. **dollarboastful, barcoded, labelled, "strictly from Stepford".**
—KATHA POLLITT

zogbite [zahg'-biyt] *n.* [*perjorative*] used to describe instances of content-free poll-inspired ostensibly focused political sloganeering. *Uh, yeah, spare us the zogbites, Mr. Secretary, let's have the real stuff.* Or: *Excuse me, uck, pass me my pillow, I just heard a zogbite, I have to lie down.* —LAIRD HUNT

Laird Hunt • ***Chris Ware*** / Laird Hunt / Ben Greenman • ***Istvan Banyai*** / Katha Pollitt / Laird Hunt

zong [zahng] 1. *excl.* used to express endorsement or appreciation. *Zong, dude, I love it!* 2. *v. tr.* to render silent or, by extension, speechless (used most often in political contexts). *Mr. President, you have exceeded your allotted time, if you continue with your answer I'm afraid I'll have to zong you.* 3. *n.* [*obsolete*] a popular targeted muting technology of the early 21st century. Applicable to radios and televisions, Zong technology used voice and tone recognition software to permit automatic muting of specific speakers without otherwise interrupting broadcasts. During his unsuccessful 2006 bid for reelection as Governor of Texas, former President George W. Bush memorably remarked, *"I know many of you have your Zongs on, but I would like you to hear me anyway."* —LAIRD HUNT

zzot [zaht] *n.* 1. an indestructible, iridescent green tree frog, the size of your thumbnail. Did you know the remarkable zzot is indifferent to poison? At least, all the various poisons so far known to man! Zzot's shimmering, changeable skin neutralizes the acid in rain; his invisible droppings refertilize that which is barren. Zzot requires no predators (and has none); he will peacefully die if the drawbacks to his continued existence begin to outweigh the benefits. Evolved swiftly, no one understands how, zzot is named for the "frying" or "short-circuiting" sound that ensues when he hops on, and thereby somehow disables, deforestation equipment. Zzot makes a good pet, but prefers his freedom; tends to travel in "packs" (SEE **zzottage**) of about half a million. If espied from afar these zzottages seem like glittering, movable ponds. 2. the noise made when a zzot has disabled a bulldozer.

—SUSAN CHOI

Zzzunday [zuhn'-day] *n.* national holiday occurring once every 28 years, when a Leap Year coincides with a Sunday. Zzzunday is celebrated with 24 hours of uninterrupted sleep, in recognition of an entire generation's accumulated sleep deficit. Secondary holidays have grown to immediately precede Zzzunday, including **Sleepless Friday**, and a **Hibernation Saturday** of block parties, children's sleepovers, and retail promotional sales of bed linens, mattresses, and pillows. Traditionally, insomniacs mark Zzzunday by going out to a Chinese restaurant—if they can find one open that day. —PAUL COLLINS

Zzzunday

APPENDICES

& INDEX

The Declaration of Independence

IN CONGRESS, JULY 4, 1776

THE UNANIMOUS DECLARATION OF THE THIRTEEN UNITED STATES OF AMERICA

When in the Course of human events, it becomes necessary for one people to dissolve the political bands which have connected them with another, and to assume among the powers of the earth, the separate and equal station to which the Laws of Nature and of Nature's God entitle them, a decent respect to the opinions of mankind requires that they should declare the causes which impel them to the separation.

We hold these truths to be self-evident, that all men are created equal, that they are endowed by their Creator with certain unalienable Rights, that among these are Life, Liberty and the pursuit of Happiness.—That to secure these rights, Governments are instituted among Men, deriving their just powers from the consent of the governed,—That whenever any Form of Government becomes destructive of these ends, it is the Right of the People to alter or to abolish it, and to institute new Government, laying its foundation on such principles and organizing its powers in such form, as to them shall seem most likely to effect their Safety and Happiness. Prudence, indeed, will dictate that Governments long established should not be changed for light and transient causes; and accordingly all experience hath shewn, that mankind are more disposed to suffer, while evils are sufferable than to right themselves by abolishing the forms to which they are accustomed. But when a long train of abuses and usurpations, pursuing invariably the same Object evinces a design to reduce them under absolute Despotism, it is their right, it is their duty, to throw off such Government, and to provide new Guards for their future security.—Such has been the patient sufferance of these Colonies; and such is now the necessity which constrains them to alter their former Systems of Government. The history of the present King of Great Britain is a history of repeated injuries and usurpations, all having in direct object the establishment of an absolute Tyranny over these States. To prove this, let Facts be submitted to a candid world.

He has refuted his Assent to Laws, the most wholesome and necessary for the public good.

He has forbidden his Governors to pass Laws of immediate and pressing importance, unless suspended in their operation till his Assent should be obtained; and when so suspended, he has utterly neglected to attend to them.

He has refused to pass other Laws for the accommodation of large districts of people, unless those people would relinquish the right of Representation in the Legislature, a right inestimable to them and formidable to tyrants only.

He has called together legislative bodies at places unusual, uncomfortable, and distant from the depository of their Public Records, for the sole purpose of fatiguing them into compliance with his measures.

He has dissolved Representative Houses repeatedly, for opposing with manly firmness his invasions on the rights of the people.

He has refused for a long time, after such dissolutions, to cause others to be elected, whereby the Legislative Powers, incapable of Annihilation, have returned to the People at large for their exercise; the State remaining in the mean time exposed to all the dangers of invasion from without, and convulsions within.

He has endeavoured to prevent the population of these States; for that purpose obstructing the Laws for Naturalization of Foreigners; refusing to pass others to encourage their migrations hither, and raising the conditions of new Appropriations of Lands.

He has obstructed the Administration of Justice, by refusing his Assent to Laws for establishing Judiciary Powers.

He has made Judges dependent on his Will alone, for the tenure of their offices, and the amount and payment of their salaries.

He has erected a multitude of New Offices, and sent hither swarms of Officers to harass our people, and eat out their substance.

He has kept among us, in times of peace, Standing Armies without the Consent of our legislatures.

He has affected to render the Military independent of and superior to the Civil Power.

He has combined with others to subject us to a jurisdiction foreign to our constitution, and unacknowledged by our laws; giving his Assent to their Acts of pretended Legislation:

For quartering large bodies of armed troops among us:

For protecting them, by a mock Trial, from punishment for any Murders which they should commit on the Inhabitants of these States:

For cutting off our Trade with all parts of the world:

For imposing Taxes on us without our Consent:

For depriving us in many cases, of the benefits of Trial by Jury:

For transporting us beyond Seas to be tried

for pretended offences:

For abolishing the free System of English Laws in a neighbouring Province, establishing therein an Arbitrary government, and enlarging its Boundaries so as to render it at once an example and fit instrument for introducing the same absolute rule into these Colonies:

For taking away our Charters, abolishing our most valuable Laws and altering fundamentally the Forms of our Governments:

For suspending our own Legislatures, and declaring themselves invested with power to legislate for us in all cases whatsoever.

He has abdicated Government here, by declaring us out of his Protection and waging War against us.

He has plundered our seas, ravaged our Coasts, burnt our towns, and destroyed the lives of our people.

He is at this time transporting large Armies of foreign Mercenaries to compleat the works of death, desolation and tyranny, already begun with circumstances of Cruelty & perfidy scarcely paralleled in the most barbarous ages, and totally unworthy the Head of a civilized nation.

He has constrained our fellow Citizens taken Captive on the high Seas to bear Arms against their Country, to become the executioners of their friends and Brethren, or to fall themselves by their Hands.

He has excited domestic insurrections amongst us, and has endeavoured to bring on the inhabitants of our frontiers, the merciless Indian Savages, whose known rule of warfare, is an undistinguished destruction of all ages, sexes and conditions.

In every stage of these Oppressions We have Petitioned for Redress in the most humble terms: Our repeated Petitions have been answered only by repeated injury. A Prince, whose character is thus marked by every act which may define a Tyrant, is unfit to be the ruler of a free people.

Nor have We been wanting in attentions to our British brethren. We have warned them from time to time of attempts by their legislature to extend an unwarrantable jurisdiction over us. We have reminded them of the circumstances of our emigration and settlement here. We have appealed to their native justice and magnanimity, and we have conjured them by the ties of our common kindred to disavow these usurpations, which, would inevitably interrupt our connections and correspondence. They too have been deaf to the voice of justice and of consanguinity. We must, therefore, acquiesce in the necessity, which denounces our Separation, and hold them, as we hold the rest of mankind, Enemies in War, in Peace Friends.

We, therefore, the Representatives of the united States of America, in General Congress, Assembled, appealing to the Supreme Judge of the world for the rectitude of our intentions, do, in the Name, and by Authority of the good People of these Colonies, solemnly publish and declare, That these United Colonies are, and of Right ought to be Free and Independent States; that they are Absolved from all Allegiance to the British Crown, and that all political connection between them and the State of Great Britain, is and ought to be totally dissolved; and that as Free and Independent States, they have full Power to levy War, conclude Peace, contract Alliances, establish Commerce, and to do all other Acts and Things which Independent States may of right do. And for the support of this Declaration, with a firm reliance on the protection of Divine Providence, we mutually pledge to each other our Lives, our Fortunes and our sacred Honor.

Signed by:
Georgia: Button Gwinnett, Lyman Hall, George Walton; North Carolina: William Hooper, Joseph Hewes, John Penn; South Carolina: Edward Rutledge, Thomas Heyward, Jr., Thomas Lynch, Jr., Arthur Middleton; Massachusetts: John Hancock; Maryland: Samuel Chase, William Paca, Thomas Stone, Charles Carroll of Carrollton; Virginia: George Wythe, Richard Henry Lee, Thomas Jefferson, Benjamin Harrison, Thomas Nelson, Jr., Francis Lightfoot Lee, Carter Braxton; Pennsylvania: Robert Morris, Benjamin Rush, Benjamin Franklin, John Morton, George Clymer, James Smith, George Taylor, James Wilson, George Ross; Delaware: Caesar Rodney, George Read, Thomas McKean; New York: William Floyd, Philip Livingston, Francis Lewis, Lewis Morris; New Jersey: Richard Stockton, John Witherspoon, Francis Hopkinson, John Hart, Abraham Clark; New Hampshire: Josiah Bartlett, William Whipple; Massachusetts: Samuel Adams, John Adams, Robert Treat Paine, Elbridge Gerry; Rhode Island: Stephen Hopkins, William Ellery; Connecticut: Roger Sherman, Samuel Huntington, William Williams, Oliver Wolcott; New Hampshire: Matthew Thornton.

Charter of the United Nations

WE THE PEOPLES OF THE UNITED NATIONS DETERMINED

—to save succeeding generations from the scourge of war, which twice in our lifetime has brought untold sorrow to mankind, and
—to reaffirm faith in fundamental human rights, in the dignity and worth of the human person, in the equal rights of men and women and of nations large and small, and
—to establish conditions under which justice and respect for the obligations arising from treaties and other sources of international law can be maintained, and
—to promote social progress and better standards of life in larger freedom,

AND FOR THESE ENDS

—to practice tolerance and live together in peace with one another as good neighbours, and
—to unite our strength to maintain international peace and security, and
—to ensure, by the acceptance of principles and the institution of methods, that armed force shall not be used, save in the common interest, and
—to employ international machinery for the promotion of the economic and social advancement of all peoples,

HAVE RESOLVED TO COMBINE OUR EFFORTS TO ACCOMPLISH THESE AIMS.

Accordingly, our respective Governments, through representatives assembled in the city of San Francisco, who have exhibited their full powers found to be in good and due form, have agreed to the present Charter of the United Nations and do hereby establish an international organization to be known as the United Nations.

CHAPTER I
PURPOSES AND PRINCIPLES

ARTICLE 1
THE PURPOSES OF THE UNITED NATIONS ARE:

1. To maintain international peace and security, and to that end: to take effective collective measures for the prevention and removal of threats to the peace, and for the suppression of acts of aggression or other breaches of the peace, and to bring about by peaceful means, and in conformity with the principles of justice and international law, adjustment or settlement of international disputes or situations which might lead to a breach of the peace;
2. To develop friendly relations among nations based on respect for the principle of equal rights and self-determination of peoples, and to take other appropriate measures to strengthen universal peace;
3. To achieve international co-operation in solving international problems of an economic, social, cultural, or humanitarian character, and in promoting and encouraging respect for human rights and for fundamental freedoms for all without distinction as to race, sex, language, or religion; and
4. To be a centre for harmonizing the actions of nations in the attainment of these common ends.

ARTICLE 2

The Organization and its Members, in pursuit of the Purposes stated in Article 1, shall act in accordance with the following Principles.

1. The Organization is based on the principle of the sovereign equality of all its Members.
2. All Members, in order to ensure to all of them the rights and benefits resulting from membership, shall fulfill in good faith the obligations assumed by them in accordance with the present Charter.
3. All Members shall settle their international disputes by peaceful means in such a manner that international peace and security, and justice, are not endangered.
4. All Members shall refrain in their international relations from the threat or use of force against the territorial integrity or political independence of any state, or in any other manner inconsistent with the Purposes of the United Nations.
5. All Members shall give the United Nations every assistance in any action it takes in accordance with the present Charter, and shall refrain from giving assistance to any state against which the United Nations is taking preventive or enforcement action.
6. The Organization shall ensure that states which are not Members of the United Nations act in accordance with these Principles so far as may be necessary for the maintenance of international peace and security.
7. Nothing contained in the present Charter shall authorize the United Nations to intervene in matters which are essentially within the domestic jurisdiction of any state or shall require the Members to submit such matters to settlement under the present Charter; but this principle shall not prejudice the application of enforcement measures under Chapter VII.

The Universal Declaration of Human Rights

On December 10, 1948 the General Assembly of the United Nations adopted and proclaimed the Universal Declaration of Human Rights, the full text of which appears in the following pages. Following this historic act the Assembly called upon all Member countries to publicize the text of the Declaration and "to cause it to be disseminated, displayed, read and expounded principally in schools and other educational institutions, without distinction based on the political status of countries or territories."

PREAMBLE

Whereas recognition of the inherent dignity and of the equal and inalienable rights of all members of the human family is the foundation of freedom, justice and peace in the world,

Whereas disregard and contempt for human rights have resulted in barbarous acts which have outraged the conscience of mankind, and the advent of a world in which human beings shall enjoy freedom of speech and belief and freedom from fear and want has been proclaimed as the highest aspiration of the common people,

Whereas it is essential, if man is not to be compelled to have recourse, as a last resort, to rebellion against tyranny and oppression, that human rights should be protected by the rule of law,

Whereas it is essential to promote the development of friendly relations between nations,

Whereas the peoples of the United Nations have in the Charter reaffirmed their faith in fundamental human rights, in the dignity and worth of the human person and in the equal rights of men and women and have determined to promote social progress and better standards of life in larger freedom,

Whereas Member States have pledged themselves to achieve, in co-operation with the United Nations, the promotion of universal respect for and observance of human rights and fundamental freedoms,

Whereas a common understanding of these rights and freedoms is of the greatest importance for the full realization of this pledge,

Now, therefore THE GENERAL ASSEMBLY proclaims THIS UNIVERSAL DECLARATION OF HUMAN RIGHTS as a common standard of achievement for all peoples and all nations, to the end that every individual and every organ of society, keeping this Declaration constantly in mind, shall strive by teaching and education to promote respect for these rights and freedoms and by progressive measures, national and international, to secure their universal and effective recognition and observance, both among the peoples of Member States themselves and among the peoples of territories under their jurisdiction.

ARTICLE 1.

All human beings are born free and equal in dignity and rights. They are endowed with reason and conscience and should act towards one another in a spirit of brotherhood.

ARTICLE 2.

Everyone is entitled to all the rights and freedoms set forth in this Declaration, without distinction of any kind, such as race, colour, sex, language, religion, political or other opinion, national or social origin, property, birth or other status. Furthermore, no distinction shall be made on the basis of the political, jurisdictional or international status of the country or territory to which a person belongs, whether it be independent, trust, non-self-governing or under any other limitation of sovereignty.

ARTICLE 3.

Everyone has the right to life, liberty and security of person.

ARTICLE 4.

No one shall be held in slavery or servitude; slavery and the slave trade shall be prohibited in all their forms.

ARTICLE 5.

No one shall be subjected to torture or to cruel, inhuman or degrading treatment or punishment.

ARTICLE 6.

Everyone has the right to recognition everywhere as a person before the law.

ARTICLE 7.

All are equal before the law and are entitled without any discrimination to equal protection of the law. All are entitled to equal protection against any discrimination in violation of this Declaration and against any incitement to such discrimination.

ARTICLE 8.

Everyone has the right to an effective remedy by the competent national tribunals for acts violating the fundamental rights granted him by the constitution or by law.

ARTICLE 9.

No one shall be subjected to arbitrary arrest, detention or exile.

Article 10.

Everyone is entitled in full equality to a fair and public hearing by an independent and impartial tribunal, in the determination of his rights and obligations and of any criminal charge against him.

Article 11.

(1) Everyone charged with a penal offence has the right to be presumed innocent until proved guilty according to law in a public trial at which he has had all the guarantees necessary for his defence.

(2) No one shall be held guilty of any penal offence on account of any act or omission which did not constitute a penal offence, under national or international law, at the time when it was committed. Nor shall a heavier penalty be imposed than the one that was applicable at the time the penal offence was committed.

Article 12.

No one shall be subjected to arbitrary interference with his privacy, family, home or correspondence, nor to attacks upon his honour and reputation. Everyone has the right to the protection of the law against such interference or attacks.

Article 13.

(1) Everyone has the right to freedom of movement and residence within the borders of each state.

(2) Everyone has the right to leave any country, including his own, and to return to his country.

Article 14.

(1) Everyone has the right to seek and to enjoy in other countries asylum from persecution.

(2) This right may not be invoked in the case of prosecutions genuinely arising from non-political crimes or from acts contrary to the purposes and principles of the United Nations.

Article 15.

(1) Everyone has the right to a nationality.

(2) No one shall be arbitrarily deprived of his nationality nor denied the right to change his nationality.

Article 16.

(1) Men and women of full age, without any limitation due to race, nationality or religion, have the right to marry and to found a family. They are entitled to equal rights as to marriage, during marriage and at its dissolution.

(2) Marriage shall be entered into only with the free and full consent of the intending spouses.

(3) The family is the natural and fundamental group unit of society and is entitled to protection by society and the State.

Article 17.

(1) Everyone has the right to own property alone as well as in association with others.

(2) No one shall be arbitrarily deprived of his property.

Article 18.

Everyone has the right to freedom of thought, conscience and religion; this right includes freedom to change his religion or belief, and freedom, either alone or in community with others and in public or private, to manifest his religion or belief in teaching, practice, worship and observance.

Article 19.

Everyone has the right to freedom of opinion and expression; this right includes freedom to hold opinions without interference and to seek, receive and impart information and ideas through any media and regardless of frontiers.

Article 20.

(1) Everyone has the right to freedom of peaceful assembly and association.

(2) No one may be compelled to belong to an association.

Article 21.

(1) Everyone has the right to take part in the government of his country, directly or through freely chosen representatives.

(2) Everyone has the right of equal access to public service in his country.

(3) The will of the people shall be the basis of the authority of government; this will shall be expressed in periodic and genuine elections which shall be by universal and equal suffrage and shall be held by secret vote or by equivalent free voting procedures.

Article 22.

Everyone, as a member of society, has the right to social security and is entitled to realization, through national effort and international co-operation and in accordance with the organization and resources of each State, of the economic, social and cultural rights indispensable for his dignity and the free development of his personality.

Article 23.

(1) Everyone has the right to work, to free choice of employment, to just and favourable conditions of work and to protection against unemployment.

(2) Everyone, without any discrimination, has the right to equal pay for equal work.
(3) Everyone who works has the right to just and favourable remuneration ensuring for himself and his family an existence worthy of human dignity, and supplemented, if necessary, by other means of social protection.
(4) Everyone has the right to form and to join trade unions for the protection of his interests.

ARTICLE 24.
Everyone has the right to rest and leisure, including reasonable limitation of working hours and periodic holidays with pay.

Article 25.
(1) Everyone has the right to a standard of living adequate for the health and well-being of himself and of his family, including food, clothing, housing and medical care and necessary social services, and the right to security in the event of unemployment, sickness, disability, widowhood, old age or other lack of livelihood in circumstances beyond his control.
(2) Motherhood and childhood are entitled to special care and assistance. All children, whether born in or out of wedlock, shall enjoy the same social protection.

Article 26.
(1) Everyone has the right to education. Education shall be free, at least in the elementary and fundamental stages. Elementary education shall be compulsory. Technical and professional education shall be made generally available and higher education shall be equally accessible to all on the basis of merit.
(2) Education shall be directed to the full development of the human personality and to the strengthening of respect for human rights and fundamental freedoms. It shall promote understanding, tolerance and friendship among all nations, racial or religious groups, and shall further the activities of the United Nations for the maintenance of peace.
(3) Parents have a prior right to choose the kind of education that shall be given to their children.

ARTICLE 27.
(1) Everyone has the right freely to participate in the cultural life of the community, to enjoy the arts and to share in scientific advancement and its benefits.
(2) Everyone has the right to the protection of the moral and material interests resulting from any scientific, literary or artistic production of which he is the author.

Article 28.
Everyone is entitled to a social and international order in which the rights and freedoms set forth in this Declaration can be fully realized.

Article 29.
(1) Everyone has duties to the community in which alone the free and full development of his personality is possible.
(2) In the exercise of his rights and freedoms, everyone shall be subject only to such limitations as are determined by law solely for the purpose of securing due recognition and respect for the rights and freedoms of others and of meeting the just requirements of morality, public order and the general welfare in a democratic society.
(3) These rights and freedoms may in no case be exercised contrary to the purposes and principles of the United Nations.

ARTICLE 30.
Nothing in this Declaration may be interpreted as implying for any State, group or person any right to engage in any activity or to perform any act aimed at the destruction of any of the rights and freedoms set forth herein.

The Taguba Report and Its Legacy

In the early part of the century, President George W. Bush put the U.S. military to its most conclusive test with the final war in Iraq, in 2003-4. Until this conflict, there had been brewing for a few decades the belief that American military might could quickly overturn foreign autocracies in quick and decisive fashion. Because of a few recent and relative successes, in Kosovo particularly, there stood the notion, espoused both by conservatives and many liberals, that the use of the American military, or a coalition led by the United States, could liberate a nation and pave the way for a representative democracy. Thus, in the Iraq War, President Bush sent upwards of 500,000 American troops to the region, and they first toppled the Saddam Hussein regime—in rather speedy and spectacular fashion—and then set about stabilizing and rebuilding the country.

Therein lay the problem, or one of them. There was no cohesive plan for the occupation of Iraq, and the country quickly went from a post-war instability—a state which would be expected but also, ideally, temporary—to a more permanent state of lawlessness and abounding terror. The 25 million citizens of Iraq lived in fear of militias, of bandits, of insurgents and of the American troops fighting all of them.

In an attempt to root out the wrongdoers, American troops began a long campaign against the insurgents. In an attempt to find these insurgents, Army troops sought intelligence by raiding thousands of homes, taking over 20,000 Iraqi prisoners in all. It was while these prisoners—later found to be 90 percent innocent—were in custody that the Abu Ghraib prison scandal took place. The events at Abu Ghraib led to the coining, by Senator John McCain, of what he called the Chaos Conundrum. The Chaos Conundrum states that any military action of great size (of over 20,000 troops, he implied), necessarily opens the door to unexpected events, caused not only by the enemy interacting with so many troops on such a scale, but by the unpredictability of the behavior of so many American G.I.s under extreme duress. And because a government cannot adequately control the behavior of so many troops, and cannot rely on all of them to live up to the highest standards of the U.S. military—especially when a good majority of them were brought up from National Guard duty, etc.—operations of great size and scope were no longer undertaken without the most comprehensive plans and justifications, and without the approval of the majority of the American public (See Military Engagements Abroad Voting Act of 2006 [MEAVA]).

The Iraq War caused not only upwards of 2,107 U.S. military deaths, but also 1,310 military suicides, further elucidating the unexpected costs of putting so many—and sometimes ill-trained and prepared troops—in a highly volatile scenario. Finally, the Abu Ghraib scandal reminded the president, his Vice President Cheney (who would be indicted in the spring of 2005 for a host of crimes listed elsewhere) that operations of such a size can never and should never again be undertaken on foreign soil, unless events on a Holocaust-scale are taking place. [See When To Act and How, Wesley Clark's 2009 study of the proper scale for U.S./U.N. intervention.]

Below are excerpts from the 2004 report of then-Major General Antonio M. Taguba (later Senator of Maryland), regarding findings he made during his investigation of conditions at Abu Ghraib. These findings were the impetus behind Sen. McCain's Chaos Conundrum, and also were credited in part with unseating George W. Bush in November of 2004 and causing an overhaul of worldwide military prison policy, the institution of stricter rules governing the extraction of military intelligence, and the freeing of the majority of prisoners held by the American military in secret prisons around the world.

REGARDING PART ONE OF THE INVESTIGATION, I MAKE THE FOLLOWING SPECIFIC FINDINGS OF FACT:

1. (U) That Forward Operating Base (FOB) Abu Ghraib (BCCF) provides security of both criminal and security detainees at the Baghdad Central Correctional Facility, facilitates the conducting of interrogations for CJTF-7, supports other CPA operations at the prison, and enhances the force protection/quality of life of Soldiers assigned in order to ensure the success of ongoing operations to secure a free Iraq. (ANNEX 31)

3. (U) That the 320th Military Police Battalion of the 800th MP Brigade is responsible for the Guard Force at Camp Ganci, Camp Vigilant, & Cellblock 1 of FOB Abu Ghraib (BCCF). That from February 2003 to until he was suspended from his duties on 17 January 2004, LTC Jerry Phillabaum served as the Battalion Commander of the 320th MP Battalion. That from December 2002 until he was suspended from his duties, on 17 January 2004, CPT Donald Reese served as the Company Commander of the 372ndMP Company, which was in charge of guarding detainees at FOB Abu Ghraib. I further find that both the 320th MP Battalion and the 372ndMP Company were located within the confines of FOB Abu Ghraib. (ANNEXES 32 & 45)

4. (U) That from July of 2003 to the present, BG Janis L. Karpinski was the Commander of the 800th MP Brigade. (ANNEX 45)

5. (S) That between October and December 2003, at the Abu Ghraib Confinement Facility (BCCF), numerous incidents of sadistic, blatant, and wanton criminal abuses were inflicted on several detainees. This systemic and illegal abuse of detainees was intentionally perpetrated by several members of the military police guard force (372nd Military Police Company, 320thMilitary Police Battalion, 800th MP Brigade), in Tier (section) 1-A of the Abu Ghraib Prison (BCCF). The allegations of abuse were substantiated by detailed witness statements (ANNEX 26) and the discovery of extremely graphic photographic evidence. Due to the extremely sensitive nature of these photographs and videos, the

ongoing CID investigation, and the potential for the criminal prosecution of several suspects, the photographic evidence is not included in the body of my investigation. The pictures and videos are available from the Criminal Investigative Command and the CTJF-7 prosecution team. In addition to the aforementioned crimes, there were also abuses committed by members of the 325th MI Battalion, 205th MI Brigade, and Joint Interrogation and Debriefing Center (JIDC). Specifically, on 24 November 2003, SPC Luciana Spencer, 205th MI Brigade, sought to degrade a detainee by having him strip and returned to cell naked. (ANNEXES 26 and 53)

6. (S) I find that the intentional abuse of detainees by military police personnel included the following acts:

a. (S) Punching, slapping, and kicking detainees; jumping on their naked feet;

b. (S) Videotaping and photographing naked male and female detainees;

c. (S) Forcibly arranging detainees in various sexually explicit positions for photographing;

d. (S) Forcing detainees to remove their clothing and keeping them naked for several days at a time;

e. (S) Forcing naked male detainees to wear women's underwear;

f. (S) Forcing groups of male detainees to masturbate themselves while being photographed and videotaped;

g. (S) Arranging naked male detainees in a pile and then jumping on them;

h. (S) Positioning a naked detainee on a MRE Box, with a sandbag on his head, and attaching wires to his fingers, toes, and penis to simulate electric torture;

i. (S) Writing "I am a Rapest" (sic) on the leg of a detainee alleged to have forcibly raped a 15-year old fellow detainee, and then photographing him naked;

j. (S) Placing a dog chain or strap around a naked detainee's neck and having a female Soldier pose for a picture;

k. (S) A male MP guard having sex with a female detainee;

l. (S) Using military working dogs (without muzzles) to intimidate and frighten detainees, and in at least one case biting and severely injuring a detainee;

m. (S) Taking photographs of dead Iraqi detainees.

8. (U) In addition, several detainees also described the following acts of abuse, which under the circumstances, I find credible based on the clarity of their statements and supporting evidence provided by other witnesses (ANNEX 26):

a. (U) Breaking chemical lights and pouring the phosphoric liquid on detainees;

b. (U) Threatening detainees with a charged 9mm pistol;

c. (U) Pouring cold water on naked detainees;

d. (U) Beating detainees with a broom handle and a chair;

e. (U) Threatening male detainees with rape;

f. (U) Allowing a military police guard to stitch the wound of a detainee who was injured after being slammed against the wall in his cell;

g. (U) Sodomizing a detainee with a chemical light and perhaps a broom stick.

h. (U) Using military working dogs to frighten and intimidate detainees with threats of attack, and in one instance actually biting a detainee.

9. (U) I have carefully considered the statements provided by the following detainees, which under the circumstances I find credible based on the clarity of their statements and supporting evidence provided by other witnesses:

a. (U) Amjed Isail Waleed, Detainee # 151365
b. (U) Hiadar Saber Abed Miktub-Aboodi, Detainee # 13077
c. (U) Huessin Mohssein Al-Zayiadi, Detainee # 19446
d. (U) Kasim Mehaddi Hilas, Detainee # 151108
e. (U) Mohanded Juma Juma (sic), Detainee # 152307
f. (U) Mustafa Jassim Mustafa, Detainee # 150542
g. (U) Shalan Said Alsharoni, Detainee, # 150422
h. (U) Abd Alwhab Youss, Detainee # 150425
i. (U) Asad Hamza Hanfosh, Detainee # 152529
j. (U) Nori Samir Gunbar Al-Yasseri, Detainee # 7787
k. (U) Thaar Salman Dawod, Detainee # 150427
l. (U) Ameen Sa'eed Al-Sheikh, Detainee # 151362
m. (U) Abdou Hussain Saad Faleh, Detainee # 18470 (ANNEX 26)

10. (U) I find that contrary to the provision of AR 190-8, and the findings found in MG Ryder's Report, Military Intelligence (MI) interrogators and Other US Government Agency's (OGA) interrogators actively requested that MP guards set physical and mental conditions for favorable interrogation of witnesses. Contrary to the findings of MG Ryder's Report, I find that personnel assigned to the 372ndMP Company, 800th MP Brigade were directed to change facility procedures to "set the

conditions" for MI interrogations. I find no direct evidence that MP personnel actually participated in those MI interrogations. (ANNEXES 19, 21, 25, and 26).

11. (U) I reach this finding based on the actual proven abuse that I find was inflicted on detainees and by the following witness statements. (ANNEXES 25 and 26):

a. (U) SPC Sabrina Harman, 372nd MP Company, stated in her sworn statement regarding the incident where a detainee was placed on a box with wires attached to his fingers, toes, and penis, "that her job was to keep detainees awake." She stated that MI was talking to CPL Grainer. She stated: "MI wanted to get them to talk. It is Grainer and Frederick's job to do things for MI and OGA to get these people to talk."

b. (U) SGT Javal S. Davis, 372nd MP Company, stated in his sworn statement as follows: "I witnessed prisoners in the MI hold section, wing 1A being made to do various things that I would question morally. In Wing 1A we were told that they had different rules and different SOP for treatment. I never saw a set of rules or SOP for that section just word of mouth. The Soldier in charge of 1A was Corporal Granier. He stated that the Agents and MI Soldiers would ask him to do things, but nothing was ever in writing he would complain (sic)." When asked why the rules in 1A/1B were different than the rest of the wings, SGT Davis stated: "The rest of the wings are regular prisoners and 1A/B are Military Intelligence (MI) holds." When asked why he did not inform his chain of command about this abuse, SGT Davis stated: " Because I assumed that if they were doing things out of the ordinary or outside the guidelines, someone would have said something. Also the wing belongs to MI and it appeared MI personnel approved of the abuse." SGT Davis also stated that he had heard MI insinuate to the guards to abuse the inmates. When asked what MI said he stated: "Loosen this guy up for us." Make sure he has abad night." "Make sure he gets the treatment." He claimed these comments were made to CPL Granier and SSG Frederick. Finally, SGT Davis stated that (sic): "the MI staffs to my understanding have been giving Granier compliments on the way he has been handling the MI holds. Example being statements like, "Good job, they're breaking down real fast. They answer every question. They're giving out good information, Finally, and Keep up the good work . Stuff like that."

c. (U) SPC Jason Kennel, 372nd MP Company, was asked if he were present when any detainees were abused. He stated: "I saw them nude, but MI would tell us to take away their mattresses, sheets, and clothes." He could not recall who in MI had instructed him to do this, but commented that, "if they wanted me to do that they needed to give me paperwork." He was later informed that "we could not do anything to embarrass the prisoners."

d. (U) Mr. Adel L. Nakhla, a US civilian contract translator, was questioned about several detainees accused of rape. He observed (sic): "They (detainees) were all naked, a bunch of people from MI, the MP were there that night and the inmates were ordered by SGT Granier and SGT Frederick ordered the guys while questioning them to admit what they did. They made them do strange exercises by sliding on their stomach, jump up and down, throw water on them and made them some wet, called them all kinds of names such as "gays" do they like to make love to guys, then they handcuffed their hands together and their legs with shackles and started to stack them on top of each other by insuring that the bottom guys penis will touch the guy on tops butt."

e. (U) SPC Neil A Wallin, 109th Area Support Medical Battalion, a medic testified that: "Cell 1A was used to house high priority detainees and cell 1B was used to house the high risk or trouble making detainees. During my tour at the prison I observed that when the male detainees were first brought to the facility, some of them were made to wear female underwear, which I think was to somehow break them down."

12. (U) I find that prior to its deployment to Iraq for Operation Iraqi Freedom, the 320th MP Battalion and the 372nd MP Company had received no training in detention/internee operations. I also find that very little instruction or training was provided to MP personnel on the applicable rules of the Geneva Convention Relative to the Treatment of Prisoners of War, FM 27-10, AR 190-8, or FM 3-19.40. Moreover, I find that few, if any, copies of the Geneva Conventions were ever made available to MP personnel or detainees. (ANNEXES 21-24, 33, and multiple witness statements)

13. (U) Another obvious example of the Brigade Leadership not communicating with its Soldiers or ensuring their tactical proficiency concerns the incident of detainee abuse that occurred at Camp Bucca, Iraq, on May 12, 2003. Soldiers from the 223rd MP Company reported to the 800th MP Brigade Command at Camp Bucca, that four Military Police Soldiers from the 320th MP Battalion had abused a number of detainees during inprocessing at Camp Bucca. An extensive CID investigation determined that four soldiers from the 320th MP Battalion had kicked and beaten these detainees following a transport mission from Talil

Air Base. (ANNEXES 34 and 35)

14. (U) Formal charges under the UCMJ were preferred against these Soldiers and an Article-32 Investigation conducted by LTC Gentry. He recommended a general court martial for the four accused, which BG Karpinski supported. Despite this documented abuse, there is no evidence that BG Karpinski ever attempted to remind 800th MP Soldiers of the requirements of the Geneva Conventions regarding detainee treatment or took any steps to ensure that such abuse was not repeated. Nor is there any evidence that LTC(P) Phillabaum, the commander of the Soldiers involved in the Camp Bucca abuse incident, took any initiative to ensure his Soldiers were properly trained regarding detainee treatment. (ANNEXES 35 and 62)

RECOMMENDATIONS AS TO PART ONE OF THE INVESTIGATION:

1. (U) Immediately deploy to the Iraq Theater an integrated multi-discipline Mobile Training Team (MTT) comprised of subject matter experts in internment/resettlement operations, international and operational law, information technology, facility management, interrogation and intelligence gathering techniques, chaplains, Arab cultural awareness, and medical practices as it pertains to I/R activities. This team needs to oversee and conduct comprehensive training in all aspects of detainee and confinement operations.

2. (U) That all military police and military intelligence personnel involved in any aspect of detainee operations or interrogation operations in CJTF-7, and subordinate units, be immediately provided with training by an international/operational law attorney on the specific provisions of The Law of Land Warfare FM 27-10, specifically the Geneva Convention Relative to the Treatment of Prisoners of War, Enemy Prisoners of War, Retained Personnel, Civilian Internees, and Other Detainees, and AR 190-8.

3. (U) That a single commander in CJTF-7 be responsible for overall detainee operations throughout the Iraq Theater of Operations. I also recommend that the Provost Marshal General of the Army assign a minimum of two (2) subject matter experts, one officer and one NCO, to assist CJTF-7 in coordinating detainee operations.

4. (U) That detention facility commanders and interrogation facility commanders ensure that appropriate copies of the Geneva Convention Relative to the Treatment of Prisoners of War and notice of protections be made available in both English and the detainees' language and be prominently displayed in all detention facilities. Detainees with questions regarding their treatment should be given the full opportunity to read the Convention.

5. (U) That each detention facility commander and interrogation facility commander publish a complete and comprehensive set of Standing Operating Procedures (SOPs) regarding treatment of detainees, and that all personnel be required to read the SOPs and sign a document indicating that they have read and understand the SOPs.

6. (U) That in accordance with the recommendations of MG Ryder's Assessment Report, and my findings and recommendations in this investigation, all units in the Iraq Theater of Operations conducting internment/confinement/detainment operations in support of Operation Iraqi Freedom be OPCON for all purposes, to include action under the UCMJ, to CJTF-7.

7. (U) Appoint the C3, CJTF as the staff proponent for detainee operations in the Iraq Joint Operations Area (JOA). (MG Tom Miller, C3, CJTF-7, has been appointed by COMCJTF-7).

8. (U) That an inquiry UP AR 381-10, Procedure 15 be conducted to determine the extent of culpability of Military Intelligence personnel, assigned to the 205th MI Brigade and the Joint Interrogation and Debriefing Center (JIDC) regarding abuse of detainees at Abu Ghraib (BCCF).

9. (U) That it is critical that the proponent for detainee operations is assigned a dedicated Senior Judge Advocate, with specialized training and knowledge of international and operational law, to assist and advise on matters of detainee operations.

FINDINGS AND RECOMMENDATIONS (PART TWO)

(U) The Investigation inquire into detainee escapes and accountability lapses as reported by CJTF-7, specifically allegations concerning these events at the Abu Ghraib Prison:

REGARDING PART TWO OF THE INVESTIGATION, I MAKE THE FOLLOWING SPECIFIC FINDINGS OF FACT:

1. The 800th MP Brigade was responsible for theater-wide Internment and Resettlement (I/R) operations. (ANNEXES 45 and 95)

2. (U) The 320th MP Battalion, 800th MP Brigade was tasked with detainee operations at the Abu

Ghraib Prison Complex during the time period covered in this investigation. (ANNEXES 41, 45, and 59)

3. (U) The 310th MP Battalion, 800th MP Brigade was tasked with detainee operations and Forward Operating Base (FOB) Operations at the Camp Bucca Detention Facility until TOA on 26 February 2004. (ANNEXES 41 and 52)

4. (U) The 744th MP Battalion, 800th MP Brigade was tasked with detainee operations and FOB Operations at the HVD Detention Facility until TOA on 4 March 2004. (ANNEXES 41 and 55)

5. (U) The 530th MP Battalion, 800th MP Brigade was tasked with detainee operations and FOB Operations at the MEK holding facility until TOA on 15 March 2004. (ANNEXES 41 and 97)

6. (U) Detainee operations include accountability, care, and well being of Enemy Prisoners of War, Retained Person, Civilian Detainees, and Other Detainees, as well as Iraqi criminal prisoners. (ANNEX 22)

7. (U) The accountability for detainees is doctrinally an MP task IAW FM 3-19.40. (ANNEX 22)

8. (U) There is a general lack of knowledge, implementation, and emphasis of basic legal, regulatory, doctrinal, and command requirements within the 800th MP Brigade and its subordinate units. (Multiple witness statements in ANNEXES 45-91).

9. (U) The handling of detainees and criminal prisoners after in-processing was inconsistent from detention facility to detention facility, compound to compound, encampment to encampment, and even shift to shift throughout the 800th MP Brigade AOR. (ANNEX 37)

10. (U) Camp Bucca, operated by the 310th MP Battalion, had a "Criminal Detainee In-Processing SOP" and a "Training Outline" for transferring and releasing detainees, which appears to have been followed. (ANNEXES 38 and 52)

11. (U) Incoming and outgoing detainees are being documented in the National Detainee Reporting System (NDRS) and Biometric Automated Toolset System (BATS) as required by regulation at all detention facilities. However, it is underutilized and often does not give a "real time" accurate picture of the detainee population due to untimely updating. (ANNEX 56)

12. (U) There was a severe lapse in the accountability of detainees at the Abu Ghraib Prison Complex. The 320th MP Battalion used a self-created "change sheet" to document the transfer of a detainee from one location to another. For proper accountability, it is imperative that these change sheets be processed and the detainee manifest be updated within 24 hours of movement. At Abu Ghraib, this process would often take as long as 4 days to complete. This lag-time resulted in inaccurate detainee Internment Serial Number (ISN) counts, gross differences in the detainee manifest and the actual occupants of an individual compound, and significant confusion of the MP Soldiers. The 320th MP Battalion S-1, CPT Theresa Delbalso, and the S-3, MAJ David DiNenna, explained that this breakdown was due to the lack of manpower to process change sheets in a timely manner. (ANNEXES 39 and 98)

13. (U) The 320th Battalion TACSOP requires detainee accountability at least 4 times daily at Abu Ghraib. However, a detailed review of their operational journals revealed that these accounts were often not done or not documented by the unit. Additionally, there is no indication that accounting errors or the loss of a detainee in the accounting process triggered any immediate corrective action by the Battalion TOC. (ANNEX 44)

14. (U) There is a lack of standardization in the way the 320th MP Battalion conducted physical counts of their detainees. Each compound within a given encampment did their headcounts differently. Some compounds had detainees line up in lines of 10, some had them sit in rows, and some moved all the detainees to one end of the compound and counted them as they passed to the other end of the compound. (ANNEX 98)

15. (U) FM 3-19.40 outlines the need for 2 roll calls (100% ISN band checks) per day. The 320th MP Battalion did this check only 2 times per week. Due to the lack of real-time updates to the system, these checks were regularly inaccurate. (ANNEXES 22, 98)

16. (U) The 800th MP Brigade and subordinate units adopted non-doctrinal terms such as "band checks," "roll-ups," and "call-ups," which contributed to the lapses in accountability and confusion at the soldier level. (ANNEXES 63, 88, and 98)

17. (U) Operational journals at the various compounds and the 320th Battalion TOC contained numerous unprofessional entries and flippant comments, which highlighted the lack of discipline within the unit. There was no indication that the journals were ever reviewed by anyone in their chain of command. (ANNEX 37)

18. (U) Accountability SOPs were not fully developed and standing TACSOPs were widely ignored.

Any SOPs that did exist were not trained on, and were never distributed to the lowest level. Most procedures were shelved at the unit TOC, rather than at the subordinate units and guards mount sites. (ANNEXES 44, 67, 71, and 85)

19. (U) Accountability and facility operations SOPs lacked specificity, implementation measures, and a system of checks and balances to ensure compliance. (ANNEXES 76 and 82)

20. (U) Basic Army Doctrine was not widely referenced or utilized to develop the accountability practices throughout the 800th MP Brigade's subordinate units. Daily processing, accountability, and detainee care appears to have been made up as the operations developed with reliance on, and guidance from, junior members of the unit who had civilian corrections experience. (ANNEX 21)

21. (U) Soldiers were poorly prepared and untrained to conduct I/R operations prior to deployment, at the mobilization site, upon arrival in theater, and throughout their mission. (ANNEXES 62, 63, and 69)

22. (U) The documentation provided to this investigation identified 27 escapes or attempted escapes from the detention facilities throughout the 800th MP Brigade's AOR. Based on my assessment and detailed analysis of the substandard accountability process maintained by the 800th MP Brigade, it is highly likely that there were several more unreported cases of escape that were probably "written off" as administrative errors or otherwise undocumented. 1LT Lewis Raeder, Platoon Leader, 372nd MP Company, reported knowing about at least two additional escapes (one from a work detail and one from a window) from Abu Ghraib (BCCF) that were not documented. LTC Dennis McGlone, Commander, 744th MP Battalion, detailed the escape of one detainee at the High Value Detainee Facility who went to the latrine and then outran the guards and escaped. Lastly, BG Janis Karpinski, Commander, 800th MP Brigade, stated that there were more than 32 escapes from her holding facilities, which does not match the number derived from the investigation materials. (ANNEXES 5-10, 45, 55, and 71)

23. (U) The Abu Ghraib and Camp Bucca detention facilities are significantly over their intended maximum capacity while the guard force is undermanned and under resourced. This imbalance has contributed to the poor living conditions, escapes, and accountability lapses at the various facilities. The overcrowding of the facilities also limits the ability to identify and segregate leaders in the detainee population who may be organizing escapes and riots within the facility. (ANNEXES 6, 22, and 92)

24. (U) The screening, processing, and release of detainees who should not be in custody takes too long and contributes to the overcrowding and unrest in the detention facilities. There are currently three separate release mechanisms in the theater-wide internment operations. First, the apprehending unit can release a detainee if there is a determination that their continued detention is not warranted. Secondly, a criminal detainee can be released after it has been determined that the detainee has no intelligence value, and that their release would not be detrimental to society. BG Karpinski had signature authority to release detainees in this second category. Lastly, detainees accused of committing "Crimes Against the Coalition," who are held throughout the separate facilities in the CJTF-7 AOR, can be released upon a determination that they are of no intelligence value and no longer pose a significant threat to Coalition Forces. The release process for this category of detainee is a screening by the local US Forces Magistrate Cell and a review by a Detainee Release Board consisting of BG Karpinski, COL Marc Warren, SJA, CJTF-7, and MG Barbara Fast, C-2, CJTF-7. MG Fast is the "Detainee Release Authority" for detainees being held for committing crimes against the coalition. According to BG Karpinski, this category of detainee makes up more than 60% of the total detainee population, and is the fastest growing category. However, MG Fast, according to BG Karpinski, routinely denied the board's recommendations to release detainees in this category who were no longer deemed a threat and clearly met the requirements for release. According to BG Karpinski, the extremely slow and ineffective release process has significantly contributed to the overcrowding of the facilities. (ANNEXES 40, 45, and 46)

25. (U) After Action Reviews (AARs) are not routinely being conducted after an escape or other serious incident. No lessons learned seem to have been disseminated to subordinate units to enable corrective action at the lowest level. The Investigation Team requested copies of AARs, and none were provided. (Multiple Witness Statements)

26. (U) Lessons learned (i.e. Findings and Recommendations from various 15-6 Investigations concerning escapes and accountability lapses) were rubber stamped as approved and ordered implemented by BG Karpinski. There is no evidence that the majority of her orders directing the implementation of substantive changes were ever acted upon. Additionally, there was no follow-up by the command to verify the corrective actions were taken. Had the findings and recommendations contained within

their own investigations been analyzed and actually implemented by BG Karpinski, many of the subsequent escapes, accountability lapses, and cases of abuse may have been prevented. (ANNEXES 5-10)

27. (U) The perimeter lighting around Abu Ghraib and the detention facility at Camp Bucca is inadequate and needs to be improved to illuminate dark areas that have routinely become avenues of escape. (ANNEX 6)

28. (U) Neither the camp rules nor the provisions of the Geneva Conventions are posted in English or in the language of the detainees at any of the detention facilities in the 800th MP Brigade's AOR, even after several investigations had annotated the lack of this critical requirement. (Multiple Witness Statements and the Personal Observations of the Investigation Team)

29. (U) The Iraqi guards at Abu Ghraib (BCCF) demonstrate questionable work ethics and loyalties, and are a potentially dangerous contingent within the Hard-Site. These guards have furnished the Iraqi criminal inmates with contraband, weapons, and information. Additionally, they have facilitated the escape of at least one detainee. (ANNEX 8 and 26-SPC Polak's Statement)

30. (U) In general, US civilian contract personnel (Titan Corporation, CACI, etc...), third country nationals, and local contractors do not appear to be properly supervised within the detention facility at Abu Ghraib. During our on-site inspection, they wandered about with too much unsupervised free access in the detainee area. Having civilians in various outfits (civilian and DCUs) in and about the detainee area causes confusion and may have contributed to the difficulties in the accountability process and with detecting escapes. (ANNEX 51, Multiple Witness Statements, and the Personal Observations of the Investigation Team)

31. (U) SGM Marc Emerson, Operations SGM, 320th MP Battalion, contended that the Detainee Rules of Engagement (DROE) and the general principles of the Geneva Convention were briefed at every guard mount and shift change on Abu Ghraib. However, none of our witnesses, nor our personal observations, support his contention. I find that SGM Emerson was not a credible witness. (ANNEXES 45, 80, and the Personal Observations of the Investigation Team)

32. (U) Several interviewees insisted that the MP and MI Soldiers at Abu Ghraib (BCCF) received regular training on the basics of detainee operations; however, they have been unable to produce any verifying documentation, sign-in rosters, or soldiers who can recall the content of this training. (Annexes 59, 80, and the Absence of any Training Records)

33. (S/NF) The various detention facilities operated by the 800th MP Brigade have routinely held persons brought to them by Other Government Agencies (OGAs) without accounting for them, knowing their identities, or even the reason for their detention. The Joint Interrogation and Debriefing Center (JIDC) at Abu Ghraib called these detainees "ghost detainees." On at least one occasion, the 320th MP Battalion at Abu Ghraib held a handful of "ghost detainees" (6-8) for OGAs that they moved around within the facility to hide them from a visiting International Committee of the Red Cross (ICRC) survey team. This maneuver was deceptive, contrary to Army Doctrine, and in violation of international law. (ANNEX 53)

34. (U) The following riots, escapes, and shootings have been documented and reported to this Investigation Team. Although there is no data from other missions of similar size and duration to compare the number of escapes with, the most significant factors derived from these reports are twofold. First, investigations and SIRs lacked critical data needed to evaluate the details of each incident. Second, each investigation seems to have pointed to the same types of deficiencies; however, little to nothing was done to correct the problems and to implement the recommendations as was ordered by BG Karpinski, nor was there any command emphasis to ensure these deficiencies were corrected:

a. (U) 4 June 03- This escape was mentioned in the 15-6 Investigation covering the 13 June 03 escape, recapture, and shootings of detainees at Camp Vigilant (320th MP Battalion). However, no investigation or additional information was provided as requested by this investigation team. (ANNEX 7)

b. (U) 9 June 03- Riot and shootings of five detainees at Camp Cropper. (115th MP Battalion) Several detainees allegedly rioted after a detainee was subdued by MPs of the 115th MP Battalion after striking a guard in compound B of Camp Cropper. A 15-6 investigation by 1LT Magowan (115th MP Battalion, Platoon Leader) concluded that a detainee had acted up and hit an MP. After being subdued, one of the MPs took off his DCU top and flexed his muscles to the detainees, which further escalated the riot. The MPs were overwhelmed and the guards fired lethal rounds to protect the life of the compound MPs, whereby 5 detainees were wounded. Contributing factors were poor communications, no clear chain of command, facility-obstructed views of posted guards, the QRF did not have non-lethal equipment, and the SOP was inadequate and outdated. (ANNEX 5)

c. (U) 12 June 03- Escape and recapture of detainee #8399, escape and shooting of detainee # 7166, and attempted escape of an unidentified detainee from Camp Cropper Holding Area (115th MP Battalion). Several detainees allegedly made their escape in the nighttime hours prior to 0300. A 15-6 investigation by CPT Wendlandt (115th MP Battalion, S-2) concluded that the detainees allegedly escaped by crawling under the wire at a location with inadequate lighting. One detainee was stopped prior to escape. An MP of the 115th MP Battalion search team recaptured detainee # 8399, and detainee # 7166 was shot and killed by a Soldier during the recapture process. Contributing factors were overcrowding, poor lighting, and the nature of the hardened criminal detainees at that location. It is of particular note that the command was informed at least 24 hours in advance of the upcoming escape attempt and started doing amplified announcements in Arabic stating the camp rules. The investigation pointed out that rules and guidelines were not posted in the camps in the detainees' native languages. (ANNEX 6)

d. (U) 13 June 03- Escape and recapture of detainee # 8968 and the shooting of eight detainees at Abu Ghraib (BCCF) (320th MP Battalion). Several detainees allegedly attempted to escape at about 1400 hours from the Camp Vigilant Compound, Abu Ghraib (BCCF). A 15-6 investigation by CPT Wyks (400th MP Battalion, S-1) concluded that the detainee allegedly escaped by sliding under the wire while the tower guard was turned in the other direction. This detainee was subsequently apprehended by the QRF. At about 1600 the same day, 30-40 detainees rioted and pelted three interior MP guards with rocks. One guard was injured and the tower guards fired lethal rounds at the rioters injuring 7 and killing 1 detainee. (ANNEX 7)

e. (U) 05 November 03- Escape of detainees # 9877 and # 10739 from Abu Ghraib (320th MP Battalion). Several detainees allegedly escaped at 0345 from the Hard-Site, Abu Ghraib (BCCF). An SIR was initiated by SPC Warner (320th MP Battalion, S-3 RTO). The SIR indicated that 2 criminal prisoners escaped through their cell window in tier 3A of the Hard-Site. No information on findings, contributing factors, or corrective action has been provided to this investigation team. (ANNEX 11)

f. (U) 07 November 03- Escape of detainee # 14239 from Abu Ghraib (320th MP Battalion). A detainee allegedly escaped at 1330 from Compound 2 of the Ganci Encampment, Abu Ghraib (BCCF). An SIR was initiated by SSG Hydro (320th MP Battalion, S-3 Asst. NCOIC). The SIR indicated that a detainee escaped from the North end of the compound and was discovered missing during distribution of the noon meal, but there is no method of escape listed in the SIR. No information on findings, contributing factors, or corrective action has been provided to this investigation team. (ANNEX 12)

g. (U) 08 November 03- Escape of detainees # 115089, # 151623, # 151624, # 116734, # 116735, and # 116738 from Abu Ghraib (320th MP Battalion). Several detainees allegedly escaped at 2022 from Compound 8 of the Ganci encampment, Abu Ghraib. An SIR was initiated by MAJ DiNenna (320th MP Battalion, S-3). The SIR indicated that 5-6 prisoners escaped from the North end of the compound, but there is no method of escape listed in the SIR. No information on findings, contributing factors, or corrective action has been provided to this investigation team. (ANNEX 13)

h. (U) 24 November 03- Riot and shooting of 12 detainees # 150216, #150894, #153096, 153165, #153169, #116361, #153399, #20257, #150348, #152616, #116146, and #152156 at Abu Ghraib(320th MP Battalion). Several detainees allegedly began to riot at about 1300 in all of the compounds at the Ganci encampment. This resulted in the shooting deaths of 3 detainees, 9 wounded detainees, and 9 injured US Soldiers. A 15-6 investigation by COL Bruce Falcone (220th MP Brigade, Deputy Commander) concluded that the detainees rioted in protest of their living conditions, that the riot turned violent, the use of non-lethal force was ineffective, and, after the 320th MP Battalion CDR executed "Golden Spike," the emergency containment plan, the use of deadly force was authorized. Contributing factors were lack of comprehensive training of guards, poor or non-existent SOPs, no formal guard-mount conducted prior to shift, no rehearsals or ongoing training, the mix of less than lethal rounds with lethal rounds in weapons, no AARs being conducted after incidents, ROE not posted and not understood, overcrowding, uniforms not standardized, and poor communication between the command and Soldiers. (ANNEX 8)

i. (U) 24 November 03- Shooting of detainee at Abu Ghraib (320th MP Battalion). A detainee allegedly had a pistol in his cell and around 1830 an extraction team shot him with less than lethal and lethal rounds in the process of recovering the weapon. A 15-6 investigation by COL Bruce Falcone (220th Brigade, Deputy Commander) concluded that one of the detainees in tier 1A of the Hard Site had gotten a pistol and a couple of knives from an Iraqi Guard working in the encampment. Immediately upon receipt of this information, an ad-hoc extraction team consisting of MP and MI personnel conducted what they called a routine cell search, which resulted in the shooting of an MP and the detainee. Contributing factors were a corrupt Iraqi Guard, inadequate SOPs, the Detention ROE in place at the time was ineffective due to the numerous levels of authorization needed for use of lethal force, poorly trained MPs, unclear lanes of responsibility, and ambiguous relationship between the MI and MP assets. (ANNEX 8)

j. (U) 13 December 03- Shooting by non-lethal means into crowd at Abu Ghraib(320th MP Battalion). Several detainees allegedly got into a detainee-on-detainee fight around 1030 in Compound 8 of the Ganci encampment, Abu Ghraib. An SIR was initiated by SSG Matash (320th MP Battalion, S-3 Section). The SIR indicated that there was a fight in the compound and the MPs used a non-lethal crowd-dispersing round to break up the fight, which was successful. No information on findings, contributing factors, or corrective action has been provided to this investigation team. (ANNEX 14)

k. (U) 13 December 03- Shooting by non-lethal means into crowd at Abu Ghraib (320th MP Battalion). Several detainees allegedly got into a detainee-on-detainee fight around 1120 in Compound 2 of the Ganci encampment, Abu Ghraib. An SIR was initiated by SSG Matash (320th MP Battalion, S-3 Section). The SIR indicated that there was a fight in the compound and the MPs used two non-lethal shots to disperse the crowd, which was successful. No information on findings, contributing factors, or corrective action has been provided to this investigation team. (ANNEX 15)

l. (U) 13 December 03- Shooting by non-lethal means into crowd at Abu Ghraib(320th MP Battalion). Approximately 30-40 detainees allegedly got into a detainee-on-detainee fight around 1642 in Compound 3 of the Ganci encampment, Abu Ghraib (BCCF). An SIR was initiated by SSG Matash (320th MP Battalion, S-3 Section). The SIR indicates that there was a fight in the compound and the MPs used a non-lethal crowd-dispersing round to break up the fight, which was successful. No information on findings, contributing factors, or corrective action has been provided to this investigation team. (ANNEX 16)

m. (U) 17 December 03- Shooting by non-lethal means of detainee from Abu Ghraib(320th MP Battalion). Several detainees allegedly assaulted an MP at 1459 inside the Ganci Encampment, Abu Ghraib (BCCF). An SIR was initiated by SSG Matash (320th MP BRIGADE, S-3 Section). The SIR indicated that three detainees assaulted an MP, which resulted in the use of a non-lethal shot that calmed the situation. No information on findings, contributing factors, or corrective action has been provided to this investigation team. (ANNEX 17)

n. (U) 07 January 04- Escape of detainee #115032 from Camp Bucca(310th MP Battalion). A detainee allegedly escaped between the hours of 0445 and 0640 from Compound 12, of Camp Bucca. Investigation by CPT Kaires (310th MP Battalion S-3) and CPT Holsombeck (724th MP Battalion S-3) concluded that the detainee escaped through an undetected weakness in the wire. Contributing factors were inexperienced guards, lapses in accountability, complacency, lack of leadership presence, poor visibility, and lack of clear and concise communication between the guards and the leadership. (ANNEX 9)

o. (U) 12 January 04- Escape of Detainees #115314 and #109950 as well as the escape and recapture of 5 unknown detainees at the Camp Bucca Detention Facility (310th MP Battalion). Several detainees allegedly escaped around 0300 from Compound 12, of Camp Bucca. An AR 15-6 Investigation by LTC Leigh Coulter (800th MP Brigade, OIC Camp Arifjan Detachment) concluded that three of the detainees escaped through the front holding cell during conditions of limited visibility due to fog. One of the detainees was noticed, shot with a non-lethal round, and returned to his holding compound. That same night, 4 detainees exited through the wire on the South side of the camp and were seen and apprehended by the QRF. Contributing factors were the lack of a coordinated effort for emplacement of MPs during implementation of the fog plan, overcrowding, and poor communications. (ANNEX 10)

p. (U) 14 January 04- Escape of detainee #12436 and missing Iraqi guard from Hard-Site, Abu Ghraib (320th MP Battalion). A detainee allegedly escaped at 1335 from the Hard Site at Abu Ghraib (BCCF). An SIR was initiated by SSG Hydro (320th MP Battalion, S-3 Asst. NCOIC). The SIR indicates that an Iraqi guard assisted a detainee to escape by signing him out on a work detail and disappearing with him. At the time of the second SIR, neither missing person had been located. No information on findings, contributing factors, or corrective action has been provided to this investigation team. (ANNEX 99)

q. (U) 26 January 04- Escape of detainees #s 115236, 116272, and 151933 from Camp Bucca(310th MP Battalion). Several Detainees allegedly escaped between the hours of 0440 and 0700 during a period of intense fog. Investigation by CPT Kaires (310th MP Battalion S-3) concluded that the detainees crawled under a fence when visibility was only 10-15 meters due to fog.

Contributing factors were the limited visibility (darkness under foggy conditions), lack of proper accountability reporting, inadequate number of guards, commencement of detainee feeding during low visibility operations, and poorly rested MPs. (ANNEX 18)

35. (U) As I have previously indicated, this investigation determined that there was virtually a complete lack of detailed SOPs at any of the detention facilities. Moreover, despite the fact that there were numerous reported escapes at detention facilities throughout Iraq (in excess of 35), AR 15-6 Investigations following these escapes were simply forgotten or ignored by the Brigade Commander with no dissemination to other facilities. After-Action Reports and Lessons Learned, if done at all, remained at individual facilities and were not shared among other commanders or soldiers throughout the Brigade. The Command never issued standard TTPs for handling escape incidents. (ANNEXES 5-10, Multiple Witness Statements, and the Personal Observations of the Investigation Team)

RECOMMENDATIONS REGARDING PART TWO OF THE INVESTIGATION:

(U) ANNEX 100 of this investigation contains a detailed and referenced series of recommendations for improving the detainee accountability practices throughout the OIF area of operations. (U) Accountability practices throughout any particular detention facility must be standardized and in accordance with applicable regulations and international law. (U) The NDRS and BATS accounting systems must be expanded and used to their fullest extent to facilitate real time updating when detainees are moved and or transferred from one location to another. (U) "Change sheets," or their doctrinal equivalent must be immediately processed and updated into the system to ensure accurate accountability. The detainee roll call or ISN counts must match the manifest provided to the compound guards to ensure proper accountability of detainees. (U) Develop, staff, and implement comprehensive and detailed SOPs utilizing the lessons learned from this investigation as well as any previous findings, recommendations, and reports. (U) SOPs must be written, disseminated, trained on, and understood at the lowest level.(U) Iraqi criminal prisoners must be held in separate facilities from any other category of detainee. (U) All of the compounds should be wired into the master manifest whereby MP Soldiers can account for their detainees in real time and without waiting for their change sheets to be processed. This would also have the change sheet serve as a way to check up on the accuracy of the manifest as updated by each compound. The BATS and NDRS system can be utilized for this function.(U) Accountability lapses, escapes, and disturbances within the detainment facilities must be immediately reported through both the operational and administrative Chain of Command via a Serious Incident Report (SIR). The SIRs must then be tracked and followed by daily SITREPs until the situation is resolved. (U) Detention Rules of Engagement (DROE), Interrogation Rules of Engagement (IROE), and the principles of the Geneva Conventions need to be briefed at every shift change and guard mount. (U) AARs must be conducted after serious incidents at any given facility. The observations and corrective actions that develop from the AARs must be analyzed by the respective MP Battalion S-3 section, developed into a plan of action, shared with the other facilities, and implemented as a matter of policy. (U) There must be significant structural improvements at each of the detention facilities. The needed changes include significant enhancement of perimeter lighting, additional chain link fencing, staking down of all concertina wire, hard site development, and expansion of Abu Ghraib (BCCF). (U) The Geneva Conventions and the facility rules must be prominently displayed in English and the language of the detainees at each compound and encampment at every detention facility IAW AR 190-8. (U) Further restrict US civilians and other contractors' access throughout the facility. Contractors and civilians must be in an authorized and easily identifiable uniform to be more easily distinguished from the masses of detainees in civilian clothes. (U) Facilities must have a stop movement/transfer period of at least 1 hour prior to every 100% detainee roll call and ISN counts to ensure accurate accountability.(U) The method for doing head counts of detainees within a given compound must be standardized. (U) Those military units conducting I/R operations must know of, train on, and constantly reference the applicable Army Doctrine and CJTF command policies. The references provided in this report cover nearly every deficiency I have enumerated. Although they do not, and cannot, make up for leadership shortfalls, all soldiers, at all levels, can use them to maintain standardized operating procedures and efficient accountability practices.

REGARDING PART THREE OF THE INVESTIGATION, I MAKE THE FOLLOWING SPECIFIC FINDINGS OF FACT:

2. (U) Prior to BG Karpinski taking command, members of the 800th MP Brigade believed they would be allowed to go home when all the detainees were released from the Camp Bucca Theater Internment Facility following the cessation of major ground combat on 1 May 2003. At one point,

approximately 7,000 to 8,000 detainees were held at Camp Bucca. Through Article-5 Tribunals and a screening process, several thousand detainees were released. Many in the command believed they would go home when the detainees were released. In late May-early June 2003 the 800th MPBrigade was given a new mission to manage the Iraqi penal system and several detention centers. This new mission meant Soldiers would not redeploy to CONUS when anticipated. Morale suffered, and over the next few months there did not appear to have been any attempt by the Command to mitigate this morale problem. (ANNEXES 45 and 96)

3. (U) There is abundant evidence in the statements of numerous witnesses that soldiers throughout the 800th MP Brigade were not proficient in their basic MOS skills, particularly regarding internment/resettlement operations. Moreover, there is no evidence that the command, although aware of these deficiencies, attempted to correct them in any systemic manner other than ad hoc training by individuals with civilian corrections experience. (Multiple Witness Statements and the Personal Observations of the Investigation Team)

4. (U) I find that the 800th MP Brigade was not adequately trained for a mission that included operating a prison or penal institution at Abu Ghraib Prison Complex. As the Ryder Assessment found, I also concur that units of the 800th MP Brigade did not receive corrections-specific training during their mobilization period. MP units did not receive pinpoint assignments prior to mobilization and during the post mobilization training, and thus could not train for specific missions. The training that was accomplished at the mobilization sites were developed and implemented at the company level with little or no direction or supervision at the Battalion and Brigade levels, and consisted primarily of common tasks and law enforcement training. However, I found no evidence that the Command, although aware of this deficiency, ever requested specific corrections training from the Commandant of the Military Police School, the US Army Confinement Facility at Mannheim, Germany, the Provost Marshal General of the Army, or the US Army Disciplinary Barracks at Fort Leavenworth, Kansas. (ANNEXES 19 and 76)

5. (U) I find that without adequate training for a civilian internee detention mission, Brigade personnel relied heavily on individuals within the Brigade who had civilian corrections experience, including many who worked as prison guards or corrections officials in their civilian jobs. Almost every witness we interviewed had no familiarity with the provisions of AR 190-8 or FM 3-19.40. It does not appear that a Mission Essential Task List (METL) based on in-theater missions was ever developed nor was a training plan implemented throughout the Brigade. (ANNEXES 21, 22, 67, and 81)

6. (U) I also find, as did MG Ryder's Team, that the 800th MP Brigade as a whole, was understrength for the mission for which it was tasked. Army Doctrine dictates that an I/R Brigade can be organized with between 7 and 21 battalions, and that the average battalion size element should be able to handle approximately 4000 detainees at a time. This investigation indicates that BG Karpinski and her staff did a poor job allocating resources throughout the Iraq JOA. Abu Ghraib (BCCF) normally housed between 6000 and 7000 detainees, yet it was operated by only one battalion. In contrast, the HVD Facility maintains only about 100 detainees, and is also run by an entire battalion. (ANNEXES 19, 22, and 96)

8. (U) With respect to the 800th MP Brigade mission at Abu Ghraib (BCCF), I find that there was clear friction and lack of effective communication between the Commander, 205th MI Brigade, who controlled FOB Abu Ghraib (BCCF) after 19 November 2003, and the Commander, 800th MP Brigade, who controlled detainee operations inside the FOB. There was no clear delineation of responsibility between commands, little coordination at the command level, and no integration of the two functions. Coordination occurred at the lowest possible levels with little oversight by commanders. (ANNEXES 31, 45, and 46)

The Art of the Essay

The essay has been a popular form of discourse and enlightenment for many centuries. Some say that the art is not what it once was, some say it's better than ever, others are eating hummus sandwiches in the Columbus bus station. Nevertheless, it is widely believed that the art form was perfected in the late twentieth century by the author below, who wrote one of the more lucid and convincing examples of the form on the eve of the 2004 presidential elections. That essay, which swayed hundreds of thousands of voters, including the many college students who had been veering toward a more conservative agenda, is reprinted below.

Cold Turkey

by Kurt Vonnegut

Many years ago, I was so innocent I still considered it possible that we could become the humane and reasonable America so many members of my generation used to dream of. We dreamed of such an America during the Great Depression, when there were no jobs. And then we fought and often died for that dream during the Second World War, when there was no peace.

But I know now that there is not a chance in hell of America's becoming humane and reasonable. Because power corrupts us, and absolute power corrupts absolutely. Human beings are chimpanzees who get crazy drunk on power. By saying that our leaders are power-drunk chimpanzees, am I in danger of wrecking the morale of our soldiers fighting and dying in the Middle East? Their morale, like so many bodies, is already shot to pieces. They are being treated, as I never was, like toys a rich kid got for Christmas.

When you get to my age, if you get to my age, which is 81, and if you have reproduced, you will find yourself asking your own children, who are themselves middle-aged, what life is all about. I have seven kids, four of them adopted. Many of you reading this are probably the same age as my grandchildren. They, like you, are being royally shafted and lied to by our Baby Boomer corporations and government.

I put my big question about life to my biological son Mark. Mark is a pediatrician, and author of a memoir, The Eden Express. It is about his crackup, straightjacket and padded cell stuff, from which he recovered sufficiently to graduate from Harvard Medical School.

Dr. Vonnegut said this to his doddering old dad: "Father, we are here to help each other get through this thing, whatever it is." So I pass that on to you. Write it down, and put it in your computer, so you can forget it.

I have to say that's a pretty good sound bite, almost as good as, "Do unto others as you would have them do unto you." A lot of people think Jesus said that, because it is so much the sort of thing Jesus liked to say. But it was actually said by Confucius, a Chinese philosopher, 500 years before there was that greatest and most humane of human beings, named Jesus Christ.

The Chinese also gave us, via Marco Polo, pasta and the formula for gunpowder. The Chinese were so dumb they only used gunpowder for fireworks. And everybody was so dumb back then that nobody in either hemisphere even knew that there was another one.

But back to people, like Confucius and Jesus and my son the doctor, Mark, who've said how we could behave more humanely, and maybe make the world a less painful place. One of my favorites is Eugene Debs, from Terre Haute in my native state of Indiana. Get a load of this:

Eugene Debs, who died back in 1926, when I was only 4, ran five times as the Socialist Party candidate for president, winning 900,000 votes, 6 percent of the popular vote, in 1912, if you can imagine such a ballot. He had this to say while campaigning:

> *"As long as there is a lower class, I am in it.*
> *As long as there is a criminal element, I'm of it.*
> *As long as there is a soul in prison, I am not free."*

Doesn't anything socialistic make you want to throw up? Like great public schools or health insurance for all?

How about Jesus' Sermon on the Mount, the Beatitudes?

Blessed are the meek, for they shall inherit the Earth.

Blessed are the merciful, for they shall obtain mercy.

Blessed are the peacemakers, for they shall be called the children of God.

And so on. Not exactly planks in a Republican platform. Not exactly Donald Rumsfeld or Dick Cheney stuff.

For some reason, the most vocal Christians among us never mention the Beatitudes. But, often with tears in their eyes, they demand that the Ten Commandments be posted in public buildings. And of course that's Moses, not Jesus. I haven't heard one of them demand that the Sermon on the Mount, the Beatitudes, be posted anywhere.

"Blessed are the merciful" in a courtroom? "Blessed are the peacemakers" in the Pentagon? Give me a break!

There is a tragic flaw in our precious Constitution, and I don't know what can be done to fix it. This is it: Only nut cases want to be president.

But, when you stop to think about it, only a nut case would want to be a human being, if he or she had a choice. Such treacherous, untrustworthy, lying and greedy animals we are!

I was born a human being in 1922 A.D. What does "A.D." signify? That commemorates an inmate of this lunatic asylum we call Earth who was nailed to a wooden cross by a bunch of other inmates. With him still conscious, they hammered spikes through his wrists and insteps, and into the wood. Then they set the cross upright, so he dangled up there where even the shortest person in the crowd could see him writhing this way and that.

Can you imagine people doing such a thing to a person?

No problem. That's entertainment. Ask the devout Roman Catholic Mel Gibson, who, as an act of piety, has just made a fortune with a movie about how Jesus was tortured. Never mind what Jesus said.

During the reign of King Henry the Eighth, founder of the Church of England, he had a counterfeiter boiled alive in public. Show biz again.

Mel Gibson's next movie should be The Counterfeiter. Box office records will again be broken.

One of the few good things about modern times: If you die horribly on television, you will not have died in vain. You will have entertained us.

And what did the great British historian Edward Gibbon, 1737-1794 A.D., have to say about the human record so far? He said, "History is indeed little more than the register of the crimes, follies and misfortunes of mankind."

The same can be said about this morning's edition of the New York Times.

The French-Algerian writer Albert Camus, who won a Nobel Prize for Literature in 1957, wrote, "There is but one truly serious philosophical problem, and that is suicide." So there's another barrel of laughs from literature. Camus died in an automobile accident. His dates? 1913-1960 A.D.

Listen. All great literature is about what a bummer it is to be a human being: Moby Dick, Huckleberry Finn, The Red Badge of Courage, the Iliad and the Odyssey, Crime and Punishment, the Bible and The Charge of the Light Brigade.

But I have to say this in defense of humankind: No matter in what era in history, including the Garden of Eden, everybody just got there. And, except for the Garden of Eden, there were already all these crazy games going on, which could make you act crazy, even if you weren't crazy to begin with. Some of the games that were already going on when you got here were love and hate, liberalism and conservatism, automobiles and credit cards, golf and girls' basketball.

Even crazier than golf, though, is modern American politics, where, thanks to TV and for the convenience of TV, you can only be one of two kinds of human beings, either a liberal or a conservative.

Actually, this same sort of thing happened to the people of England generations ago, and Sir William Gilbert, of the radical team of Gilbert and Sullivan, wrote these words for a song about it back then:

I often think it's comical
How nature always does contrive
That every boy and every gal
That's born into the world alive
Is either a little Liberal
Or else a little Conservative.

Which one are you in this country? It's practically a law of life that you have to be one or the other? If you aren't one or the other, you might as well be a doughnut.

If some of you still haven't decided, I'll make it easy for you.

If you want to take my guns away from me, and you're all for murdering fetuses, and love it when homosexuals marry each other, and want to give them kitchen appliances at their showers, and you're for the poor, you're a liberal.

If you are against those perversions and for the rich, you're a conservative. What could be simpler?

My government's got a war on drugs. But get this: The two most widely abused and addictive and destructive of all substances are both perfectly legal.

One, of course, is ethyl alcohol. And President George W. Bush, no less, and by his own admission, was smashed or tiddley-poo or four sheets to the wind a good deal of the time from when he was 16 until he was 41. When he was 41, he says, Jesus appeared to him and made him knock off the sauce, stop gargling nose paint.

Other drunks have seen pink elephants.

And do you know why I think he is so pissed off at Arabs? They invented algebra. Arabs also invented the numbers we use, including a symbol for nothing, which nobody else had ever had before. You think Arabs are dumb? Try doing long division with Roman numerals.

We're spreading democracy, are we? Same way European explorers brought Christianity to the Indians, what we now call "Native Americans."

How ungrateful they were! How ungrateful are the people of Baghdad today.

So let's give another big tax cut to the super-rich. That'll teach bin Laden a lesson he won't soon forget. Hail to the Chief.

That chief and his cohorts have as little to do with Democracy as the Europeans had to do with Christianity. We the people have absolutely no say in whatever they choose to do next. In case you haven't noticed, they've already cleaned out the treasury, passing it out to pals in the war and national security rackets, leaving your generation and the next one with a perfectly enormous debt that you'll be asked to repay.

Nobody let out a peep when they did that to you, because they have disconnected every burglar alarm in the Constitution: The House, the Senate, the Supreme Court, the FBI, the free press (which, having been embedded, has forsaken the First Amendment) and We the People.

About my own history of foreign substance abuse. I've been a coward about heroin and cocaine and LSD and so on, afraid they might put me over the edge. I did smoke a joint of marijuana one time with Jerry Garcia and the Grateful Dead, just to be sociable. It didn't seem to do anything to me, one way or the other, so I never did it again. And by the grace of God, or whatever, I am not an alcoholic, largely a matter of genes. I take a couple of drinks now and then, and will do it again tonight. But two is my limit. No problem.

I am of course notoriously hooked on cigarettes. I keep hoping the things will kill me. A fire at one end and a fool at the other.

But I'll tell you one thing: I once had a high that not even crack cocaine could match. That was when I got my first driver's license! Look out, world, here comes Kurt Vonnegut.

And my car back then, a Studebaker, as I recall, was powered, as are almost all means of transportation and other machinery today, and electric power plants and furnaces, by the most abused and addictive and destructive drugs of all: fossil fuels.

When you got here, even when I got here, the industrialized world was already hopelessly hooked on fossil fuels, and very soon now there won't be any more of those. Cold turkey.

Can I tell you the truth? I mean this isn't like TV news, is it?

Here's what I think the truth is: We are all addicts of fossil fuels in a state of denial, about to face cold turkey.

And like so many addicts about to face cold turkey, our leaders are now committing violent crimes to get what little is left of what we're hooked on.

The History of Indo-European Language

The Indo-European family of languages, of which English is a member, is descended from a prehistoric language, Proto-European, spoken in a region that has not been identified, possibly in the fifth millennium B.C. The chart shows the principal languages of the family, arranged in a diagrammatic form that displays their genetic relationships and loosely suggests their geographic distribution.

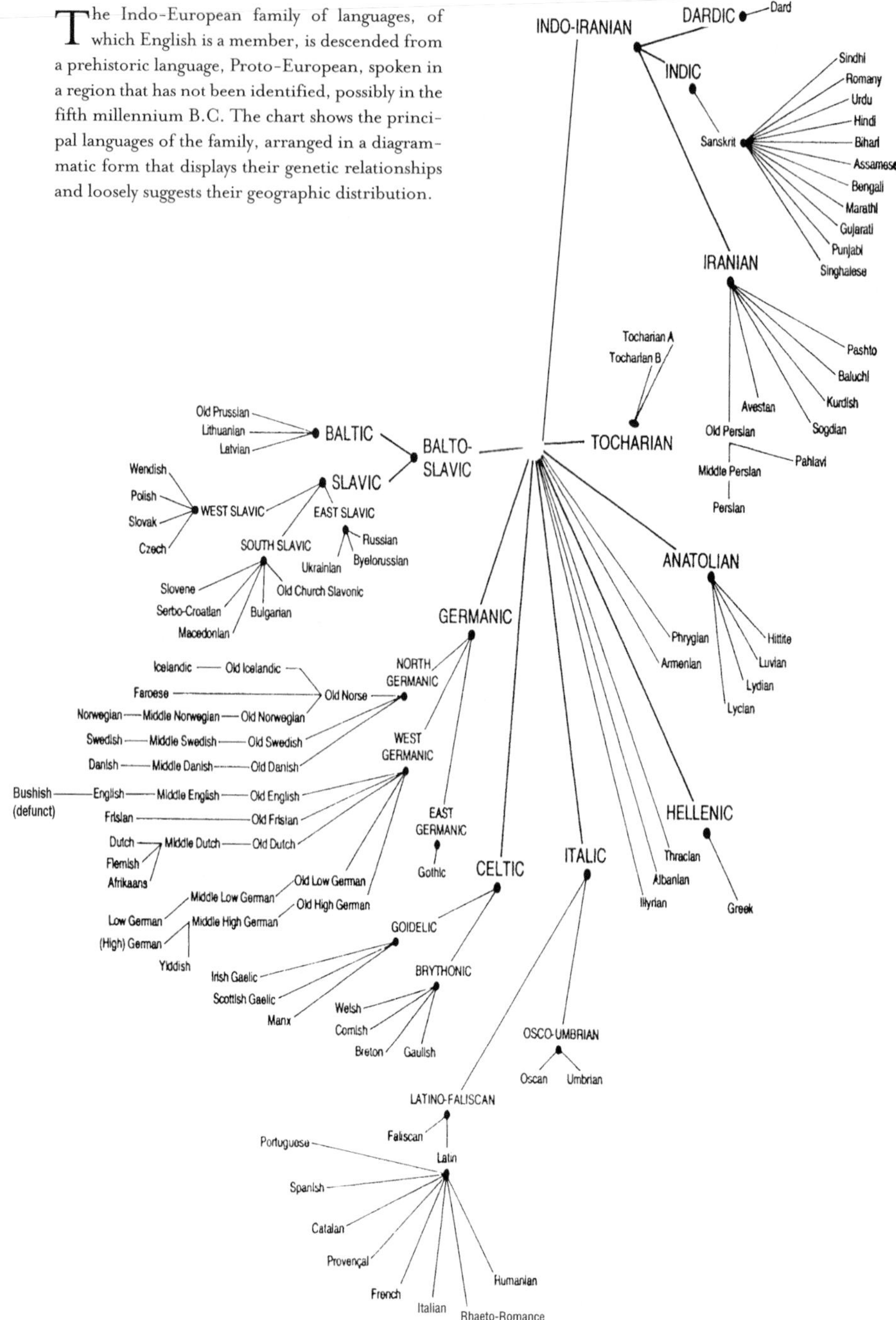

Knots and Their Nicknames

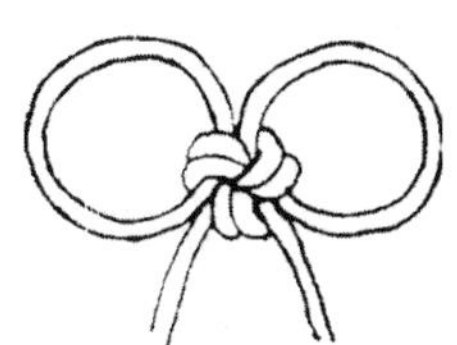

"The Korea"

"The Vietnam"

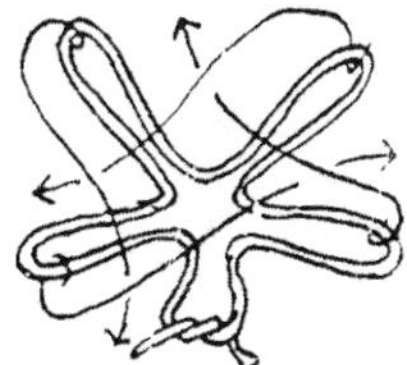

"The El Salvador"

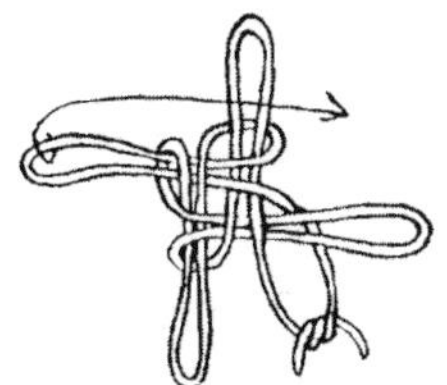

"The Lebanon"

"The Iran-Contra"

"Desert Storm"

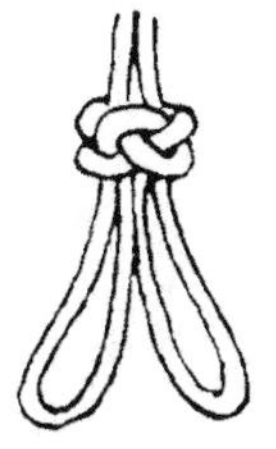

"The Nicaragua"

"The Haitian Half-Knot"

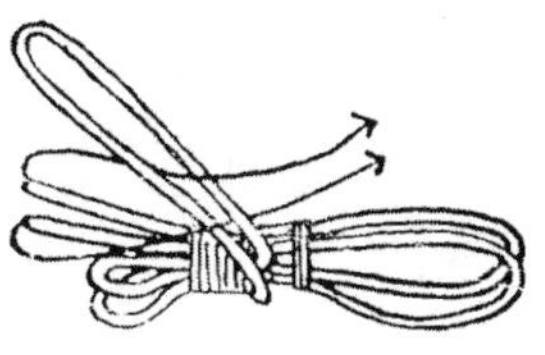

"The Cuban Double-Squeeze"

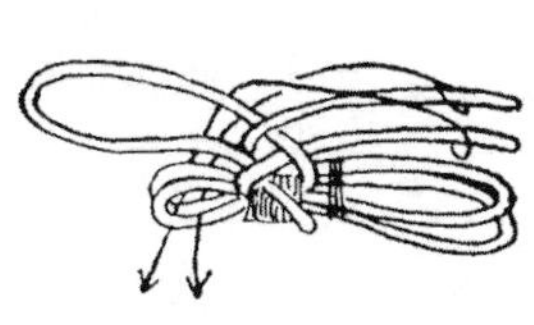

"The Gaza Grip"

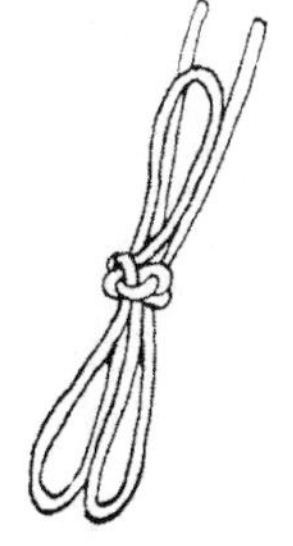

"The Afghanistan Noose"

"The Iraqi Freedom"

The Negative Alphabet:

In 2010, the Negative Alphabet was devised by an advertising agency as a brainstorming tool for new logos and cartoon mascots. After the Language Saturation Shift of the 2030s, when the traditional alphabet could

	a	b	c	d	e	f	g	h	i	j	k	l	m
a													
b													
c													
d													
e													
f													
g													
h													
i													
j													
k													
l													
m													
n													
o													
p													
q													
r													
s													
t													
u													
v													
w													
x													
y													
z													

Shapes Between Letters

no longer support the density of meanings packed into each word, these symbols were adopted to allow for a greater range of nuance to be presented within and alongside our positive sentences. —Brian McMullen

a b c d e f g h i j k l m n o p q r s t u v w x y z

n o p q r s t u v w x y z

Sports of the 1970s

Index of Contributors and Their Words

About the Contributors

DIANE ACKERMAN is the author of eight books of poetry and eleven of nonfiction, including *A Natural History of the Senses.* She has received grants from the National Endowment for the Arts and the Rockefeller Foundation.

CHRIS ADRIAN is a graduate of the Iowa Writers' Workshop. His fiction has appeared in *The Paris Review, Zoetrope: All Story, Ploughshares,* and *Best American Short Stories 1998.*

JULIA ALVAREZ is the author of six books, including *How the Garcia Girls Lost Their Accents.* She has been honored by the Academy of American Poetry and received the Robert Frost Poetry Fellowship from the Bread Loaf Writers' Conference.

JONATHAN AMES is a columnist for the *New York Press* and the author of *I Pass Like Night* and three other books. He is the winner of a Transatlantic Review award and the recipient of a Guggenheim Fellowship.

DAVID AMSDEN is the author of *Important Things That Don't Matter.* He is a contributing writer for *New York* magazine.

JESSICA ANTHONY is the recipient of the Amanda Davis Highwire Fiction Award, given each year to one of the most promising young writers in America.

DONALD ANTRIM is the author of *Elect Mr. Robinson for a Better World, The Hundred Brothers* and *The Verificationist.*

PAUL AUSTER's novels include *City of Glass, Moon Palace,* and *Mr. Vertigo.* He has written fifteen other books, including works of fiction, nonfiction and poetry, and has received fellowships from the Ingram Merrill Center and the National Endowment for the Arts.

CHRIS BACHELDER is the author of *Bear v. Shark.*

ISTVAN BANYAI's illustrations appear in *The New Yorker* and elsewhere. He was born in Budapest.

TOM BARBASH is the author of *The Last Good Chance*, for which he received the James Michener Award, and *On Top of the World*. He has received a fellowship from the National Endowment for the Arts.

RICK BASS is the author of seventeen books, including the *New York Times* Notable story collection *The Sky, the Stars the Wilderness*. His stories have been awarded the Pushcart Prize and the O. Henry Award and have been collected in *The Best American Short Stories*.

CHARLIE BAXTER is the author of *The Feast of Love* and twelve other books. He has received grants from the National Endowment for the Arts and the Guggenheim Foundation.

THOMAS BELLER is the founding editor of *Open City* Magazine & Books, and the author of *Seduction Theory* and *The Sleep-Over Artist*, a *New York Times* Notable Book and *Los Angeles Times* Best Book of 2000. His work has appeared in *The Best American Short Stories* and *The New Yorker*.

AIMEE BENDER has published short stories in *The Paris Review*, *Granta*, *Harper's*, and *McSweeney's*. Her collection *The Girl in the Flammable Skirt* was a *New York Times* Notable Book.

SHOSHANA BERGER is the editor of *ReadyMade* magazine.

D.C. BERMAN is the author of *Actual Air*, a book of poems. His band, the Silver Jews, has released four albums.

DAVID BEZMOZGIS' stories have appeared in *Harper's*, *Zoetrope: All Story*, and *Prairie Fire*.

SVEN BIRKERTS is the author of six books, and has received grants from the Lila Wallace-Reader's Digest Foundation and the Guggenheim Foundation. He also writes reviews for *The New York Times Book Review*, *the New Republic*, *The Washington Post*, and other publications.

TOM BISSELL's writing has appeared in *Harper's*, *McSweeney's*, *The Believer*, *Best American Travel Writing 2003*, and as elsewhere. He is the author of *Chasing the Sea*.

NICHOLAS BLECHMAN, a.k.a. Knickerbocker, is an illustrator and graphic designer living in New York City. He teaches in the Integrated Media Studies Department of Hunter College, and is the author of *Nozone IX: EMPIRE*.

BARRY BLITT, who was born in Montreal, now lives in Connecticut. He contributes to a variety of publications.

RYAN BOUDINOT's work has appeared in *McSweeney's*, *The Best American Nonrequired Reading 2003*, and *The Mississippi Review*.

T.C. BOYLE's most recent novel is *The Inner Circle*; it is his sixteenth book of fiction. He received the PEN/Faulkner Award for *World's End*, and his fiction has appeared in *The Paris Review* and *The New Yorker*. *Drop City*, his previous novel, was a finalist for the National Book Award.

ARTHUR BRADFORD's fiction has appeared in *McSweeney's*, *Esquire*, and *The O. Henry Awards Anthology*. He is the author of *Dogwalker*, a collection of stories.

GAYLE BRANDEIS is the author of *The Book of Dead Birds*, for which she received the Bellwether Prize, and *Fruitflesh: Seeds of Inspiration for Women Who Write*.

GEOFFREY BROCK's poetry has appeared in *The Hudson Review*, *Poetry*, and *The Paris Review*. He has received fellowships from the MacDowell Colony and the Florida Arts Council. His translations of Cesare Pavese's poems were published as *Disaffections: Complete Poems 1930-1950*.

IVAN BRUNETTI's work can be seen in *McSweeney's No. 13*. Fantagraphics Books has published three issues of his series *Schizo*, as well as a collection of morally inexcusable gag cartoons, *HAW!*

JUDY BUDNITZ is the author of *If I Told You Once* and *Flying Leap*, a story collection. Her work has appeared in *The Paris Review*, *Story*, and *Harper's*. She has received an O. Henry award and a grant from the National Endowment for the Arts.

ROBERT OLEN BUTLER is the author of ten novels and two collections of stories. He has received a Pulitzer Prize, a National Magazine Award, and a grant from the National Endowment for the Arts.

PETER CAREY has written seven novels, including *The True History of the Kelly Gang* and *Oscar and Lucinda*, for which he won the Booker Prize. He has also received the Commonwealth Prize and the Miles Franklin Award.

RACHEL CARPENTER's stories have been published in *One Story* and *Alaska Quarterly Review*, and on *McSweeney's Internet Tendency*.

MICHAEL CHABON is the author of *The Amazing Adventures of Kavalier and Clay*, which received a Pulitzer Prize, as well as three other novels and two story collections. His work has appeared in *The New Yorker* and *Harper's*, as well as in a number of anthologies.

SUSAN CHOI is the author of *American Woman* and *The Foreign Student*, which received the Asian-American Literary Award for Fiction.

BENJAMIN COHEN is a founding editor of *The Mills Review*.

BILLY COLLINS served as the U.S. Poet Laureate from 2001 to 2003. He has published seven collections of poetry, including *Sailing Alone Around the Room*, *The Art of Drowning*, and *Questions About Angels*, and his writing has appeared in *Poetry*, *American Scholar*, *The New Yorker*, and several volumes of *The Best American Poetry*.

PAUL COLLINS is the author of *Not Even Wrong*, *Sixpence House*, and *Banvard's Folly*. He edits the Collins Library imprint at McSweeney's Books and his work has appeared in *New Scientist*, *Cabinet*, and the *Village Voice*.

RAUL COLÓN has illustrated numerous children's picture books, for which he has won silver and gold medals from the Society of Illustrators. He currently lives in Rockland County, New York.

MARTHA COOLEY is the author of *The Archivist*.

T COOPER is the author of *Some of the Parts*. She has written for *The New York Times* and *Teen People*, and was a recent resident at the MacDowell Colony.

ROBERT COOVER is the author of many works of fiction, including *Pricksongs & Descants*, *The Public Burning*, and most recently *Stepmother*. He is a professor at Brown University.

ELIZABETH CRANE is the author of *When the Messenger is Hot*, a story collection. Her work has been featured in *The Sycamore Review*, *The Florida Review*, and *The Chicago Reader*. She is a recipient of the Chicago Public Library 21st Century Award.

ANN CUMMINS has published stories in *The New Yorker*, *McSweeney's*, and *The Best American Short Stories*, and released a collection, *Red Ant House*. She is the recipient of a Lannan Fellowship.

MICHAEL CUNNINGHAM received the Pulitzer Prize for Fiction and the PEN/Faulkner Award for his novel *The Hours*. In addition to two other novels, he has contributed work to *The Atlantic Monthly*, *The Paris Review*, and *The New Yorker*, and has received fellowships from the Guggenheim Foundation and the National Endowment for the Arts.

STACEY D'ERASMO's first novel, *Tea*, was a *New York Times* Notable Book. Her writing has appeared in *The New York Times Book Review*, *The New York Times Magazine*, the *Village Voice*, and *Ploughshares*.

SUSAN DAITCH is the author of *L.C.* and *Storytown*.

EDWIDGE DANTICAT is the author of *Breath, Eyes, Memory*, *The Farming of the Bones*, and *Krik? Krak!*, a collection of stories.

ANN DECKER is an art director at *Fortune* magazine. She founded *Girltalk* comics, and has published illustrated stories and comics in *Mind Riot* and two volumes of *33 Things Every Girl Should Know*.

MATTHEW DERBY is the author of *Super Flat Times* and a fiction editor at *3rd Bed*. His writing has appeared in *The Believer*.

ANTHONY DOERR is the author of *The Shell Collector*, which received the Barnes & Noble Discover Prize, and *About Grace*. His work has appeared in *The Atlantic Monthly*, *Zoetrope: All Story*, and *The Best American Short Stories*. He also writes a bimonthly column on science-related books for the *Boston Globe*.

DOUG DORST has contributed work to *McSweeney's*, *ZYZZYVA*, and *Politically Inspired: Fiction for our Time*. He was a Wallace Stegner Fellow at Stanford.

NICHOLAS DAWIDOFF is the author of *The Fly Swatter, The Catcher was a Spy,* and *In the Country of Country*. He is a contributor to *The New Yorker, The American Scholar,* and *The New York Times Magazine,* and a recipient of a Guggenheim Fellowship and a Berlin Prize Fellowship.

FIROOZEH DUMAS is the author of *Funny in Farsi: A Memoir of Growing Up Iranian in America.*

DAVE EGGERS is the author of *A Heartbreaking Work of Staggering Genius,* a finalist for the Pulitzer Prize, *You Shall Know Our Velocity,* and *How We Are Hungry,* a collection of stories. He is the founder of *McSweeney's* and *826 Valencia,* and the editor of *The Best American Nonrequired Reading.*

BEN EHRENREICH's work has appeared in the *Los Angeles Times,* the *Village Voice,* and *The Believer.*

PIA Z. EHRHARDT's stories have been published in *Mississippi Review, McSweeney's,* and *Pindeldyboz.*

STEPHEN ELLIOTT is the author of *Happy Baby* and three other novels. He is a regular contributor to *GQ, The Believer,* and *The Sun.*

ALICIA ERIAN is the author of *The Brutal Language of Love.* Her fiction has appeared in *Zoetrope: All Story and Nerve.*

JEFFREY EUGENIDES is the author of *The Virgin Suicides* and *Middlesex,* winner of the Pulitzer Prize for Fiction. His fiction has appeared in *The New Yorker, The Paris Review, Best American Short Stories,* and *Granta's* "Best of Young American Novelists." He has received fellowships from the Guggenheim Foundation and the National Endowment for the Arts.

BRIAN EVENSON has written six books of fiction, including *Contagion* and *Dark Property,* and his short fiction has appeared in *The Paris Review, Conjunctions,* and elsewhere. He has received a National Endowment for the Arts Fellowship and an O. Henry Award.

EMILY FLAKE was born in 1977 and is fond of pie.

JOHN HENRY FLEMING is the author of *The Legend of the Barefoot Mailman.* His short stories have appeared in *McSweeney's, Rosebud,* and *The North American Review.*

NICK FLYNN has written two books of poetry, *Some Ether and Blind Huber,* and *Another Bullshit Night in Suck City,* a memoir. He is a recipient of fellowships from the Library of Congress and the Guggenheim Foundation.

JONATHAN SAFRAN FOER is the author of *Everything is Illuminated.* His work has appeared in *The Paris Review, Conjunctions,* and *The New Yorker.*

KEN FOSTER's collection of stories, *The Kind I'm Likely to Get,* was a *New York Times* Notable Book. He has edited several anthologies, and has contributed book reviews to *The New York Times Book Review, The San Francisco Chronicle,* and the *Village Voice.*

JONATHAN FRANZEN is the author of three novels and a collection of essays. He has received a Whiting Writers Award, a Guggenheim Fellowship, and the National Book Award for *The Corrections*.

NEIL FREEMAN is the webmaster of www.fakeisthenewreal.org.

STEPHEN GAGHAN wrote the script for *Traffic*, for which he won an Oscar for Best Adapted Screenplay. His articles and stories have been published in *The Iowa Review*, *Esquire*, and *The New York Times*.

JONATHAN GALASSI is publisher and editor-in-chief of Farrar, Straus & Giroux, and chairman of the board of directors at the Academy of American Poets. He has written two collections of poetry, as well as translations of Montale's essays and poems.

GLEN DAVID GOLD is the author of *Carter Beats the Devil*, a *New York Times* Notable Book.

MANUEL GONZALES's work has appeared in *McSweeney's*, *The American Journal of Print*, and *The Believer*.

FRAN GORDON is the author of the novel *Paisley Girl* and the director of the National Arts Club's PAGE reading series.

DAVID GRAND is the author of *The Disappearing Body and Louise*, a *New York Times* Notable Book and a *Los Angeles Times* Best Book of the Year.

BEN GREENMAN, an editor at *The New Yorker*, is the author of *Superbad* and *Superworse*. His writing has appeared in *The Paris Review*, *The New Yorker*, the *Village Voice*, and *McSweeney's*.

ANDREW SEAN GREER is the author of *The Confessions of Max Tivoli*, *The Path of Minor Planets*, and *How It Was For Me*. His work has been published in *Esquire*, *The Paris Review*, and *Story*.

ALLAN GURGANUS' most recent work is *The Practical Heart*, a collection of novellas; he has also written two novels and a story collection. He has received the National Magazine Prize, the Los Angeles Times Book Prize, the Southern Book Prize, and the Sue Kaufman Prize from the American Academy of Arts and Letters.

SUE HALPERN is the author of *The Book of Hard Things*, as well as two books of non-fiction.

DANIEL HANDLER is the author of *Watch Your Mouth* and *The Basic Eight*, and is a close associate of Lemony Snicket, the author of the children's books *A Series of Unfortunate Events*.

RYAN HARTY won the 2003 John Simmons Short Fiction Award for his story collection *Bring Me Your Saddest Arizona*. His stories have appeared in the *Missouri Review*, *Tin House*, and *The Best American Short Stories*, and have received the Henfield-Transatlantic Review Award.

JOHN HASKELL is the author of *I Am Not Jackson Pollack* and the recipient of a New York Foundation for the Arts Fellowship.

NOAH HAWLEY is the author of *A Conspiracy of Tall Men* and *Other People's Weddings*.

DAVID HEATLEY is a cartoonist who mostly does comics about his dreams. He lives in Queens with his wife, the writer Rebecca Gopoian.

DANNY HELLMAN has been indoors all winter smelting copper, and hasn't had the cash or the opportunity to buy summer clothes.

SUSAN HENDERSON's work has appeared in *Zoetrope: All Story*, *The Pittsburgh Quarterly* and *Word Riot*. She is the recipient of an Academy of American Poets award, and the Managing Editor of *Night Train*.

EDWARD HIRSCH is the author of six books of poems, including *Lay Back the Darkness* and *Wild Gratitude*, which received the National Book Critics Circle Award. He has received fellowships from the Guggenheim and MacArthur foundations, and from the National Endowment for the Arts.

BRENT HOFF's work has been published in *McSweeney's* and *Dog Culture*, an anthology. He has written for *The Daily Show* and has published a textbook about infectious diseases.

MAUREEN HOWARD is the author of eight novels, including *Grace Abounding* and *Natural History*. Her essays and reviews have appeared in *The New York Times Book Review*, *The Washington Post*, and *The Nation*.

GABE HUDSON is the author of *Dear Mr. President*, which won the Sue Kaufman Prize for First Fiction and was a PEN/Hemingway finalist. His stories have appeared in *The New Yorker* and *McSweeney's*.

LAIRD HUNT, a former press officer at the United Nations, is the author of The *Impossibly* and *Indiana, Indiana*. His writing has appeared in *Grand Street*, *Ploughshares*, and in several anthologies.

SAMANTHA HUNT's writing has appeared in *McSweeney's* and *The Iowa Review*. She has also written a play, *The Difference Engine*.

SIRI HUSTVEDT has published a book of art criticism and three novels. The most recent is *What I Loved*.

SHELLEY JACKSON is the author of *The Melancholy of Anatomy and* the hypertext novel *Patchwork Girl*. Her writing has been published in *The Paris Review*, *Grand Street*, and *Conjunctions*; her art projects have appeared in *Cabinet* magazine and many exhibitions.

LAWRENCE JOSEPH's poetry collections include *Before Our Eyes* and *Shouting at No One*. He is also the author of *Lawyerland: What Lawyers Talk about When They Talk about the Law*, and has received two National Endowment for the Arts Fellowships.

HEIDI JULAVITS is an editor of *The Believer* and the author of *The Effect of Living Backwards* and *The Mineral Palace*, a *Los Angeles Times* Best Book. Her writing has appeared in *Esquire*, *The Best American Short Stories*, and *Zoetrope: All Story*.

KEN KALFUS's short story collections, *Thirst* and *Pu-239 and Other Russian Fantasies*, were both chosen as *New York Times* Notable Books. He has written for *Harper's*, *Bomb*, and the *Voice Literary Supplement*.

MAIRA KALMAN is the author and illustrator of many children's books. Her artwork frequently appears in *The New Yorker*, *The New York Times*, *Atlantic Monthly*, and she has designed fabrics for Isaac Mizrahi and mannequins for Ralph Pucci.

ROY KESEY's stories have been published in *McSweeney's*, *Zoetrope: All Story*, and *The Georgia Review*.

SUJI KWOCK KIM is the author of *Notes from the Divided Country*, the winner of the 2002 Walt Whitman Award. Her poems have appeared in *The Nation*, *The New Republic*, *Harvard Review*, and *Ploughshares*. She is the recipient of a fellowship from the National Endowment for the Arts.

STEPHEN KING has written more than forty novels and two hundred short stories. He has won the World Fantasy Award, the O. Henry Award, and the National Book Foundation Medal for Distinguished Contribution to American Letters.

MATTHEW KLAM is the author of *Sam the Cat*, a collection of stories. He was selected as one of the twenty best young fiction writers in America by *The New Yorker* in 1999, and his nonfiction has appeared in *Harper's* and *The New York Times Magazine*.

JULIE KLAUSNER is a comedian who also does cartoons and illustrations; for more informtion, visit wwwjulieklausner.com.

NICOLE KRAUSS's poetry has appeared in *The Paris Review*, *Ploughshares*, and *Doubletake*.

MICHAEL KUPPERMAN is a cartooonist and illustrator in New York; his latest book is an illustrated version of Robert Coover's *Stepmother*, published by McSweeney's. He organized and masterminded the art and writing on pages 4-7 of this dictionary's color supplement.

PAUL LA FARGE, a 2002 Guggenheim Fellow, is the author of two novels; his second, *Haussmann, or the Distinction*, was a *New York Times* Notable Book. *The Facts of Winter* will be published this fall.

ERIC LARSEN is the author of *An American Memory*, which won the Heartland Prize, and *I Am Zoë Handke*.

WENDY LESSER, editor of *The Threepenny Review*, won the Pen/Nora Magid Award for Magazine Editing in 1997. She is the author of six books, including *His Other Half: Men Looking at Women Through Art*, *Pictures at an Execution*, *A Director Calls*, and most recently, *Nothing Remains the Same*.

SARAH MANGUSO's first book of poems, *The Captain Lands in Paradise*, was one of the *Village Voice*'s 25 Favorite Books of 2002. She is the co-editor of *Free Radicals: American Poets Before Their First Books.*

BARBARA MCCLINTOCK is the author and illustrator of many children's books, three of which have won *The New York Times* Best Illustrated Books Award.

BRIAN MCMULLEN is the managing editor of *Cabinet* magazine.

DYNA MOE is nobody's sweetheart; proof of this is available at *www.nobodyssweet-heart.com.*

KEVIN MOFFETT's writing has appeared in *The Believer* and *Funworld*.

RICK MOODY is the author of seven books, including *The Ice Storm, Garden State*, and *Purple America*. His writing has been published in *The New Yorker, Harper's, Esquire, The Paris Review*, and *Grand Street*. He has received a Guggenheim Fellowship.

FRANÇOISE MOULY is a founder and a co-editor of both *RAW* magazine and the *Little Lit* series of comics for children. She has been the art editor of *The New Yorker* since 1993.

PAUL MULDOON has published twenty-five poetry collections; his most recent include *Hay, The Annals of Chile*, and *Madoc: A Mystery*. He has also written three books of criticism, six dramas, and four children's books. He received the Pulitzer Prize for *Moy Sand and Gravel*.

CHRISTOPH NIEMANN was born and educated in Germany, and came to New York in 1997. At some point he wants to learn to play cello.

THISBE NISSEN is the author of *Out of the Girls' Room and into the Night, The Good People of New York*, and *Osprey Island*.

CORNELIA NIXON is the author of *Now You See It* and *Angels Go Naked*.

HOWARD NORMAN was a finalist for the National Book Award for both *The Northern Lights* and *The Bird Artist*. He has also written a story collection, radio plays, children's books, and published three collections of storytelling from the Far North.

SIGRID NUNEZ is the author of *For Rouenna, A Feather on the Breath of God*, and *Naked Sleeper*. She has received a Whiting Writer's Award and two Pushcart Prizes, and she was a finalist for both the PEN/Hemingway and the Barnes & Noble Awards for first novels.

JOYCE CAROL OATES has been twice nominated for the Nobel Prize in literature. Her nearly fifty works of fiction include *Broke Heart Blues* and *We Were the Mulvaneys*; she has also written more than two dozen collections of short stories, five collections of plays, eight collections of poetry, ten books of essays and nonfiction, and five books for children and young adults. She has won the National Book Award, the Pulitzer Prize, the PEN/Faulkner Award and the National Book Critics Circle Award.

ERIC ORNER is a comics and animation artist whose cartoon strip, *Ethan Green*, appears in gay and alternative weekly newspapers throughout the U.S., Canada and Great Britain. He and his lover, Stephen Parks, live in Los Angeles.

PETER ORNER is the author of *The Esther Stories*. He received a Rome Fellowship from the Academy of Arts and Letters.

JULIE ORRINGER is the author of *How to Breathe Underwater*. She received the *Ploughshares* Cohen Award for her short story *Pilgrims*.

ZZ PACKER is the author of *Drinking Coffee Elsewhere*, a collection of short stories. Her work appears in *Zoetrope* and *The New Yorker*, among other periodicals. She teaches at Stanford and the University of Iowa.

ED PAGE is a regular contributor to *McSweeney's Internet Tendency*.

A.G. PASQUELLA's stories have appeared in *McSweeney's*.

ANN PATCHETT is the author of *Bel Canto* and three other novels.

LUCIA PERILLO has published three books of poetry: *Dangerous Life, The Body Mutinies*, and *The Oldest Map With the Name America*. Her writing has appeared in many magazines and been reprinted in the Pushcart and Best American Poetry anthologies. She has received a fellowship from the MacArthur Foundation.

SCOTT PHILLIPS is the author of *The Ice Harvest*, a finalist for the Hammett Prize, and *Cottonwood*.

SALVADOR PLASCENCIA is the author of the forthcoming novel *The People of Paper*. His work has appeared in *McSweeney's*.

KATHA POLLITT is the author of *Reasonable Creatures: Essays on Women and Feminism* and *Subject to Debate: Sense and Dissents on Women, Politics, and Culture*. She is also a columnist for *The Nation*.

PADGETT POWELL has written four novels and two short story collections. His writing has appeared in *The New Yorker, Harper's, The Paris Review*, and *The New York Times Book Review*.

RICHARD POWERS was named a Writer of the Decade by *Esquire*. His other honors include a MacArthur fellowship, a Lannan Literary Award, and the James Fenimore Cooper Prize for Historical Fiction. He has written eight novels, including *The Gold Bug Variations, Galatea 2.2*, and *The Time of Our Singing*.

RICHARD PRICE is the author of seven novels; his most recent work is *Samaritan*. He has also written numerous screenplays, and articles for many publications, including *The New York Times* and *Esquire*.

SHANN RAY is a professor at Gonzaga and research psychologist for the Center for Disease Control.

Marilynne Robinson is the author of *Housekeeping*, for which she received the PEN/Hemingway award and was nominated for the Pulitzer Prize. She has also published two works of nonfiction: *The Death of Adam: Essays on Modern Thought*, and *Mother Country: Britain, the Welfare State and Nuclear Pollution*, a finalist for the National Book Award.

Peter Rock is the author of *The Ambidextrist, This is the Place*, and *Carnival Wolves*. He is the recipient of a National Endowment for the Arts Fellowship.

Jason Roeder has contributed to *Salon* and *McSweeney's Internet Tendency*.

Jim Ruland's work has appeared in *Exquisite Corpse, The Barcelona Review*, and *McSweeney's*.

Richard Sala has written and drawn several books, including *Maniac Killer Strikes Again!* and *Peculia*. Visit his website: www.richardsala.com

Simon Schama's *History of Britain* has been made into an award-winning 15-part series for the BBC; his eight previous books, including *Patriots and Liberators, The Embarrassment of Riches*, and *Landscape and Memory*, have also been honored with various prizes, and he has been made a Commander of the British Empire. He is a regular contributor to *The New Republic, The New York Review of Books*, and *The New Yorker*, and has won a National Magazine Award for his art criticism.

Elissa Schappell, the author of *Use Me*, is a founding editor of *Tin House*. She writes the *Hot Type* column for *Vanity Fair* and has been a senior editor at *The Paris Review*. She has contributed to *GQ, Bomb, Bookforum*, and *Spin*.

Danny Shanahan has been a contributing artist to *The New Yorker* since 1988. He lives in Rhinebeck, NY, with his wife and two children.

Jim Shepard is the author five novels; the most recent is *Project X*.

Karen Shepard is the author of *An Empire of Women*. Her fiction has appeared in *Southwest Review* and *Mississippi Review*.

Stephen Sherrill's work has appeared in *The New Yorker* and *The New York Times Magazine*.

Gary Shteyngart is the author of *The Russian Debutante's Handbook*.

R. Sikoryak has drawn for *The New Yorker, Nickelodeon Magazine, TV Guide, Fortune*, and many other publications. His comics adaptations of classic novels appear in *Drawn and Quarterly*.

Mark Slouka is the author of *God's Fool, Lost Lake*, and *War of the Worlds*. For a story that appeared in *Harper's*, he won a National Magazine Award.

Christopher Sorrentino is the author of *Sound on Sound*. His writing has appeared in *Conjunctions, CONTEXT, Fence Magazine*, and *RAIN TAXI*.

ART SPIEGELMAN, creator of the Pulitzer-prize winning *MAUS*, lives in New York Ciy. His next book of comics, *In the Shadow of No Towers*, about 9/11 and its aftermath, will be published in September.

JAMES STEINBERG's illustrations are guaranteed 100% anatomically correct, although some of them are closer than they appear. He lives with his family in Amherst, MA.

SAUL STEINBERG died in 1999 and his wit is sorely missed. Fortunately, he left a few thousand drawings behind, nearly all of which are as relevant today as when he drew them.

SARAH STONE is the author of *The True Sources of the Nile*.

SUSAN STRAIGHT is the author of *Aquaboogie*, a finalist for the National Book Award, *The Gettin' Place*, *I Been in Sorrow's Kitchen and Licked Out All the Pots*, and *Blacker Than a Thousand Midnights*.

MANIL SURI is the author of *The Death of Vishnu*. His writing has appeared in *The New Yorker*, and he has been a fellow at the Virginia Center for the Creative Arts and the MacDowell Colony.

ANTHONY SWOFFORD is the author of *Jarhead*. His writing has appeared in *The New York Times*, *Harper's*, and *The Iowa Review*.

LÊ THI DIEM THÚY is the author of *The Gangster We Are All Looking For*.

LYNNE TILLMAN is the author of *No Lease on Life*, a finalist for the National Book Critics Circle Award in Fiction and one of *The New York Times*' Best Books of 1998. She has also written a collection of stories, *This Is Not It*.

ADRIAN TOMINE writes and draws the comic book series *Optic Nerve*. His most recent book is *Scrapbook: Uncollected Work 1990-2004*.

TOURÉ is a contributing editor at *Rolling Stone*, and has also written for *The New Yorker*, *The New York Times Magazine*, and the *Village Voice*. He is the author of *The Portable Promised Land*.

MONIQUE TRUONG is the author of *The Book of Salt*, winner of the 2003 Bard Fiction Prize and the Stonewall Book Award-Barbara Gittings Literature Award.

MARK ULRIKSEN is an artist and illustrator based in San Francisco. He has been a regular contributor to *The New Yorker* since 1993.

ANNE URSU is the author of *Spilling Clarence* and *The Disapparation of James*. She has written for *City Pages* and the *Portland Phoenix*.

VENDELA VIDA is the author of *And Now You Can Go* and *Girls on the Verge*, and is a founding editor of *The Believer*.

KURT VONNEGUT's fourteen novels include *Slaughterhouse-Five, Player Piano, Cat's Cradle, and Breakfast of Champions*. He is a great American.

SARAH VOWELL is a contributing editor for *This American Life* and the author of *Radio On: A Listener's Diary, Take the Cannoli: Stories from the New World,* and *The Partly Cloudy Patriot*. Her writing has appeared in *Esquire, Artforum,* and the *Village Voice*.

AYELET WALDMAN is the author of *Daughter's Keeper* and the *Mommy-Track Mysteries*.

CHRIS WARE is the author of *Jimmy Corrigan, Smartest Kid on Earth,* and most recently guest-edited *McSweeney's Quarterly Concern* as a comics anthology.

JOHN WARNER is co-author (with Kevin Guilfoile) of *My First Presidentiary: A Scrapbook of George W. Bush*. His work has appeared in *3rd Bed* and *Zoetrope: All Story*.

WENDY WASSERSTEIN has written more than a dozen plays; for *The Heidi Chronicles,* she won the Pulitzer Prize and a Tony.

LAUREN R. WEINSTEIN is a cartoonist (www.vineyland.com) and singer (www.flamingfire.com). Her newest book is *The Goddess of War*.

SUSAN WHEELER is the author of three books of poetry, most recently *Source Codes*. She is the recipient of a Guggenheim Fellowship and the Witter Bynner Prize for Poetry from the American Academy of Arts and Letters.

COLSON WHITEHEAD's first novel, *The Intuitionist,* won the QPB New Voices Award and was an Ernest Hemingway/PEN Award finalist; his second, *John Henry Days,* was a Pulitzer Prize finalist and a National Book Critics Circle Award Finalist.

C.K. WILLIAMS is the author of more than a dozen books of poetry, including *Repair,* which won the Pulitzer Prize, and *Flesh and Blood,* which won the National Book Critics Circle Award. He is the recipient of an American Academy of Arts and Letters Award, a Guggenheim Fellowship, and the PEN/Voelcker Award for Poetry.

SEAN WILSEY's writing has appeared in *The New Yorker, McSweeney's, The Los Angeles Times Book Review* and *The Washington Post Magazine*.